Praise for Jim Lynch's

Truth Like the Sun

"Addictive." —*The Seattle Times*

"Lynch takes the drizzly history of modern Seattle and spins it into this colorful novel." —*Entertainment Weekly*

"A swirling portrait of a place . . . equal parts huckster-ism, genuine civilizational hope, profiteering racket and progressive mecca." —*The Oregonian*

"A beautifully crafted, fictional remembrance of the Seattle World's Fair and a cleverly plotted tale of the very public death of one man's political ambitions. . . . Lynch is a sparkling host, rendering history in glorious technicolor and the recent past in absolute and black-and-white moral tones." —*The National* (London)

"A tremendously entertaining yet serious political novel." —*The Edmonton Journal*

"Alternating between the two periods, Jim Lynch's novel is a brilliantly disturbing dissection of political morality, where right and wrong are, like Seattle itself, blurred in a grey mist." —*Daily Mail* (London)

JIM LYNCH
Truth Like the Sun

Jim Lynch is the author of the novels *Border Songs* and *The Highest Tide*, both of which have been adapted for the stage. His prizes include the 2010 Indies Choice Honor Book Award, the 2010 Washington State Book Award for Fiction, the Pacific Northwest Booksellers Award in 2006, and the Livingston Young Journalist Award for National Reporting. Lynch grew up in the Seattle area and now lives in Olympia, Washington, with his wife and daughter.

ALSO BY JIM LYNCH

The Highest Tide

Border Songs

Truth Like the Sun

Truth Like the Sun

JIM LYNCH

VINTAGE CONTEMPORARIES
Vintage Books
A Division of Random House, Inc.
New York

FIRST VINTAGE CONTEMPORARIES EDITION, FEBRUARY 2013

Grateful acknowledgment is made to Doubleday for permission
to reprint excerpts from the following:
"My Papa's Waltz," copyright 1942 by Hearst Magazines, Inc.;
"The Adamant," copyright 1938 by Theodore Roethke;
"I Knew a Woman," copyright 1954 by Theodore Roethke;
from *Collected Poems of Theodore Roethke* by Theodore Roethke.
Reprinted by permission of Doubleday, a division of Random House, Inc.

The Library of Congress has cataloged the Knopf edition as follows:
Lynch, Jim, 1961–
Truth like the sun / by Jim Lynch.–1st ed.
p. cm.
1. Women journalists—Fiction. 2. Seattle (Wash.)—Fiction. I. Title.
PS3612.Y542T78 2012
813'.6–dc23 2011050564

Vintage ISBN: 978-0-307-94934-9

Book design by Robert C. Olsson

Printed in the United States of America
10 9 8 7 6 5 4 3 2 1

For my parents, Levin and Janet, and my sister, Jennie Nelson

As the hot dog stands were removed, the permanent buildings of the civic center, the dream behind the dream of the fair, took their planned relationship. Something permanent, something beautiful had been created: Something to build on.

—Murray Morgan, author of *Century 21: The Story of the Seattle World's Fair, 1962*

I started believing that Seattle in the latter half of the twentieth century was a nexus, a magic confluence of physical and temporal forces, a place and time where lives were changed more dramatically and more for the better than anywhere else on earth.

—Fred Moody, author of *Seattle and the Demons of Ambition: From Boom to Bust in the Number One City of the Future*

Truth Like the Sun

Chapter One

THIS IS WHEN and where it begins, with all the dreamers champagne-drunk and stumbling on the head of the Needle. Look back further all you want, but this renaissance starts right here when the dreamers get everyone to take one long gawk at this place. Look! Just, just look at this brash metropolis surrounded by postcard summits and all that boat-loving water. Up here in the dark, five hundred feet above it all, downtown looks like it's on fire again, though it's just showing off this time, flaunting cheap hydropower, everyone flipping on their lights to greet the world, all those bulbs straining to make the city look bigger than it actually is. Taste that salty air. Smell the clam spit. Where better to start afresh? A whole new way of living in a city of things to come. That's right. A city so short on history it's mostly all future anyway. So climb on board and go, go, go!

The elevator doors glide open seven minutes before midnight, everyone spilling out, men dressed like penguins, women like peacocks, an older crowd, bloodshot and slack-jawed, up past bedtime, bumping into radiant waitresses in gold lamé passing out flutes of champagne. Roger Morgan, the grand exalted dreamer himself, grabs a glass, thanks the waitress, takes in the chaos. Dozens of people—and it sounds like hundreds—are already here, seeing their city for the first time from this height, shouting, crowding the windows, exclaiming *Good God!* at the spectacle of lights and water below while others marvel at how the dining area spins around the elevators and kitchen just slowly enough to make you think you're losing your marbles. A busty woman returns from the bathroom and can't find her friends, who've rotated eighty feet clockwise, until she hears them roaring at her confusion. A drink spills, a glass breaks, a man retches and blames it on the spinning. More shouts. More stampeding laughter.

Roger parts a gaggle, turning more heads—*so damn young, isn't he?*—into another flurry of handshakes and hugs from people who've already embraced him tonight, but they want more contact now that they're loaded and up in *his* Space Needle. Everybody wants his blessings, whether it's the etiquette committee urging local ladies to wear dresses during the fair or the beautification committee telling school kids to keep those candy wrappers in their pockets. The fair's coming! Clean the streets and shine your shoes. The fair is coming!

Roger continues grabbing shoulders and, depending on the recipient, offering one of his nimble smiles—gracious, mischievous, reassuring. Boyishly jug-eared, he comes off as a careful listener who agrees with you even while explaining why he doesn't. Pushing words through his head now, he tries them out against this dizzy backdrop. Plan a toast all you want, but when the mood shifts you'd better adjust. "Every endeavor, big and small," he whispers to himself, "begins with an idea."

Where the hell is Teddy?

More overdressed drunks stumble out of the elevator into a fresh round of exclamations and squabbles over the exact whereabouts of various landmarks. Dapper men surround him. The only one he recognizes is Malcolm Turner, to whom he recently gave most of his savings. "Looks like the world's your oyster," a bullet-headed man tells him through a menacing smile. A camera flashes with each shake of his hand. Is that a *Times* photographer? It's past midnight. Toasts were supposed to start already, but Roger knows when to stall. A meeting runs on schedule or tempers flicker, while a roast, a tribute or any boozy gathering moves to a slower beat. You wait until they're itching for someone to make sense of it all, then you wait a bit longer.

He hears Linda's laugh, gauging her inebriation by its volume: *plastered*. He'd considered her gregarious before she'd wheedled him into proposing. Since then, she's struck him as loud, especially when she drinks. He finds his mother, as far away from his fiancée as she can get, telling a story about her childhood that he knows isn't true.

He wraps an arm around her as if to brace her, though she's probably the sturdiest woman up here, her sober regality as out of sync with this teetering mob as her fake British accent.

Teddy Severson finally strides over, tall, hipless and lipless. "You ready?"

The sound system squeaks before Teddy's throaty voice comes through louder than necessary. "Thanks for joining us." Reporters set their champagne aside and flip open notebooks as everybody packs into this curve of the dining area. "Thanks for joining us," he repeats over the lingering chatter, "on the eve of something that most people didn't think was possible." Laughter ripples, glasses clink, the city sparkles, a cigarette smolders toward his wedding band. "Along the way, I heard from enough doubters and doomsayers to make me forget that all we were trying to do was throw a nifty fair, not ruin this city." Laughter mixes with gossipy murmurs. Everyone knows this crowd holds more than its share of doomsayers. "I too miss the quiet Seattle of yesteryear," he continues woodenly, reading now, "but we can't keep this place in curls and a Buster Brown suit much longer." He blushes, waiting out the polite chuckles. "This city has done amazing things. It rose from ashes, flattened hills, dug canals, bridged lakes and shipped its products to every major port. And for the next six months, it will, my friends, become the capital of the world." He pauses, as if expecting more than golf claps. "But let me shut up and get Roger up here to christen this place up right, because without his gift of gab we wouldn't be here, and we certainly couldn't have coaxed thirty-five countries into helping us throw a fair in some city they still think rhymes with *beetle*."

"Jus' a few words," Roger says to amuse those familiar with his rambling, noteless speeches. Easy to see in this light that he's younger than everybody: loose-limbed, bushy-haired, dimpled. "First time I experienced this view," he begins, "was when Teddy, Mr. Vierling and I rented a helicopter and hovered up here to see what it might be like to actually have a restaurant in the sky." Roger makes helicopter noises, then mimics the pilot. "'Four hundred, four-fifty, five hundred feet. Holding.' Teddy kept muttering *Jesus,* while Mr. Vierling calculated aloud what it would cost to build this thing. The numbers, of course, kept going up, but it was obvious to all of us that this not only *could* happen, but *needed* to happen. So, what do you think? Pretty marvelous, huh?" Opening his arms, as if to hug everyone, he notices the county prosecutor, the city attorney, the police chief, two doomsaying councilmen and the head of Boeing all studying him. While cameras flash, it occurs to him that he still doesn't know the full price of the deals he's struck and the *friends* he's made.

"I've been warned that frankly we're not *sophisticated* enough to pull this thing off, that we have a champagne appetite and a beer budget. Well"—he hoists his glass—"I disagree."

His gratitude rattles on for five minutes without notes, thanking architects, contractors and engineers by name. "All ambitious endeavors," he says slowly now, "begin with a suggestion, a kiss, a daydream—whether it's to build a freeway, a relationship or a world's fair." He lowers his eyes and waits out the murmurs. "This unique building was put up in four hundred and seven days. It can take longer than that to remodel your kitchen, yet it's already well on its way to becoming one of the world's most recognizable icons." He pauses, letting the words prick the bastards who want to tear it down after the fair. "We even put a forty-foot flame on top of it. That's right. We built the tallest building west of the Mississippi, slapped a spinning restaurant on top and lit the whole damn thing on fire. Sound smart?" He grins and shrugs. "I confess to having some moments of profound doubt. 'What if this is the stupidest thing anybody's ever tried?' Look at us! Look at this audacity!" He steps back, inhales, then continues. "It's amazing how many bad ideas we've had to overcome. Somebody suggested we fill Mount Rainier's crater with oil and keep it burning through the fair. Another genius recommended that we tell NASA to land a rocket in Elliott Bay. Others offered conspiracy theories. The Committee Hoping for Extraterrestrial Encounters to Save the Earth—aptly nicknamed CHEESE— claims the Needle was designed to, and I quote, 'send transmissions to beings in other solar systems.'" He cuts into the rising mirth. "Can I get a moment of silence here?" As the room settles, he takes everything in—the strange gleaming faces and lopsided chandeliers, the counterclockwise drift of the lights below, the bright-lipped brunette seemingly modeling ringless fingers for him. He waits a few more beats. "We are simultaneously at the end of something challenging and magnificent and at the beginning of something challenging and magnificent. So let's commit this moment to memory, okay? Look around. Remember what our city looked like on this night from up here. Remember how *young* we all were." He leans back to milk the laughter. "Remember *this* moment," he insists, "before the eyes of the world take a good long look at us."

ANOTHER WHIRLWIND of good-night hugs and handshakes. Roger takes his time on each one, matching each grip and embrace with his oversize hands. He's great with good-byes, having noticed long ago that most people aren't.

Soon it's down to just him and Teddy staring at the moonlit silhouette of the Olympic range with dishes clanking behind them in the kitchen. Teddy coughs, clears his throat and frisks himself until he finds a pack of Chesterfields. He taps one out, flips open a lighter, spins the wheel, watches the flame, hesitates, then shuts it and slides the cigarette back into its pack.

"Been thinking," he ruminates, dragging a palm through his graying hair. "When you really look closely, you realize that just about every goddamn thing begins with a *kiss.*"

"Screw you." Roger chuckles. "But you know what?"

"What's that?"

"Seriously, all BS aside."

"Yeah."

"Seeing how at least one of us needs to keep our mind on what matters?"

"Right."

"Well, what I've been thinking—"

"Uh-huh."

"—is how we can't keep this city in short pants any longer. Know what I mean?"

Teddy taps a cigarette back out and lights it. "Go to hell."

Roger waits for whatever's coming, knowing his friend often

turns serious when he drinks. Starts out sarcastic, goes philosophical, grave, then personal.

"You know I still get people asking me about you." Teddy mimics voices: " 'What's his story? Where'd he come from? How'd you let a youngster run things?' "

"Don't they read the papers?"

"What do they ever say other than the obvious? Rising star in the restaurant biz who drew the Needle on a napkin, blah, blah, blah."

"So, what do you tell 'em?"

"That you came here on a spaceship from some planet where they're a whole lot smarter than we are."

"C'mon."

"I tell 'em your age doesn't matter, that you can't be outworked, that you could sell snow to Eskimos and you don't need any sleep. Sometimes I just tell 'em you're the future, or the city's good luck charm, or that Jackie V. swore by you. Basically, I encourage 'em all to go directly to hell. Don't pass *Go*. Don't collect two hundred dollars."

Roger watches tiny red taillights crawling up Capitol Hill.

"Know something, though," Teddy says on the inhale. "Been meaning to tell you this: enough is never enough with you. And it's not healthy. It's like an addiction."

"To what?"

"To *more*." Smoke flares out his nostrils. "You can't get enough of anything."

Roger rubs his cheeks and averts his eyes, wondering if it's that obvious he's increasingly driven half-mad by the limitations of having only one life. All the things he'll never see or do or understand. All the people he'll never know. "Whatever you say," he finally says.

"Think about it."

Roger squints in mock contemplation.

"Hell with ya." Teddy straightens the jacket over his bony shoulders. "But tell me, how *do* you win over people so quickly?"

Roger smiles slowly. "By finding out what they want."

"Ahhh. Like a good waiter."

"Not really."

"Because you don't always give it to 'em."

"Right, but at least I know what it is."

Teddy snickers. "Gonna grab a few hours of shut-eye, so *I* can function in the morning." He snubs the half-smoked Chesterfield on the heel of his dress shoe, sets it on the table, smoldering end up. "You should too, but you won't because how else will people possibly find the fair if you're not sitting up here guiding them in?"

"Teddy?"

"Yeah?"

"We ready?"

He sighs. "By the time we're ready it'll be over. You really gonna stay up here till morning?"

"Maybe."

Teddy shakes his head and wobbles off in a pigeon-toed shuffle. "Remember," he shouts without looking back, "there won't be anybody to work the elevator till eight or so."

"Thanks for what you said tonight," Roger says, "even if I don't deserve it."

Teddy waves it off. "I lie about all sorts of things, but not about you."

FOG SHROUDS the sunrise and turns the brightening sky into what looks like yet another champagne illusion before he hears the city waking below—downshifting garbage trucks, belching ferries, the faint gargle of incoming cars. He can't see well enough to reassure himself that anything is actually happening. What if everybody stays home because the doomsayers told them there won't be anywhere to park?

Soon Teddy and the gang join him up here, everybody puffy-eyed, slurping coffee, listening to the muted city stir until the fog thins enough to confirm what in truth looks like any other morning. What'd they expect? An invasion of foreign autos and luxury liners? Still, the day looks embarrassingly ordinary for the grand opening of what the governor has been calling—at Roger's suggestion—*the most imaginative and spectacular show of our time!*

"Where is everybody?" Teddy finally says aloud.

An hour later the men drop solemnly to their fairground offices as subdued crowds waddle toward the stadium beneath the ominous sky. Before Roger can get there himself, he hears that the west gate opened twenty-two minutes late because of a lost key, and that the Philippine and German entourages are furious with their assigned seats. Other gripes include electrical problems, delivery delays and passport snafus. A letter from the local St. Matthew's Church condemns the girlie shows that haven't even opened yet: *Such pagan displays will show the world what they already suspect: that Americans are amoral, materialistic, sex-conscious, pleasure-seeking people!*

His vision reels—too much champagne and coffee, too little sleep—as he enters the stadium and heads for the stage where the governor, the senator, the mayor and other bulky, suited men are checking wristwatches and chortling at each other's shoulder-clutching jokes. Everything has a clumsy small-town feel to it. The stage is too far away, making the speakers look like midgets. And the crowd is mousy, polite at best. Politicians drone through the scratchy PA. Unable to make out half the words, the audience fidgets, waiting to hear Kennedy himself.

Finally, Roger theatrically wheels his arm and points at the jumbo countdown clock, which has been ticking toward this moment for a year now. When it hits all zeros, an ancient Swedish cannon thumps the air with a half pound of gunpowder followed by a twenty-one-gun salute. Then an old steam whistle sounds and ten thundering F-102 fighter jets shred the sky, joined by sirens, church bells, fireworks, car horns and just about every other noisemaker within a mile.

Once the pandemonium subsides, the president's nasal voice crackles through the speakers. "May we open an era of peace and understanding among all mankind," he says by phone from a Florida getaway. Amazingly, it takes him just a dozen words to say what everybody's thinking but nobody's saying, that it's a wee bit ironic to be throwing a party about the world's rosy future in a city that's building battleships, bombers and bunkers as fast as it can.

"Let the fair begin!" Kennedy commands. The Space Needle carillon clangs 538 bells, and two thousand *See you in Seattle* balloons rise into the clearing sky. Then the freak show really begins. Water-skiers in tutus slalom and flip in the huge oval moat around the field as Circus Berlin motorcyclists accelerate up a cable strung between the stadium roof and the Needle. He hears the crowd's hesitancy, its collective disappointment. *Is this all there is?*

Roger floats out of the ceremonies with the exiting mob, his gut twitching over either the lackluster turnout or Kennedy's words. From his vantage, the president just raised the stakes. The fair must not only entertain the world but *save* it. If this thing flops, Roger realizes, his knack for talking people into things will have backfired in the grandest fashion imaginable, and he'll be the fall guy who brought ridicule and doom upon the city he loves.

As the sun blasts through wispy clouds, he drifts past hundreds of pink begonias that the Belgians brought and watches men in dark suits and brown wingtips snapping pictures of their smiling wives in feathered hats while their kids cavort around the fountain with plumes of cotton candy bigger than their heads. Maybe the fair will help people step outside their lives, he tells himself. He looks up at the blazing newness of the Needle, and then at the Science Pavilion and the Coliseum too, everything stunningly new. He suddenly notices his face is wet. How long has he been crying? It's gotta be the lack of sleep. Even a nap would help, but not yet. Go, go, go!

A breathless assistant miraculously finds him in the mumbling horde and explains that one of the fighter jets that flew over the stadium crashed in a north Seattle neighborhood. He takes this omen in stride, as if expecting it, then jogs toward headquarters, sending iridescent pigeons into the balloon-freckled sky.

Chapter Two

APRIL 2001

SHE WHEELED onto the shoulder, hopped out and broke into an exasperated jog, passing four lanes of idling vehicles, including two TV vans, as she approached the span, hoping like hell her photographer was already there to capture the bridge shrouded in this morning funk of fog and light rain that seeped into your bones no matter what anybody said or how well you slept or how much espresso you swallowed. Once she got to the orange cones, she saw cops pacing in the lane closest to this lanky young woman standing soldierly atop the narrow concrete railing, steady as a gymnast in black Levi's and thick-heeled work boots.

A quick scan of the crowd turned up a half dozen breathless reporters and photographers. God, she hated these gangbangs, everyone's IQ halved in the frenzy to get the story, a story, *any* story. There was no getting out of this one, though. She was the closest reporter to the bridge when the "potential jumper" crackled across the newsroom scanner. So once again she was assigned to a story she wasn't hired to do, though that increasingly seemed to be the paper's MO, with younger reporters filling the news holes while veterans averted eyes, intimidated editors or feigned industry while playing computer solitaire or outlining novels about divorced journalists finding true love again. During the past few weeks, Helen had been yanked off her five-part epic on the inexplicable rise and spectacular collapse of groceriesnow.com so often that the project had been postponed indefinitely. The latest edict from above was for her to produce *enterprising* retrospectives on the 1962 World's Fair. She'd waded just deep enough into the clip files to realize it was the worst assignment imaginable.

The escalating indignation on the bridge sounded oddly misplaced in a city that was always bragging about its manners. As honks and shouts rose in the anonymous gloom, it sounded more like a hostile rush hour in Philly, D.C. or New York.

"Come on!"

Helen started collecting details so she'd have word pictures if the woman actually jumped and generated some news. Yellow caution tape. Dimpled water winking through the steambath. Three waddling cops: one twirling his flashlight like a baton, one on the radio, one small-talking the jumper in a gentle mumble.

Then, during the longest lull yet, someone about ten cars back howled, "Just jump, bitch!"

Whether the woman heard the taunt or not, she jumped or, rather, stepped.

The falling body didn't look like a full-grown woman, more like a shrinking child wheeling its arms, trying to regain balance, as if reconsidering the whole ordeal several times before audibly slapping the gray canal, her splash as curiously discreet as an Olympic dive.

Helen tried to find the heckler but got only sheepish headshakes before the flashlight cop shooed her off the bridge. She phoned the newsroom, trotted back to her car, then rolled off into heavier rain. Her defroster was no match for all this moisture, so she rubbed the windshield with her forearm; and when she cracked the window, rain pelted her face. Stopping at a blurry red, she watched commuters on bikes. There were joggers, too, and a man in a suit on a skateboard being pulled by a black Lab. Even pedestrians glided by without hats or umbrellas in fleece jackets and ultralight hiking boots, as if they might scale Rainier that afternoon if the weather cleared. Back East, exercise junkies had the decency to do it behind health-club walls. Out here everybody was an exhibitionist, though she did marvel at their rain Zen, striding into it, not *away* from or *out* of it. Her own disarray swung back into focus. A cereal bowl on the dash. Newspapers, folders, notebooks and pens strewn across the coffee-stained

passenger seat. Chipped mugs on the floor next to a toy dump truck
and the cheapest of her violins.

At times, she forgot that moving out here was her idea. The original plan was to write for a feisty daily in one of America's last competitive newspaper markets as far away from D.C. as possible. They
flew her out and seduced her with all the *ass-kicking* stories they
couldn't wait to assign to someone *with her talents.* The day she'd
interviewed, a local billionaire christened a new rock 'n' roll museum
by smashing a glass guitar in a rebellious spasm that seemed to say,
Look, even our establishment is radical! The job, the newspaper, the
city, it all seemed irresistible, especially at vivid twilight with a congratulatory cocktail and all these skyscrapers jockeying for views of
this freakishly scenic place.

But like most of her dates, it quickly fell short of expectations.
The *Post-Intelligencer* was in worse straits than anyone admitted,
and not even a bona fide daily. There was no Sunday stage for her
work. How had she glossed over that? And even the city turned out
to be a two-faced tease, a chilling rain pissing on her by the time she
returned with Elias to hunt for an apartment. Yet it was the preten-
sion that annoyed her, not the weather. She'd never seen a city this full
of itself. The most livable! The most literary! The best place to locate
a business or raise a kid or have a dog or get cancer! The capital of
the new world economy! And the locals swallowed all these national
rankings and blather, even during this current dot-com hangover. *Just
look!* they told her, as if the views alone justified the hype. Seattle
reminded her of men she'd known who'd been told too many times
how handsome they were.

She spent most of the next hour repeating and affirming what
she'd just heard and seen, the editors debating whether "Just jump,
bitch" was too inflammatory, and if there was actually a story here
at all or just a *brief,* seeing how bridge jumps were fairly common.
Those arguments were discarded, though, once KING-5 led with the
jump-bitch quote on its noon broadcast. By then it was also clear the
jumper had amazingly survived, which opened other doors. The lede
for a story on road rage? Ultimately it was deemed a punchy daily

with a follow-up for the social services reporter, who'd been looking for a peg for a story about the city's suicidal tendencies.

Still, Helen scrambled to make her twelve column inches breathe. The Aurora Bridge was second only to the Golden Gate in suicide leaps. She looked up *aurora,* and found a Roman myth about *the goddess of dawn.* Is that who the jumper was, or why she survived? She considered checking weather patterns for the last ten jumps to see if anyone ever did it on sunny days. No, she told herself, keep it simple and get back to those insufferable World's Fair archives.

Her editor, Shrontz, called her assignment an honor, explaining in vague if glowing terms how the fair was the coming-out party that launched modern Seattle. What a perfect little project, he told her, *for an enterprising reporter who can really write.* The newsroom was still getting used to Helen. She wrote fast yet colorfully, her stories often reading like news-feature hybrids that confused the copy desk. With the fortieth anniversary looming, the *Times* was gonna be *all over the fair,* Shrontz kept telling her. She was hating him again. Liked him, then hated him, respected him, then resented him for confronting her about Elias, as if she'd lied during the interview by not mentioning that she had a son.

She reloaded on espresso, then camped out in the *P-I* library, skimming books, magazines and newspaper clippings, reassuring herself that they'd let her return to her dot-com drama if she delivered a few nostalgic gems about the fair. What a long shot to beat out New York and land the first American expo in decades, back when world fairs were must-see spectacles and Seattle was a sleepy Boeing bunkhouse without a freeway. Yet from what she could tell, the fair was an artifact of the corniest of American times and, worse yet, a local sacred cow with fawning coverage shamelessly regurgitated through the ten-, twenty- and thirty-year remembrances. By now it was a myth, and with that realization she felt a rebellious desire to expose the truth about the fair.

Starting cautiously, she prepared a story about it being an unreliable crystal ball, given how the official program predicted we'd be sleeping in rotating houses, commuting in flying cars and eating scrambled eggs out of aerosol cans by now. She noticed, however, that the fair's president, Roger Morgan, had the foresight to add this qualifier for the next generation: "If we're accurate, we will have amazed you. If not, we hopefully will have amused you."

She needed to talk to Morgan but kept putting it off, knowing she'd get only one chance to catch *the silver-tongued P. R. Hercules*— as one reporter gushed—off-guard with her questions. People still called him *the father of the fair* or *Mr. Seattle* or, more often, just *Roger,* as if there were only one. *Ask Roger. Call Roger.* Everyone deferring to his memory.

Reworking her questions now, she was surprised to find his number in the white pages, but hung up mid-dial. Maybe she should start with Ted Severson or one of the other surviving notables, though they'd given bland quotes nine years ago and no doubt would encourage her to talk to the man himself. She dialed again, and a young woman casually informed her that he was at a funeral. "Although you might be able to visit with him tonight, at his party."

"His party?"

"Well, you know he's turning seventy, right?"

Helen made the mistake of mentioning this to Shrontz, who lit up and insisted she cover it—not as a daily piece, but to gather fresh material for a Roger Morgan profile.

All three of her unreliable babysitters were unavailable, as usual, so she dragged Elias along. He looked like he'd been force-fed sugar at preschool again, talking too fast, his pupils dilated. She tried to listen, but it was hard. Some bully named Cameron Falkenberg—he called every kid by his full name—wouldn't play with him, and Miss Cantrell was blowing her nose all day, and there was some elaborate conflict on the playground that didn't make any sense. Her eyes panned the glistening skyline as a cruise ship peeled away from the waterfront like an entire city block calving into the bay. Now he was talking about Buzz and Woody and the rest of the *Toy Story* cast as if they were close friends. She parked illegally near Ivar's, the only fast food he'd eat lately, and stepped onto the waterfront boardwalk amid the daily flotsam of tourists, rummies and shrieking seagulls.

Fries in hand, they rolled south on Alaskan Way with Elias pointing out the port's huge cranes—"Orange dinosaurs!"—and Helen trying to recall which east-west street wasn't a luge run. Locals climbed these comically steep sidewalks like brainless mountain goats, as if there was nothing ludicrous about building a city on cliffs. She guessed wrong on Spring and smoked the clutch on the lip of Third, waiting for the light, before speeding to University and then up to Sixth, where she parked in a loading zone and jaywalked, Elias clinging to her hand and jogging to keep up as they slipped past bellmen dressed like third-world dictators onto the white marble floors of the Olympic Hotel.

Shrontz guessed the location. *Where else would Roger Morgan party?* Shiny new escalators aside, the brick and terra-cotta hotel was a time capsule, exuding the 1920s, with an elegant balcony surrounding the massive lobby. Holding hands again, Helen and Elias scampered up marble stairs to the Spanish Ballroom, where tall double doors opened to a noisy banquet hall the size of a basketball court with bejeweled chandeliers, paisley carpet and more than thirty tables surrounded by dapper seniors.

Helen couldn't recall seeing so many old people in one place before, and just about everyone was laughing, their delighted cackles bouncing off the high ceiling. A commanding amplified voice rose above the ruckus, followed by more life-threatening laughter.

She hand-combed Elias's hair and led him to the only empty table in the back as the short, bald speaker clutched the microphone as if to steady himself on the little stage. "Will you *look* at him," he said wistfully. She saw where he was pointing now and matched Roger Morgan's silver hair and still-bright smile with his clippings. "Ahhh," the speaker said, "to be seventy again. Wouldn't that be nice?"

Helen slowed her eyes and noticed all the pearls, diamonds, shawls and elbow-length gloves, all the pinstripes and tiepins and cuff links. She wished she had a photographer and a guest list of all these fading doctors, lawyers, tycoons and their wives. She tried to take it all in at once. The black bunting skirting the stage. The mirrored wall seemingly doubling the crowd size. Twenty-foot arched windows framed by columns carved with winged horses. Almost any crescendo of detail absorbed and soothed her. No need to *tell* the readers much. Just be their eyes.

The speaker was now rattling off a story about Morgan that didn't track. People looked distracted, laughed out, older. She watched a tiny woman pop pills, then lean across the table to wipe her husband's cheek. When Helen turned back, Elias had vanished. Rising, she spotted him stomping stiff-legged and unnoticed across the floor. When she caught up, he shifted into high whine. He wanted to leave. She fished a deck of cards from her purse and told him to sit *still* until he found all four aces.

Parched and sweaty, she released her ponytail and threw her head around like a horse, her thick locks springing free and settling wider than her shoulders like the roots of a toppled oak. When she looked up again, she saw bug-eyed grandpas staring at her as if she'd just exposed her breasts.

Another old man hobbled to the microphone, this one tall and angular with the raspy voice of a smoker. "I'm gonna keep this short because there isn't much to say about this fella other than that he's been a better friend than I deserve going on forty-two years now." Helen assumed this must be Ted Severson, though he didn't look anything like his fair photos. "Roger is so beloved people often overlook the fact that I'm a surly bastard." People were chuckling and engaged again. "He's got such a relentlessly good disposition that even I can't tell when he's bent out of shape. But making him happy, that's easy: just ask him about anything that's ever happened in this city. As you know, Roger suffers from an attention *surplus* disorder. Nothing escapes his interest, including the welfare of old coots like us. And that's all I've got to say about this SOB other than to state the obvious, which is that he's still the finest civic man this city has to offer and has been for four decades now."

She watched Morgan mosey toward the podium until Elias waved four aces in front of her nose. She grabbed him and the cards and speed-walked around the tables for a closer look, oddly exhilarated that the man she'd been studying in the abstract of 1962 was actually about to speak in public tonight, right *now*. She watched him shake hands, everybody reaching for him, swinging his arm to give the point of contact a slight pop the way younger men do, his left hand working shoulders, forearms, necks. He was more dashing than she'd expected, a blue handkerchief angling from his breast pocket, silver cuff links pecking from his suit sleeves. He looked built to last and too young for this crowd, with smile lines that suggested the good life and teeth too white to be natural but not so bright as to look fake.

Elias vied for her attention by chewing on the ace of clubs. She pried it from his mouth and collected more details. A wife shouting at her husband to turn up his hearing aid. A couple in their eighties with identical blue-black hair dye. A palsied woman near the stage pulling a plastic neck brace out of her purse, hurrying to tighten the strap until it stopped her head from trembling. Helen glanced at Morgan and at the other tables, trying not to miss anything, but she couldn't resist watching this neck-braced woman reaching in her purse now for Altoids, the can rattling hopelessly in her hand. Helen glanced back to Morgan, who was closing in on the stage. Somehow the woman popped the lid, bounced a mint into her mouth and dropped the tin into her purse just as he arrived at her table. "Wonderful to see you, Blanche," he said, bending down to kiss her steady forehead before stepping up to the podium.

"Thanks to Teddy and Evan for still lying about me after all these years," Morgan began. "By now, I really can't tell if they forget how many times I've ticked them off or if they're just getting nostalgic for all the aggravation I've inflicted." He let the room settle. "There was a time—and I remember it better than I recall last week—when all of us together in this room could constitute a revolution." He grinned through laughter. "Anyone remember my seven a.m. *working* break-fasts?" Groans mixed with chortles. "Well, it pains me to think that us gathering here tonight doesn't give a governor, or even a mayor, any indigestion. Hell, in the day, six of us could meet for a drink and change the course of history."

He let them revel in that. "But we're not running this city any-more. And, for the most part, that's a good thing. *But,*" he said, tap-ping his fingertips as if praying, "that doesn't mean we're done yet, does it?"

His stridency startled people, though not the prior speaker, whom Helen saw nodding and smiling, tapping a box of cigarettes against his palm.

"When we see this city going off the rails we still feel the call, don't we? Well, old friends, this city is off its rails."

The hubbub rose as Morgan rambled on, the responses increasingly out of proportion to what was actually being said. Gunshot laughter where there should have been chuckles. Affirmative groans where there should have been silence. Helen wrote what she saw and heard, her pen gliding across the page without her looking at it, trying to pinpoint the man's unusual tone.

"This has never *ever* been a city where people encourage a suicidal woman to jump off a bridge rather than hold up rush hour any longer. But that's what happened this morning, if you didn't hear. Luckily, the young lady survived, but the point is, this used to be a place where people *helped* each other. And I'm personally tired of all the inconsiderates, people who leave briefcases in the seats next to them on buses and don't acknowledge the presence of an elderly woman. We've accomplished remarkable things here with people of all ages and backgrounds working together and embracing newcomers and fresh ideas. Yet here we are coming off yet another boom with little to show for it other than more insensitivity and hostility. *Am I wrong?*"

The resounding "No!" carried more oomph than Helen had figured this crowd could summon. Morgan didn't sound quite like any politician she'd heard before. A more intimate voice, it sounded like your favorite truth-telling uncle after he'd had a few beers. She found the prior speaker's face again—Ted Severson, she was now certain, with an unlit cigarette dangling from his grinning lips.

"I tell you one thing: I'm sick and tired of city hall being a place where great ideas go to die," Roger said softly now. "This city needs vision again." The ballroom stirred with murmurs. "For many years many of you used to call me *the real mayor*. And I admit I enjoyed it, but I haven't heard that in a while. And I've been thinking that now just might be the right time to run while I've still got the energy and most of my original joints and organs." Severson started to rise, fell back into his chair, then tried again. More people rose, confusion careening toward excitement.

"All I will need," he said, suddenly defiant, "is one term." He let the words linger as disjointed cheers and clapping spread and more people struggled to stand up. "That's right," he said, louder still. "I'm asking for your help once again." He smiled and took a breath. *"Are you with me?"*

Helen punched the numbers into her cell for the newsroom, feeling as if she'd inadvertently overheard a coup conspiracy less than a half hour before the paper's second deadline. By the time the irritable night editor picked up—"City Desk"—the ballroom was too loud for her to be heard over the shouts and croaks and hoots. She watched men and women in their eighties and nineties fighting to their feet, others tiring and plopping back down like a poorly executed wave of undulating sports fans. People started banging coffee cups on tables. Canes thumped the floor. A large woman in a handicapped scooter pounded her horn. Three women danced a slow jig, people tapped forks against glasses and one table started a "Ro-ger! Ro-ger!" chant that spread across the room.

Helen broke toward the exit doors so she could be heard before realizing she'd lost sight of Elias again, then hung up and frantically looked for him in the ruckus. A plate fell and shattered. Thinking it was on purpose, a thin man whooped and hurled a water glass against the wall, though not hard enough to break it. Then his friend threw a wineglass and succeeded. When Helen finally spotted her son he was standing across the ballroom next to Morgan himself, coming up to his waist, the two of them seemingly enjoying a casual interchange amid the madness. The city's newest mayoral candidate pulled some sort of doll out of his pocket and handed it to Elias. Behind them, Ted Severson calmly lit his cigarette, the smoke billowing from his smile.

When the shouting and laughter reached a climax, servers, cooks and dishwashers burst through the kitchen doors into the back of the room to witness the bedlam that rose up and over the thick walls into Seattle's oldest streets.

Chapter Three

MAY 1962

THE SLOW START quiets the alarmists who warned that the Century 21 Exposition would paralyze downtown, and the smaller crowds give the staff a chance to develop a rhythm in herding people into exhibits, shows, rides and up the Needle. And, deep into the second week now, Roger is finding his stride as the master of ceremonies, introducing luminaries, regaling journalists and hawking the city to visiting tycoons.

For once, his provincial port shimmers with worldliness. Filipino dancers, Thai silk, Frenchwomen dousing everybody with perfume. And the food! The sudden aroma of Danish sausages, Belgian waffles and Mongolian steaks in a place accustomed to burgers, fish sticks and hot dogs. As all the strange license plates suggest, the fair is rapidly becoming the new destination of the great American road trip, with families puttering into town in bug-smeared Valiants, Skylarks and Bel Airs, just curious as hell ever since they saw the Space Needle on the cover of *Time, Sunset* or *Life.* They come by train and Boeing airliners too, thousands flying for the first time on gleaming new 707s. And Roger sees all these visitors as potential residents, straining their necks to gape at the views. And there is so much to do! Ride the silent monorail, then spend a few hours in the Science Pavilion, or how about the World of Art—*never before, never again?* Or meander over to Show Street for a futuristic striptease while the wife checks out the fashion exhibit—*new models every two hours.* Then throw a few pennies into the reflecting pool, recharge in the Food Circus and loosen your tie or slip off those heels. Hear that background jingle? *Hi-ho, come to the fair. See the world of tomorrow today!*

Roger's days start at his fairgrounds office, where the cheerful secretary he'd instantly nicknamed Jenny Sunshine brought him stacks of reports, requests and complaints. It would be hard to beat the opening-day air force disaster, which demolished three homes and killed two citizens, but there is a daily onslaught of snafus. And most mornings, shortly before eleven, he speed-walks to the Plaza of the States, where the marching band plays the same songs, over and over again, before and after his effusive introductions of visiting notables. Crowds for these formalities vary wildly. The governor of Alabama gets skunked. The shah of Iran gets mobbed. Then come the astronauts. First Gherman Titov shows up, boasting about his space travels and poking fun at Western religious notions. "I saw neither angels nor gods up there," he smugly observes. People are appalled, particularly Teddy, though still awed until John Glenn shows up. Having just orbited the earth three times in five hours, he attracts far bigger throngs scrambling for a glimpse of America's freshly minted hero.

After the meet-and-greets, Roger usually whisks the VIPs to Club 21, the exclusive expo lounge, for lunch or cocktails, and tries to get their impressions, though they are rarely illuminating. This time it's Ed Sullivan prattling over martinis about how Los Angeles is dying until Roger interrupts. "So, what do you make of Seattle, Mr. Sullivan?"

Hunched and neckless, Sullivan glares at his martini. "Feels like Nevada to me." He sucks the olive and spits it back into his glass.

Roger fakes a chuckle, but the variety-show king remains hunkered down like a grumpy turtle. "Whole lot of gambling," he finally mutters.

Smiling and nodding, Roger leaves open the possibility that this is a crafty setup for some joke about Seattle or Nevada or gambling in general, but that's all there is.

Journalists are so much easier to read. He loads them into vans and hauls them around, exaggerating the city's growth rate and insisting it's on its way to being, in Teddy's words, *big league,* with an expanding economy and people eyeballing it for pro sports franchises and, well, everything else, really, nailing the expectant tone without crowing. It's not all that different from selling the idea of the fair in the first place, a matter of weaving the urban history into a flattering narrative until lines like *Seattle is the ripest city for development in the most dynamic state in the West* are accepted as fact. He shows off all-American neighborhoods full of roomy homes with daylight basements and blooming rhododendrons. "Ten-thousand-dollar houses with ten-million-dollar views," he says, knowing reporters can't resist superlatives. He isn't sure where he heard this one, though he spins it as gospel: *Seattle has gone from a wilderness to a big city faster than any place in the world.*

Positive press begets more of the same and then gets recycled in local papers, the echo continuing with visiting celebrities feeling obliged to praise this "jewel box of a fair." Walt Disney raved about it, and John Wayne called it fantastic. Sure, the theme is sanguine— Science is coming to the rescue!—but it's not all happy talk, either, otherwise it wouldn't indulge the specter of bomb shelters in every home, would it? And if it isn't a serious venue, why is NASA brass and the vice president himself flying out here to chat about "the peaceful uses of space"?

On the morning of the conference, John Glenn asks to see the World of Tomorrow. As Roger leads him into the Coliseum, Glenn smiles and waves at fans and cameras and carries himself like a patriotic superhero, as if recognizing that his role—*Spaceman*—has never been played before. He's also the breathing, wholesome, square-jawed proof that America will get to the future first. Yet he rubs his nose, gets food caught in his teeth and loses his hair just like the rest of us, which makes us all potential spacemen, right?

Glenn and Roger lay beside each other on the carpeted floor of the Bubbleator, a massive glass elevator rising through images of twenty-first-century life. Houses with push-button windows, disposable dishes and helicopter pads in cities shielded by weather domes. "Pretty nifty," Glenn mumbled afterward, though nothing seems to have really registered.

"What do you think of our city?" Roger asks, now escorting him to the NASA exhibit, matching his stride and posture so well that they look like *two* famous spacemen strolling the grounds.

"It's your city," Glenn responds. "You tell me."

"What I want it to be, sir," Roger explains, "is a different kind of city, a big city that still feels like it's on the edge of the forest, yet a true cosmopolis with opera and clams and symphonies and deer and Major League Baseball, if you know what I mean."

Glenn stares through him with eyes as unresponsive as marbles.

"Well, in your opinion, sir," Roger prods awkwardly, "what do you think makes a city great?"

Glenn offers him a clumsy wink. "I'd start with an honest police force."

Roger forces a laugh, but isn't sure if Glenn's joking.

The astronaut beams for more cameras, muttering through his strangely even teeth. "Saw the headlines on my way in."

Roger nods with false understanding, then later rifles the papers, skipping stories about China getting its own bomb and the Birchers calling city hall's fluoridation plan a Communist ploy until he finds a short piece inside the *P-I* about the note a Pioneer Square tavern owner posted in his window: *Thank you for your patronage for the past three years. This tavern has been forced to close because I refused to make further extortion payments to the racket whose enforcers are members of the city's police force. I am willing to take a lie detector test, though I know the great white chief and the lord high mayor dare not.*

There was nothing more from the bar owner, Charlie McDaniel, and little from the police other than a brief comment that his accusation lacked credibility.

"The guy's a crackpot," Teddy says, reading over his shoulder. "A real nut job."

At the NASA conference that afternoon, Lyndon Baines Johnson's opening speech is instantly forgettable, but that doesn't matter. The place is overrun with reporters as attention swings from Glenn to unknown pilots and scientists, then back to the famous astronaut. People shout questions, drowning out reporters. "See any UFOs up there, John?"

Afterward, amid a dizzying crush, the vice president and other politicos are served Olympia oysters and Dungeness crab legs atop the Needle. This is where Roger has most of his meals now, usually with out-of-town CEOs fishing for tax breaks and cheap properties. He softens them with his recruitment chatter, gets them drunk, finds out their needs and timelines, then watches their excitement build during the hour it takes the dining room to make a complete revolution. As the sun sinks behind the Olympics, he hears himself making promises he can't keep, but it's festive handshakes all around with everyone vowing to do their damnedest. Then he's off to work on the grain exporters or the auto dealers or the aluminum manufacturers. But this is a political gathering, with LBJ's presence attracting a senator, the mayor, a congressman and the local U.S. attorney. And the more festive it gets, the darker Roger's mood becomes, his worries going well beyond the fair. It's what wasn't said at the conference that alarms him, such as Kennedy's announcement this morning that atomic testing will resume and, almost as an aside, that the Pentagon is installing long-range missiles about a hundred miles southeast of Seattle.

He studies Johnson's furrowed face, his jowly mug a vault of secrets. His aides had cryptically hinted that he almost didn't fly out at all. As if sensing the scrutiny, he suddenly focuses his hound-dog eyes on Roger. "Let's pop outside and chew the fat."

They excuse themselves and head up to the observation deck, where LBJ sticks out a big hand, keeping his security boys out of earshot, then breaks wind noisily. Roger braces himself for whatever he intends to confide, desperately wanting the conversation to develop before someone interrupts them. Teddy's right. Everything *is* starting to piece together. Kennedy's oddly foreboding words at the opening ceremony. The jarheads insisting on a bomb shelter beneath the Science Pavilion as well as the sudden construction of an underground hideout on Sixty-fifth Street to house as many as two hundred people during an attack. It occurs to him in a hot flash that the word *Seattle* might come to mean something entirely different in the future, as *Hiroshima* would never again be just a Japanese city. He can't resist asking, "Is there any reason to think, sir, that Seattle is a target?"

LBJ looks away, smacking his lips. "Lots of mustaches in this town."

Roger counts to five, then says, "So, sir, is—"

"I almost couldn't fly out here, son," he twangs, squinting at the anchored freighters bobbing like toys in Elliott Bay.

Here we go, Roger thinks, grabbing the railing. "Why's that, sir?" he drawls, as if they hailed from the same sun-baked Texas county.

"Got a swollen right testicle," Johnson tells him. "Ain't supposed to fly."

Roger can't tell if the big man is kidding or just getting at whatever needs to be said in roundabout Texan fashion. So Roger matches his neutral expression and waits, studying the city, neighborhood by neighborhood, as if for the first time—Wallingford, Montlake, Laurelhurst—and the new freeway sections being laid out to the north. It's hard to imagine people doing sixty through the heart of the city, yet he feels excited all over again by all the change this will bring. Most of the buildings in its path have already been bulldozed. The Hotel Kalamar at James and Sixth, gone. Likewise, St. Spiridon's Russian Orthodox Church and some of the city's oldest homes on Sixth and Seventh. Closer to the canal, he notices a large yellow crane hovering over a cleared lot off Roanoke Street and feels his pulse quicken. Construction isn't supposed to begin until *after* the fair. The sight of this crane makes him think about how the senator just called him *his boy* and how the chamber president patted him on the head as if he were a clever cocker spaniel, and how he might have no idea to what extent he's being used.

He catches LBJ measuring him through those slitted eyes and thinks their conversation is about to get somewhere. "Got my tailor to make six pairs of these trousers last year with a little extra in the pockets so my knife and keys don't fall out every time I sit down, see?" He shows off his roomy hip pockets with his fingers. "But I also got a little extra room for the nuts. Told him to put another inch in there between the zipper and my bunghole. Could use a couple more inches now," he adds, rearranging himself and scanning the hills with sudden interest. "Can't get over how there's no goddamn bugs. Any octopus in these lakes?"

Roger struggles to connect the dots: the significance of the crane, the absurdity of the tailoring asides and the octopus question and, above all, how Kennedy could've picked this clodhopper, out of *everybody,* to be his right-hand man.

"What in God's name?" Johnson mutters, distracted by the enormous Goodyear blimp that Teddy has apparently sent up to rescue his friend. Once it reaches restaurant level, the blimp's electronic screen is easily readable: "Welcome to the Space Needle, Mr. Vice President!"

Chapter Four

APRIL 2001

AFTER MONTHS of damp gloom, the low clouds finally lifted and bureaucrats and bums alike leaned against City Hall, their eyes closed, savoring the feeling of sunshine on their faces. It was only sixty-three degrees, but they wanted to strip off their clothes and sacrifice themselves to the stingy sun god. And when they finally opened their eyes again, the bay was brighter and the looming snowball of Mount Rainier had rolled a little closer to downtown.

Helen tried not to fall for the scenery, but it was hard. The upside to all this background drizzle was that the ever-present moisture essentially backlit everything, which was why the grass looked greener and the sky bluer and the pavement blacker; why apples appeared juicier and skin healthier, why Chevrolet and Honda, she'd read, shot their commercials here and why just about everywhere else you went suddenly looked drab.

This seasonal jolt of warmth and clear skies drew more Californians looking for tech jobs, as if they hadn't heard or didn't believe that the boom city had crashed once again. The highest unemployment in the country didn't scare them off because they'd been told Seattle was *different*, a city that *reinvents* the world, right? That *Newsweek* cover was five years old, but the message lingered: *Swimming to Seattle: Everybody else is moving there. Should you?* The answer then and now was *Hell yes!* Sure, Microsoft was getting spanked by judges, and Boeing was mumbling about moving its headquarters to the Midwest. And while this wasn't the same start-up Valhalla it was even a year ago, the venture caps would be back. They got rich even on bad ideas here, so everybody's gearing up for the next big thing. Three of the world's ten richest men still live here for a reason. *Three!*

Helen passed the sun worshipers and went inside to watch the mayor. Douglas Rooney looked bigger than he did the last time she saw him, his suit bunching on his thighs and warping across his meaty back. Word had it he was a carb junkie—not a chip he could resist—yet it all added to his forcefulness. After running the show for seven years, he didn't peek into rooms before entering, his head rarely swiveling on his expanding neck. He looked and moved *forward,* now toward the podium, pretending to engage the overflow of supporters, gophers and advisers who cornered reporters and whispered—*not for attribution, okay?*—that while the mayor didn't suffer fools gladly, he's a *brilliant* tactician. A third term? they asked rhetorically. *Fait accompli.*

He hadn't officially begun running, other than to set up The Nonpartisan Committee for Re-electing Mayor Rooney. Yet he'd been in campaign mode for months now, with a barrage of mailings touting all the new streetlights, sewer extensions and police substations. His flacks had fended off the media for a day and a half, promising the mayor would answer *all* questions—including those about the *new entrant* in the race—at his weekly briefing.

He began, however, by stalling, first giving a numbing update on a feasibility study into replacing a treatment plant north of downtown, then an excruciatingly vague analysis of the upsides and downsides to potential light-rail routes before discussing his meaningless correspondence with sister cities in Costa Rica and Vietnam. Reporters rolled their eyes and feigned wrist slits, reminding Helen of the bridge jumper stepping into space. Snapping back to the present, she wondered how much the mayor's haircut had cost. When he finally opened it up to questions, everybody shouted the same name.

His lips curled into a snarl that bordered on a smile, so the cameras snapped. "I welcome anyone into the race who sincerely believes he has the skills and experience to do this job well."

"How well do you know Mr. Morgan?"

"I know him"—he hesitated—"fairly well." After a pause, he added, "Always welcomed his input through the years."

"Is he dissatisfied with how you're running the city?"

"You'd have to ask him, wouldn't you?" He bristled. "Never said anything of the sort to me."

The mayor glowered as the *Roger* questions continued, the reporters knowing his quotes improve the more riled he gets. "Is he qualified?" Rooney asked, as if that was the stupidest question yet. "Any resident of this city is *qualified*. Look, nobody can diminish his role in bringing the fair here. What all he's done since then that makes him believe he can lead this city in this new century, I'm not as clear on." He paused, sweat glistening above his upper lip. "In fact, I don't even know if he's a Democrat or a Republican."

He never once mentioned Roger or the other candidates by name, apparently hoping voters would think he didn't have any challengers if he avoided naming them.

"Were you at the World's Fair?" Helen asked, and heads spun. Most city hall reporters didn't recognize her, but they knew her byline, especially after her little front-page stunner about Morgan's surprise announcement at the Olympic Hotel.

The mayor found her face in the crowd and sighed, grateful for the digression. "I was thirteen. And I remember the Wild Mouse roller coaster and going up in the Space Needle, of course. And I remember the Roy Rogers show." He brightened. "And eating with chopsticks! That was the very first time I ever used chopsticks."

It didn't surprise her that the mayor gushed on cue. She'd heard similar responses a dozen times now. Ask people what they remembered about the fair and they smiled. Even Helen felt herself getting sucked in after reading an apparently sober historian claim the fair was at its core an act of *rebellion*, that Morgan and Severson went around city hall to make it happen. The Needle itself, he'd suggested, was *a dagger to the belly of stuffy, postwar Seattle*.

After the news conference, she prowled antique shops until she found—tucked amid old books, necklaces, posters and art deco lamps—a junkyard shrine to the fair with Century 21 plates, teacups, shot glasses and cigarette lighters, a *Seattle '62* seat cushion, a World's Fair bolo tie and three slender champagne flutes—at $50 a pop—that helped christen the Space Needle the night before the fair began. She held one up, marveling at the thought of it in someone's hand—perhaps Morgan's—up *there*, on *that* night.

The shop owner hovered nearby, smirking beneath slicked-back hair. "You know where the Bubbleator ended up, right?"

She looked up. "Tell me."

"Some old hippie couple uses it as a greenhouse in West Seattle now," he said in an odd stage whisper. "Growing banana trees and orchids and God knows what else."

"Were you there?"

"The fair? Of course."

"What sticks with you?"

"Everything. Bird's nest soup. A microwave oven. Polynesian dancers. Jackson Pollock's paintings. Elvis."

"You saw him?"

"No, but he was there." She looked away from his yellow smile to the Farrah Fawcett poster behind him. "The King was definitely there. And so was I."

ROGER MORGAN rode shotgun across downtown, his new assistant at the wheel, Teddy napping in the back. He felt strangely alert and anxious from his toes to his scalp, noticing all the block-size craters, half-completed garages, idle cranes and other signs that the city was on hold. What better time to try to lead? He'd been bombarded with congratulations since the party, as if he'd already won something, though there weren't even any notable endorsements yet. He tried to relax by noticing all the changes along Third Avenue.

"Used to be Woolworth's on that side of Pike, and Kress on the other side," he told Annie. "Bookends for thirty or forty years at least, gone without a trace. And twenty-five years ago nobody could've imagined Fifth and Pine without Frederick & Nelson and its Frango mints. About the only thing that hasn't changed is the Bon. But even that looks different."

"You know what?" Annie said. "You should give tours."

"Don't encourage him," Teddy mumbled. "We don't need the eldery candidate reminiscing about the good old days."

Roger laughed but continued. "Used to be billboards all along here. Remember, Teddy?" His voice lowered into 1960s ad-man tenor: " 'Pan Am—the world's most experienced airline.' Chandler's Shoes was over there. And a couple blocks over we had Ernst, Pay 'n Save and Abruzzi's Pizza. Used to have all our own stuff, see. Now we've got what everybody else has. So people like me see ghosts whenever we drive through here. Remember Nick Abruzzi's pizza pies, Teddy?" He glanced back and saw his pal's head slumped awkwardly to the side, his eyes closed, his face worn thin by time, its once vast capacity for expression reduced to this scowling hatchet. Roger watched him until his chest rose, then recalled Nick shuffling out from behind the counter, flour misting off him, his voice a high giggle. *Excuse me, but I want to make sure you all realize you have the good fortune of dining today with the great Roger Morgan, the real mayor of our soggy city.*

"That right there used to be Lamonts," he whispered. "Never got used to that. For me, it'll always be Rhodes—'Seattle's home-owned department store.' Or what about the Polynesian Restaurant on Pier Fifty-one? Had a great run before they barged it to the Duwamish in '81 and torched it for the firefighters. Everything has to be new, understand? So we tear down the old or blow it up. Just ask the Kingdome."

"Roger," Teddy grumbled. "*Focus.* What're you gonna tell these people?"

He laughed. "The truth. What else do I got?" He shuts up, though, and tries to imagine everything that might entail.

A couple moments later, Teddy rested a cold hand on his shoulder, slid it to his neck and squeezed. "Let 'em know you've always been on their side, and you hope they'll be on yours. You've got it. Just don't fly off the handle on the mayor or the police, for Chrissakes."

Of the many times he'd accompanied candidates into this conference room, he'd never seen it this packed. Fifteen burly men crowded the table. Another dozen lined the walls. Roger shook the closest hands, instantly feeling ancient and brittle as Teddy dropped too swiftly onto a wooden chair and muzzled a groan.

As the room quieted, Roger thanked everyone for meeting on such short notice. They fidgeted, muscles twitching beneath hairy forearms. "As some of you may have noticed, I've been around awhile." He expected snickers, at least grins, but missed entirely, then heard himself listing former union leaders he'd known. He knew how gauche this must sound. Ambition is fine, he used to tell candidates, as long as you don't show it. "I've watched the power of unions shrink around here," Roger said, wishing he'd shut up and listen. "Yet this is still a stronghold and just needs to be stronger."

Making eye contact wasn't getting any easier, and he knew he was saying the same things politicians had said in this room since the beginning of time. So he cut to the companies he'd heard might be *amenable*—he almost said *vulnerable*—to organizing. The chairman yawned without opening his mouth. "Thanks, Mr. Morgan, but we've been working on them for years now."

When Roger asked what they were looking for in a mayor, they shifted in their seats until the chairman softly said, "I think you know."

"Then can we just lay it on the table here?" He bit off a smile that he knew looked phony. "What do I need to do to get your support?"

He listened to the chairman tell him what he already knew while scolding himself for rushing this meeting in the first place. These people weren't here to meet the next mayor. They were here to see a relic. His suit, his shoes, his hair—everything about him straight out of some wax museum. He heard belly laughs through the walls as they strolled out.

"Blew that one," he said once they stepped outside and Teddy lit a Pall Mall. He'd cut back during his sixties, but once he'd turned seventy he'd said the hell with it and went back to burgers, ice cream and unfiltered cigarettes.

"You'll find your way," Teddy said, his breath catching on the smoke. "You were better in there than you think you were."

"Nah, I didn't connect. Not even close. They didn't know who I was."

"You kiddin' me?" Teddy licked a knuckle to remove a tobacco speck from the tip of his tongue. "Why you think so many showed up? But you know what, I'm not helping you any. You should bring in that young hotshot Ryan what's-his-name who ran Gilbey's campaign. That kid is a shark, and he'd come cheap."

"Yeah, but I wouldn't listen to him." Roger started toward the car. "I barely listen to you."

Driving away, the city suddenly felt oddly foreign. Everywhere he looked people were muttering to themselves or mumbling on cell phones. Who could tell the difference anymore? And the half-empty office towers looked generic and disposable, like they'd get knocked down and hauled to the dump once the party was really over. Even the new street signs seemed hostile—*Click it or Ticket! Litter and it hurts!* Why the hell, he wondered, would anyone want to be mayor of a city he no longer recognized?

"The machinists matter more anyhow," Teddy volunteered. "What you just did was your practice round, okay? But you think you can get me home? I'm dragging a bit here, in case you haven't noticed."

HELEN SAT ACROSS from a smiling, ponytailed man and read the button on his hemp jacket: *I'll have a mocha vodka marijuana latte to go, please.*

Omar Duran was the executive director of Small Footprint, a one-man nonprofit advocating tiny cars and houses, less trash and fewer possessions. When Helen called for a quote on a global-warming story, she'd found him so entertaining that she profiled him a week later. The photos alone were worth it—six-foot-three Omar crammed inside his Smart Car, and another of him standing next to his tiny houseboat.

"I'm no fan of the mayor, but at least we know what he'll do." He leaned across the table so only she could hear. "He's into *appearing* green, not *being* green." His eyes scanned hers for comprehension. "Makes pledges he has no intention of fulfilling. There's no real commitment to anything beyond stroking his own carrot."

"Charming endorsement," Helen said, increasingly impatient,

though her tone remained gentle. "But I'm not writing about the mayor."

Having learned long ago not to socialize with radicals, she'd ducked Omar's prior attempts to coax her out for coffee, yet here she was with this uncompromising enviro-madman on the edge of Pioneer Square sitting outside Café Bengodi in brilliant rush-hour daylight, a pint of Guinness on his side of the table, an ice water on hers, all because he'd hinted that he might have something on Roger Morgan.

The sudden screech of a violin somewhere in the square launched a flock of pigeons into the sky behind him, followed by a messy two-octave scale in A minor and another piercingly high G sharp. Helen chided herself that this was how bad she'd sound if she didn't practice more. Glancing back down, she caught Omar staring at the scar that ran like a pink bead of caulk across the base of her neck and resisted offering her standard explanation that the noose broke.

"Look, I'm not an environmental reporter, and I'm not even covering this race, okay? I wrote a quickie daily because Morgan announced when I happened to be there. I'm writing about the fair, not . . ." She glanced at her ringing phone, saw her mother's number flashing on the screen. "My editor," she said. "I've gotta run, but please tell me what you've heard."

"Can I tell you something else first?"

Checking her watch, she felt the mounting pressure to go pick up her son before she got trapped in traffic. Eight joggers grunted past, followed by the whoosh of three bicyclists in skin-tight neon. "No," she said softly, "you can't. And I'm sorry, but I doubt you've got anything really useful anyway."

He laughed and finished his beer. "O ye of no faith."

She grabbed her satchel, slid her chair back without any intention of leaving and listened to the deranged outdoor violinist make the opening to Bach's Sonata no. 1 in G Minor sound like a wounded cat.

"There's an old gadfly I've known ever since I moved here," he said. "Used to make a career out of suing the city for this and that. Probably in his mid-seventies by now. Not an altogether appealing guy, to be honest, but his shit checks out."

She held her bag across her chest, as if she was still about to flee. "He challenged the cruise ships coming in here. Lots of people were pissed, though he's the only one to give 'em hell at every turn. But he does everything behind the scenes. Practically nobody's heard of him."

There was no obvious reason to find Omar appealing, especially if you broke him into parts—gap-toothed smile, boxer's nose, sunken eyes and a receding hairline yanked back into a short ponytail he obsessively retightened. Maybe it was his irreverence, how he left price tags on his Value Village shirts so you could see how little he paid for them. Or perhaps his boyish enthusiasm reminded her of Elias. His Midwest roots also probably helped, though almost every-body she'd met came from somewhere else, which made this the per-fect city, she thought, for fugitives like herself.

"This guy lives alone on the backside of Queen Anne in a little dump *filled* with papers," Omar continued, patting the air next to his chair to help her visualize the stacks. "It's not that he's insane, you know. Just a pack rat. Well, maybe he is nuts, but he keeps meticu-lous files on *everyone* he doesn't like."

Helen had always been able to sense when somebody was about to say something that might give a story life. The catch was, you had to be the sort of person they wanted to tell it to, and everyone's different. Some need to be shoved. With others you just hunkered down and waited quietly, like birds do when they feel the air thinning before a storm.

Her phone went off again. It was Shrontz now. She turned off the ringer and looked back to Omar. "Yes?"

"He doesn't forget or forgive anything."

"Okay."

"He's known Morgan since before the fair. Claims he's got a file he's been compiling since back then just in case he was ever dumb enough—*his words*—to run for anything."

Helen sipped water to hide her excitement. The streets had gone strangely quiet, as if all the cars had picked another route and some-one had paid the violinist to shut up.

"Know what he calls Morgan?" Omar asked.

She shook her head, unable to block her smile.

"The False Prince."

ROGER CHECKED his voice messages, half of them from reporters requesting interviews. "Wake up, Teddy."

"Huh?"

"We're almost at your place." He turned to face him. "What do you know about that young *P-I* woman who showed up at the party?"

Teddy smacked his lips. "The new girl?"

"Yeah. She wants an interview. What do we know about her?"

"Well, she's got an amazing head of hair, that's for sure."

"Thanks, pal. That's a big help. Can you call your favorite columnist over there and find out about her?"

Teddy groaned himself upright. "She looks like she stepped right out of a shampoo commercial."

Chapter Five

MAY 1962

ROGER TRIES to keep it to two whiskeys, but a third slides down and it's all he can do to stop himself from hugging everyone as Club 21 overflows with suited men and perfumed women waiting to pay homage, to get a picture or have a word with him, or more likely to request a favor now that the fair's such a hit—in the words of *Life* magazine, "an exposition of soaring beauty and unique impact." He tries to say yes to everything. Yes to tickets to the Ice Follies, San Francisco Ballet and Count Basie Orchestra. Yes to arranging meetings with the chamber, the mayor and, perhaps, the governor. Yes to more passes into this VIP lounge. Yes, yes, yes! He'll do what he can, and usually does while simultaneously squeezing as much as he can into his days, running on reminders in a pocket notebook and three hours of sleep. Even his dreams don't give him a break anymore. He's always at the fair.

Mostly local notables in here tonight—the city attorney, the public-works gang, the rumpled mayor, the nearly blind city planner chatting with the nearly bald Malcolm Turner. Roger waits for an opening to speak with the manic little developer while absorbing praise. *Good God, you must be tickled to death!* Nimbly bouncing from person to person; he recalls his father working crowds like this, rolling up his sleeves and pointing at you, his thumb cocked, as if toasting or shooting you, engaging everyone without committing to anyone. Teddy, as usual, takes the opposite tack, cornering key people in deep conversations while occasionally swapping eyebrow-shrugging status reports with Roger, who finds Count Basie himself in a back booth with friends. He hopes like hell he hasn't already missed all of Basie's shows. He doesn't want to *miss* anything. The more he sees, the more he needs to see.

A portly man with a bowling ball head and milky blue eyes blocks his path and offers his hand without extending it, forcing Roger to step closer. "Mr. Morgan," he says. "Dave Beck."

"Of course," Roger says, recognizing the Teamsters boss once he gets over being startled.

Beck pulls him closer. "I'm told you run one heck of a fair," he says in a boyish whisper.

The compliment feels suspect, seeing how everyone says Beck runs everything and had all the fair workers signed up with one of his unions. "Thank you, sir," Roger says, matching Beck's sustained grip and wondering when he'll get his hand back.

He glimpses Malcolm Turner talking the ear off another bureaucrat, and also notices Meredith Stein in animated conversation, her large glass of red suggesting she occasionally slips out of character as the fair's imposing arts director. He'd dropped into her galleries again this afternoon, striding past the classics to the mods, where half an hour blew by in what felt like a few minutes. The man she's talking to pivots enough for Roger to see it's Sid Chambliss. Almost three years had passed since he'd told the feisty attorney that the fair needed the Freemasons' Nile Temple at Third and Thomas. He'd played a similar unpopular role with the state board picking the freeway route, his name burbling through subsequent lawsuits claiming unlawful condemnation, as if he alone decided which buildings lived and died.

"Let me know if you need *anything*," Beck says, finally releasing his hand, narrowing his eyes. "You hear?"

"Same goes for you, Mr. Beck." Part of looking comfortably in charge, Roger has learned, requires offering help, not requesting it. "You let *me* know."

He intercepts Chambliss by cutting in front of a business columnist for the *Times*.

"Sid!" Roger says festively, grabbing his shoulder. "Glad you made it!"

Chambliss looks aghast. "I suggest," he says, leaning in with his bourbon breath, "that you don't misread things. Business, not plea-sure, brings me here."

"Never understood that distinction," Roger mock-whispers back.

Chambliss hesitates and leans closer, his freckles looking like some tropical disease running into his hairline. "We're going ahead with the suit. You know that, right?"

Roger rocks backward and laughs, noticing Teddy watching, feel-ing the *Times* man listening. "You're very welcome," he half-shouts. "Enjoy yourself!" He turns and starts for Malcolm Turner but is way-laid by women demanding photos with him, their intoxication and the lighting making them all look far chummier than they actually are. When he turns to look past the shapely woman next to him, her bright smile blocks his view, and his left hand, he realizes, is lingering on the small of her back. If he makes eye contact and doesn't keep moving, he knows he might wake up with her. He excuses himself and feels overheated now, wishing he hadn't provoked Chambliss. He signs three fair programs and grants more pleas for passes, tickets and appearances. Sure, he'll try to make it. Yes, *of course!*

The governor lumbers inside now and draws an immediate posse. Jovial and inarticulate, Big Ed Lopresti often shows up at the club and, to Roger's surprise, occasionally closes the place.

Several more men crowd Malcolm Turner, hinged at their hips, hanging on the little man's words. Roger's view gets blocked, and again a large hand is dangled in front of him.

"Mr. Morgan, just wanted to reintroduce myself. Clive Buchanan."

"Of course." Roger shakes enthusiastically, staring up into the county prosecutor's nostrils.

"Congrats," Buchanan says coolly, then picks his words without releasing his grip. "Seems you know what you're doing."

"Glad it appears that way."

"I didn't realize you and Malcolm were friends." Buchanan's chin twitches toward the developer. "That's terrific."

"Why's that?" he asks, but the prosecutor has nothing to add and fi-nally yields to a sweaty-palmed council candidate angling for Roger's support, followed by a mass-transit advocate pushing for a September levy, an auto lobbyist soliciting advice on how to kill the same measure, and a sociology professor who, at Roger's convenience, of course, would like to discuss the fair's impact on the city. Then a man who doesn't bother to introduce himself informs him that the French exhibit, particularly its movie, is *an absolute travesty*! Roger's face remains wide-eyed and curious long after he quits listening. He finally excuses himself, spots Teddy entertaining the mayor—waving both hands the way he does whenever he's telling stories—and peels off toward Malcolm, moving too briskly for anything beyond smiles and nods, pretending not to hear his name being called, bottling his mounting irritations—all these doubters and doomsayers sucking at his trough. The self-righteousness of Sid Chambliss flickers inside him like a severed power line. And now, watching Malcolm Turner in action, he senses something reckless and loose-lipped about him that he'd mistaken for enlightenment.

Perhaps he'd placed too much stock in their similar ages and backgrounds. Both dropped out of the U and rose rapidly, Roger in restaurants, Malcolm in real estate. Yet the differences were more telling. Malcolm was married, had four children, drove a new Cadillac and owned a suburban mansion. Roger had a fiancée, no kids, a dented Impala and a Queen Anne bungalow he shared with his mother. Still, they were both good at dreaming aloud. Mal flipped downtown properties the way other developers bought and sold suburban houses—demolishing, rebuilding, reselling and leapfrogging into bigger buildings. And listening to him babble at times, Roger could imagine the entire skyline filling in. It was Mal's relentless pestering that persuaded him to invest in a project near the incoming freeway. What else was he going to do with the money that was piling up for the first time in his life? Mal had a fancy name for his future apartment complex—*The Borgata: A Villa by the Sea*—even before he'd figured out where it would be built, which was where Roger kicked in. Unfurling a battered map, Mal had circled four intersections with a red pen and asked which would ultimately become the most convenient location. All Roger did was point a trembling pinky at the circle a block away from the future Roanoke Street on-ramp.

By the time Roger gets to him now, Malcolm is doubled over, glassy-eyed with mirth, raising his hands in mock surrender. "The man of the hour! You know everybody, right?"

Roger surveys the unfamiliar smirkers as Malcolm rattles off names and titles: "Jon Reitan, undersheriff, Rudy Costello, Northwest Games, and Michael Vitullo, tavern owner and notorious rascal."

Roger shakes hands and matches names to faces as cameras flash—who's photographing him now?—and the muttering men praise the fair, the lounge, the weather, everything. When he can't take it anymore, he points at Malcolm. "Talk to you for a minute?"

"Certainly! Honored to get an audience. 'Scuse me, fellas."

The crowd noise forces Roger to speak louder. "Would appreciate it if you'd return my calls."

Malcolm looks dumbfounded. "If anybody understands what it's like to be *ridiculously busy,* I'd have thought it'd be you."

Roger bends closer. "Why are you building already?"

"The apartments? Prep work," he says slowly, as if to a child. "These things don't pop up overnight, Roger. Gotta clear the land and lay the foundation while the weather holds."

"You bought, cleared *and* started faster than you said you would. Nobody else is building."

Malcolm starts to laugh, closes his mouth, smacks his lips and leans in. "Everybody's snapping up properties, okay? Everything's fine. More investors hopping on board all the time." He snickers. "Never had someone gripe that I'm building too fast before. *C'mon,* Roger. You're running the greatest show on earth here, and you're worrying about what little old me is doing in my sandbox?"

Roger senses people just beyond his peripheral vision. "I just like it," he says softly, "when people do what they say they're going to."

Malcolm nods sympathetically, as if the real issue is Roger's temperament.

"Hilton Hotels," Roger mumbles, "wants an acre between Forty-fifth and Fiftieth just west of the freeway. If you can piece together a proposal they like within ninety days, they'll pay well over appraisal." He fishes a card from an interior pocket. "President's name is Sizemore." He glances up in time to see Teddy waving him over.

"Thanks," Malcolm says, beaming once again. "Trust me, if I even take a leak on that Roanoke site, you'll be the first to know."

Teddy leans into him when he arrives. "Looked like you needed to be rescued from that weasel. Walk me out?"

Free at last, they stroll beneath muted stars. "These people all want a piece of you, Rog. You know that, right? You're not stupid enough to think they *like* you. I mean, where were they even a year ago? Now they're already asking, what's next? If Roger can pull this off, what's next? Did you have to glad-hand Vitullo?"

Roger squints. "The tavern owner?"

"Yeah, right. He runs strip clubs. The Firelight's his cash cow. And he wants to open more."

"How'd he get in here?"

"You tell me."

"What'd the mayor have to say?"

" 'What a great fair!' He's a cheerleader now like the rest of 'em. And he, of course, *desperately* wants to meet Elvis if he shows up. Blah, blah, blah. Says this new U.S. attorney's got his dick in a knot over what that bar owner said about the police. Guess he's astonished," Teddy whispers, "that in a state where gambling is illegal— surprise, surprise—there's still a little wagering going on."

"Ed Sullivan told me this place reminds him of Nevada."

"Right. And I'm Marlon Brando's twin brother. He was pulling your leg."

"He's not a joker."

Teddy relights a cigarette he'd forgotten about.

"Weren't you surprised to see Beck in there?" Roger asks.

"As good a place as any for people to kiss his ring."

"He actually seems pretty harmless."

Teddy laughs. "Be sure to mention that when you visit him in the clink."

"He'll get off, won't he?"

"Not even Dave Beck gets off this time."

"Bob Hope said he might swing by later."

Teddy snorts. "Not a fan. Linda waiting up for you?"

"Yeah, I'll get there eventually."

Teddy grins. "You'll hit the wall one of these days is what you're gonna do." He steps back, spins gracefully and starts off, flicking his Chesterfield ahead of him and squishing it under his heel without breaking stride.

"Who can sleep," Roger half-shouts, revived and exuberant all over again, "when there's only one hundred and fifty-one days left of this damn thing?"

Teddy raises a thumb up high without looking back.

Charging back inside, Roger notices six tables cluttered with dirty glasses and overflowing ashtrays. He doesn't want to complain, so he grabs a tub and busses them himself, his swift efficiency clearing his head.

Afterward, he finds the governor off by himself, his eyes grazing on three young women at a nearby table, his smoldering cigarette confirming that he's well into his second scotch. "Like to meet Count Basie?" Roger asks.

Big Ed's eyes widen. "He's here?"

"Follow me."

Basie's table is packed with new drunks, the lone holdover from his earlier entourage being the woman beside him, her luminous skin reflecting the light.

Before making introductions, Roger asks the governor what Teddy has been wanting him to ask for months now. "You hear anything to make you think the city or the fair could be a target?"

The governor squints to get a better look at Basie's woman. "How do you mean?"

"Well, we're putting in all these shelters and silos, right, and this is where the bombers are made," Roger says reasonably. "And the Soviets didn't want an exhibit, didn't want to be here, period. So is there anything LBJ or anybody else told you beyond what the papers say?"

"Hard to know," Big Ed says sheepishly. "I don't read the papers."

After the governor finishes flattering Basie and ogling his date, he meanders off. Then Roger grabs another whiskey and plops down across from the bandleader.

"What makes a city great, Mr. Basie?"

"To tell the truth," he says in a deep voice, "yours is a bit white for me." His ice-sucking woman joins him in a smile.

"That's changing," Roger says. "What do you look for in a city?"

"The right amount of sin, I guess. Not too much, not too little. Excitement without corruption. Though they're all corrupt, right?— least the ones worth living in. You can get anything you want here in ten minutes, so I'm told."

"*So I'm told,*" his woman mimics, then laughs an ice cube right out of her delighted mouth that skates across the table and spins in front of Roger, who pops it in his mouth before she can apologize— her ringed fingers suspended in midair astonishment—and realizes as the laughter rises and he swallows the ice that he'd better not have another drink.

The lounge fills with yet another wave of boozy VIPs and favor seekers. Surprisingly, the fair's arts director is still around, smoking while waiting in line for the restroom. He ambles over and asks her how the moderns are faring versus the classics.

"You mean the *pompous trivia*?" she says.

It wasn't just the deep tone of Meredith Stein's voice that stood out, but its swagger.

"That *Times* critic is an idiot," he says. "The mods are marvelous." She smiles warily. "I agree, of course, but most don't." He watches her slow exhale. Beamy and full-cheeked, she's straddling the line between chubby and voluptuous with the devil-may-care confidence that alcohol gives some people, one spiked heel toppled to the side so her left foot can rub the wall behind her like a cat clawing a couch. She switches the black cigarette holder to her right hand and swings a diamond into view as if she was reading his mind.

"I'd love to spend some time with those paintings when nobody else is around," Roger hears himself saying, noticing the perfect print of her lips along the rim of her half-empty glass.

Laughter crests behind him, but her eyes don't let go. A thick eyebrow rises, her puffy lips loosen around the long cigarette. Out comes more smoke. "It's your fair."

"Well no, it sure isn't, but I'd like to just the same. I think, by the way," he says, gently but positively, "that one of your Pollocks is upside-down."

On the way out, he watches the strip-club guy cornering Governor Lopresti. He feels he ought to protect Big Ed, but he seems to be enjoying himself, so Roger strolls by them and through the closed fairgrounds and waves down a taxi.

"Just visiting?" the cabbie asks before he can spit out Linda's address.

He pictures her waiting for him, her hair in curlers, puffing a cigarette, flipping through fashion magazines. "Yeah," he says now. "Here for the fair and whatever else I can find."

"What you lookin' for?"

"Whaddaya got?"

The cabbie laughs, pulling away from the curb. "Had this fat guy climb in here a week ago and ask me where the flagellants are. That's right, *flagellants*. I couldn't help him, but I can probably get you what you need. Something for your head? That's easy. If it's girls, let me know if you want young or old. It gets pricier the higher you go up the hill. The best of the eight houses I know of is near Broadway and Harrison. Actually got red carpet in there—New Orleans–style. Business is great all over, though. And no discounts during the fair. No, sir. Boys? Men? Cards? Small stakes, high stakes, punchboards, pinball, bingo—we've got a dozen parlors. Porno, slots?"

"Cards," Roger says, feeling an exhilarating loss of control. "The biggest card game that's close by."

"Well, take your pick. They're all close, and I'm not sure which is the biggest. The New Caledonia, the Turf, the J&M, the Seaport . . ."

"Seaport."

The taxi coasts down Denny to First, then descends into Pioneer Square. Drop a bag of marbles almost anywhere in Seattle and they'll end up down here. It's been years since Roger has seen this part of town after midnight, and back then it'd been just a smattering of honky-tonks and hobos. But there's a rich mix of people now, in rags and suits, even some dresses. He feels as if he's dropped into a different city altogether or slipped through the wall from West into East Berlin.

He tips the cabbie and steps out into curb trash—an empty pint, a crushed Rainier can, a soiled T-shirt. Up the street, a uniformed cop jokes with a leggy, booted blonde while Roger ducks into a dimly lit, windowless bar shuddering with the crash, rattle and bells of too many games. The far-right wall, he slowly realizes, is covered with pinball machines and the men lined up to use them. Following the cabbie's advice on what to mumble to the bartender, and how generously to tip her, he's directed into the card room.

Surprisingly, it's bigger and smellier than the bar out front, reeking of cigars, armpits and something vaguely tidal, with eleven octagonal felt tables, each surrounded by as many as seven silent men. The card-room manager signals him over.

"Three or five?" he asks without looking up, as the cabbie said he would.

"Let's start with five," Roger mumbles.

The manager takes the money, hands him the chips and points to an empty seat at a game with bids up to five dollars.

Half the men at his table look like they've been sleeping outside. The others are clean-shaven, two of them wearing suits. He wishes he had a hat and avoids everyone's eyes until he notices they're already ducking his. It's five-card stud, and they take turns dealing. He orders another drink, mimics the prevailing slouch and watches his chips get raked away, not minding the loss, feeling only a flickering thrill.

When he finally stands up, his head spinning slightly, he veers toward the manager. "Know a man named Robert Dawkins?" he asks, and something flashes in the man's bored eyes. "I'm his nephew," Roger lies. "Might not've been around for quite a while. Played lots of cards, though."

The manager looks past him to the tables, shaking his bearded head.

"What about Charlie McDaniel, that bar owner who complained about the police when he shut down? Know where I'd find him?"

"You a cop or a snitch?"

Roger laughs. "Neither, sir."

"Then why you askin'?"

"So you do know them."

"*Beat* it."

To the left of the exit, there's a filthy aquarium. He gets close enough to see a dozen giant goldfish floating on the surface, with another dozen desperately sucking the air above the foul water. He wants to tell someone the fish are suffocating, but it's all he can do to wobble into the reviving air of the cooling night.

He passes a crowd of men in suits he doesn't recognize and relishes the anonymity, feeling like a double agent, a drunken one, yes, but a man fully capable of indulging multiple lives. He lifts his head and strides up First Avenue, half-expecting his father to step out from an awning and say, in an uplifting tone, "Helluva fair you're runnin' here, sport."

Chapter Six

"WHAT DO WE really know about him? Is he a serious candidate? Isn't he too old?" The managing editor, Charles Birnbaum, paced in front of the packed conference room cradling his Stanford mug with both hands while Helen Gulanos and a dozen editors and columnists waited for his questions to end. "Is this a pipe dream or a stunt? What do we truly know except that he's a seventy-year-old legend who ran our World's Fair?"

The morning meeting was hijacked by the *Times* article, which didn't actually break new ground, but its then-and-now photos of Morgan in the exact same pose, pointing with his left forefinger as if shooting the photographer, were provocative enough to spread consternation that, God forbid, they were getting beat here.

Birnbaum stared at Lundberg, a multichinned walrus who'd been ruminating over city and state politics both in and out of his column for twenty-three years now. "So, who is this guy, *really?*"

Lundberg didn't burn a calorie summoning a reply before Webster, a blue-blazered editorial writer who'd been here even longer, blurted, "He was the most important guy to have on your side if you wanted to get any civic project off the ground for two or three decades after the fair. Led the defense of the Market, helped turn Gas Works into a park, played a role in saving farmlands and got the Kingdome built, among other things. Then, I guess, he helped establish height limits on skyscrapers in the mid-eighties and . . . I don't know what else." Webster scanned the room, palms up. "Guess you'd have to call him a political consultant, too, though he's never publicly endorsed anyone I know of." He glanced at Lundberg, who was preoccupied with balancing a loafer on his toes. "Also been told he's advised all sorts of companies," Webster added, less confidently now, "on how to deal with the city, state and feds, though I don't know that he's ever registered as a lobbyist. Lundy?"

The columnist let his shoe fall and nudged his glasses higher on his nose. "Hell no," he said in a breathy falsetto. "He's a handshake guy. Never signs contracts. Won't find his name on anything since the fair." He sat up, though his voice remained a smug whisper, forcing everyone to lean in. "He's got no staff, no real political base, yet he's probably advised the last five governors and mayors, including the one he now wants to unseat. If Rooney wasn't worried about him, he wouldn't have bothered to hint that he might be a Republican."

"Yes, yes!" Birnbaum said, knocking everyone back with his volume. "So he's an old-money, behind-the-scenes guy who's also one of the best public speakers the city's ever seen, right? That's unusual in itself, isn't it? Granted, most of those speeches were a long time ago, but he was known to light up crowds—wasn't he, Lundy?"

"I've only heard him on a few occasions," Lundberg reluctantly admitted, "but he's as good as anyone I've seen without notes. He's got an *incredible* memory. Names, faces, conversations. People've seen him take a blank map of the state and pencil in all forty-nine legislative districts. And he knows the story behind every building in this city—who built it, who owns it, who leases it. He doesn't grant many interviews, but when he does, he's a straight shooter. Best time to talk to him is on one of his downtown walks. He's a Mariners fanatic. Polite as a prince, too, and dresses like he's heading to a funeral, which he often is, seeing how he's the youngster of his crowd. Not a name-dropper, but a real storyteller. And he's got something going for him that very few politicians ever have—even his *opponents* love him." Helen watched everyone suck on this nugget. "He's a *straight* shooter," Lundberg repeated, louder this time.

As hard as she tried to play it calm and neutral, her tone got away from her. "Is there such a thing as a straight shooter who's been involved in politics at every level for the past forty years?"

Everybody stared at her, taking her in as if for the first time. She was still *the new girl* to them, more than half of whom were elderly mutes who exhibited all the side effects of spending decades in this brevity mill. From what she could tell, they'd been snipping color and humor and emotion out of stories for so long, they had inadvertently started pruning their personalities as well. One got so drowsy during a planning session several years ago that he tipped his chair over backward and crashed through the floor-to-ceiling window. As newsroom lore had it, he didn't cuss or even mention it to his wife until she noticed the tiny cuts in his hairline.

"You'd think so, wouldn't you, Helen?" Webster said now. "But you gotta remember this isn't Chicago or D.C. This is a *consensus* city, a compromise city, perhaps to a fault, but not a corrupt"—his fingers formed quote marks in the air—*"machine."*

Shrontz nodded, his grin saying, *See what she's like?*

"Hold on." Birnbaum made a steeple with his fingers. "Why hasn't he run before? The two theories I've always heard are: it'd be a demotion, and he's got skeletons. Just listen to what we've heard here already: We've got a de facto mayor—at least he used to be—and an aging political consultant who's somehow never bothered to register to lobby. And so now we've got a guy who's always been effective, partly because he had no political ambitions, suddenly, finally, wanting to be mayor?"

Postures stiffened and throats cleared. Marguerite, the deputy managing editor and the only other woman in the room, nodded emphatically. She'd been Helen's advocate since she arrived, though seemingly lobbied for everyone. Still, when her effusion was aimed at you, it was hard not to feel the lift. "Helen?" she said. "Go on. What're you suggesting?"

"I'm not saying he has to be a crook," Helen began gently, "but it's hard to do all he's done and not get dirty, no matter what city you're in, isn't it? And from what I can tell, nobody's ever taken a real close look at him, probably because he's never run for anything before," she added diplomatically before turning toward Birnbaum. "If there are skeletons to be found, I think we'd all rather assess them before the *Times* does it for us."

Chins and foreheads were rocking fiercely now. Even Lundberg and Webster brightened at the prospect of exhuming corpses.

But now that she had their attention, what should she say next? That she'd heard about some old guy who calls Morgan the *false prince*? Omar's latest update was that his gadfly wouldn't come forward until he was convinced Morgan actually had a chance. She half-suspected he didn't even exist.

"So what do you think we should look at?" Marguerite prodded her.

"Everything," Helen said, "starting with his childhood. His mother's still alive, I believe, but apparently hasn't been interviewed since the fair. His investments and consultant work—over and under the table. And his divorce papers, assuming he's been married."

"Last I checked," Webster observed, "there's no crime in getting divorced."

"Good," Birnbaum offered. "Otherwise I'm a two-time offender."

"He never got married," Lundberg said after the obligatory chortling. "Got close several times, though."

"Maybe," Helen dared to suggest, "even his role in the fair needs to be looked at in a different way."

Webster's groan was followed by Lundberg's snicker, before Birnbaum silenced them with, "Good, good, I like it."

"Terrific!" Marguerite chimed.

Discussions erupted over divisions of labor for interviewing friends and foes as well as checking lobbying and court records.

"Never trusted the guy," muttered a sullen copy editor. "I think he probably made a bundle for himself as our pseudo-mayor. Always heard he was a BS-er and a gambler."

"A gambler?" Birnbaum chirped. "Perfect. Love it! How soon can we get a sit-down with him?"

"We already requested one, right?" a perspiring Shrontz asked Helen.

"Several times. He's hard to get ahold of. His campaign staff, so far, consists of an answering machine and his old—and I mean very old—sidekick from his fair days who—"

"Severson," Lundberg said. "Teddy Severson. Corporate lawyer. Ran for governor in 'sixty-four as a Republican and bailed early, as I recall. I'll make some calls and see who Morgan advised over the years. Maybe I can piece together his de facto public record so he can't run as a blank slate."

"Good!" Birnbaum shouted. "Brilliant!"

An editor who helped oversee cops and courts timidly poked her head into the meeting.

"What is it?" Birnbaum demanded.

"Seattle PD just confirmed an officer shot and killed an intoxicated—and apparently unarmed—African-American driver in the Central District early this morning."

"Driving while black," Marguerite whispered.

"And Starbucks," the mousy editor added, "just got its windows smashed on Twenty-third."

Reporters drifted toward Helen's desk after the meeting to ask how the clusterfuck went, and to offer their assessments of Roger Morgan, assuring her either that he was a straight shooter or as corrupt as they come though confessing not even secondhand knowledge of any of it. Once the crowd thinned out, Bill Steele strolled up.

The paper's oldest reporter, Steele still wore a suit every day and wouldn't make eye contact with anyone until he'd unlocked his files, drunk his thermos of coffee and read the morning papers. His phone rang, he didn't answer. People approached, he wouldn't look up. After he finished refolding his papers, he'd whisper "Uh-huh, uh-huh" into his phone, as if the newsroom was bugged.

A two-time Pulitzer finalist, Steele was seen by most of the reporters as a dated action hero of sorts. Not everyone enjoyed hearing him shout information-access laws into the phone, but Helen did. Most of his recent tussles had been with bankruptcy court clerks, ever since a prominent builder blindsided a couple hundred "investor friends" by filing Chapter 11. Regardless, it was Malcolm Turner *this* and Malcolm Turner *that* every day, all day. Early on, when Turner refused to speak to him, Steele had staked out his Eastside mansion for three days, hoping an ambush might provoke a response from the man who'd built four of the city's ten tallest skyscrapers. She'd never seen Steele more delighted than when the developer filed a restraining order. "Let me guess," he began now, "they took turns kissing Morgan's ass until one of them got mildly tough—maybe you—and then they all got fired up to do some *public service* journalism, by God. Then somebody suggested putting me on the story with you, and half the room groaned."

"Not too far off, but your name didn't come up."

"*Yet.*" He noticed Marguerite was closing in on them. "Look out, here comes Mary Poppins."

The newsroom's second-in-command crouched close enough for Helen to smell her shampoo. "You were *awesome* in there," she purred. "This story is *so* overdue. Let's kick some booty!"

Adrenaline spiking, Helen started calling people she wasn't even ready to interview just so her coworkers would leave her alone. Another call to Morgan's office got the answering machine yet again. She noticed Shrontz hovering, waiting for her to hang up.

"The MLK Center's holding a community meeting in an hour," he said, excitement twitching in his face. "Roger Morgan has asked to speak. Birnbaum wants you there."

"I'll be damned," Steele interjected from behind. "That crafty old dog's running for real."

Helen grabbed a notebook, two pens, her phone and a tape recorder, then loped toward the elevator, trying not to break into a noticeable jog.

THE DIAGONAL RAIN made it hard to see the freshly boarded-up Starbucks as she drove down Twenty-third toward a three-story brick fortress that looked more like a detention facility than a community center. She parked in the gravel lot next to the netless basketball hoop among older American cars that reminded her of Ohio and watched families shuffle toward the entrance, their necks bowed against the rain. A KIRO-7 news van pulled up, followed by one from KING-5.

She could hear clanking metal chairs and sharp voices as she entered the old, wood-floored auditorium, asking people why they came. The responses ranged from confusion and hostility to thoughtful or flip commentaries about the police. Finally, a stout woman mentioned that she came to hear what this Roger Morgan had to say. As others chimed in, Helen turned on her recorder.

"He's just pandering," another woman said.

"Patronizing," her friend corrected her. "Patronizing, not pandering."

"Least he wants to talk," a third added. "Doesn't want to *think* about it and get back to us with some *statement*. He wants to talk. And I wanna listen."

"Fishin' for votes like the rest of 'em."

"Yeah, least his ass will be here. Where's the mayor? Where's Rooney's big butt? Seen the size of that man lately?"

By now Helen sensed the crowd growing around her and, looking up, saw other recorders and microphones and a shoulder-held TV camera.

"Try to find a seat," shouted the director, a tall, reedy-voiced woman.

"Hope nobody's here from the fire department," a man muttered as damp faces lined the walls.

The director welcomed everyone, through a microphone now, extending her condolences to the family and friends of Michael Alan Shelton. She talked vaguely about tragedies and injustices, then suggested, "But I hope we can all agree there needs to be a more thoughtful response than the vandalizing of businesses that bring jobs to our community."

A man shouted, "Starbucks ain't run *by* us or *for* us!"

"*Three* businesses had their windows broken this morning," she replied forcefully, "which ones aren't the point." When she recommended writing letters to the police oversight board, people started murmuring and eyeing the door.

Next up was a reverend, short and loud and off subject. People fanned themselves and monitored the entrance until Roger Morgan stepped through it dressed like the father of the bride in a charcoal suit and champagne tie, followed by a blushing young woman in a dark pantsuit and by a gimpy Ted Severson. The rev gabbled on about how hard times can bring out the best in us, but everyone's eyes were on Roger. When the whispering grew louder, the preacher got the hint and closed with a generic prayer.

"As many of you may know," the director announced, "we received a request today from a new mayoral candidate to address this group. Given our unsuccessful efforts to get the mayor and the police chief here today, the board swiftly agreed to let Mr. Roger Morgan speak. Mr. Morgan?"

There was no applause but rapt attention as he strolled up to the microphone, adjusted it patiently, licked his lips once and finally looked slowly around the auditorium. Body language, Helen knew, was more important than words at times like these.

"I'm not looking for votes today," he began with a somber ease that struck her as pitch perfect. "I'm looking for answers. I'm looking for *help* in understanding not only this morning's tragedy, but the daily travesties that go on around here."

Helen watched the expressions in the crowd, some insolent or distrustful—just another politician, blah, blah, blah—and others sensing something *different.*

"I don't understand, for example, how so many landlords in this area are allowed to raise their rents while they let their properties go to hell." He paused, meeting eye contact from one side of the room then the other. "How is *that* okay?"

"I heard that!" a man yelled.

"Problem is, they pay less taxes, you see, when their houses and apartments drop in value. So what's the incentive to keep them up? Not a lot we can do about that except to enforce the codes, right? So why don't we? From what I can tell, too many of our building inspectors are either incompetent or unethical. I prefer to assume the former. What I know for sure is that this goes on and on and on, and no mayor or city councilman has ever tried very hard to stop it. Don't let anybody tell you otherwise."

Several gasps punctuated the rising buzz of agreement before a man hollered, "What about the shooting?"

"I'm getting to that." Morgan blew out his cheeks, as if limbering his mouth for what needed to be said, then softly asked, "You think this is easy?"

The room quit fidgeting, and Helen was transfixed. He'd walked into a volatile scene without any rehearsal time, a scenario most politicians duck at all costs, and he somehow was making it appear *personal*.

"The oldest among you probably remember—and I'm sure some of you've been told—that the police have a shaky history when it comes to your neighborhoods."

Hadn't Morgan's voice, Helen suddenly wondered, subtly adopted the reverend's inflections?

"Graft was rampant at one time. A whole lot of cops were taking bribes. That's a fact, not an accusation. And during the sixties, vice cops working this area got caught confiscating drugs and reselling them through the dealers of their choice. Look it up. Several did time. And I believe there's been ample evidence of an ongoing lack of leadership and restraint, such as this seemingly unnecessary shooting last night." He paused, waiting out the murmurs.

"Don't get me wrong. Most of the force is made up of brave and honorable officers protecting us as I speak. And Mr. Shelton was apparently driving erratically before he was pulled over, and he did have an outstanding warrant on a weapons charge."

He quieted the grumbles by raising a hand. "Regardless of what actually happened, I think it's fair to ask, if he'd been a white man driving erratically in Laurelhurst or Broadmoor, do you think he would've been shot?" He was talking over a chorus of *unh-uhh*s now. "I don't think so either, and that's not right."

The grunts and sighs subsided as he started up again. Nobody wanted to miss whatever he'd say next, no matter how full of it they thought he was. Helen had seen crafty politicians come off as truth-telling outsiders many times before, but she'd never witnessed anything so seemingly genuine and spontaneous.

"Some of you are still thinking," he said, voice rising, " 'See, I knew he was here for votes.' But you know what? You're *still* wrong. Think about it. There are TV cameras and all sorts of reporters here. What I've already said will cost me far more than it'll help me. But see, when I decided to finally run, I vowed to do it the only way I know how, which is to be as honest as I can and not worry about what anybody—including all of you—thinks of what I'm saying. Today, I simply wanted to see you people and tell you that I'm very, very sorry about what happened this morning, and that you've got good reasons to be suspicious and even angry, but that I hope you'll take some deep breaths and act peacefully and constructively."

He dropped his head in an abbreviated, Japanese-like bow and stepped aside. The response was more astonishment than applause, but there was some of that too as he pumped the director's hand and bounded toward the door with long youthful strides, his whole body rising and falling, his silver hair flopping, just ahead of the media scrum that abandoned the rest of the meeting to follow him into the narcotic rain.

Ted Severson attempted to wave off the reporters, claiming they were already late for another appointment, but Roger fielded questions anyway while a young aide propped an umbrella over his head.

When Helen introduced herself to Severson, he stared past her at Roger, still yakking just out of earshot, the rain pelting everyone. "He's booked."

"I understand," she said. "But could I ride with you guys to your next appointment?"

He looked like he was about to spit, glanced down and then away, either weighing things or ignoring her. He cupped his hands around a cigarette, lit it and exhaled. "Wait next to the black SUV," he grumbled, pointing his long, thin nose at it. "Backseat, driver's side. Don't be obvious. We can't play favorites."

She called Shrontz to get the editor on her side as Morgan, Severson and the young assistant strode toward the rig in what was now a downpour. When the aide clicked the locks open, Helen couldn't resist exchanging glares with the retreating journalists before climbing into the backseat.

"Did you just pick a fight with the police, Mr. Morgan?" she asked casually as the car slalomed through puddles.

"Not at all," he said just as calmly. "I have great respect for the police, but they screw up too, Ms. Gulanos." He even pronounced it correctly, *Gu-lawn-ose*. "And somebody needed to say to those folks,

'You're not being crazy.' " He glanced out the window, then turned back to her. "How's Elias?"

"Fine," she said, startled and annoyed by his presumption they'd already bonded over her son. And she was suddenly keenly aware of the importance of her demeanor with men his age. If she looked too casual, she was dizzy. Too stiff, a bitch.

He handed his cell phone to Severson, who fumbled it onto the floor mats, and then started expressing his deep appreciation of good police work. She took notes, though not on what he was saying. Up front, Severson was talking on the cell. "Huh? Right. Right. He'll call you."

"Same with the building inspectors?" she prodded gently. "You admire them too?"

"Of course. That's hard work, but I won't take back anything I said, if that's what you're asking. In fact, write this down: I would gladly debate the head of that department any time, any place."

She didn't write that down and instead asked questions about his past that he gracefully dodged. He told her verbatim what she'd already read, as if all he knew about himself was what he saw in the papers.

It struck her as odd that Severson was staring at the driver until she realized he was actually aiming his good ear at their conversation, eavesdropping, waiting for an opening to say, "Larry can do it at three-fifteen if—"

"We'll meet him at his place," Morgan said.

Helen listened to their back-and-forth on several cryptic scheduling matters, finishing each other's sentences like an old couple. He apologized, then returned to his tell-nothing autobiography before interrupting himself to educate her about Yesler Way, which they'd turned onto and were now descending toward the bay in the slackening rain.

"This was the first divot in the forest where they slid all these big ol' firs down to the mill. We had as much timber as San Fran could possibly want just waiting to be felled." Without pause or transition, he pointed at the bone-white Smith Tower. "Built in nineteen fourteen. Think about it. Forty-two stories and horses still on the street. Must've looked like some New York skyscraper lost in the Wild West, huh?"

Helen's efforts to interrupt were no match for this *straight shooter*'s ability to explain things to death so there was no time to talk about anything that mattered. Most people will eventually talk their way into the meat of what you need, but skilled politicians—much less this guy—have got enough slogans and asides and stories to fill whatever time you've been allotted with meaningless jabber.

"And this street," Roger continued gaily, "for some time divided *good* from *bad* Seattle. The brothels and shanties clustered south of Yesler, the businesses and better neighborhoods to the north. Who knows how long it would've taken for the city to get a toehold if Henry Yesler hadn't built his mill at the bottom of this chute, proving once again that history often hinges on the decisions of a few greedy bastards." Teddy cleared his throat now, a phlegmy three-step procedure. Roger glanced up warily, then carried on. "But that didn't stop us from putting a plaque up on the courthouse 'in recognition of his public spirit and helpful generosity.' "

"Seems to be a recurring theme," Helen interjected firmly. "No offense, but the history of the fair feels a bit glorified too."

He measured her, then laughed abruptly. "*Touché!* This city lacks honest introspection. Always has. Still a booster town in many ways."

Does he really believe this, she wondered, or is he just playing me too? "So how do you win this thing, Mr. Morgan?"

He laughed again. "Doesn't pencil out, huh? Well, basically five legislative districts decide the mayoral race—thirty-six, forty-six, forty-three, thirty-seven and eleven. And the district chairs work like ward bosses, see. Not supposed to say that out loud, but that's what they are. The chairs shepherd the votes through loyal precinct captains who do the doorbelling and mailings. We're off to see three chairs today, right?"

Severson nodded grimly, his neck still twisted for eavesdropping.

"And then there's the city's often-underestimated voting blocs—twenty percent Asians, ten percent blacks, ten percent gays, and so on," he continued. "And you gotta keep in mind that the city's made up of neighborhoods that operate like small towns—Queen Anne, Magnolia, Capitol Hill, Seward Park, and so on, each with its own diners, funeral parlors, taverns, churches and—"

"But how do *you* win?"

He chuckled. "You've gotta remember there are times when voters prefer change and unpredictability, and I'm offering plenty of both."

He pointed vaguely out the window. "We're in the old brick soul of this city now, which for me is like looking at the stump rings on a big old tree." She looked outside and saw an old neon sign: *State Rooms 75 cents.*

"What do you look for in a city?" he asked.

"Humility," she said.

"Ha! Hear that, Teddy? Spoken like a true Midwesterner. It can be so much more, Ms. Gulanos. A city can be downright magical."

Helen felt simultaneously charmed, flustered and conned as the SUV slowed near the ferry dock. In this short ride, he'd guessed her roots, indulged her with his mock candor and colorful history lessons and listened to her questions so intensely his ears seemed to bend toward her. Yet she knew this was all part of his subliminal goodwill campaign, and the expected reciprocity that went along with it.

"When can I talk to you again, Mr. Morgan?"

"Just ring Annie here and get on the schedule."

"I'd also like to talk to people about you." She tried to hide her urgency. "People who know you well," she added, as Annie deftly parked the large vehicle.

"Nobody knows me much better than Teddy, though you're not much of a talker, old man, are you?"

Severson gave no sign of hearing any of this.

"I'd like to talk to other friends—your mother, your relatives, former fiancées."

Roger smiled. "What could they possibly know about me?"

"We'll get you some names and numbers," Annie said coolly, "but we're running behind now."

Helen glanced around, wondering where, exactly, they were running, then thanked Morgan and shook his surprisingly large hand. "Could I have your cell number, sir?"

"Call me *Roger*," he said, then gave her the number.

HE WATCHED her brisk walk, which had a slight swing and strut to it that belied her respectful manner. Her voice was the same way, and her questions too, all hinting at a confidence and ambition beneath her cool, shy facade.

"You don't give out your cell to the press, for God's sake," Teddy muttered. "That's all you'll be giving her anyway."

"Why's that?"

"Got a rundown on her this morning."

"Yeah?"

"Not good."

"Then why'd you invite her along?"

"So she can't claim we shut her out. But that's it for one-on-ones. Went too far with the police today, Roger. *Way* too far. This is a campaign not a vendetta."

"Thought we agreed I wasn't gonna censor myself." He wished he had more people to talk to right now than just Teddy and Annie. He was surging, invigorated, bursting. *Let's go!* he wanted to shout.

"Thought we agreed you were gonna try to *win*," Teddy said. "Nobody wins anything picking fights with cops. Felons can't vote."

Roger watched the reporter mosey toward the waterfront. "What did your pal at the *P-I* say about her?"

Teddy rattled off what he'd heard. Daughter of a laid-off steelworker. Won a Mencken award at the Youngstown *Vindicator* for exposing a contracting scandal. Then worked in D.C. for *Roll Call,* an aggressive rag where she specialized in embarrassing congressmen. "Then she got hired to dig up dirt out here. Lundy says she's only been here seven months, mostly writing tech stuff, but has a nose for big stories. And she's *hungry*. She's a muckraker, Roger. A moralist."

"C'mon. She's too young and—"

"She's the perfect age," Teddy scolded him. "Old enough to know how to make you look like hell, young enough to think she's justified. She plays with sharp knives."

Roger paused. "I kind of like her."

"Get over it," Teddy grumbled. "You're playing with dynamite here."

"Pick a metaphor and stick with it, Teddy. Knives or dynamite, not both." He unlatched his door. "I think she likes me."

"Oh, for Chrissakes." When they piled out of the SUV, Teddy glared at the little Turkish restaurant. "Why'd you pick this place? No room in there for a private conversation."

"No, but there's plenty of baba ghanoush, old man." Roger strode toward the door, feeling like far more than a *candidate*, with his springy steps, nimble mind, the effortless pulse of his heart. He felt—he mouthed the four syllables—*unbeatable*.

Teddy hobbled pigeon-toed, trying to catch up, until Annie offered her elbow, which he waved off, then snapped at Roger, "Quit your goddamn smiling."

HELEN STOOD in the shadows of the roaring double-decker highway stacked near the seawall, watching Roger Morgan strut across Seattle's oldest street toward one of its oldest buildings, bounding toward the Café Paloma. She watched him yank open the door for his side-kicks and heard him shout what sounded like "Baba ghanoush!"

Chapter Seven

JUNE 1962

THE RELENTLESS SCHEDULE rescues him from his guilt. There's no time to wallow amid this daily onslaught of business recruitment, needy VIPs and astonishing acts. Last week it was the Benny Goodman Orchestra and the Ukrainian dancers. Next week it's Roy Rogers, Edward R. Murrow and Billy Graham.

Today it's Prince Philip, and the spectacle is ten times what Roger expects as people swarm Boeing field to glimpse British royalty in person for the first time. The prince doesn't disappoint, dropping out of the infinite blue at the helm of a flamingo-pink Royal Air Force ten-seater. Women swoon as he steps onto the tarmac with slicked-back hair and a jaunty smile. Even his tweedy bodyguard, grim-faced and inscrutable, is perfectly cast, lighting a curve-stemmed pipe as they pile into a brand-new powder-blue Oldsmobile and roll off to the fair with a hungover Roger Morgan at the wheel.

The prince is all wit and manners as he cheerfully disregards the itineraries, which suits Roger just fine since he feels a comforting sense of order and predictability no matter where he is on the grounds. Kids darting and shrieking in and out of the fountain. Men watching women inspect their stockings. Decent people waiting patiently in hourlong lines.

"No Soviet exhibit?" the prince says. "Good! The bastards murdered half my family." Roger nods, as if they'd slaughtered half of his too. They're running behind by the time he coaxes Philip up in the Needle, where the governor, the senator, the mayor, Teddy, Roger's mother and a dozen others are fidgeting in anticipation, making sure the napkins and silverware are laid out properly, unsure of what to say or drink.

Once the prince is seated, Roger's hand-picked maître d' approaches with the opening line he'd scripted: "Your Majesty, would you like something before lunch?"

He feigns dismay. "A gin and tonic, of course!"

Laughter cracks like gunfire, and Roger detonates as well. God, he's sick of himself today.

Everyone defers to the prince, who shares anecdotes from his navy days, his hunting and fishing exploits, with cocksure delivery. "Let cats and lizards rejoice in basking in everlasting sunshine," he says of London's and Seattle's similar weather, "but mists and drizzles and even occasional light rains make sunshine all the more welcome and constitute the proper environment of man, wouldn't you say?" Or, after sampling the crab: "Worth crossing the pond just for this food. Unfortunately, our problem is genetic: British women can't cook."

Most of his asides tend toward jokes so dry he has to emphasize them by stomping his foot, everyone then roaring on cue, desperately striving for the appropriate response in hopes of bathing even briefly in his royal approval. A prince, a goddamn prince!

Roger's mother's fixation with the Brits has always seemed excessive to him. She mimicked the accent and favored English movies, poetry and theater, and always wanted him to call her *Mummy*. After hearing the prince ask her if he didn't detect a familiar accent, Roger excused himself.

He finds a *P-I* in the bathroom and trudges up to the observation deck, spinning on gin. He's heard about it, but it looks different in print: *Teamsters boss Dave Beck was sentenced Wednesday to two years at the McNeil Island Penitentiary for grand larceny and four counts of evading taxes totaling almost $330,000.*

A seaplane lifts off Lake Union, a 707 floats southbound over the city, another jet airliner heads east—every day, more planes in the sky. Maybe it's his hangover, but he feels like everything's slipping out of his control. He can't sleep nor resist the card rooms now, much less summon the nerve to call off Linda's elaborate wedding preparations, though their engagement has become his daily lie.

He drifts to the southern deck, where people are packed eight deep behind the coin-operated telescopes—taking in the homely backside of downtown, acres of car lots, windowless warehouses, rusty fire escapes and gas stations. He imagines how pathetic, even ghastly, it must look to people from Paris or London or even New York.

He calls the office on a Needle phone to get the latest dozen messages, including one from Malcolm Turner. He tries to resist glancing at the job site, though it's hard to miss that huge vacant lot and the only construction crane in sight.

Returning to the table, he finds Prince Philip politely insisting that his mother pay him a visit the next time she's in London, *by Jove.* Then he shares a story over tea about his son, Charles, sneaking out in his sports car, which ends in a toast to the charming recklessness of children on this gin-soaked afternoon in a revolving restaurant in the bright sky. The prince stomps his foot again, and Roger feels the Needle sway with laughter.

Back at headquarters, he scans the latest consultant report: The average fairgoer spends $5.19 a day—two bucks for admission, fifty cents for the monorail and $2.69 for food, rides and games. Expenditures double or triple that if they have a meal in the Needle. The consultant suggests offering more music, clowns and outdoor activities, arguing that people spend most of their time between exhibits. And so on. He flips through the stack of new complaints. *The movie in the French exhibit is atrocious and should be canceled immediately! Almost $7 for crab legs in the Space Needle restaurant!?* There's also a letter signed by more than half of the burlesque proprietors, pleading for lower leases.

He puts everything aside and heads out early to clear his head before meeting Teddy for dinner. He'd tried to get out of it, but Teddy had insisted. Roger feels a scolding coming and knows he deserves it. He's not even trying to keep up with the workload now and has visited the card rooms just about every night. Part of it is his growing obsession with this *other* Seattle; the more he sees, the more he wants to see. The rest of it is what he's avoiding—Linda.

Dazed with self-loathing, he doesn't notice a thing in the dozen blocks he walks to the Pike Place Market, where he browses through the clothes, jewelry and produce, then loiters beneath the big clock to read the fresh fish menu: kippered salmon, scallops, steamer clams, Pacific oysters, lingcod, mussels and more. Ten minutes later, he's enjoying the closing bustle, falling prices being called out before the rustle and clank of everything getting packed away for the night. He catches a thin, pale man staring at him, then ambling off before risking a furtive glance back over his shoulder. Who the hell is he? The wind shifts, now carrying the stink of raw fish. Turning to go, he hears someone shout "Dawkins!" in his direction. He flinches at the sound of his family name, but keeps walking. It might've been *Hawkins*. Realizing he was already late, he hustles down First until he's breathless, then slows down and braces himself for Teddy's lecture. He's sweating so profusely by the time he gets to Rosellini's that his collar is soaked, and the large crowd and raucous applause all make it instantly clear that this isn't just an unpleasant meal with Teddy.

"Surprise!" everyone shouts in unison.

Most of the day's illustrious lunch crew—minus the prince, thank God, but including his mother—is here, as well as the mayor, the prosecutor, five councilmen, three legislators, assorted businessmen, a dozen fair staffers and a smattering of wives, all of them grinning and snorting as if seeing him sweaty and unhinged was high entertainment. What the hell? It's not his birthday or the anniversary of anything that he can recall. Regardless, he wishes he'd showered, shaved and changed, and that he had a few more moments to manufacture an appropriate response.

Finally, Teddy's cigarette breath closes in. "Sorry, Rog, but the guv ordered me not to warn you. I told everyone to make sure Linda heard about this, but I haven't seen her yet."

Looking hopelessly now for his fiancée, Roger finally understands that some honor has arrived at the least appropriate hour. He's lost control of his expressions, his wits, his galloping heart.

"You look less than thrilled," Teddy whispers as a waiter slides a tumbler of Old Crow into Roger's palm. He spills some and gulps the rest, and the world softens enough for him to kiss his mother and give her the detached British hug that she prefers. He can tell by the sudden hardening of her eyes that Linda has in fact arrived and is standing right behind him. He turns around and feels so grateful she's here that he almost weeps—her eyes glittering, her hair luxuriously curled, her sleek yellow dress flared at the ankles.

Governor Lopresti starts the evening off by joking that people who insist that Roger would make such a terrific governor need to realize there's a little-known age minimum of thirty-five, "so the kid can't run for another four years. Plus, from what the papers say, this summer he's making more money than I am anyhow." He then haltingly reads telegrams from congressmen who clumsily assert that Roger's imagination and determination woke this city up and made the fair possible, that he's earned a spot in Seattle's history books. Everybody's eyes are fixed on Roger, gauging his reaction to each and every compliment, dig and quip. Fortunately, by now he's composed himself and is able to look grateful and humble and good-humored about the whole thing. The mayor, the senator, Teddy and others then take turns toasting and roasting him while the guests polish off their crêpes Martinique and roast tenderloin of beef. Finally, it's Roger's turn.

He thanks the usual suspects, lingering on his deceased mentor and boss, Jackie Vaughn, though moving on before he calls him the father he never really had. He takes a long breath and widens his stance. He's been crafting this speech in his head since before the fair opened, figuring he'd wait until the final days to deliver it, yet this is the perfect audience. "As grand as it is, this is just a fair. One hell of a fair, but *just a fair.* We're still such a young city, and pretty soon it's gonna be important to figure out what we want to be when we grow up. Everybody has their own vision, but it's clear to me that if we invest in downtown, the rest will follow. We need better schools and safer streets and less reliance on Boeing. We need swimming pools, a new aquarium, a multipurpose stadium. And we've gotta continue cleaning our lakes and give mass transit a chance. What I'm saying is that this fair can't be the pinnacle of our community resolve, but rather an example of a new way of getting things done."

Even the waiters are listening now, cradling bottles of champagne, not wanting to break the spell he's casting. "We need to keep and preserve what we love and what needs to be kept, like the Market," he says slowly, then waits out a few boos and grumbles. "We also need to seriously consider expanding this monorail up to Everett and down to Olympia. We need a city that lives up to its setting without losing its soul or this'll soon feel just like any other impersonal western city. We need to strive to not only be a hub for world commerce, but for technology and innovation and culture too. What we have right now is a green light, and hopefully the inclusive spirit, to build a city unlike any this world has ever seen." He scans the faces in front of him, most rapt, some confused, and a few people start clapping. "Wait a minute," Roger jokes. "You think I'm done talkin' already?" After a final flurry of observations and ideas, he realizes he's on the brink of announcing that he eventually intends to run for mayor, but instead he simply raises his empty glass.

AFTERWARD, he's hugging everyone, his faith in himself at least temporarily revived. He knows that a half-true rendition of his life story will now be passed around like brandy. How he waited tables at Vaughn's while going to the university, then dropped out to manage restaurants for Jackie V., who made him VP and dragged him into his World's Fair pipe dream once his throat cancer spread. How, the more meetings he ran, the clearer it became that he had the persuasive powers to pitch the dream. And how, after the governor appointed him fair president in '60, his enthusiasm spread like an epidemic and he sketched the idea of the Needle on a cocktail napkin late one night. Amazingly, he still lives with his mother and is engaged to that knockout right over *there*.

He feels bigger than his daily self, as if, at this very moment, he could address and inspire thousands. Even Victor Rosellini shuffles over for a photo. As the owner's arm settles across his shoulders, Roger realizes he'll soon join the luminaries—the actors, athletes and politicians—whose autographed pictures hang on these walls. And that years later, he'll walk in and wince at how young and confident he looked; or, worse, not find himself at all. Talking with three women at once now, floating on whiskey, he feels their heat, the proximity of their breath, eyes, lips and breasts, the warmth and ease of their hands on his forearms. This anarchic desire to show married women a good time is something he doesn't like to admit, even to himself.

Teddy corners him to suggest that he have a chat with the senator about the U.S. attorney's ridiculous gambling inquiry, an opinion that he hasn't softened even after Roger shared a bit of what he'd seen on his late-night forays. "You must've gone to the biggest joints on their busiest nights," Teddy had grumbled.

"Tell him the timing stinks," he says now. "It's not just the fair we're worried about. We've got all these relocations hanging, right? Tell him about that. And remind him that grand juries are unpredictable as hell. There's just a U.S. attorney telling jurors to charge people with crimes. A good one could indict Jesus."

"Why don't you tell him?"

"You're his boy." He winks. "Plus it's *your* night, not mine."

Minutes later, waiting for the senator to finish a conversation, Roger overhears his mother lying about where he'd grown up and things he'd said and done as a child. Across the room, Malcolm Turner is chatting with the police chief, and apparently he feels the scrutiny because he suddenly turns and salutes him.

Then the senator pivots and smiles. "Hell of an impromptu speech you fired off there." He clinks his glass against Roger's. "Been meaning to ask what you made of LBJ."

"He farts like a bugle."

Caught off-guard, the senator spittle-mists the air between them with laughter.

Roger resists mopping his face, then says, "Do you know anything about the new U.S. attorney here, Senator?"

"Stockton? He's a go-getter." He smiles, dabbing at the corners of his mouth with a hanky. "Kind of like you."

Roger rephrases Teddy's concern that gambling headlines could cost the city its wholesome reputation at the worst possible time. The senator studies him, having no doubt heard every direct and obtuse pitch and plea a thousand times by now. He tilts his glass until ice clanks against his teeth, then mutters something about blue laws creating more problems than they solve.

"Maybe there's someone in that office who could at least keep me posted," Roger ventures, his voice tightening. "Just until the fair closes."

The senator's head bobs so slightly it could be an affirmation or just the jostling of his pulse before they're interrupted by the tipsy governor.

Roger accepts another whiskey and watches these successful men interact woodenly, as if they're still developing skills he himself never had to learn. And with this revelation comes the notion that perhaps running for mayor is thinking too small. Sidestepping away now, he finds the fair's arts director blocking his path with a hand on her hip.

"Tuesday nights, at six," she says, "right after closing, you could get some quiet time with the mods." There's nothing in Meredith Stein's voice or face beyond a collegial friendliness, but in Roger's mind it's provocative nonetheless, especially with his fiancée cackling nearby. Meredith arches her neck, causing her breasts to lift beneath the satin. She's just stretching, but she might as well have been pressing up against him.

"I'll definitely keep that in mind," he says.

"I bet you will," she says. He blinks first.

"Go easy," Teddy whispers as he and Judith interrupt to say good night. "Pace yourself."

Roger nods, his nose deep in Judith's hair with her long, lovely arms around his neck. "As always," he whispers for her amusement.

He walks Linda to the curb half an hour later, her anger with his growing evasiveness still mercifully suspended. Obviously tired, she resembles her mother around the eyes, which always makes him uneasy. But it's not her looks that concern him, rather a lack of curiosity or insight that he fears might also be genetic. He has to stay to the bitter end, he explains, but promises he'll get to her apartment as soon as he can. He kisses her once on the forehead, once on the lips, and lights her cigarette. They wait patiently, small-talking like strangers until a cab rolls up and he opens the door.

He watches closely, trying to imagine living with her forever, as she carefully sits on the seat and swings her heels in high enough over the door frame that she won't risk ruining her stockings.

An hour later he's loping down James Street into Pioneer Square with a roll of twenties in his front pocket. It's busier than ever, with the buzz and stink of a carnival, people of all stripes spilling in and out of honky-tonks—sober, drunk, shouting, sulking, laughing. He bounces in and out of three card rooms—the Turf, the Occidental and Bob's Chili Parlor—sticking around in each just long enough to blow a twenty and ask the gamblers and managers, as casually as possible, if anyone knew where to find Charlie McDaniel or Robert Dawkins these days, getting little in return but conversation-killing glances.

It's hard to pinpoint when these outings veered from curiosity to investigation. Maybe right from the beginning. Yet that's part of what intrigues him, not knowing, for once, exactly what he's up to. He'd spent the past decade climbing ladders, working seventy-hour weeks, right through holidays and weekends. He tells himself he's making up for lost time. At least his nights are his own now.

One card room offers strippers behind a side door, coin-operated nudie reels near the bathroom, and, by the sound of it, prostitution upstairs. He settles into another game of five-card stud while on the far side of the room people are pouring dimes into boisterous pinball machines.

"Can you believe this?" he finally asks the clear-eyed, sunburned man next to him who just won a hand. "We've got cards, pinball and porno in here, and some cop out in the street's joking with the hookers."

"That's the beauty of it," the man says without looking at him. "The city's wide open, but nobody knows it."

He wins enough, loses enough and hangs around long enough to ask where he might find some older high-dollar gamblers. When that subject dead-ends, he takes a chance. "Know how you were saying everything's wide open?"

The man carefully stacks his chips.

"That interests me," Roger tells him.

"Whaddaya mean?" the man asks, restacking the same chips while the others sneak looks at him.

"Well, I teach sociology at the U."

A gambler slides his chair back and leaves the table.

"I just like to understand the way things work, you know?"

Another player departs.

"I'd like to talk to people like that tavern owner who claimed the cops were shaking him down."

The man restacks his chips again. Cards get shuffled. The manager sends two new players to the table.

A couple hands later, the chip stacker says, "Tried the J&M?"

"What?" Roger says.

"Might find Charlie there."

An hour later, he's staring at himself through a pyramid of liquor bottles stacked against the mirror behind the bar at the J&M Café while the short, bearded bartender paces like a penned dog, acting as if he didn't hear or doesn't care. When Roger starts to introduce himself again, the man says, "Got a card, Professor?"

"In fact, I do." Roger pulls out the one given to him in Club 21, crosses out the office phone, writes his home number below it and hands it over. Then he roams the square.

A man asks him for a dime, and after giving him a quarter, Roger tails him back to a pack of men who look like they've been camping in doorways. He offers them Lucky Strikes. They light their cigarettes and study him, waiting for the catch.

"How long you guys been here?"

"You a cop?"

"No, are you?"

They love that.

"Been here three weeks," says the tall one. "Beats the hell out of Spokane."

"Why's that?"

"What do you care?"

A man with an eye patch steps closer. "Spare another quarter?"

"No, but I've got a buck for the best story of why you ended up here."

They joke among themselves as if he's not there. One coughs uncontrollably. Roger watches a cop stroll past and nods at him. "What do they actually *do* down here?"

"Besides harass us for money?"

"C'mon."

"*Pay to stay.* That's their slogan," says the tall one. "I'll go first."

"Your little Spokane story?" one of them whines.

"You'll get your chance." Roger lights himself a cigarette, savoring the woody flavor. "Fleeing Spokane for Seattle. From the top, take one. Let's hear it."

Several hours later, he feels strangely clearheaded, even clairvoyant, his ambitions and curiosities and temptations all seemingly merging, as if it's entirely possible that he might actually understand the city and life itself before sunrise, though he notices the first glimmers in the eastern tree line while climbing out of a cab on Capitol Hill near Harrison and Broadway.

He springs up cobblestone steps to the stately Victorian he'd assumed had been converted into a duplex, not a brothel. On the top step, he teeters and sways, regaining his balance as nearby robins greet the new day. When the door opens, he glides into the perfumed entryway on a red carpet so plush his steps make no sound, and all his senses rise up. He feels capable of so much *more*.

Chapter Eight

MAY 2001

HER DESK was buried in 1962; a brittle, sun-yellowed souvenir edition of the *Seattle Times* on the eve of the fair, musty *Argus* weeklies from April through October, the official guide and entertainment calendar, two cheerful books celebrating the expo, a panoramic map with a hokey introduction explaining that Paul Bunyan built Mount Rainier with his bare hands. Pinned above her desk was a photo of a shirtless Elias, flexing muscles he didn't yet have, and five of Roger Morgan—two taken in '62, one at the Market in 1972, another when he addressed the city council in 1981, the last in the rain outside the MLK Center nine days ago.

Her original assignment had merged completely with the paper's coverage of his candidacy. Lundberg was looking into his political consulting while city hall and statehouse reporters were gauging his influence in Seattle and Olympia through the years. Helen was concentrating on the fair, as everyone now agreed that it warranted more than another standard rehash. The jolt of teamwork sent a unifying current through a newsroom unnerved by the layoff of three young reporters and the closing of two bureaus that week. Along with this temporary setback, as Birnbaum spun it, was the announcement of smaller news holes—*keep stories tighter!*—and rumors of stingy buyout offers for old-timers. So what better diversion from all these harbingers of a shrinking—or dying—business than scrambling to stay ahead of the *Times* on a humdinger story like this?

Marguerite strode over and squatted next to Helen's desk and said, nearly nose-to-nose with her, "Let's rock this joint!" Helen had no idea what she meant but her scalp tingled.

She'd made the mistake of telling her about the False Prince comment. So it was no longer a secret—those two words were on everyone's lips—though Omar still hadn't produced his gadfly. She procrastinated, clearing her head, flipping through junk mail, red lining on espresso, reorganizing her final round of questions, waiting for Morgan's call, trying not to dwell on the fact that she needed to file a draft by tomorrow and cover the debate this afternoon.

Vague and anonymous tips continued to pour in. He's a womanizer, a boozer, a serial home wrecker with at least a half dozen kids out of wedlock and, worst of all in Seattle, a *Republican*. And he isn't as healthy as he looks. Ask him about his hip replacements! Just ask. And, of course, the clichéd tip she'd received everywhere she'd ever worked: Follow the money. As one caller put it: "Ask Mr. Storyteller how he got so rich."

She kept all this to herself, so the editors wouldn't panic about *Times* reporters getting the same leads—as they no doubt were—and try to rush her. The paper also was receiving bundles of handwritten letters from people who were thrilled and grateful that *the Great Roger Morgan*—a phrase several actually used—was willing to sacrifice his privacy and retirement to rescue their city.

She'd had only two brief phone calls with him since her ride-along. Yet, during those chats, he rattled off so many facts and impressions she'd already collected that it felt as if he'd written the history of the fair himself and that the city simply nodded along as he told it.

She'd already finished a draft of "Roger at the Fair." There was more sweep and bullshit than she'd like, but given how hard it was to dredge up any fresh material, it felt oddly illuminating, or at least not fawning. It conceded the consensus view that the fair transformed stodgy postwar Seattle, though she pointed out that the so-called Father of the Fair actually came late to the party, three years after the idea hatched, and that his salary of $30,000 was controversially high in 1962—the equivalent of about $250,000 today. She also noted that the Seattle expo wasn't as popular as the ones in Brussels and New York preceding and following it, and its profitability claims were exaggerated by federal subsidies. And that there was no way of knowing how many of the ten million visitors were local repeats who just couldn't get enough. Leafing through old articles, she even found nuggets of criticism lost in the avalanche of accolades. Still, it was less a reporting job than a writing exercise, largely a matter of tone, finesse and pace. Glancing at her editor, she felt herself bracing for battles over words.

TWO HOURS BEFORE the debate, Roger was trying to raise his act to high theater, his British accent in all its versatile splendor producing voices for Harry, Hermione, Dumbledore and the rest. He'd reminded himself that he was *performing* the book, not just reading it. And his audience of one was right there with him, upright and big-eyed in bed, listening intently to every word. When he described the arrival of Harry's mail-delivering owl, his mother's face brightened with delight. "Oh, I adore Hedwig," she said.

Roger slowed his pace as he neared the end of the chapter. " 'There was a long pause, during which Dumbledore stared at the slip in his hands, and everyone in the room stared at Dumbledore. And then Dumbledore cleared his throat and read out—"Harry Potter." ' "

"Oh, how wonderful," she whispered before visibly winding down from the strain of listening so intensely. "Dumbledore is such a great man," she said, her eyelids drooping. "Though I do worry that he can't protect my Harry. Don't you, Roger? Harry is still far too young to be pitted against He Who Cannot Be Named."

HE CALLED HER a half an hour before the debate, while they were both driving toward the club. She pulled over in a bus zone to take notes.

"What were you really doing during the fair?" she asked, scrambling now to find her list of questions. "I mean, besides running it? What did it mean to you? What were you getting out of it?"

Roger chuckled. "I was trying to figure things out, how the world worked, little things like that." He sounded at once fatigued and nostalgic. "I was asking lots of questions and watching everything really closely. There was this odd sense of profundity to that fair that's hard to explain. Part of it was that I was very young for my role. And everything's more profound when you're young, isn't it?" She waited through a long pause. "But see, I was trying to put my finger on something. . . . Hold on, I gotta take a left here. . . . All right, I'm back. Still there?"

"Go ahead."

"It was an odd time in my life, and in this city and the world, is what I guess I'm trying to say."

"What was so weird about it?"

"Oh my God, *everything*. We were on the brink of nuclear war, the city was flatlining and then suddenly we're the center of the universe. Least that's how it felt. It was just a fair, but . . . Well, I was meeting every big shot and learning how Seattle worked at the same time, both over and under the table. You know what it feels like to try to understand everything at once?" He laughs. "And yes, I was in charge, sure, but things were out of control."

THE NARROW LAWN in front of the Rainier Club was an exotic green flash in the city's darkest canyon of steel and glass, Helen noticed, as she followed an elderly stampede through a canopied entryway into this brick, five-story timepiece. The club hadn't admitted women until 1978, she'd read, and remained a vaunted, if waning, symbol of Seattle's good-old-boy royalty.

So many of the overdressed elderly and the underdressed media had pressed into the Heritage Room that dozens of irked old-timers were routed into a nearby room and would have to listen to the debate through loudspeakers. Finally, the moderator and the three candidates settled in front of the darkly paneled wall beneath chandeliers with fake candles.

Mayor Rooney's bulging neck had already jettisoned his collar button, which made him look scruffy in this crowd. Councilwoman Christine Norheim, the only woman besides Helen wearing pants, came off as a tomboy with her short frosted hair and muted jewelry. Roger Morgan, however, appeared to have stepped right out a decades-old Brooks Brothers catalogue in his three-piece and polished wingtips. And Norheim's tepid opening remarks about her desire to serve the city, and her sense that despite the mayor's best efforts it's time for a change, were followed by a completely different opener from Morgan.

"Many people move here as an act of hope," he began. "Or they happen upon it on a glorious day and can't resist the idea of living here. Still others come here on the run from someplace else, chased by something they probably can't describe. They pile up along our waterfront like birds tempted to follow the sun farther west, and they want more from life, which is the good side of ambition, right? Yet so many of these people who feel like they've personally discovered this city are getting priced right out of it. If only the wealthy are welcome here, we're doomed because we'll lose the mix that has always made this place original and enjoyable. We need to continue to be a destination where all kinds of people can start over. As much as we consider this place ours, it's a city of newcomers. Always has been, always should be."

The moderator hesitated, waiting to see if any more was coming, as did the journalists, who were uncertain if anything he'd said constituted news. Helen jotted down every last word—*always should be*—and was looking around the room, smiling. In this lair of old money, he was advocating for dreamers who washed up here but couldn't afford a house, once again demonstrating his willingness—no, his desire—to gamble and provoke. Yet most of the audience seemed charmed, not offended, savoring the rhythm of his words.

And the moderator was grinning as he said, "Mr. Mayor, you have thirty seconds to respond."

"I enjoyed listening to him like everybody else," Douglas Rooney said over the laughter. "I don't know if anything he just said has anything to do with overseeing ten thousand employees, but I sure did enjoy it." The mayor then explained it was essential that he be granted one more term to finish all the important work now under way. "Have we been perfect? No, we certainly have not." He then rattled off his recent accomplishments, as if an admission of imperfection provided more than enough humility, and finished in a flurry of optimism that concluded with his sincere hope that his challengers would join him in vowing to run campaigns free of innuendo.

"Are you thinking of something one of your opponents has said in particular?" the moderator asked.

"Well, I have heard Mr. Morgan make what I consider an inaccurate characterization of our police department," Rooney said gently. "I think he unfairly exploited a recent incident involving a tragic shooting to cast our officers in a very negative light. He also, according to reports, questioned the integrity of our building inspectors. Let me just say that these comments do not sound like the fair analysis of anyone with a prudent temperament."

Morgan smiled. "May I please respond?"

The moderator nodded. "Thirty seconds."

"It's pretty clear that Douglas can out-innuendo me any day of the week. By questioning my *temperament*, I believe he just innuendoed that I'm crazy, which I'd like to think would be hard to prove." He stopped the laughter with an open palm. "Truth is, we're probably as crooked as most big cities and have been for decades. Don't think so? Go ask people who've challenged city hall or crossed this mayor." He plowed on as Rooney shook his big head and raised a finger to speak. "Ask them," Morgan said, his voice climbing, "if they've had any problems getting driveway or building permits. Or, better yet, take on city hall yourself, and see if maybe you don't have troubles with your garbage pickup or getting your power turned back on or your roads plowed. My point is, the mayor shouldn't be so quick to brag about running such a fabulously clean city."

Rooney's eyes bulged. "Where are the facts, Mr. Morgan? Where are the specifics?"

"Mr. Mayor," the moderator interrupted, "we need to stick to the format here because—"

"Can I get in on this?" Norheim blurted, then conceded she, too, found some of Mr. Morgan's comments inflammatory, yet considered some of the mayor's claims misleading as well, the audience fidgeting as she described the interactive and responsive city hall she intended to lead.

Morgan finally got another chance to speak. "In the mayor's defense, his job's a bit ridiculous these days. It's not only harder to buy city hall, it's getting harder to steer it. But as for Douglas's indignation over my lack of specifics, I thought I'd mention one little thing I've noticed, which is that he recently received the maximum campaign contribution allowed from Michael Vitullo, a five-time felon and the owner of several strip clubs in our fair city."

It's not just his words, Helen told herself. It's his posture, his fingers laced casually behind his head. She'd never seen anyone push the truth-telling-candidate routine quite this far, and it thrilled every bone in her reporter's body. If she were writing about a bank robber, she'd want him to be the next Jesse James. A bootlegger? The next Capone. She wanted the best.

The moderator allotted the mayor several minutes to lecture on campaign finance rules. "Anyone can contribute up to six hundred and fifty dollars," he repeated for the hard-of-hearing. "What I can tell you, unequivocally, is that I've never done anyone *any* favors based on their support for any one of my campaigns."

Morgan snickered. "I'm sorry," he said, but couldn't stop grinning.

Rooney raised the innuendo flag again, more forcefully this time, before the moderator granted Councilwoman Norheim a chance to detail her vision of a *transparent* online government that encouraged input and scrutiny.

Asked to assess the recent dot-com implosion, Norheim and the mayor dropped the names of companies that were still hiring and discussed fruitful cross-training programs available to laid-off techies.

Then Morgan offered his take: "I know a lot of people got hurt, but we can only build so high on hype. Many of these companies were just paper tigers whose products and services, if they had any, weren't needed. The sad part is, more wealth was generated per capita in this city during the latter half of the nineties than perhaps any city ever, yet we have little to show for it other than the mayor's happy talk about us leading the new world economy."

Rooney spluttered, "The legendary booster is giving me grief for trying to make this a *world*-class city?" The crowd seemed equally amused by this, which emboldened him to add, "We don't even know how you make a living, Mr. Morgan."

After the moderator finished stammering, Morgan calmly said, "I'm a civic handyman who helps people with their campaigns and their conflicts and their ideas. Some people pay for the advice. Others get it for free, as I believe you did, Douglas. And don't get me wrong. You're not a bad mayor. You just lack original thoughts."

Rooney tried to smile, but then barked, "This is *outrageous*. I would've expected more from you than insults and the sort of campaigning voters hate." Buoyed by mild applause, he began listing his accomplishments again, then interrupted himself to say, "Please answer one simple question: What exactly have you done? What record are you running on? Congrats on the fair, but is there anything you've done in recent history that we should be aware of?"

The moderator raised his hands in mock surrender when Norheim jumped in to straddle the fence. When she was done, Morgan said, "What have I done recently? I've been alive. I kayaked down part of the Amazon. I rode a glider into the Grand Canyon. I went spelunking in Spain and sailed around Vancouver Island. I bungee-jumped at Wild Waves with my grandson a year ago. I wrote a lot of bad poetry and essays. And what I've kept coming back to is a desire to try, in my own way, to help this city live up to its potential. But, Douglas, does it really matter what we did or didn't do twenty-five or thirty years ago? Is any of that relevant to voters today?"

Rooney hesitated, like a trout that just spotted a fly too sumptuous to be real. "Well, yes, I believe so," he said. "More importantly, I think voters do too."

"Well, then I guess they'll want to know," Morgan said slowly, "that you were briefly jailed for assaulting a baseball umpire twenty-seven years ago in Petoskey, Michigan. Do I have that right, or is this just innuendo?" He was talking too fast for the mayor to have a chance to interrupt. "For you voters who care about such things, Douglas was a high-school catcher who apparently disagreed with an umpire's call. So he kicked him. Enlarged his spleen, I believe, isn't that right? I don't find it all that relevant, but according to Douglas, you might."

Delighted and startled murmurs and grumbles rolled through the crowd. Rooney curled his fingers in and out of fists before saying haltingly, "I think we can all agree that a much-regretted incident in the heat of athletics in our youth is not as germane to voters as our activities as adults on behalf of this citizenry."

Morgan bunched his lips, nodding earnestly. "A stuffy answer, but I concur. And your original question actually was a reasonable one. I've been around a long while, but most people don't really know who I am. Or if they've heard of me, I'm just a name, or I'm the *father* of the fair, which actually had many parents. So who am I? Hopefully this campaign will answer that. But to have a chance I'll need the help of the people I've helped in the past, which includes you now, doesn't it?"

The moderator smiled. "You sure look like you're enjoying this, Mr. Morgan."

"Every morning I wake up in a state of uncluttered joy." He shook his head in amazement. "For the life of me, I don't know why I waited until now."

A deep-voiced woman started chanting "Ro-ger! Ro-ger!" and a few others joined in before Morgan silenced it with a casual wave.

After filing her story, Helen escaped the newsroom and strolled around Seattle Center. She'd visited once before, but not since she began researching the fair. Despite some name changes and several new buildings and sculptures, it was essentially the same fairgrounds with the Coliseum, Science Pavilion, Opera House, and International Fountain right where Roger Morgan had left them. The grounds looked exhausted yet intact, as if this were a time capsule that nobody dared to mess with.

She studied the Space Needle with new appreciation, having read how hastily it was built on deadline—its legendary continuous pour involving 467 truckloads of concrete, its frantic dash to haul 65-foot-long steel beams from Chicago, its innovative use of turntable technology and a 1.5-horsepower engine to rotate the restaurant. She walked around it twice, jotting down her own impressions. It's a martini glass. A big-headed woman sucking in her gut. Or it's comic relief, a jester on a pogo stick. No, it's *him*. It's Roger Morgan! A provocateur turned establishment, and now a historic landmark!

And just as no fair lives up to its hype, no rookie mayoral candidate is as crafty and spontaneous as Morgan *seemed* today. A man this capable of casting spells and creating mythology couldn't have resisted politics all these years if he was clean. And if Seattle has its dark sides—such as the country's highest Prozac consumption rate—this False Prince no doubt has more than one skeleton in his closet, probably storage lockers full of them.

Juggling thoughts on how best to sharpen the opening graphs of "Roger at the Fair," she broke into a fast jog back to the newsroom.

Chapter Nine

JULY 1962

THE FAIR is so widely praised and celebrated by the daily throngs that Roger feels blindsided when critics begin trying to knock it down as they always do whenever anything takes hold. " 'The Show of Tomorrow' was put together by a team of amateurs," snipes the *New York Post.* "The needle is a monstrosity," cries the *Saturday Review;* "this pretentious and vulgar structure, sad when compared to the Eiffel Tower, does irreparable damage to the grandeur of Seattle's natural setting." And Alistair Cooke, the premier British interpreter of all things American, likens the fair to a cheap Coney Island attraction and dismisses this "drab, courteous city that labors between promotion and truth." Local grouches happily join in. The monorail is way slower than advertised. The Needle looks better the farther away you get from it. Yet tens of thousands of visitors keep coming every day. Still, Roger takes the criticism so personally, he can barely stop himself from hunting down the detractors and trying to change their minds.

He tries now to relax himself with the morning paper, but the news is anything but soothing. Linus Pauling—one of the smartest guys alive, right?—estimates there's a 40 percent chance that mankind will annihilate itself in the next four years, a prediction that's still haunting him later this same hazy morning when he finds himself alone with Edward R. Murrow.

The former TV icon keeps a cigarette lit through lunch, letting it burn down to his fingers, ash falling onto the table, his plate, his lap, his shirt and the floor, lighting fresh ones from the stubs. He looks older than Roger expected, his eyebrows not as dark or thick, his jaw not as angular, his weary, burdened face seemingly incapable of joy. Yet his distinctive voice is as authoritative as ever, full of articulate bursts and emphatic rhythms.

"What do you make of this city, Mr. Murrow?"

"She's provincial and puritanical and insecure."

Roger smiles. "She's not all that puritanical, sir."

"You're all trying so desperately to prove you're first-rate," Murrow says. "Can't you just not care what everyone else thinks?"

Roger can't resist any longer. He asks for a Camel, lights it and exhales through his nose exactly as the broadcast legend does. "And the fair?"

"Well, this cheerful glimpse into the future is a disservice to clear thinking, isn't it?" Murrow asks. "From where I'm sitting, it looks like we're closer to Armageddon than any efficient paradise you or any other dreamer can come up with."

Roger's own ashes fall in his lap as he studies the man's brooding eyes and ghostly pallor. Perhaps, now that he's charged with explaining America to the world as the new head of the United States Information Agency, he knows too much. Or maybe he's just beaten down by the doomsday gravity of his own voice.

"So you think Linus Pauling is right?" Roger asks, matching his exhale. "Is there any reason to think the fair could be a target?"

Murrow frowns and snorts. "The fair? Boeing makes you a bull's-eye, of course, but you already know that, right? The unvarnished truth is, the world's a whole lot more dangerous than people want to know." He sucks hard and squints. "Reasons to be afraid? Good God, yes. Fact is, I'm astonished something hasn't happened already."

"*Something?*" Roger feels dizzy.

"Khrushchev," Murrow says, his somber eyes pulling Roger in, "is neither predictable nor *stable.*"

Afterward, Roger wanders the grounds in a deepening funk, now seeing the expo as little more than a cheesy roadside attraction. He drifts into the Fashion Pavilion, where models pirouette on carpeted lily pads above a perfumed pool; he then visits the Bell exhibit and winces at its assertion that satellites one day will bring us live television from Africa and Asia, which fits perfectly with all the other false hopes emanating from his operation. Back outside, he watches kids frolic by clinging to balloons stuffed with pink rabbits while their parents slouch in line, drinking Orange Juliuses or waiting for rental cars, *$5 a day, 5 cents a mile.* Suddenly this overflow crowd seems like a single collective organism, an enormous, gullible beast.

Aides find him wherever he goes and pass along more requests, demands and snafus. He puts them all off and cuts in line at Boeing's Spacearium exhibit. Clearing his sore throat, he settles into a seat and waits in the nose of this imaginary rocket as a deep voice counts down the seconds. Blasting off now, he swiftly circles the earth before shooting toward the moon and beyond, planets whirling across the screens, causing him to duck. He actually loses himself in this experience, a spaceman among spacemen, until the lights return and he again sees everything through the aperture of Murrow's harsh lens. He hears a kid squealing because his parents won't buy him *the bullet that killed Jesse James!* He watches people slouching in line after line, alone with the tumble of their thoughts, chewing gum, doing their slaughterhouse shuffle. He buys a pack of Camels, lights up and gazes at another poster: *Don't miss the Roy Rogers and Dale Evans Western Show!* He feels like the mastermind of the ultimate farce.

Retreating to headquarters, he's greeted with the front of the afternoon *Times* and its confusing blend of silliness and seriousness—a photo of a fat Kentucky man who won more than a hundred stuffed animals next to an article about the U.S. attorney's announcement that he's investigating allegations of illegal gambling and police payoffs in Seattle.

Rummaging through messages, he finds one from the senator's secretary, but it's too late to reach anyone back East. Jenny Sunshine pokes her head in and says Malcolm Turner's waiting outside for him. He groans as the developer scurries in and immediately starts talking about the six parcels he's on the brink of cobbling together for the Hilton near Forty-fifth.

"Sorry," Roger interrupts him, "I've got lots going on here now."

"You don't look right. You sick?"

"Tired," he says, realizing he's no longer comfortable around this man.

"Heard anything from the senator?" Malcolm asks abruptly.

Roger hesitates.

"What's he say about this stupid gambling investigation?"

Roger shrugs. "Beats me."

"The chamber's asking about it all the time. We need this thing to go away, least for a while . . ."

We? Roger detects something in Malcolm's eyes—a flicker of desperation? He wants to ask him to be more specific, but more than anything he wants him to leave. Stalling, he takes Teddy's approach. "If a few crooked cops get busted, it's not the end of the world."

"Hey," Malcolm says, shifting his weight from foot to foot, "if Dave Beck can go to jail, anyone can."

Roger reads his pink face for a moment, then says, "Beck invested in your apartment project too, didn't he?"

Malcolm stares at him impersonally. "Lots of people are."

Roger flinches as the door swings and Teddy leads three flush-faced men toward his desk.

"Let me guess, Murrow opened right up for you!" Teddy begins loudly.

"He talked quite a bit," Roger admits, forcing a smile. Then, to Malcolm: "I'll give you a call."

"Kills me!" Teddy regales the others. "These big shots tell me next to nothing, then they tell Roger anything and everything like he's their shrink or something."

As the door shuts behind Malcolm, Teddy introduces him to these Dallas businessmen who seem trapped between a three-martini lunch and a nap. "So what'd Murrow have to say?"

"The fair's a joke. The city's insecure. Armageddon is coming. All sorts of cheerful stuff."

They laugh in unison. Teddy loosens his tie and pours five small glasses of bourbon without ice or water. "Do your LBJ for 'em, Rog."

"*Teddy.*"

"C'mon, been talkin' you up, boy."

"You just got done telling me they're from Texas."

"All the more reason. Just a sentence or two."

The Texans goad him too, and as the office quiets Roger clears his mind until he can conjure the vice president. "Tol' my tailor to gimme a couple more inches down here between the zipper and my *bung*hole, see."

The men lose it.

"Encore!" Teddy barks. "Ed Sullivan. Or John Glenn working the crowd."

An hour later, Roger abandons his to-do list and rushes to the stadium to introduce a lanky preacher named Billy Graham. When he'd asked Roger yesterday if he was a man of science or faith, he waited a beat before saying, "Just a man, Reverend." He shuts his eyes now and listens to the voice of a sensible zealot.

"As the sands of our age are falling in the hourglass, our hope and confidence should not rest alone in our mighty scientific achievement, or in space exploration, but in God." It seems to Roger that Graham's taking shots at the fair too, and moments later he sounds as grim as Murrow or Pauling. "Since the advent of the atomic bomb, man has at his disposal the weapons to bring all these prophetic things about. Man realizes we live in the shadow of the bomb and realizes how fragile man really is."

This day feels like ten crammed into one as he checks his watch and strides from the stadium, Graham's amplified sermon blending with the clunk and whir of the rides and the arcades. He stops into the club to thank Nat King Cole for coming and to glad-hand the city planner and the chamber boys, never stopping long enough to converse with anyone. Finally, he tells Teddy he's going to catch a few winks, then steps back into the illuminated fairgrounds—yellow, purple and gold geysers spouting from the fountain and the girly shows lit up with the word PEEP flashing white. He finds himself glancing overhead, wondering if we'll actually be able to see the incoming missiles before they strike.

CHARLIE McDANIEL is sitting in the corner booth where he said he'd be, his back to the wall so he can see everyone who enters the Frontier.

Built like a bouncer with a dented nose and whiskered cheeks beneath a filthy Yankees ball cap, he's sipping burnt coffee and looks to be recuperating from an illness or a hangover. "You the professor?" he says after Roger sits down. "So-ci-ol-o-gy?" he says, as if for the first time, reading from the business card in his hand.

Roger in fact feels like a prissy academic in this man's bloodshot glare. "I try to teach kids how things really are, how they really work," he says, awkwardly paraphrasing his grandfather. "I try to get at the truth."

McDaniel's giggle makes him sound like a street-corner lunatic, but then he shifts into a low mumble. "What makes you think anybody's interested in that?"

Roger offers him a cigarette. McDaniel shakes his head, sips his coffee and giggles again. "Now how'm I supposed to know you're not setting me up?"

Roger sets the pack on the table between them. "For what?"

"People want me to go away. Lots of people." He glances around the bar. "How 'bout some ID?"

Roger wishes he hadn't come. There's an underlying stench beyond stale beer and ammonia, a sharper odor no cleaning solution can conceal, and much of it, he slowly realizes, is McDaniel's BO.

"Well, you can't know," he says, recalling that the best way to reason with paranoids is to admit they might be right. "And you obviously don't have to talk to me, but I thought the note you posted in your tavern deserved more attention than it got. And from what I can see, you were actually stating the obvious."

McDaniel lowers his head as three hefty men settle in a nearby booth, talking simultaneously.

Roger leans closer, despite the odor. "The chamber brags about what a wholesome city this is. A good-government city's what they call it."

McDaniel holds the business card up to the light as if checking for counterfeit. "How 'bout a driver's license?"

Roger plucks the card from his hand. "Everybody says you're a crackpot. If you don't want to help, I'm pretty sure I can find somebody who knows what you know and more."

McDaniel reaches for the Camels. "In a little less than half an hour," he says, tapping one out, "Officer Winston Blair will walk up to the left side of this bar in plainclothes, throw back a free shot, pick up a sack of money and walk out."

He yaks for the next fifteen minutes, fast and animated in that same low mumble, smoking aggressively, twirling keys on his callused fingers. A year and a half ago, his story goes, he sold a restaurant in Everett and bought the Shipwreck on First. He knew about its card room, but not its cigar-shop bookie. It took him less than a week, he says, to learn that the city's "tolerance laws" weren't what they seemed.

Roger overhears some loud woman a couple booths away. "They're tearing it down after the fair, that's what I hear. . . . No? Well, they should. It's not architecture, it's *gimmicktecture.*"

When he tunes back in, McDaniel's explaining that he had to pay off the cops or close his card room. Claimed he paid two different bagmen $250 for each of the first three months, then refused to let the beat cop handpick his next card-room manager. Suddenly Teamsters started fights in his bar, health inspectors showed up during the dinner hour and a state liquor man framed him for selling to minors. "I'm selling to kids? Go to the Turf or Merchant's. They serve twelve-year-olds. And my kitchen was spotless, okay? Cooks complained all the time that I cared more about cleanliness than taste, which is true. People'll eat anything." By then, though, he was losing money so fast he had to pay off the cops or sell at a huge loss to the only willing buyer—the same crook who'd sold him the place. So he hired a young attorney to help him expose the shakedown. "The kid backed out in less than a week. Couldn't even interest the papers. I really don't know where it all begins and ends."

"What do you mean?"

"Like I said, for all I know you're in on it." Now he looked more desperate than tough.

"You probably know this, Charlie, but saying things like that makes you sound paranoid."

McDaniel lights another cigarette and studies him.

"Let's stick with what you know for sure," Roger says gently. "The patrolman collects the money, but where does it go from there?" He feels his pulse throbbing in his neck. "If you were getting jerked around by Teamsters and health and liquor inspectors, they're getting paid too, right? What about higher up in the police?"

McDaniel takes a long inhale, glances at the door, blows smoke at the ceiling. "One of the few honest cops I met told me there's one sergeant who figures out exactly who gets what, but that he's the only one who knows."

Roger sweats through another ten minutes as McDaniel grows even more cryptic and indecipherable. He's whispering now that the high-dollar games have moved to the New Caledonia Bridge Club on Union. "Bridge in the front," he says, "poker in the back."

Roger's attention wanders. He overhears more people talking about the fair. Somebody heard Billy Graham tonight, others rattle on about their friends' kids getting lost or all the goddamn lines. He notices two women staring at him, trying to place his face, and realizes he can't get away with much more of this. At the bottom of the hour, McDaniel points with a pinky at the bar where a strapping hatted man sidles up to a shot of whiskey. He turns it once in his fingertips, as if assessing its quality, before tossing it back and grabbing a paper bag, then strolling out like he'd just picked up his sack lunch.

Hours later, Roger's in his third different game of the night and losing again. Compared with the others, the New Caledonia is almost tasteful, with cedar paneling and dozens of nudes that suggested the owner was a collector, not a pervert. Of the six men hunched around the table, Roger is the only one under sixty. And he's had enough liquor to feel sober, so he's talking about the weather, the fair, even the bagman he'd seen taking cash right off the bar top, working it all in between hands like he was sharing, not asking. "The U.S. attorney wants to be a congressman," he suddenly volunteers. "Thinks he can make his name indicting cops."

"Not just cops," one of them says. "Bankers, councilmen, you name it."

"Shut up, Larry."

"Everybody always focuses on dirty cops. Cops, cops, cops," Larry drones. "But why in God's name would it stop there? Everybody likes money, right?"

"Hard to know what's talk and what's real," Roger says, agreeably.

"It's as real as the nose on your face. What people don't understand is that it's an industry—tax-free too." His grin's one-sided.

"Shut up, Larry."

"Sounds like a racket to me," Roger says.

"What isn't? If you're doing business, you're in a racket."

"Somebody's gotta run it," Roger says. "Things don't run themselves."

"There's a *network*. That's what they call it. The network."

"Shut it, Larry. You're blowing smoke."

"Yeah? Go see who shows up for breakfast at the Dog House on the second Tuesday of every month."

"Shut *up*, Larry."

"Cops, jewelers, realtors, staffers from the mayor's office and—"

"Shut the hell—"

"*You* shut up, Rudy."

Roger tosses in more chips, raising the pot by thirty dollars, and loses again. He stays quiet and loses some more, waits another hand, then asks, "Any of you ever know a Robert Dawkins?"

The dealer shuffles.

"Who?"

"Bobby Dawkins. Used to play a lot of cards round here maybe fifteen years ago."

Cards fly, heads shake.

"He's my uncle."

Nothing.

The men cagily organize their cards. Another hand passes, and Roger loses more money.

"He go by Doc?" asks a potbellied old-timer, speaking for the first time.

"How's that?" Roger asks.

"That uncle you're snooping around about. I knew a *Doc*, my age or older. Laughed like a cement mixer. Big old gummy smile."

Roger feels a quiver.

"Las Vegas. Least that's what I heard. Went to Vegas, didn't he, Larry?"

Larry studies his cards, suddenly mum.

Rudy glares at Roger. "Your uncle owes people a lot of money."

"Perhaps," the dealer says, "but you can't squeeze it out of his nephew." He glances at Roger's chip pile and grins. "Or maybe we already have."

Chapter Ten

JUNE 2001

THEY SLEPT in the same bed, mother and son, in their dank brick apartment in the shadow of the freeway just north of downtown. He had his own big-boy bed, but slept beside her, not out of his need so much as hers. After peeling his skinny arm off her stomach, she rolled onto her side and turned off the alarm seconds before it would have sounded at 5:29. What she craved were two uninterrupted hours before entering the Monday newsroom. Outside, the interstate roared with people speeding into the city even before the day had a chance to break.

Her apartment looked like a set for an earthquake movie—toppled stacks of dishes and cereal boxes, books and folders strewn across the floor next to newspapers, maps, notebooks and DVDs—*Toy Story, Lion King, Aladdin*—and crumpled drafts of her next Roger Morgan story. The books were split into distinct piles. *Skid Road, Seattle Heritage, See You in Seattle!, Century 21,* and *Seattle: Past to Present* in one heap. *The New Journalism, Raising Hell, Stalking the Feature Story* and instructive gems by Orlean, Kidder and Thompson in the other. She could summon their salient points from memory, yet having them within reach made her feel like she wasn't writing alone, and the same was true of her bound collections of Pulitzer-winning articles. She'd reread them often enough to know the common ingredients: original reporting, compelling prose and some irresistible intangible that often involved dragging secrets into the sunshine. From what she could tell, the Public Service Medal, the granddaddy of the *P*s, guaranteed salvation.

For years now, without ever saying it aloud, she has prowled and dredged and scratched for stories that just might—if everything fell right—be deemed Pulitzer-worthy. The dot-com saga offered some of the essentials. She'd already gathered the glitter and punch such a series needed. But she hadn't been here for the zenith, when champagne-colored Lexuses filled the streets, and her reporting began during the confessional stage with open-collared thirty-something former CEOs called Ron or Daryl or Brad (they were too cool and new-school to bother with last names) crowing about their $100,000 parties, Brazilian strippers, chain-saw jugglers and pet alligators. Some even boasted about how hard they'd crashed, hawking Ferraris, Steinways and marble-size diamonds while tumbling through divorce and bankruptcy courts. One smiled ruefully and tried to describe what it felt like to lose $1.1 billion in stock options. She'd amassed enough details that her description of the collapse alone should be as irresistible as watching a skyscraper implode in slow motion; and she had begun tying it all into the city's boom-and-bust DNA, likening it to the Yukon Gold Rush hysteria, when enough little people got ridiculously rich here to lure mobs of newcomers. And people were still coming. Just ten months ago, national reporters were telling the world that Seattle receptionists were retiring in their twenties with a few mil in options, that the rules of the old economy no longer applied in a city that was printing money. Shortly before its fall, *The Economist* called Seattle the tenth best city in *the world*. Not to be outexaggerated, *USA Today* anointed it "the number one city of the future."

The problem with her dot-com drama, she increasingly understood, was that once you peeled away the silliness and excesses, it pretty quickly boiled down to rich kids getting drunk and puking on themselves. But the mysterious father of the world's fair running for mayor forty years later? Now, there's a story that wouldn't win any prizes but was alive, unpredictable and perhaps even parabolic.

She'd written a few drafts of "Mr. Seattle" over the weekend. It still needed fact-checking, whittling and sharpening, but she'd have most of the week to get it just right. She steamed herself a latte, then stepped over dirty clothes into Elias's bedroom and turned on the computer. Once her old Compaq finally awakened, she typed *seattletimes.com,* pressed enter and up popped Morgan's jug-eared face alongside Rooney's jowly mug. *Mayoral Race Almost a Dead Heat.*

She didn't exhale until she realized it was just a poll story. Still, prior surveys showed Morgan at least ten points behind Rooney and five behind Norheim. This one had Rooney leading him by just three, Norheim by six. Once she got over the fear of being scooped—anybody can buy a poll—her heart skipped again when she noticed the *Times* had another story about the race, this one detailing campaign contributions from several strip-club owners to mayoral and council candidates over the past ten years. She read it fast, relieved the sums were inconsequential and that it was mostly a dry recounting of adult-club ordinances.

She guiltily poached the last egg for herself, knowing Elias would have to eat cereal now. She heard the *Seattle Times* thump her porch and resisted the urge to see exactly how the stories were played. Over breakfast, she condensed and recast her pitch to make "Mr. Seattle" sound original and ambitious enough to lead Friday's paper. Then she soaked her hands in hot water for three minutes, dried them off and took her Molinari out of its case.

She played three-octave scales as softly as she could. Tucking the violin under her chin always calmed her, until she heard sloppy bow work on simple études. Just playing chords and double-stops was difficult enough. She should've practiced *before* she'd read the *Times* and started rethinking her story. She pulled out one of the solos in Vivaldi's *Four Seasons* and hummed the first page to herself. Yet as soon as she began playing, it sounded strained. She was holding the bow too tightly or moving it too slowly, and her aching fingers were too tense for vibratos. Five more tries, but it only got worse, her mind wandering now between Morgan and the fact she couldn't play Vivaldi anymore, even the easier parts.

She woke her boy up and helped him dress. He brushed his teeth with his eyes closed, oblivious to her urgency, and yakked nonstop while chewing cereal about how he wanted to go to Hogwarts and be a child wizard too. When the phone rang, she saw her childhood number pop up and groaned.

"Hi, Mom."

"Oh, Helen!" her mother blurted. "I didn't expect to get you!"

"Been working hard, and now I've gotta get Elias to preschool. I'll try to call you tonight, okay?"

Elias big-eyed her. "Granny?"

She glanced at the clock. They were already late. "Elias wants to say hi."

Her parents had been clamoring to visit ever since she got settled. They couldn't grasp that her apartment was too small and that even modest hotels were too expensive out here. Plus, she didn't want them to see how far her life had fallen short of their imagination. It was easy to picture her mother tidying, cooking and ironing, desperately trying to make this place homey while her father paced, jingling keys, in between trips to the nearest Dunkin' Donuts. His voice boomed through the phone now. "That my grandson?"

The two of them talking always got to her. Elias immediately launched into a detailed account—sounding like an FAA investigator—of exactly how his cardboard Spitfire airplane broke its yellow wing. Her father's laugh was enough to push her over this morning.

"Jesus," she mutters, dabbing her eyes and firing up another latte. Glancing out the window, she watched one of her hard-drinking neighbors—the fifth-year psych major or perhaps the sixth-year philosophy student—step outside in a filthy bathrobe and gut the neighbors' *Times* of its sports section. Minutes later, she and Elias were striding through the ratty courtyard—a coffee mug in one hand, Elias clutching the other, skipping to keep up—with the freeway roaring like surf at their backs, as if the entire city were on deadline.

She noticed that just seven of the twelve apartments got morning papers now, fewer every month, and it made her anxious. People don't quit the paper, change their minds and sign back up. It was a lifestyle decision, or a pattern broken. And with papers increasingly free online now, big scoops could become as transitory as lightning bugs. Only two of the remaining seven subscribers, she noticed, got *her* paper, which gave extra personal weight to the recurring notion that she was born too late.

THE LIVING ROOM above the Ming Yen restaurant was packed, just as Roger had hoped it would be since Teddy shared the encouraging news that Chan Wu had asked to host a tea for him. The eighteen women were nibbling egg rolls and sipping gunpowder tea while Chan, pushing eighty beneath a two-tone beehive, popped the questions until they all joined in. Does he call this the International District? *No, Chinatown.* What about building a branch of the city library here? *He's all for it.* And tennis courts? *Why not?* Would he help them raise money to build a Chinatown gate? *Of course.*

The questions weren't hard, but they kept coming, and he felt awkward articulating his intentions on issues he'd never once thought about. Stalling, he nervously defaulted to storytelling and sharing his recollections of Wing Luke. He barely knew him, yet was dropping his name, which further rattled him. "Always so measured, but he had a fun side—didn't he?—with those cartoons he drew and that smile of his. First one to ever put campaign ads on buses, remember that? Looked ridiculous at first, then everyone started doing it." He knew he was dying here, rolling out two-dimensional memories of a man some of these people had counted as a friend, yet blundered ahead hoping to find somewhere to stop. "Better leader than people realized, I'd say. He fought for open housing and was the only one, as I recall, in favor of saving the Market. And then, well . . . Then he just vanished in that little plane in—what was it, 'sixty-five?" Hell, none of this was news, though it probably was insensitive and maybe even ghoulishly violated some custom about not discussing the dead. In all his previous visits here with candidates, he'd never seen a moment this awkward. "It's just that he was only forty," he continued, sweat beading his forehead. "If he could've . . . I don't know." He trailed off, all these dark eyes avoiding his, amazed anew that the gateway to the city's Asian vote still passed through the modest living room of this venerable restaurant owner.

Chan gently broke the silence. "We had Wing Luke fortune cookies for a while when he was on the council." She smiled. " 'Wing Luke says this. Wing Luke says that.' "

The room filled with oxygen, and Roger was so grateful he reached over and squeezed her hand. As they were leaving, she quietly told Teddy to put her on the endorsement list.

Two hours later, he was riding shotgun through downtown after meeting with Boeing's machinists, babbling like an excited child.

"Ever wonder how much water gets piped into this city on a daily basis? Or how much electricity gets wired in from Ross? Or how many thousands of gallons of storm water gush beneath these streets when it pours? And think of all the hundreds of garbage trucks and buses and ferry boats it takes just to keep this city moving every goddamn day. Then think of all the thousands of policemen and firemen it takes to keep us safe, and all the hospitals and doctors and ER nurses it takes to patch us up. We don't really think about it, do we? No, we just mosey along our little habit trails. But we feel it whether we think about it or not, know what I'm saying? It's what we share, all this stuff that's going on offstage. And there's an odd collective power to it that gets under our skin in a good way, don't you think? It's not just the landscape or architecture that holds us here."

Annie nodded feverishly, and even Teddy wasn't snoring. A simple bump in the polls and people listened better, even the machinists. Rooney was demanding their endorsement, but they told Roger they'd stay neutral through the primary, a vote of confidence that left Teddy baffled. "Why'd they do that?" he'd asked as they left. "You didn't *promise* them anything."

When they parked alongside a row of shops near Mercer and Eleventh, Roger noticed a young man sticking large block letters— R-O-G—in a window and slowly registered exactly where they were before following Annie into his new campaign headquarters. Close to twenty people were stacking signs, stuffing envelopes and answering landlines and cell phones in a cluttered space the size of a studio apartment. It wasn't so much the commotion on his behalf that excited him as the mix of volunteers in their twenties and eighties. Someone shouted his name, and everybody's attention swiveled toward him.

After disjointed applause, he asked everyone what exactly they thought they were doing here and then worked the room, greeting the smooth-skinned college kids first. "Extra credit?" he said. They nodded, and he laughed.

"We could've picked any campaign, though," a girl with jagged bangs explained.

"Why mine?"

"You seem honest," said an earringed boy with an armful of *Morgan for Mayor* yard signs. "We hope you'll talk on campus."

"Definitely," Roger told him, then turned to the older ladies, careful not to say *Nice to meet you* in case he simply hadn't placed them yet. Finally, he got to the large gray woman filling envelopes behind a desk. The familiar empathy in her baggy eyes made him suspect she knew him well.

"So how the hell are you?" he asked.

She rose gingerly and shuffled heavily around the desk as the commotion resumed around them. "You don't recognize me, do you?" she said softly, before wrapping her arms around him and squeezing.

She smelled like almonds and dead leaves. He knew he'd slept with her, but when? Her name began with *D*, for sure. Diane? Diana? Denise? He held on, stalling.

SHRONTZ READ HELEN'S story pitch, glanced back at the draft, then at the pitch again. It was all she could do to resist reading it aloud to him. He was painfully slow most mornings, slogging, she suspected, through pharmaceutical hangovers. Finally, he walked by, heading to the morning meeting, and mumbled, "Pretty close on the reporting?"

"Yeah, I need to double-check quite a few things and talk to several more people and see what Lundberg has for me and so on, but what I really need is a sit-down with him."

He yawned. "Think you could file by late Wednesday?"

The earlier she turned the story in the more time everyone would have to tinker and second-guess. But wanting Friday A-1 and needing Shrontz in her corner, she bobbed her head.

"Put in another call to his campaign," he muttered, as if the idea hadn't occurred to her.

A half hour later, a fully awake Shrontz rushed out of the meeting. "We're running it tomorrow."

"Tomorrow?" Helen's eyes widened. "No, I—"

"We're in a competitive market here," he said, no doubt parroting higher-ranked editors. "All barrels."

"What?"

He turned his hands into fake guns and pointed them at her. "All barrels blazing. And everything we know," he added, "about *Mr. Seattle.*"

"Wait. I've at least got to talk to him, because it's still not even—"

"Birnbaum loves it. Marguerite *really* loves it. Everyone does."

"That's a *draft*. There's still a lot of reporting. I mean—"

"You just said you were pretty close," he reminded her. "Competitive market," he repeated, hustling toward his desk. "Give Morgan a deadline."

Helen walked as slowly as she could to the drinking fountain and back. *Tomorrow?* She glanced at the first page of her draft again. A daring premise thin on facts. When the words started to blur, she looked up and saw the backlit silhouette of Marguerite strutting toward her, blowing imaginary smoke off the tips of her index fingers.

HELEN AND A SCRUM of reporters, photographers and TV crews followed Morgan and his volunteers—armed with campaign flyers, yard signs and dog biscuits—through the Phinney Ridge neighborhood, north of downtown.

"So what's your strategy?" asked an elderly woman at the corner of Fifty-second and Palatine.

"To go everywhere the mayor doesn't go and meet as many voters as I can," Morgan cheerfully replied. "And to tell the truth—all the time, every time."

"Tell your people," she said loudly, "they can put one of those big signs in my yard."

Helen tried to conceal her mounting panic. The afternoon was fading fast, and she still didn't have a formal interview set up. Ask your questions in front of everybody else, Ted Severson had suggested, or hope for a break in the schedule.

When the repetitive doorbelling—"I'm Roger Morgan, and I'm running for mayor"—continued south into the Fremont neighborhood, she broke from the pilgrimage, even though the *Times* reporter was still eavesdropping on Morgan's every utterance, and called Shrontz, pleading for more time. "Lock and load," he said. "Competitive market."

"Right."

"Huh?"

"I *came* from a *competitive market.*"

"Why are you *shouting* at me, Helen?"

She hung up and, instead of rejoining the paparazzi, tailed Severson into a neighborhood espresso shop, where she watched him lean on his cane and order a drip coffee.

"Cool," replied the sleeveless, tattooed barista. Once he got his steaming mug, Severson dropped with a groan into a chair at a tiny square table, glaring at all the red stools and the people wearing funny hats, throwback glasses and striped shirts.

"You mind?"

He shrugged, though it was clear he did. He studied the heart-shaped foam design atop her latte and then the barista, as if uncovering some lesbian tryst. He obviously wanted to get up and leave, but his coffee was still too hot to guzzle and he hadn't gotten a go-cup.

Sitting this close, she noticed just how narrow his skull was, his nose and chin coming to points, his eyes reduced to slits, as if he'd seen more than enough already. She started gently, but even the friendliest question about Roger Morgan prompted the stink-eye and a bland response. Impatiently, she prodded him about the fair's little-publicized downsides.

"Can we go off the record for a minute?" he asked.

"You mean not for attribution?"

"I mean *off the record,* as in what I'm about to say can't be printed or repeated."

She hesitated. "You're running his campaign, Mr. Severson. You're one of his closest friends. I'd like whatever you might say to be on the record."

"Who told you I'm running his campaign?" His voice rose. "You'd think *a trained observer* would've noticed by now that Roger runs his own show."

When his responses to her questions slowed down, as if his batteries were dying or he was doing his damndest to bore her to death, it crossed her mind that Severson probably didn't even think women should *be* reporters. He told her how many years—forty-six—he'd been around politics and the press, leaving the number hanging with its insinuation that he knew exactly what she was up to. She pretended to listen but mostly watched, noting how his ash-colored hair hovered like a messy halo over his freckled scalp.

"What did you want to tell me off the record?" she finally asked.

"Thought you weren't interested."

"Deep background, just for my edification."

"Call it whatever you want." He glanced out the window. "You listening to me now?"

"Of course."

"Sure?"

"Yes."

"You should be ashamed of yourself for trying to tear down such a great man."

Helen blushed. "You went off the record to scold me?"

"I'm not finished," he snarled, breathing audibly now. "I suggest you take a good look at those chips on your shoulders and see whether they factor into your sense of fairness with Roger and the others you've skewered for sport through the years, including a certain senator from South Carolina. Okay, now we're back on the record. Any more questions, Ms. Gulanos?"

She found her voice, but there wasn't much behind it and her heart was kicking. She hadn't moved all the way out here to get lectured on newspaper shit storms back East. "Mr. Severson, I'm putting a whole lot of extra time into this, to be absolutely fair. I wouldn't—"

"What are we even talking about?" He brought the cup to his

mouth again, but it was empty and he looked away. "I'll try to get you some time with him around dinner, but no promises, okay? Good day." His voice rose on *day* the way Paul Harvey's did on the radio, a squiggly vein bulging near his temple, his fingers going white as his weight shifted onto the cane, his suit coat hanging so wide open that Helen couldn't miss the dark handle of a pistol bulging from his left armpit.

PAIN HAD CRAWLED up Roger's calves into his knees and was headed for his hips by the time this doorbelling marathon approached the last house, where there was supposed to be a barbecue in his honor.

The front yard of the mustard-yellow three-story was adorned with Tibetan prayer flags, a ceramic Buddha, African masks and plastic pink flamingos. Getting closer, he saw much more—a metal sun, birdbaths, clamshells, wind chimes, sneakers wrapped around overhead telephone lines, kites and swings dangling from maple branches. The largest bumper sticker on the VW van parked out front read *Visualize One Love*. He heard excited voices rounding the far side of the house, repeating his name. People stepped outdoors to eyeball the novelty candidate in his button-down shirt, nobody knowing what to say. It was all he could do to sustain his smile, perspiring there on the cracked walkway, eager blades of grass sprouting around his wingtips. Young and old people, dozens now, tittering, waiting. He dabbed at his brow with the back of his wrist. "So what's for dinner?" he finally asked, his eyes stinging, and everyone acted like Seinfeld had just showed up.

They limply shook his hand and offered beer. What he needed was food and water, a bathroom and a couch, but he accepted a warm Pabst and stood there, his feet sizzling as if he'd scaled some peak. The chicken'll be a while, he overheard, still raw on the grill. He had trouble following questions and suggestions, everybody's eyes on him, half of them drunk and overly earnest, trying too hard to be substantive.

Nodding along, as if he knew precisely what they meant, he looked around to see how many reporters were still shadowing him.

He spotted the *Times* guy, a snide columnist with one of the week-lies, the KING-5 airhead, another who claimed he was writing for *Slate* magazine and, of course, Helen Gulanos, who was *insisting* on talking to him *today*. He desperately tried to stay alert, to be *on*, but he was finished, hopelessly repeating himself and answering questions that hadn't been asked. Finally, he excused himself to the bathroom, hoping the domineering woman he'd just abandoned wasn't in mid-question.

The tiny, windowless dollhouse bathroom made him perspire even more, the walls a frightening blood-red, the mirror a foggy antique, the sink barely large enough for his swollen hands. He splashed his face repeatedly with cold water to shake the grogginess, trying to hide the one thing an old candidate can't show: exhaustion. The day had started with such giddiness, but he should have known better. A poll this early meant less than nothing, and while the machinists and Asians were kind, it's not as if they were campaigning for him.

Cornered as soon as he stepped outside, this time by a bearded man with a *Fuck Capitalism* T-shirt, he got quizzed on same-sex marriages, organic-food certifications, the plight of polar bears and other issues he didn't much care about while overhearing drunks explain in the background that yes, they in fact had run out of propane. So yes, they'll either have to borrow a tank from a neighbor or bake the chickens in the oven. Feeling dizzy, he scanned the room for snacks but saw only potato chip crumbs. Meanwhile, he was getting grilled by a man with oven-cleaner breath and ogled by three older women too shy to approach. Behind them, another ring of gawkers monitored his availability, waiting for an opening so they could say they *met* him.

Annie finally rescued him, apologizing profusely to everyone within earshot, pulling him outside as if some emergency had arisen, whispering that Teddy insisted they get him dinner *right now*. Roger stopped at the gate to thank everyone but his voice was too weak, his words lost in the confusing bustle. They all assumed he'd come back shortly. The entire departure was muffed, his largest crowd of the day squandered.

HELEN LET HIM FINISH chewing the oyster crackers. They were in Ivar's Salmon House now, across Lake Union from downtown, waiting for his dinner while frat boys cussed at the happy-hour bar and Severson and Annie eavesdropped from an adjacent table.

She tried not to look frazzled, but she'd raced here from her apartment after explaining Elias's allergies and food and video preferences to yet another new babysitter, this one a big-eyed fourteen-year-old who kept bragging that she had a Girl Scout badge for child care. The thrill of the hunt had faded anyway, especially given that Morgan looked half-dead. Behind his head was the cityscape with the Space Needle off to the side, as if the other buildings were either in awe of it or refused to be seen with it.

HER HAIR WAS so thick and unruly that it made her face seem small and intensely focused, with a contained desperation in her eyes and unasked questions tightening her expressions. Despite all her nonchalance, he could tell she was burning inside. He pointed out a seaplane on the lake so she wouldn't notice his hand trembling as he sipped his water.

There was no rhythm to her queries. She went from asking about hobbies—mountains he'd climbed and sports he watched—to his churchgoing habits. She followed an aside about whether it was true that he'd paid bums to tell him stories with a point-blank question: Was there anything apocryphal about how he'd come up with the idea for the Space Needle?

He'd lost track of what he was saying, mumbling through what felt like yet another minefield, knowing her questions deserved more thought. Mercifully, a tray of oyster shooters was set down in front of him.

SHE LOOKED AWAY when he threw back what resembled slugs crammed into shot glasses and forced herself not to glance at her watch, breathing through her nose to slow her pulse.

"So what have you done since you moved here?" he asked. "Have you canoed through the arboretum yet?" She shook her head. "Sailed in the duck dodge?" She squinted. "Rode the Burke-Gilman Trail? Climbed Mount Si? Taken a ferry ride? Driven up to Paradise?"

"Paradise?"

"On Rainier, my dear. The lodge. You haven't been there yet either?"

She was running out of time for major changes before the first deadline. "Mr. Morgan," she said, "I just work here." She let him take a bite, waited a beat, then said, "You look tired."

He stopped chewing and grinned. "Am I too old for this? Is that the question?"

"It's a fair one, isn't it?" she said neutrally. "Doorbelling is hard work, even for young legs. That was a long day. I'm impressed you held up as well as you did. I mean, you've had some joints replaced, haven't you?"

He groaned and glanced at Teddy. "You're serious, aren't you?" He squeezed out a smile. "Left hip twice and right knee once. So far. Why? What'd you hear?"

"That you've got a pacemaker too."

"Wow!" His short, hard laugh alarmed Teddy, who cocked his good ear closer. "No, ma'am! My heart beats entirely on its own volition. But you know, my father, uncle and grandpa didn't make it out of their sixties, so this is all bonus time."

She studied him. "How'd they go?"

"Aneurysms. All of 'em. And it's a hereditary thing too, a narrowness of the blood vessels up here." He tapped his skull. "My grandfather went mid-sentence. He was a history professor at the U-Dub and explaining Manifest Destiny to me in the backyard when"— Morgan snapped his fingers—"he was suddenly gone. So either I'm likely to go at any minute or I'll take after my mother and be around forever. Anything else you'd like to know about my mortality?"

He swallowed a cup of Manhattan chowder and plowed into the halibut—"the *steak of the sea*," he informed her—and she saw a new alertness, the seafood working like a defibrillator.

Wiping his mouth, he leaned toward her and lowered his voice.

"What you need to understand, Ms. Gulanos, is that it's not my body that's having a hard time with all this. It's being old enough to smell bullshit a few miles away and yet still having to pretend it's valid. That's what I'm getting too *old* for."

She'd lost control of the interview and didn't know how to regain it, scribbling in her notebook even though the tape recorder was running. She concentrated on appearing neither friendly nor hostile and waited to see what he'd say next.

SEEING HER FLUSTERED, he offered his damn-the-consequences smile. He was used to rolling this one out to relax people, though it wasn't working on her, and he couldn't tell if that was because she was wound too tight or, worse yet, simply immune to it. "I'm clearly not used to talking so much about myself," he said finally. "So you're from Ohio?"

"Originally, yes."

"Which part?"

"Youngstown."

"Rust Belt." He resisted mentioning that her eyes were steel-gray in this light. "Parents still there?"

"Listen, I'm sorry, but I'm up against a deadline and still have more questions. And I know you have to leave in a bit to—"

"You don't like talking about yourself either."

"I'm not running for mayor, sir."

"That's a diversion not an excuse. I doubt you share much of yourself with anyone."

She stared at him, clearly weighing her options.

"Tell me something about *you*," he pressed, pointing his fork at her. "Please. Anything."

She inhaled. "I live in a small apartment a five-minute walk from here, but it feels like it could be anywhere, in any city. I rented under the freeway because it's across the street from a preschool and day care that's a 'peanut- and coconut-free zone,' which caught my eye, seeing how Elias is allergic to peanuts. The paper snowflakes the kids made in January are still up on the windows for reasons I don't understand."

He waited for more, then nodded. "Thank you for that. It wasn't much about you, but what was unsaid was actually rather generous. You're a single mom with a demanding full-time job, yet you're willing to live like a troll under the freeway if you think it's good for your boy." He wiped his mouth, his energy and imagination returning in waves, picturing her thirty years from now, still beautiful, her face rounder, less defined, the skin of her neck loosening enough to cover that fading scar. And it hit him right then—the familiar old woman volunteering at his campaign was *Deborah*. Deborah Barrows! She still even looked something like her forty-year-old self. He'd ended that one so poorly that he teared up now at her forgiveness before he could stop himself.

As he dabbed his eyes, her questions started up again, in a much firmer tone, about his consulting work through the decades. Then, out of nowhere: "Did your parent company profit off the Space Needle restaurant during and after the fair?" Obviously, she already knew the answers, which made this a lie detector test as well as an interview.

"I'd appreciate your help," she said now, "at putting me in touch with people who know you well instead of just acquaintances who admire you. I'd like to talk to your mother."

"Teddy knows me as well as anybody, and he definitely doesn't admire me."

"Mr. Severson thinks I'm out to get you."

Roger glanced at Teddy, who looked like he was about to rupture. "Loyal to the brink of paranoia, isn't he? My mother's not well. I will thank you in advance for not bothering her."

It took them forever to get the bill, but once they finally escaped her and her questions, he debriefed Teddy while Annie drove them toward a nearby retirement home.

"She's clearly under a lot of pressure to break new ground on me," Roger said. "I almost feel sorry for her."

"Don't," Teddy instructed him. "I just skimmed her stories on some poor senator from South Carolina. She chopped off his head, stuck her knife in his ass, slit open his belly and tossed him on the grill."

Roger laughed. "Maybe he deserved it."

"She thinks you all do. Don't feel sorry for her. The bunny rabbit doesn't feel sorry for the hungry eagle. She's a shark."

"Teddy, please. Pick an image and stick with it."

SPEEDING BACK to the office, she was redesigning the story so feverishly in her head that she glided through a red with that familiar rush of clear thinking that comes with attempting to not only get everything precisely right but also to make it engaging, even irresistible— maybe even artistic—without bending a single fact, *on deadline*. But truth and art are moving targets. Stories change and evolve. Bigger news breaks. And even if she did her part and lucked out with the timing, the story still had to survive several editors, a headline writer, a page designer and maybe a half dozen others with the authority to fuck it up. But if this were easy, it wouldn't be exhilarating, and she wouldn't be blowing through red lights rewriting in her head. Her thoughts hopped into the future, picturing tomorrow's readers. Marguerite, Birnbaum, Steele and, of course, Morgan himself, Teddy and Annie, then her parents, friends at *Roll Call* and the only two people in her courtyard who get the *P-I* every morning. Probably only six inches of copy on the front, the other fifty inside, but people would read every word. The phony way Morgan had teared up at the restaurant over her plight as an overworked single mom suddenly infuriated her all over again.

She realized she hadn't checked her phone messages in more than an hour. *Four.* Two from Shrontz demanding updates, in that Morse-code brevity of his. One from Omar Duran: "My guy saw the poll this morning and says he'll talk to you next week about Morgan—off the record." The last one, yet another from Shrontz: "Birnbaum's holding it. You've got another day or two." She was so distracted by this news, so simultaneously disappointed and relieved that she crossed the center line into oncoming traffic until the medley of horns revived her and she swerved back on course.

· · ·

"ALL I'M ASKING is that you just say hello to a few people," Teddy said as they pulled up to the Grand Firs Retirement Community.

Roger didn't respond, listening to Dave Niehaus on the radio describing a blooper single that loaded the bases in the bottom of the eighth.

"Bill Hogan lives here," Teddy explained. "Claims he's turned a bunch of these folks into activists."

Roger shushed him. "It's tied," he said. "Let's just hear the end of this inning. That too much to ask?"

"Yes. We're late as it is, and we're not running your campaign around the Mariners' schedule."

Roger held up his hand to listen as Nichaus described Piniella's glum stroll to the mound, signaling the bullpen to send in the big right-hander. "You don't get it," he said, unhitching his seat belt. "It's not just baseball. It's *Niehaus*. And haven't we done enough today? Do we really need to do this now? Don't we already have the Alzheimer's vote locked up?"

"Not if you take it for granted, dummy. Everybody likes to be asked. And some of these people might do more than vote for you."

Roger climbed out and tried to rise to the moment, to look bigger and smarter and better than he felt, but his body was stiffening and his mind already spent.

"Must be something going on tonight," Teddy murmured once they stepped inside and heard voices through the walls. "Let's just peek in here. I'll ask around for Hogan."

Applause broke out as they entered the dining hall. Roger looked around for a speaker or a performer, but as the room swung into focus he saw what had to be a hundred and fifty people older than himself huddled around tables, not eating, just sitting, clapping and staring at him. Finally he spotted the homemade *Morgan for Mayor!* banner above the kitchen door and staggered backward in a combination of real and mock surprise. Laughter strafed the room. Some woman started chanting "Ro-ger! Ro-ger!" and as it spread across all the tables he felt the scratchy voices and happy faces practically lifting him off the floor.

Chapter Eleven

AUGUST 1962

THE MORNING Marilyn Monroe doesn't wake up, Roger opens his eyes next to his fiancée, her curls spilling across his pillow. He'd taken her to hear Ella Fitzgerald the night before, though she'd explained in advance that she wasn't actually much of a jazz fan. He wasn't as dismayed by her lack of interest as he was by *his* interest in a woman who wasn't moved by jazz. How had he got to this brink without realizing that she didn't have the slightest weakness for Miles, Coltrane and Ella? When pressed, she'd admitted she rarely noticed or cared what music was playing. Lawrence Welk, Mozart, Elvis, what does it matter? Yet once they'd dropped into their seats and Ella began humming, she was big-eyed and beaming like a delighted child. That's what had attracted him in the first place, her kidlike euphoria. And when Ella's voice rose inside him, he saw Linda swaying. But just as he began to feel undeserving of her affection and loyalty, and ridiculously lucky that he apparently hadn't screwed everything up yet, she'd started spinning her engagement ring—the size of which so clearly disappointed her—and then turned to him and said, "Ready?"

"For what?"

"Let's go, sweetie, before the rush."

"But she's still singing."

"Haven't we heard enough?"

He'd tried to will himself back into the music but couldn't, and they'd filed out midsong, as if tending to some personal emergency. Once outside, she'd babbled about wanting to see the Ringling Brothers.

After some unimaginative lovemaking at her apartment, he'd passed out until he woke at dawn after a variation of a recurring dream involving JFK. As in the others, they were strolling the fairgrounds together, but in this one Roger was a boy too short to be heard. A full-size version of Linda, however, suddenly joined them and loudly asked the president whether he and Jackie had driven out to Seattle. Roger woke right then, with the lingering embarrassment that he'd taken the attractive blank slate of a Frederick & Nelson jewelry saleswoman and tried to invent the woman he'd wanted.

He dresses quietly and putters up the hill to his house, then shaves and showers, singing Ella off-key—*Your daddy's rich, and your momma's good lookin'*—and thinking about how his grandfather had always savored these morning interludes. In fact, he'd adopted many of the old man's habits, eating toast with jam and drinking a pot of Folgers while reading the newspaper front-to-back in silence, which is exactly what he was doing now, sitting in his grandfather's chair, though the quiet is interrupted by his mother's manlike snore down the hall. Five months from his wedding, he still can't imagine her moving out or Linda moving in, much less both of them milling around in curlers.

The house sits on the steep southern incline of Queen Anne Hill, just above the fairgrounds. He can almost somersault to work if he has to. And from this vantage, it's easy to see the monorail track winding like an IV tube from the Needle to the shopping district, where Freddie's, he reads in this morning's paper, is now boasting that its workers speak thirty-eight different languages, further proof that truth in advertising is suspended as everyone scrambles to make a buck off the exposition.

Returning to the *P-I*, he reads that the new dictator of Cuba has announced that any direct U.S. attack on his country would spark a world war. Roger writes his mother a quick note and is coasting down the hill in his Impala, trying to imagine U.S. platoons invading that little island, when the announcer on the radio casually mentions Monroe's death. Why does it feel so personal? He never met her and was hardly an adoring fan. Yet there is—*was*—something so intimate about her. Everybody remembered her singing happy birthday to *Mr. President* just a couple months ago. Was it suicide, an accident or murder?

Instead of preparing to introduce the governor of Louisiana—or was it Nebraska?—he goes for a drive, veering past the Market and the deserted card rooms and honky-tonks before rolling through Pioneer Square and turning east on King Street to watch another trainload of rumpled out-of-towners shuffle into the morning glare with stiff necks and drowsy toddlers in their arms. They keep coming, more every day, as if it's become a national mandate to haul your family all the way out here to see the fair at the end of the road.

He parks on Bell Street and feels ridiculous snooping past the windows of the Dog House before stepping into the aroma of bacon and pancakes. "Just meeting someone," he tells the hostess, wandering toward the back, where the tables can't be seen from the street. A German or Austrian family is barking consonants in one booth, with mostly American couples in the others. Roger recognizes several older businessmen but can't place their names. Walking out, though, he notices two tables he'd overlooked. A large family at one and seven men crowding the other—a city councilman, a deputy county prosecutor, a prominent jeweler and the pushy Teamster who'd brokered the labor deal with the fair. All regulars at Club 21, all guys whose hands Roger shook on a regular basis these days. He turns away as the Teamster's bald skull swivels toward him, then strides outside beneath a hopeful sky.

With a few worn-out puns and generic flattery, he introduces the Louisiana governor to a tiny, disinterested crowd, then returns to yet another stack of complaints—including several more about the *appalling* French film—and the results of yet another study, which Teddy summarizes aloud to him. "The Science Pavilion is easily the most popular attraction. Overall attendance is, curiously, better on cloudy days, and far more people are paying to enter the World of Art than the nudie shows. The most popular rides are Calypso, the Olympic Bobsled and Wild Mouse."

Roger's barely listening. Finally, he tells him what he saw at the Dog House.

Teddy goes silent, as if double-checking to see what, if anything, he'd just missed. "So?"

Roger sheepishly shares an abbreviated version of what Charlie McDaniel told him.

"You met with that crackpot?" Teddy hisses. "Jesus H. Christ, you're naïve. A little gambling's *good* for a city. It's just a little god-damn vent. If anything big was going on we'd have the mob involved. And who gives a damn who eats breakfast together? A city coun-cilman knows a cop who golfs with a Teamster who buys his wife bracelets from a jeweler who went to high school with a prosecutor." He leans back and studies Roger again. "Isn't there enough on your plate?" He waits, but Roger won't meet his stare. Then, as if recalling his main point, "So what the hell's the senator doing about that U.S. attorney, anyway?"

"Haven't heard."

"Then maybe you should put in another call."

"I don't think so."

"You don't?" Teddy inhales, still looking at him.

"You hear about Marilyn Monroe?"

Teddy hesitates, then nods. "Are you finally showing your youth? Is that it?"

Roger rises, leans across the desk, lifts the pack of Chesterfields out of Teddy's breast pocket, taps one out, lights it and slides the pack back in, all without making any eye contact.

"And now you're smoking?" Teddy says.

Later that afternoon he avoids the office and strolls the grounds, chain-smoking in the anonymous mob before drifting into the French exhibit to see what all the fuss is about. The movie starts calmly enough, with a soft-sell promo on the achievements of French scientists, then shifts into an ominous portrayal of modern life—brawling street mobs, flashing lights, sirens and machine guns—before ending grace-fully, with the "seven keys" to a promising future. Roger sits through it a second time before concluding it might be the most honest enter-tainment the fair offers. He's still thinking about it, while simulta-neously appreciating an impossibly tall blonde in the fashion tent, when it occurs to him that it's Tuesday and approaching six o'clock.

Without the crowds, it's a far more intimate one-on-one with Calder, Tomlin, Tobey, Pollock and the others. The longer he studies these paintings, the more convinced he is that many of these modern works resemble cities, no less chaotic or preconceived than New York, Paris or Seattle. Whether they intended to or not, they capture the pleasing asymmetry of . . .

"You're wound up."

He spins, startled to see her, broad-hipped, buxom and imposing. He doesn't know how long it has been since she led him back here and told him to take his time.

She points at the cushioned bench next to Tobey's *Serpentine*. "Sit down, keep looking," she says.

He obeys.

"Most people won't give this stuff a chance," she says. "It's like a revolution only some people can see."

He flinches when she comes closer and presses down on his shoulders. "Relax," she says, working her thumbs into the stress knots between his shoulders and neck.

"They're cities," he says, trying to remember her husband's name. "At least for me they are. They show us what cities are like, and why they move us."

"Keep looking."

Her thumbs crawl up his neck, then descend along his spine, through his shirt, vertebra by vertebra, until the paintings start to move and look like forests or rivers or oceans or . . .

"They can be anything you want them to be," she whispers, close enough that he can feel her breath on his ear.

She explains how Pollock paints, her words now a low, rumbling accompaniment to whatever she's doing to his back with her elbow. "Most people give these ten seconds at best, shake their heads and move on. Sad about Marilyn, huh."

"I didn't even know I cared about her."

"She cut a half inch off all her left heels to exaggerate her butt-wiggle," Meredith says.

"It worked."

"Must've been hell on her ankles, though," she purrs. "Sure was on mine when I tried it." Her fingers work below his belt.

"I really like your voice," he hears himself saying, his eyes closing.

"You know what Pollock should've called this one?" she whispers into his left ear.

"What?"

"*Foreplay.*"

He opens his eyes, turns his head and her smile covers his.

"No janitors?" he asks when he can breathe again.

"Not till seven."

"Or assistants?"

"Nope."

Afterward, he's sitting on the same bench slipping his slacks back on, not wanting to overthink, much less discuss, what just happened. Fortunately, a comfortable silence lingers, as if they've been naked around each other plenty of times before. He hopes like hell they can get through this without talking, but she starts in so gently the words feel harmless.

"You're engaged, right?"

"Uh-huh."

"Lisa?"

"Linda."

"Very pretty."

"Yeah."

He changes the subject and inexplicably begins sharing some of what he's seen and heard about cops on the take.

"And you're surprised?" she asks, her heavy breasts swinging toward him. "How could anything like that happen in this sweet little city of yours?"

"Your husband's a cop, right?" he suddenly remembers.

Even that doesn't trip her. "A lawyer, but my brother-in-law is one of the assistant chiefs now."

"Is he honest?"

She smirks. "To a fault."

"He ever talk about the gambling and crooked cops and all that?"

"He can't stand it. Won't let anyone buy him a cup of coffee, okay? Straight as a fence post. Keeps transferring people out of his division if he thinks they're not. I worry about him all the time." She inches her panties higher on her smooth thighs, not bashfully, not turning away as Linda would, but facing him.

"Tell your brother-in-law I'd like to help him," Roger says, surprising himself.

She smiles as if he were a child. "You haven't heard a word I've said. This never happened, understand? None of it. I never mentioned him to you. This is all in your imagination."

Time slows as he takes everything in at once. The pleasing curve of her hips, the swirling art, the deep nook of her navel, her candor and infidelity, the delicate hairs on her upper thighs—all crammed into this swollen moment and calling into question everything about his known world.

She slides a finger under the elastic and holds it until he meets her gaze, looking down at him without affection or familiarity. And in this instant he can see her future resentment and the both of them blushing whenever they meet each other in public twenty or thirty years from now, when she's larger than a mule and he'll walk up to her knowing he has nothing to say.

An hour later, Roger pulls up outside Linda's apartment, ready at last to tell her a gentle version of the truth and plead with her to at least hold off on the invitations.

She greets him in her casual blue sun dress, his favorite, and immediately breaks into a glassy-eyed apology for being such a simpleton—he's surprised she knew the word—and dragging him out of the concert last night. He sits silently on the love seat beside her, smelling salmon and potatoes—also his favorite—in the kitchen, her long, slender fingers trembling inside his.

Chapter Twelve

IT'S IMPOSSIBLE to know for sure how a story will play outside the newsroom. Sometimes the hardest ones to report and craft, those designed to expose and outrage, are greeted with yawns while cheesy no-brainers capture the public's mood like catchy songs. And occasionally there are stories crafted well enough to jolt your colleagues and blessed with enough timing to enter the zeitgeist and become *talkers*.

Helen's "Mr. Seattle" was one of those.

Even the large front-page photo was provocative, with Morgan staring thoughtfully—righteously?—back at the reader, the left side of his lips curling toward a grin, the right side flat and stern, as if he were shifting from amused to concerned. It was taken three days ago, during his doorbelling expedition, his expression hinting at fatigue, his shirtsleeves rolled to mid-forearm, his tie slack around his open collar. And the story itself read more like a freewheeling magazine piece than a standard newspaper profile, asserting up high that Roger Morgan might be as close as anyone to the human incarnation of this city.

Think about it. He's ambitious, photogenic, courteous and agnostic. He's a Gore-Tex-wearing, novel-reading, Mariners-loving, daily-exercising former mountaineer who seemingly reinvents himself at will. He's advised Boeing and Microsoft and five of the last six mayors. He's arguably played as much of a background or foreground role in shaping this city as anyone alive.

And like the city's Pied Pipers before him, she wrote, he sold the notion that Seattle exists beyond the humdrum limitations of the rest of the country. Doc Maynard pitched it to easterners in the 1850s as an Eden with winter flowers. Fifty years later, Erastus Brainerd spun the illusion that this city was only a brief stroll from the Yukon gold mines. And after another half century, young Roger Morgan coaxed everyone out to the unlikeliest of world's fairs. At times, she wrote, the city seems like his alter ego. "I've always taken this place very personally. When it's thriving, I thrive. When it's struggling, I struggle. Right now I feel like hell, which is part of why I'm running."

Inside the *P-I*, some editors marveled over a political feature that, for once, was hard to put down. Young reporters discussed Helen's daring style while older ones pondered how her story slipped past the butchers and pruners, speculating that someone with a glass office— probably Marguerite—must fancy her. Regardless, the story generated a battle-cry buzz, as if a salty profile had somehow raised the stakes in one of America's last daily newspaper wars. The *P-I*, Helen learned early on, pretended it competed with the *Times* every single day. Actually, the *Times* had twice the staff, and it usually showed. So when the *P-I* won a news cycle, it celebrated and the *Times* feigned oblivion.

Yet this hubbub wasn't enough to alter Bill Steele's morning ritual. When he finally got to her article, she watched him slide his glasses lower on his nose to assess the visual placement of the story. Then he slowly read the lede and his eyes widened. When he smirked a few beats later, she knew exactly which sentence he was on. Once he finished, he carefully recreased the section, set it in his tidy stack, unlocked his Rolodex, dialed a number and said "Hey." Then: "Uh-huh, uh-huh, uh-huh . . ."

By 10 a.m., circulation reported that street sales were *ridiculously* high, and Steele finally shuffled up to her desk. "Solid story," he said, glancing at the crowded fishbowl. "But I hope they're not stupid enough to think this is as good as we can get on this guy."

She nodded, fending off deflation. An electronic message from Marguerite flashed onto her screen. "YOU ABSOLUTELY ROCK!!!!!!"

Steele leaned closer, squinting over his glasses. "Hmmm. Six exclamation points. In Marguerite-speak that means 'not bad.' She sent me a note once without a single exclamation point. I almost offed myself. Talk to Morgan's mother yet?"

"He won't give me her number," she said. "Practically begged me not to bother her."

"Good for him." He tore a page from his notebook. "Personally, I'd much rather beg for forgiveness than ask him for anything. Here's her address."

ROGER READ the obits every morning though was rarely surprised. With most of his friends a decade older, he spent more time discussing lung, brain, liver, breast, thyroid and prostate cancer than most doctors. If not the big C, it was the big D or all the mental slippage associated with the A word. What could he offer beyond sympathy? Though today everything hurt, but that still wasn't something to bring up with dying friends. *I tell ya, Vern, this doorbellin's a son of a bitch.*

Most of his funeralgoing cohorts exuded grim obligation. They signed the book and rehearsed the clichés—*You have my condolences*—though by the time they got through the grieving line they often broke down or became inappropriately chatty. *How the hell are you?* Afterward, they exited ASAP, hunkered, spent, apocalyptic. Roger came early, stayed late. Often asked to speak, he knew how to exaggerate the right amount, to sum up complicated lives and to resuscitate poignant stories that left audiences teary, chuckling and wondering if he'd made them up.

Yet when Patricia Lange's son asked him to speak today, he graciously declined. He didn't want to come off as a politician in front of all these artsy big shots, and he knew her husband, Jonas, probably wanted him to keep his mouth shut. He felt awkward afterward when more people lined up to talk to him than to Jonas, but they were clamoring to hear what he thought of the *P-I* article. Some called it *marvelous* publicity—don't you think?—and others considered it proof that the paper was in the tank for Rooney. "They're obviously doing everything possible to make you look bad, Rog, even the *picture*."

He grinned through it and didn't let on that Teddy missed the funeral so he could scare the piss out of the boys and girls who ran the *P-I*. "Could've been worse," Roger told them. "They didn't call me a pedophile."

"Why in God's name did you tell 'em you like to gamble?"

"They asked."

"I know, Rog, but . . ."

He missed whatever came next because he was scrambling to put a name to a large, familiar woman in her seventies barreling toward him. Her mischievous smirk gave her away. He hadn't seen Meredith Stein since the thirtieth anniversary of the fair, but it was definitely her, flabby-necked, breathing heavily and stuffed into a black dress.

"Finally," she said, after casually displacing his questioners. "You're actually running."

"Great to see you, Meredith."

"Yeah, right."

"Sorry about your husband," he said. "Would've gone, but it didn't seem appropriate."

She grinned. "Seeing how he hated you?"

"How 'bout your brother-in-law," he asked, "the honest cop? How's he making it?"

"Could've thrown his retirement party in a phone booth. The stubborn bastard moved to the peninsula and refuses to take chemo."

Their heads swiveled toward the baritone thump of Mayor Douglas H. Rooney's voice.

"I hope you kill that jackass," she muttered.

"Thank you, Meredith. You look fantastic."

"Yeah, right. You should see me naked."

"I'll take your word for it."

She gently grabbed one of his shoulders and pulled him to her so she could kiss his cheek nice and slow, then exited with the calculated lift of a penciled eyebrow.

Seconds later, Rooney thundered past in his too-tight suit, signed the book, gave Jonas and his sons his *deepest* condolences, then—after a blizzard of handshakes that excluded Roger—forcefully departed.

As the crowd thinned, he quietly answered questions about his views on various neighborhood issues until it was just he and Jonas, who was single-handedly draining a liter of Spanish red that his wife loved. *Everyone* knew Patricia. If Jonas had croaked first, there'd still be a mob here to comfort the generous arts benefactor. But who knew Jonas Lange? Roger had squeezed just enough conversation out of him over the decades to admire his loyalty to his wife and his disdain for his own class. Despite being a pricey lawyer who specialized in avoiding capital gains taxes, he clearly despised the elites.

"You don't have to hang around out of guilt for sleeping with my wife," Jonas said.

"I'm not," Roger replied, after recovering. "You were separated at the time, and you know it."

"Still . . ." He took a breath to say more, but didn't.

"Yeah, I know," Roger conceded. "But that has nothing to do with me being here now." He grabbed a second long-necked Budweiser out of the ice and rolled it over his cheek and forehead until he noticed Jonas staring at him. "Guess I've never quite got over the thrill of a midday beer." He missed the widower's rare grin while gesturing to his kid volunteers to relax. His university visit would have to wait.

He helped Jonas carry framed photos of his wife out to her white Jaguar with its OPERA vanity plate. "Can't wait to sell this piece of shit," Jonas muttered.

Roger laughed. "You know when I enjoyed Patricia the most?"

Jonas stopped organizing the boxes to listen.

"When she got all ticked off and cussed people out," he said. "She was a force to behold when she was pissed. Know what I'm saying? She was all of five feet and a hundred pounds but she could scare the hell out of me when she'd go off."

"Me too," Jonas warbled. "Me too."

"One hell of a woman," Roger added, looking away to signal *one more minute* to the college kids.

SHRONTZ STORMED OUT of the fishbowl toward Helen's desk, where she was on the phone instructing Omar Duran to tell his coy gadfly to quit playing games and talk.

"Hold on." She palmed the mouthpiece.

"We've got problems," Shrontz said.

"How's that?"

"Morgan's demanding *corrections*." He pointed at the phone, then slashed the same finger across his neck. "Conference room *now*."

She cleared her throat, told Omar she'd call him back, then followed her editor like a prisoner toward the fishbowl.

"What?" she ventured. "What're they saying?"

"That they'll sue if we don't correct things."

"Correct *what*?"

He turned and glared without slowing down. "*Don't* take an attitude."

Conversation halted as they entered. The same editors who'd praised her an hour ago now wouldn't look at her—including Marguerite, who was sliding a finger along the edge of a homicidally long silver letter opener.

"What's the problem?" Helen asked meekly.

"Please sit down," Birnbaum told her, though there wasn't an empty chair. So she leaned against the glass wall, folding her arms before realizing how defensive this looked. "Morgan's campaign says we got some things wrong," he said. *We.* Ever the diplomat.

She wondered why all these editors—even two reporters, Lundberg and Steele—needed to hear this. At least Steele faced her, counseling her with his slow blinks to stay calm, which wasn't easy, given this felt like the prelude to an execution.

"They say he never in any way personally profited from the Space Needle restaurant, as the story implies," Birnbaum said, lacing his fingers across the Stanford mug. "They also say he *never* was paid to advise any Republicans, and that while he does enjoy cards he never said he enjoyed *gambling*. His attorney—Sullivan, or whatever his name is—is demanding front-page corrections, or he's basically threatening to sue."

Helen exhaled, but the palpitations continued. "I wouldn't know what to correct."

Webster groaned, and others rolled their eyes.

"We didn't say he profited from the restaurant," she said slowly. "We said the company he'd been working for did."

"Hold on." Birnbaum hunted for the exact paragraph, then shrugged and nodded for her to continue.

"When I told him that people say he's been paid to advise both Ds and Rs, he didn't object or clarify," Helen said. "I named three Republicans, and he nodded. As for his gambling, he did say, 'I enjoy a good game of cards.' And I said, 'Well, I'm told your game of choice is poker.' He didn't deny or clarify. I mean, what do I have to—"

"I'm afraid," Birnbaum interrupted, "the story lacked precision, that it needlessly overreached based on nods and nondenials and vague language. And I feel uncomfortable about that." His eyes swung over to Shrontz.

"I tried to peel it back to what felt *solid,*" Shrontz said ruefully. "Probably should've cut deeper."

A glum Marguerite spoke up. "What I'm wondering is why we felt we had to rush this into the paper in the first place."

Heads bobbed, and Birnbaum turned to Shrontz. "Why did it have to run today?"

"Helen said it was ready to go on Monday," he mumbled. "I suggested she take another day or two to tighten things up, which she indicated she had."

Helen stared holes into the side of his head as Birnbaum passed her a flyer. "This, no doubt, set 'em off."

She looked at it blindly, her vision pulsing. "Don't have my contacts in," she said desperately.

"The State Dems are sending this out to sixty-six thousand households today," Webster explained, then read from it: " 'Roger Morgan's mysterious past includes getting paid to advise Republican candidates and a gambling habit, according to the *Seattle Post-Intelligencer.* Don't gamble on Morgan. Re-elect Mayor Rooney.' "

Birnbaum turned to Helen. "There are facts and there are instincts. In this case, I think your instincts should've told you this was too much too soon. Sometimes"—he dragged this word out—"you go with instincts over facts."

Helen nodded, willing to swallow any medicine to get through this.

"Personally," Steele interjected, "I don't think there's anything wrong with Helen's story."

Webster, Lundberg and others mumbled inaudibly.

"His people are freaking out," Steele continued, "because the state party twisted our story into a Rooney mailing. *So what?* We just gave Morgan the sort of exposure most politicians would pay for if we'd let them. We told everyone he's *Mr. Seattle.* And now we're wringing our hands because it wasn't quite the blow job he'd hoped for? I mean, what're we gonna do when we get something truly damaging on this guy?"

"Well," Webster countered, holding up a stack of paper, "we're hearing from a lot of people who think we're in Rooney's pocket already."

"I see," Steele said. "So we should run corrections because his friends are upset."

"For once," Webster asked, "could we try to be something other than defensive?"

"Try reporting sometime, Webbie. Maybe you'll get what it means to defend your story."

"We'll tell 'em," Birnbaum intervened, "that we are standing by the story, *for now,* and continuing to report. And if we conclude that any correction or clarification is warranted, we'll do so in a prompt and prominent manner. Otherwise, any nuances that may have been misunderstood by readers will be more thoroughly explained in subsequent coverage. We'll call their bluff without saying as much. Okay?"

Strolling out, pulse settling, Helen thanked Steele.

He vibrated his lips. "*Instincts over facts.* Fuck me. Birnbaum has the instincts of a lemming."

ROGER WAS SHOUTING at more than a hundred students eating lunch on the brick steps of Red Square while his young volunteers passed out *Vote for the Old Guy!* pamphlets.

"Seattle's a big city now, but it's still ridiculously young, if you think about it," he said, reheating one of his grandfather's mini-lectures. "In the grand scheme of things, it's been around about a week. Seven days ago it was a few thousand Indians and fir trees growing right down to the tidal flats. Six days ago, a persuasive alco-holic doctor coaxed people into trekking out here from the East. Five days ago, downtown burned and had to be rebuilt. Four days ago, we threw a big fair on this campus to exploit the gold rush in the Yukon. Three days ago, we became the airplane manufacturing capital of the world. Two days ago, we built the Needle and threw another audacious fair. Yesterday, we built too many skyscrapers and became a hip high-tech hub. Today, we're an overcrowded city that has the second-worst traffic in the country and a housing market that's too expensive for normal people."

He bowed as hesitant applause broke out. "Our current mayor treats this university as if it were its own sovereign nation, a place to be feared and ignored. I see it as the future." He also saw that he was losing them, some walking away, others talking among themselves or flipping open cell phones. "Ten or twenty years from now, some of you will be running this city," he continued desperately. "Problem is, the city needs your help now. It needs your imagination and your idealism and your common sense—even if you haven't cornered the market on that yet."

SHE ENTERED an elegantly furnished room with an adjustable twin bed that looked like a double because the old woman was so thin. Her tiny triangular face was mostly eyes, and she was oddly dressed up for being prone, with rouge and pearls and a handsome sweater buttoned to the neck.

The stout nurse at Helen's side said, "Mrs. Morgan? This news-paper woman is here to speak with you about your son. Do you want to talk to her?"

The old woman pressed a button. A motor whined and her head rose. She studied Helen with her big eyes until her face broke into a warm smile. "Why, of course."

Left alone with her, Helen pulled up a chair and listened to her prattle on for ten minutes about how the chaplain came into her room and gave her communion *right here.* "A fine young man, don't you see." The more she talked, the more British she sounded. She told Helen that she tried to open that window months ago and cracked a vertebra, then described all the people she *cherished* in the home, including several delightful women who come from *good families,* and how terrific the help is, including Sara, "whom you just met, and of course Mrs. Truman, who comes by every Wednesday afternoon to discuss world affairs. A delightful conversationalist, don't you know."

Helen was convinced Morgan had to be blowing ten grand a month to keep his mother here.

Without transition, Eleanor Morgan suddenly started in on the Duke of Edinburgh. "*What a raconteur,* that man. You've never met a better talker. Invited me to come stay with him. The prince himself. He certainly did."

"Did you ever go?"

"Where?"

"To England."

"Not *yet,* but an offer like that doesn't expire, now does it?" She smiled and blinked slowly, as if agreeing with herself. "But, truth be told, you know who I'd rather visit?"

"Who's that?"

"Albus Dumbledore." Her teeth were false, but her smile was genuine. "He is an absolute marvel. So clever, so wise, so warm, don't you see."

Helen smiled along, uncertain whether the woman was being playful or delusional. How could she have known that Helen would know who Dumbledore even is? "What do you think of your son getting into politics?" she asked

"The unexamined life," Mrs. Morgan responded, "is not worth living."

"Socrates?" Helen asked, flustered.

"Excuse me, dear?"

"Are you happy Roger is getting into politics, ma'am?"

She blinked rapidly. "He could have been a senator," she whispered. "*Should* have been. Nobody believes it, but he started out so awkwardly. Couldn't tell what he was saying till he was five. The words came out too quickly, don't you see. It didn't fall into place until he started acting."

Helen tried to smile. "What do you think," she asked loudly and succinctly, "of Roger running for mayor?"

Her forehead clenched. "Oh, no. Not that it's beneath him, but we know who we are."

Helen nodded along, waiting for more, then took a shot. "What ever happened to Roger's father?"

"Oh, Robert passed away long ago, of course. Soon after he got out."

Helen hesitated. "What was his full name again?"

"Robert Ignatius Dawkins."

She studied her. "You mean, Robert Ignatius *Morgan*?"

"No, dear. Morgans are *my* side. Robert was most definitely a Dawkins."

"But Roger—"

"Took my maiden name, of course. Changed it, don't you know, when he turned eighteen."

Helen bobbed her chin, as if she'd simply forgotten. "You said Robert died after he got *out*—of what?"

"Why the penitentiary, of course."

"That's right." Helen hated herself for playing this game, but couldn't stop now. "Why was he there again?"

"Oh, any number of things. He was never a man of in-*teg*-ri-ty. What did you say your name was?"

"Helen. Helen Gu-la-nos."

She smiled. "It's so nice to visit with one of Roger's friends. But if Sara does come in again, please do stand up. Out of respect, my dear. I can't, of course, but you should."

Helen sat up taller. "Ma'am, I'm not a *friend* of your son. As the nurse tried to explain, I'm a newspaper reporter. That's why I'm taking notes." She held up her notebook. "I'm working on an article about your son because he's running for mayor."

Mrs. Morgan's rapid blinks resumed. "Of course," she said, her voice suddenly officious. "Now do leave your name and phone number on the dresser before you go."

"Certainly." Helen wrote it out, very large, and ripped out the page. When she looked up, Mrs. Morgan was smiling again. "Roger has always had a lot of newspaper friends. You people love him, don't you? If it's no great inconvenience, would you please send Sara back with some *black* tea, dear? Not to rush you, but I am tiring from all this talking. You mustn't let me go on like this. And make sure it's piping hot, if you would. Sara knows full well that I will send it back if it's not *piping* hot."

Helen took in the room one last time, saw a thick hardback in the nightstand and moved close enough to read the title: *Harry Potter and the Goblet of Fire.* "Do you have grandchildren you read to?"

"Pardon me? Grandchildren? Oh heavens." She grinned. "How old do you think I am?"

HIS NECK WAS BOWED, chin low, ears jutting like funnels, as he pulled questions out of the students.

"It felt like reading my obit," he said of today's article. "I just kept picturing people saying to themselves, 'Isn't he dead already?'"

A student nervously asked if he had a gambling problem.

He smiled. "My problem is I don't win as often as I'd like, but I do enjoy a good game of poker on occasion with the right company—Elvis Presley, for example."

"Before or after he died?" asked another student.

As the questions dwindled, he strained to sustain their interest by recalling how students used to smoke pot on the grassy knoll behind Kane Hall and taunt the cops who weren't allowed on campus. "I remember driving out to a rock concert on the Eastside back then. And before the bands started up there was this *piano drop* out in the field. That's right. They dropped a piano from a helicopter just to hear what it would sound like. Everyone was on drugs, of course."

"Were you?" asked a girl who looked too young to be in college yet. "Did you smoke pot?"

"Experimented," he clarified, raising an index finger, "but I never exhaled."

The laughter attracted more students. He realized it was nearing the top of the hour and said, "Look, it's time for me to do something good for this city. I need your help, obviously, but more importantly, the city needs it."

Someone shouted, "Vote for the old guy!" A disjointed cheer rose and fell.

The crowd had dispersed by the time Helen Gulanos jogged into the square and found the intern Shrontz had dispatched to interview students about Morgan.

"What'd he say?" she demanded.

"Lots of stuff." He flipped anxiously through scribbled pages. "People really liked him."

"Forget your notes. Just talk to me."

He smiled awkwardly. "Well, he kind of said he smoked pot with Elvis."

"What?"

He riffled through his notes again. "Gambled with him for sure, I think. *Experimented* with pot. 'Never exhaled.' Elvis was at the fair, right?"

"Never exhaled or *inhaled?*"

"Think he said exhaled, but—"

"You recorded it, right?"

"No, I, uh, just wrote it out . . . and not that well, apparently."

Helen took a breath. "These kinds of scenes aren't easy. Any other reporters here?"

"I only saw one. Works for *The Daily*. I know her."

"If she recorded, get her to loan it to you, okay? Where'd Morgan go?"

HE WAS REGALING volunteers and students with stories about Seattle goofballs, including a man who claimed he'd climbed Mount Rainier barefoot. "When a photo of him shoeless on the summit didn't satisfy people, he put on demonstrations around town, standing on blocks of ice until his bare feet melted through to the concrete." He noticed her midway into his next story about a perennial mayoral candidate who always wore a suit and top hat when he jumped into Elliott Bay after every defeat.

She looked older in this context, like a distraught young mother instead of a kid reporter, her messy mound of hair bouncing along like tumbleweed on a pogo stick. He briefly hoped she hadn't spotted him, but it was obvious she had. He glanced back at the students crowding his table in the food court. "Give me a few minutes here, please." They turned in unison to see her closing in, jean jacket swung wide, sweat glistening, her neck scar gleaming like a strand of pearls.

"What a coincidence," he said as the kids scattered.

Catching her breath, she slid her satchel off her shoulder and sat down. "Sorry to interrupt, but I know you're upset about the story," she began, her chest heaving, "and I wanted to talk to you about it."

"Teddy's upset," he said.

She took a moment to digest that. "Your attorney's asking for corrections."

"That's true." This had been Roger's idea. Let Teddy vent and Sully threaten while he stayed cordial. The catch was that Teddy didn't have to fake anything. He was furious.

"So are *you* asking for corrections?" she asked, setting a tape recorder on the table that was already recording.

He shrugged. Teddy had made him promise to duck any more interviews with her.

"You consider the story accurate?"

"Not particularly, but that's the nature of being written about, isn't it? You work with what you have, and I'm certainly not an easy study. So given all that, I thought it was . . . amusing."

She exhaled. "Mr. Severson says you never represented any Republican campaigns."

"He's technically right," he said finally. "I never was paid during their election cycles, but I did offer advice, as I indicated, and I've done other things for them."

"And your gambling comment?"

"Blown out of proportion, in my opinion, but that's the way these things go."

"What about the Space Needle restaurant? They say—"

"Again, you're both right. What you wrote isn't false, but the insinuation isn't fair."

She took off her jacket, slid one sleeve up to her elbow and moved closer. "I'm sorry I missed your campus talk, but did you just tell the students you gambled and smoked pot with Elvis?"

"See?" He chuckled. "Jokes and asides rarely survive translation."

"So you were joking?"

"Ms. Gulanos, do you have anything substantive you'd like to discuss before I have to go to my next song and dance?"

She looked away, then swung back at him, knowing it was best to ask delicate questions as directly as possible. "Did you change your name when you were eighteen from Dawkins to Morgan?"

His head jerked as if he'd caught himself dozing. "How do you even come up with something like that?"

"I visited your mother today."

His eyes widened. "Now, *that* surprises me." The tightening of his jaw made him look like a ventriloquist when he said, "I mistook you for a . . . Didn't I *specifically* ask you not to bother her?"

"Sorry to agitate you, Mr. Morgan, but you're not in charge of me." Her voice dipped into an almost sympathetic tone. "You can't tell me who I can talk to."

He stared at her for a few breaths. "You don't understand. She doesn't have a firm handle. You can't just take what she says and—"

"I might not quote her at all, but I have to ask you about some things she said."

"No, you certainly do not." He kept staring. "She used to invent stories to pass the time, to put me to sleep. Understand? I don't know when the lines blurred, but by now they're gone. I asked you, plain as day, not to bother her."

"Okay," Helen said gently. "We've already discussed that. I'm asking you now, on the record, did you legally change your name? And, if so, why?"

"What I did," he began sharply, then stopped and reconsidered, "is nobody's business and of no interest to anyone."

"I disagree," she said. "I think people would want to know why."

"Let them wonder."

"That's your choice, but people might find it odd that someone who's waged such a candid campaign won't talk about something as basic as his name. I mean, I imagine you'd agree that it's one thing if you changed your name because you're running from something, and another if you did it for a stage career or whatever."

He looked away. "You intend to write a story about this."

"I don't know what this is yet."

"But you'll write about it."

"If we think it's relevant, yes, we'll probably mention it."

"Does a sense of fairness ever play into your thinking?"

"I'm here *right now* out of fairness." Her voice rose. "This whole discussion is out of a sense of fairness."

Her defiance surprised him. He didn't know whether to get up and leave or not. Perhaps if he calmed himself he could talk his way out of this. "My grandfather Morgan was a professor here."

"I know," she said, "you already told me."

"I'm telling you again." He then patiently described the little man, his bowlegged walk, his missing thumbnail, his ever-present odor of rum-cured pipe tobacco.

Helen noticed that his posture had improved and how carefully he was selecting his words, as if his grandfather had just sat down at the table behind them.

"He was very comfortable with silence," he said, "but nobody could talk much better. He had more wisdom than the next ten men combined and a voice like an airline pilot."

Helen waited for him to reach some relevant point, but he seemed to be finished. "And what about your father?" she asked. "You grew up with him?"

Roger hesitated. "Till I was thirteen."

"You two get along?"

He reached toward his sports coat. "We're not gonna do this."

"Sorry, but I have to ask the questions. It's up to you whether you respond."

"My feelings about him are mine."

"But if you changed your name—"

"To honor my grandpa, which is why I just described him to you."

"Thank you for that, but how did you feel about your father? Perhaps you don't even have any clear memories of him."

He shook his head and leaned forward. "He wore cuffed pants and rolled his shirtsleeves midway up his biceps and had a gold bracelet he'd twirl when he was nervous and a mole right here on the left side of his chin that went from brown to black when he got angry. And he always sang off-key, but he didn't care. He had a whole lot of personality. That's what people said about him: *What a charming man.* He had no problem getting sales jobs, but couldn't hold them. So we kept moving every few months. He smelled like Listerine in the morning and aftershave at night. I hated the smell of Aqua Velva because it meant he was going out. More? He was a jokester. He could wiggle his ears, fart on command and convincingly turn his head all the way around like an owl. He'd bring home used toys from Goodwill, and he'd call my mother *Sweetie* right before he started insulting her. When he really yelled at her, I felt like a coward because I didn't try to stop him. My grandfather was there, finally, for one of those, and he rose up on those bowed legs and spoke real calmly, as if he had a gun in his hand. 'Pack it up, Robert.'"

Roger paused and looked up. "We through?"

Helen cleared her throat. "Your mother says," she whispered, "that he died shortly after getting out of prison."

He blushed. "That's what I'm talking about."

"What?"

"She makes things up."

"I'll let you know," Helen said, "what our research librarians find."

"No, *please* don't, though that probably won't stop you."

"That depends."

"On what?"

"What they find."

He stood up and grabbed his coat, then leaned over the table. "I do have one question for you."

She smelled beer on his breath. His smile was unconvincing but not menacing, his voice level, his eyes aglitter.

"Why would any sane person run for anything?"

She stared up at him, all eight pints of her blood racing.

"Well?" he prodded. "Cat got your tongue?"

She didn't speak at first, just held on to the table. "I'm gonna need to talk to you again soon, Mr. Morgan, about a variety of things, including your finances."

She waited for the moment to pass, but he hadn't budged, still close enough to slap her.

Five minutes later, he was on the phone with Teddy, his voice shaking slightly. "She talked to my mother! . . . What? . . . Yes! What? . . . Yes, it was on the record. . . . Uh-huh. She had a tape recorder going. . . . Calm down!"

INSTEAD OF HEADING back to the newsroom, Helen stayed on campus and dropped down into the special-collections reading room in the bomb-shelter-like basement of the Allen Library. She remembered Bill Steele telling her about this fussy place as she relinquished her jacket, purse, book bag and cell phone before being admitted through a locked door with nothing more than a pencil and a yellow pad.

She requested boxes of various World's Fair files, then watched a silent eight-millimeter home movie shot by some Texan whose wife kept popping her big head into the frame. It started, camera jostling, with her buying tickets for the monorail, then showed them gliding toward the burnt-orange Space Needle. Everything looked amazingly new and clean, the bone-white arches of the Science Pavilion, the gold-and-silver roof of the arena, the yellow elevators climbing like ladybugs up the Needle's white stem. Out on the fairgrounds, every woman was wearing a dress, nylons and heels. Even most of the kids were formally dressed, with short hair and thick, black eyeglasses.

The movie skipped abruptly to the stadium, where water-skiers flew off jumps. It must have been opening day, and Helen felt oddly exhilarated. Suddenly, the wife was on top of the Space Needle staring south over the city, and the Smith Tower was the only building Helen recognized. Everything else looked small and plain. A blimp floated nearby, and that must have been a novelty given all the footage of it. Now it was getting dark, the fountains shooting orange, gold and purple geysers, the girlie shows beckoning with neon, the amusement rides lighting up the sky in the distance. The wife leaned her head into the camera with a tired smile and a thumbs-up before the movie abruptly ended.

One of the whispering librarians rolled up a cartload of boxes, and Helen instantly felt embarrassed that she'd taken this long to mine these archives. She spent an hour reading schedules, itineraries and testimonials, then found an envelope stuffed with photos of Morgan and Severson—usually with drinks in their hands—alongside other happy men in suits. She asked for paper copies of every photo that included Morgan, then found a recording of an interview with him at the beginning of the fair. He sounded like himself—but so young! It struck her that he was just about exactly her age at the time. She was almost excited for him, to hear him explain how the fair came about and what it took to build the Needle so quickly. "It was a desperate race against time, and none of us were sure we could get it done." He chuckled. Helen smiled. "Guess you could say," he added, "it was a day when the dreamers prevailed."

Chapter Thirteen

THE CROWDS should dwindle once school starts, but the spectacle snowballs and the city continues to light up and cash out like a friendly slot machine. Frederick & Nelson, I. Magnin and the Bon Marché are all smashing monthly sales records. A luxury liner docked along the waterfront to offer more lodging options also sells out. And beyond Seattle, the entire region overflows with travelers discovering the Great Northwest as capacity crowds tour the sandstone capitol building and visit the Olympia brewery, which triples its staff to slake the thirst, and weekend traffic jams stretch from Oregon to Canada as fairground admissions exceed 100,000 people a day.

At some juncture that Roger can't pinpoint, his expo has turned into a pilgrimage. A shaggy eighty-year-old calling himself Old Iron Legs walks there all the way from San Francisco. A sixteen-year-old pedals from Kansas without telling his parents. Newlyweds paddle down from Alaska in kayaks. Dozens of deaf and blind kids arrive from Great Falls, and hundreds of beret-wearing members of the Caravan Club park their trailers on the outskirts of town. Thousands more arrive by jet, including Koreans, Brits, Germans, Scandinavians and Japanese, who can't stop exclaiming that the green landscape reminds them of home. It occurs to Roger that the more dangerous the world feels—*A U.S. senator has just claimed there is ample evidence of Soviet missile installations in Cuba*—the more popular the fair becomes.

He watches the workers get high on this crescendo, catching their second, fourth or eighth wind amid the mounting sensation that there's something unforgettable, perhaps even *honorable*, in play here, that through alchemy, timing or luck this fair is transcending its predecessors, and if not actually saving the world, at the very least distracting it. At night after closing, workers from a dozen countries form conga lines and dance through the grounds. The fair never truly sleeps anymore. And beyond its gates, downtown is more awake than ever too. The grander the fair the bigger the vice. Card rooms, pinball halls and bordellos bubble into the streets as if the whole city were pulling an all-nighter, careening toward nirvana or a crash, whichever comes first, everything about it exhilarating and unsustainable, like accelerating your car until the steering wheel vibrates, then flooring it.

Roger and Teddy are increasingly mentioned as potential favorites for Congress or the governor's mansion. Columnists speculate that Teddy would run as a Republican, while Roger's politics remain a mystery. His perceived lack of bias, as well as his burgeoning reputation as a PR-savant, has turned him into an oracle. Chamber boys, port commissioners, city councilmen, zoning officials, labor bosses, gadflies and monkey-wrenchers line up to run ideas past him. His asides, quips and advice, he notices, increasingly pop up in ads and campaigns and speeches. Aware of his growing public image, he tries to limit his late-night forays to drive-bys and walk-throughs and fielding phone calls in the small hours from Charlie McDaniel.

"They want me to name cops," Charlie tells him. "I'm thinking about testifying, but for the right amount I'd go away. Made that plenty clear too."

"To who?"

"Not gonna put a bigger target on my back. Know what I'm saying? I sleep with two guns these days. Know what else?"

"What's that, Charlie?"

"I know who you are."

He doesn't know how to reply other than to say, "Sorry 'bout that. Didn't think you'd talk to me otherwise."

"So what exactly is Mr. World's Fair doing with our conversations?"

"Educating myself. I want to know everything there is to know about this city."

McDaniel snorts. "In case you want to run for mayor or something."

"Maybe something like that."

McDaniel laughs but keeps talking, as if this disclosure means little to him, though he never calls again.

The next morning Roger is jittery and dragging through yet another cool blue dawn, strung out anew on wedding dread and a mounting sense of pressure, when the fair hand-delivers Elvis Presley to him on its 144th day.

Governor Lopresti is beyond giddy, blurting cheerful fragments and laughing at nothing in particular while dragging his hands through his thinning hair during an increasingly awkward photo op. Elvis is handing him a Tennessee ham, and for the money shot their arms are bowed with effort as if it were made of lead. While the cameras fire away, the governor gleefully rocks back and forth over what he apparently considers the most hilarious gift on earth. Elvis can't hold his smile any longer, and the disconnect between the agitated super celebrity and the thrilled politician grows until some young woman in the rapidly swelling crowd recognizes Presley and shrieks as if someone were swinging a machete at her neck.

Once her awkward scream passes, Elvis looks relaxed again, moving with the athletic grace of a boxer in the best-fitting suit and whitest shirt around, his shiny, slicked-back hair and twinkling eyes flashing in the sunlight, his skin so smooth it looks polished, his gold cufflinks twinkling on his wrists. Yet, amazingly, when Roger introduces himself, he not only looks him in the eye but also gives him a *rescue-me* eye roll, as if they already knew each other well enough to share exasperation. But then the governor drags them all off toward the Science Pavilion, clinging to his plan to personally guide Elvis everywhere even though it's obvious to Roger that the rubberneckers will make that impossible.

MGM was considerate enough to delay filming until the kids returned to school, but hundreds apparently skipped class today to climb fences and stand on garbage cans for a glimpse of the man who'd just spun away to buy a sno-cone with extra cherry syrup.

Roger spots an empty flatbed rolling behind the booths, flags it down and a few minutes later is loading the pouting governor, Elvis and his four bodyguards into the back for an abbreviated tour, the growing mob of fans jogging to keep up. Roger never considered himself an Elvis man. Yes, he'd wasted almost an hour in the privacy of his living room trying to dance like him, but the so-called King didn't play jazz and he came across as shallow and cocky on television. But now that he's sitting right next to him in this truck, Roger feels like an adoring teen and starts spouting fairground facts and even mentions that the city has sixteen FM stations, as if this might coax Elvis into moving here.

"So this is your show, then?" Elvis asks, surprising Roger that he's actually been listening. "Can't be easy."

"Compared to what you do it is."

"You mean *this*?" he asks, pointing absently at the trailing crowd. "Once you get involved in this racket your life's public," he says, in a Southern mumble. "People are gonna wanna know what you eat. It's natural. I try to remember that, but of course there are times I'd really like to just walk into a crummy bar for a little Jack Daniel's and some cards."

Roger's eyes widen. "You need a break while you're here, just ask for me."

When the truck slows near a corner, Elvis flings his sno-cone wrapper into a trash can, and three squealing girls sprint over to the can.

Two hours later, Roger is doodling on napkins and sipping a beer in the Blue Moon on Forty-fifth, sizing up each man who enters. Most of them look like afternoon drunks, so when Assistant U.S. Attorney Ned Gance finally looms in the doorway in patched jeans and a new green-and-white plaid shirt, he might as well have been wearing his three-piece with the gold chain looping out of his vest pocket. Yet it isn't his clothes so much as his albino complexion—he clearly isn't accustomed to natural light—that blows his cover. Even more revealing are his too-alert eyes, which take all of three seconds to find Morgan sitting in a booth with two foamy pints, one of which he slides toward the other side of the graffiti-engraved table as Gance approaches.

"I don't drink," the attorney says dismissively, then pulls out a handkerchief, wipes off the bench and sits down.

"We'll make a great team." Roger smiles, pulling the beer back to his side. "I don't eat." When he sticks out his hand, Gance frowns and offers a moist, reluctant shake. "Thanks for coming," Roger says, squeezing the man's bony fingers.

"Please understand," Gance says quietly, his close-set eyes boring into Roger, "that I'm here strictly as a favor to the senator and against my own better judgment."

"Why's that?"

"The senator's initial inquiry, which I assume you prompted, essentially backfired, at least from your perspective."

"How so?" Roger asks hesitantly.

Gance stares even harder, as if gauging whether Roger's bright enough to understand this answer. "It only made Stockton go harder." He smacks his bloodless lips. "And I'm telling you this in confidence, and only because the senator made a personal request. Cops are on the take all over the city, not just in the square and along First. The Chinese, Japs, Negroes and Filipinos got their games too. Stockton's moving as fast as he can to convene. Understand?"

"How soon'll that happen?"

"Next week, next month, next year? Who knows? Whenever it comes together. If I had to guess, I'd say next month."

"We've got lots of balls in the air right now with corporate relocations and all," Roger says, sounding more nervous than he'd like. "It'd just be a lot easier on everyone if we could finish the fair before this sideshow gets under way."

Gance glares at him like he's a blathering child. "Are you asking me to slow down an investigation?"

Roger hesitates. "I'm telling you what concerns people."

"And I," Gance says, "am telling you what I know, which is all I was asked to do. I'm not concerned with your PR problems."

Roger gulps down half his beer. "So is it true that Stockton's rushing because he wants the spotlight that the fair gives him?"

"Keep your voice down." Gance scowls. "Look, he wants to be a congressman. What do you think?"

Roger suddenly thinks he knows more than he should, which is that the U.S. attorney and a few honest cops are in a race to see who can expose this city first.

When he'd seen Meredith Stein for the third time this week, she'd told him that her brother-in-law's coup was coming soon. "His *what*?" Roger had pressed. "You heard me," she'd said. "His revolt, his insurrection. The word he used was *coup,* and I'm not speaking French just to arouse you. He wants to police his own before anyone else does."

"Are you guys," Roger asks Gance now, "just going after card-room owners and crooked cops?"

"What do you mean by that?"

Roger tells him what he'd heard about the breakfast gatherings at the Dog House.

"Who told you that?"

Roger hesitates. "I don't know that I can say."

Gance strokes his chin. "Because you don't know or you won't share?"

Roger feels something fundamental shift, as if he's fallen from the senator's pal to potential suspect in Gance's eyes.

"Who'd you see there?" he presses.

Roger finishes his beer and slides it aside, weighing his options. "Look, I don't know anything for sure."

Gance pops out a tiny black leather notebook. A slender pen materializes in the other hand, and he writes something in such small letters that Roger can't read them. "Who? Names."

Roger chuckles, but his pulse is rising. "I don't work for you, Counselor."

The way Gance's Adam's apple moves reminds Roger of a snake swallowing a mouse. Then his words pop out fast and hushed. "The only reason I'm here is the senator asked. Period. Actually, he had his aide ask me, but it amounts to the same thing. Said he'd *greatly appreciate* it if I spoke with you, which I'm willing to do strictly under the conditions of my choosing, which definitely don't include a one-way relationship. Regardless, I fully expect you to tell the senator what a huge help I've been. Understand?"

Roger takes a long drink from the second beer and tries to smile. "Are you always this much fun to be around?"

Gance stares at him, flat-eyed. "Names."

"The deputy county prosecutor," Roger says quietly. "Winston Edgell. He was there."

"Can you swear to that?"

"*Swear?*"

"Yes, potentially. And the others, the ones you recognized. Their names."

THE SHOOTING SCHEDULE is kept confidential, but by midweek the fans have figured out when and where to find Elvis Presley. His eyes are puffy slits now as he strides over to Roger near the close of the fourth day and asks if there's someplace they might grab a drink.

Roger tries not to look too thrilled. He's already handpicked the Club 21 waitress—*no fawning!*—to serve them cocktails if this opportunity ever arose, and he's double-checked to make sure there's an extra bottle of Jack Daniel's in the cabinet.

After giving Elvis's security boss a tour of the sealed-off lounge, they finally sit down. "How's the film coming?" Roger asks, instantly regretting his question.

"Like the others, I guess." Elvis looks into his drink, clutching it with both hands. "Got people all the time saying, 'Why don't you do an artistic picture?' I'd like to do that, sure, but if I can entertain people in the meanwhile, well, I'd be a fool to tamper with that, wouldn't I? You don't get many chances in this racket, but this one really does feel like the worst one yet." He chuckles. "I fly into town in a crop duster then hitchhike to the fair in the back of this Oriental fella's truck, and then he asks me to take care of his little niece. So I get stuck with her at the fair, and use her to try to score, of course. Cornball stuff. Rather not think about it."

Roger can't imagine what to say next, and he's second-guessing his decision to put Sinatra on the hi-fi, though he doesn't want to change the music now and draw even more attention to how hard he's trying. He waits for Elvis to break the silence.

"You get older," he finally says, "you see people differently."

Roger smiles and mumbles back, "You're all of twenty-seven."

"That's as old as I've ever been." He grins. "I've experienced a lot, actually—wealth and the lonely side of life. And I've had a little tragedy." He pauses again, then looks up. "Just trying to be a better human being."

"Me too," Roger says, stunned to be sharing this odd moment of candor with a young man who's sold seventy-five million records. Then, as if the two subjects are linked: "I'm engaged."

"Well, well." His teeth are big and bright. "Congratulations."

Roger exhales. "Yeah?"

"Sure," Elvis says. "Who'd want to be alone forever?"

Roger laughs. "You could have any wife you want. As many as you want."

"Takes me a while to trust somebody, to find someone who understands me," he mumbles. "Gotta surround yourself with people who bring you a little happiness, though, don't you? Only go through life once, Jack. Can't come back for an encore."

Roger notes every last detail about him so he won't forget. His mumbled Tennessee accent, his slow, expressive hands, his wide-set eyes, tapered eyebrows, plump lips and bouffant of hair. He'd expected him to come off as an arrogant buffoon up close, not as this thoughtful and respectful young man. They talk football and politics until Roger shares his plan for the evening, which sounds ridiculous, even reckless, when he says it aloud. Elvis chuckles and slaps the table gently. "Why not?"

He picks him up near sunset at the back of the New Washington Hotel to avoid the horde of girls rioting out front after they got ousted from the lobby for trying to storm the stairs. Elvis sinks low in the front seat, looking larger cooped up like this, smiling across at him, his dimples and everything about him absurdly recognizable despite the large blue sweatshirt and worn-out Cubs cap. Roger pulls off into the night, coasting down Madison toward the water. He usually drives with the radio on but is too self-conscious to turn it on now, especially after bragging about the city's stations. He resists delivering his recruitment pitch when their view opens up to the sun sliding behind the Olympics and the mirrored water reflecting pink clouds.

Elvis clenches and unclenches fists, studies them, twirls a ring, then looks up. "This place is something else."

Now off his leash, Roger admits how the city dazzles him, how he can't resist reading its history again and again, how sometimes he sees the whole city—past, present and future—all at once and how this almost overwhelms him. He rattles on about the dreamers who leveled hills, filled tidal flats and brought in electricity and railroads, Elvis's head bobbing along to his words.

"I feel the same way about Memphis," he says when Roger finally stops. "Came home from the army, and they ask me what I missed about it. 'Everything,' I said. 'I missed everything.'"

Now they're filling a booth at the Turf, staring across at each other through blue smoke, heads low, sipping cocktails, dozens of voices bouncing off the low ceiling. Elvis can't stop smiling and has his face cocked to the side, but even semi-disguised he's attracting the attention of people in booths all around the room. Roger glares at the gawkers until they finally notice him, then raises a finger to his lips. They nod hypnotically and, amazingly, stay put.

"I don't have a plan," Elvis volunteers. "I just have a feel. Trying to get a better understanding of myself. The mistakes I make always come back around. Truth is like the sun, isn't it? You can shut it out for a time, but it ain't going away."

Roger nods emphatically with no idea of what he's talking about. He has a sudden giddy impulse to ask him to sing the opening lines of "Jailhouse Rock," about the warden throwing a party in that county jail. Once they finish their second drink, he leads him into the back room, where they join a table of five players. Cards disperse, Elvis checks his hand, fiddles with his chips, can't stop smiling.

Two hands later, Roger notices a pack of gawkers growing near the back. So does the card-room manager, who hobbles grumpily over and shoos them out, meeting Roger's glance before resting his eyes on Elvis and nodding reassuringly.

Deep into the next hand, a stocky, clear-eyed man sidles up to Roger's left shoulder, squats down and whispers, "Mr. Morgan,

Seattle PD. I suggest you and your friend get out of here within the next five minutes."

Roger tells Elvis to fold, and they push their chips into the center and take the nearest exit into the alley.

"People don't understand what a nuisance I am to bring along," Elvis apologizes once they're outside.

"Has nothing to do with you," Roger says.

"But goddamn was that fun!" Elvis says, hooting lightly.

Film him *now*, Roger thinks, in this alley with all the colorful graffiti on these brick walls. Cast him as a handsome young man elated after a little poker, whiskey and conversation, a man hoping to improve himself.

Elvis gives him a long look when he drops him off, as if he doesn't want to get out of the car. Finally, though, he grins and says good night without a handshake, as if they'll meet again the next evening.

Once he gets home, Roger calls the six numbers he'd copied out of the Las Vegas phone directory he found in the library. The first three sound too old or too young. The fourth and fifth don't answer at all. The sixth—"Hello?"—sounds possible.

"Robert?" Roger asks, careful to keep his voice low enough to not wake his mother down the hall.

"Who's this?"

"Dad?"

The unfamiliar laugh rules this one out. *Click*.

He falls asleep in front of the television, wakes up to the national-anthem sign-off, then turns off the buzzing static and trudges to bed.

Chapter Fourteen

JULY 2001

A FUNNY THING happened during the run-up to the primary. Alongside updates on the volatile race was a puzzler in the *Times,* a photograph with a long caption on the front of the local section that captured, in gangster-movie twilight, the stripper king himself, Michael Vitullo, standing outside his club Fluffers next to a gangly, suited man who happened to be Edward "Big Ed" Lopresti, the ninety-two-year-old former governor. In the caption, Vitullo characterized the parking lot chat as "two old acquaintances shooting the breeze," and it also noted that he'd served twenty-six months on racketeering charges during Lopresti's reign as governor (1960–64). Sure, it was just a photo, but it rattled the fishbowl. Why was the *Times* shadowing either of these men, and what did this hint that they were working on? Apparently the photo had been deemed too provocative to hold any longer.

Birnbaum summoned Bill Steele into the morning meeting, seeing how the city's past and present were colliding on multiple fronts. According to Steele's improvised history lesson, the city council passed a "tolerance" law in 1954 to allow some small-time gaming downtown—despite state laws forbidding gambling—and started licensing card rooms in exchange for a small tax and an adherence to strict rules such as no bets over a dollar. This supposedly was just common sense, but it essentially sanctioned shakedowns. Card rooms had to accept far higher bids to turn a profit, so the cops decided which ones could break the rules based on who was willing to pay monthly bribes. This went on for years, and by the early '60s, dozens of card rooms—and thousands of pinball machines rigged to pay out like slots—were crammed into bars and restaurants throughout downtown. "Many cops doubled their salaries with these payoffs," Steele explained. "And there were sheriffs and jailers, liquor regulators and councilmen pocketing the money too. And good old Vitullo not only was bribing cops but working as their bagman for the bingo parlors. Everything peaked during the fair," he said, "when the city had seventy-five licensed card rooms and more documented gambling than any city outside Nevada." He then summarized the subsequent mutiny within the police department and the grand-jury probe that blew it all wide open.

What everyone wanted to know, of course, was what the former governor was doing with Vitullo the other night.

"That's easy." Steele smiled. "They're old pals."

AGAINST TEDDY'S ADVICE, Roger agreed to talk to Helen Gulanos again. There was something about her gentle tenacity that he couldn't resist. She'd flinched when his voice rose during their testy interchange at the university, but she'd kept doing her job as she saw it and had the prudence not to write anything his mother had said, at least not yet. Plus, he was feeling bulletproof. His campaign had begun to look like a movement, with his volunteer army doubling weekly now. On his drive home today, just about every rush-hour corner had been commandeered with seniors holding *Time for Roger* signs and a smattering of youngsters waving *Vote for the Old Guy!* placards. Even the *New York Times* had taken notice, calling Roger "a new old voice on the Northwest political landscape."

And here she was, big-haired, wide-eyed and pointing at the small photo of him and Elvis framed on the living room wall of his apartment. "So what was he like?" she asked. "Full of himself?"

"Quite the contrary." He couldn't hide his irritation. "He was an engaging and considerate young man when I was with him. A gentleman."

Her photographer, a bearded gum chewer who kept saying *Got-*

cha or *Cool* whenever Roger told him anything, snapped a close-up of the picture, then asked if he could take it off the wall—*Cool?*— and took more point-blank shots.

They scanned the room like anthropologists, as if his possessions were so archaic that everything needed to be inventoried so future generations could understand how he lived. She held up a hunk of concrete the size of her fist. "What's this?"

"Part of the Kingdome."

"What about all these tiny spoons?"

"I bring one back from every big city I visit."

She fingered through the bowl. *Caracas. Cairo. Istanbul. Jakarta.* "Where's next?"

"Buenos Aires, I hope."

She pointed at another photo. "Who's this?"

"My gramps."

"Morgan?"

He nodded. "Shortly before he died."

"Pretty young, huh? How'd he go?"

He remeasured her. "Already told you."

"Sorry. Aneurysm."

He wished he could rewind and insist they meet somewhere else or decline this interrogation altogether. He'd vacuumed the rug, stuffed laundry in a closet and boxed the toys, but he hadn't wiped the counters or emptied the trash. Books, he noticed now, were stacked precariously on every surface that wasn't destabilized by magazines and newspapers.

EVERYTHING ABOUT his apartment startled her. She'd heard he lived in a condo, but expected a swanky Belltown penthouse with a possessive view of the city, not a bland two-bedroom unit in a two-story lower–Queen Anne complex with what cheery realtors might call a "peekaboo" view of the Space Needle, the top of which could be glimpsed from the kitchen window through the tangle of power lines. The furniture was dated and far from regal—a scarred table, a worn leather recliner, a musty avocado-green sofa that would be hard to give away in this century. It astounded her that a man who was delighting large crowds everywhere he went—whether pushing for cheaper housing and monorail expansions or simply talking about the city—lived in a dump the same size as hers.

There was a nineteen-inch Zenith from the '80s, a large abstract painting and a naked ceramic woman performing a cartwheel, but mostly there were books in floor-to-ceiling cases and freestanding stacks. Old, new, hardcovers, paperbacks, coffee-table books and countless titles about cities. She spotted a small framed photo of JFK, looking young, thoughtful and very single, wind playing in his hair. Returning to the shot of Elvis, his left elbow resting on Morgan's shoulder, she wanted to ask more about him but knew she'd already shut that door.

He backpedaled as she turned toward him. "Feel free to snoop around," he said, "while I brew some coffee here."

She nodded and blushed, realizing how nosey she must seem.

"Cool," the photographer said.

Morgan's bedroom smelled sour and looked humble with its double bed, leather rocker and stacks of the *Wall Street Journal,* the *Washington Post,* and the latest copies of *The Atlantic, The Economist, The Nation, The Weekly Standard, Cities and Municipalities, National Geographic* and others. An old turntable sat on top of a small bookcase with large speakers in the corners. Opening the armoire, she found albums instead of clothes, and she had no idea Coltrane, Monk, Davis and Mingus had put out so many records. A painting of a slender, tanned woman about Helen's age hung above the bed. "That's got to be his mother," she whispered to the cameraman.

"Gotcha," he said and fired away. As he'd explained on the drive over, he was a "volume shooter" who tried to capture as many images as possible for fear he'd miss the one that later proved most relevant.

The bathroom was tidy, if not clean, with a standup shower the size of a phone booth and a medicine cabinet that doubled as a time capsule. Milk of Magnesia, Vitalis, Vicks VapoRub, Castile soap. His small office was dominated by a stately oak desk too cluttered to use, and nothing on its walls advertised who he was or what he'd done.

Yet she jotted it all down. Everything about Morgan was of interest since last Friday's poll showed him leading Rooney by two points and Norheim by four—despite being outspent ten-to-one by both of them.

Rooney had tried to shout his way back into front-runner status at his weekly briefing, and Norheim doubled her TV ad buys and bristled on camera after a council meeting when asked to explain Morgan's popularity. "I think it's high time he comes out of the closet and admits that he's a Republican." Morgan had strolled amiably into the TV studio later that evening. "I see myself as an independent who loves good ideas no matter where they come from, which seems appropriate for a nonpartisan job like being the mayor of this city. But please tell Ms. Norheim that if I had to pick a party, which I don't, I'd be a Democrat who believes Republicans shouldn't be treated like lepers."

Helen listed more book titles and noticed a phone line attached to the back of an old computer. Unbelievably, Morgan didn't even have cable Internet. She took one last look around and saw two neatly folded obituary pages with six names circled in blue pen, at which the photographer started blasting as if his Nikon were an automatic weapon.

"Unfortunately, I'll need to leave somewhat soon," Roger explained when she came back into the living room. "Got another funeral to get to."

"I saw you had quite a few obits circled in there." She tried not to panic about time and reassured herself that he was just creating an early-exit excuse in case he needed one.

"My voters," he said and sighed, "are dying much faster than my opponents' voters."

Helen pulled out a small recording device. "Mind?" She pressed a button, "Have you always subscribed to so many magazines and newspapers?"

He chuckled while watching her scribble down his flip quote about dying supporters. "Had to downsize, actually."

"Excuse me," the shooter said, emerging from the office with a large multicolored plastic structure, which Helen slowly realized was made out of LEGOs. Helen wanted to intervene and mute him, but it was too late. "This what I think it is?" he asked.

"Depends," Roger said, with one of his mixed-message smiles, "on what you think it is."

The shooter pointed toward downtown. "The skyline?"

"Good," Roger said. "So there is some resemblance. It's mostly just boxes, you know, so how tough can that be? I'm told LEGO is coming out with a Space Needle, which would certainly help matters."

"Did you do this?" the photographer asks, setting the model on the table. "Or do you have a—"

"Grandson," Roger said. "Miguel."

Helen was about to interrupt when she saw photos of a small Hispanic boy on the refrigerator door.

He followed her eyes. "One of my daughters adopted him."

"And *he* did this?" the shooter asked.

"You could say we did it together."

"Gotcha." He was behind the lens now, snapping shots of Roger's face directly behind and above the LEGOs. "Still working on it, huh?"

Roger sighed. "I don't particularly want a picture of me playing with LEGOs in the newspaper."

"Gotcha." *Snap-snap-snap.* He then unfolded and extended what looked like a translucent umbrella behind Roger's head.

"So what other properties do you own, Mr. Morgan?" she asked, bringing the conversation back on track while the camera kept clicking. "You still have a house on Queen Anne, right?"

"Sold it in 'ninety-seven."

The photographer switched to a wide angle lens and moved back, shooting from the kitchen doorway.

"What about your beach house on Hoods Canal?"

"*Hood*—no *s.*" Morgan set the LEGO structure on the floor behind him. "Sold it two years ago."

"Rentals in Ballard? You're a landlord, right?"

"No, never." He laughed and looked around. "Is this that big of a letdown?"

"It's just that people seem to think, you know, that you're wealthy. And maybe you are, of course, but I think they'd assume that you could afford a lot more than . . ."

He waited, letting her flail.

"Many people figure you're financing your own campaign, or at least that you could if you wanted to," she said, finally taking a breath, "but you're not, are you, not unless you've dumped something into it since the last filing. Meanwhile, Norheim's spending forty grand a month on campaign staff alone, and Rooney's forking out even more. You have only one person on salary, at about four thousand a month, right?"

"Annie gets paid that no matter what. And now that she's doing mostly campaign work, it comes out of that pot."

"And the rest are volunteers?"

He nodded.

"If you did have more savings, would you be running this differently?"

"No."

"Well, then, why aren't you soliciting more contributions?"

"Because I'm not selling anything, and I don't like asking people for money, which is amusing given how many candidates I've urged to get over that. But I've never understood why people are so interested in other people's money anyway." He stood up. "I've been rich, and I've been broke." He grabbed three mugs and the coffeepot before adding, "I've never felt much different either way."

"Your critics might say that sounds like more crowd-pleasing bullshit," she said gently. "Money doesn't have any effect on how you feel?"

"Of course not."

"Then why do you drive a Lexus SUV?"

"Teddy leased it for the campaign. Ask him."

"And your mother's in that . . . impressive home, which I assume costs a bundle."

"She deserves it."

"And you recently lost at least eighty grand in groceriesnow.com, right?"

His smile was lopsided, showing teeth just on her side. "Must be dreadfully boring wasting so much energy looking into stuff like that. What do you do on your days off, Ms. Gulanos?"

"Play with my son," she lied. She now was investigating Morgan on weekends too. "Sorry to keep reminding you, sir, but you are the one who's—"

"Running for mayor. Yes, yes. But what are you running *from*?" he asked. "Your son's father? Or is it Youngstown itself?"

She was so blindsided that it took her a beat to muster a response. "What could you possibly know about—"

"I know it's a pit stop for presidential candidates trying to gain credibility with laid-off workers. Bet you were the first in your family to go to college."

She hesitated, overwhelmed.

He flipped his palms up. "Like I said, I've got this funeral, so how 'bout I save us some time by offering you my brief, dull financial history."

"Yes," she said quietly. "Please."

Some of what he said jibed with her research, but he volunteered more that she could double-check later and surprised her with such asides as admitting that he no longer had an office in the Smith Tower. "Only a mailbox now. Guess I don't want to give up that address. If that's a vanity, so be it." His office phone bounced to Annie's cell, and she ran his schedule from wherever she was, he explained.

After he finished, she brought him back to groceriesnow.com. "Doesn't your investment there make you a participant in the same dot-com craze that strikes you as so foolish?"

"Yes."

"But isn't it hypocritical to mock something you tried to profit from?"

"No, it's being human. 'I'm like you' is what that says. 'I can be a sucker too.'" He laughed.

"People vote for suckers?"

He studied her. "I'm sorry to put so much pressure on you."

"How do you mean?"

"To write something *terrific*, preferably damning, about me. It must be exhausting."

"I'm not. I'm just trying . . . to do what I can to explain you as well as I can. That's why I'm here."

He smiled again, just with his eyes. "C'mon. What're the chances anyone can boil me down into a newspaper story and get it right?"

Ignoring the question, she asked him to recount his history with alimony and children out of wedlock, then pretended not to notice how closely he was scrutinizing her.

"Even Mother Teresa had some off days," he said in a detached whisper. "You understand that, right? Why can't you accept contradictions instead of warping what you find to fit some naïve thesis? You take half facts and coincidences and attribute some pattern to them, or you take a flip comment and shake it up with current events and create someone else altogether. Now that I'm reading all about myself, I'm rethinking sixty years of reading newspapers, and there's a vague distrust settling over all that. Know what I'm saying? All those people—and I should've known this—probably weren't as rotten and corrupt or as pure and virtuous as they were made out to be."

"What do you make," Helen asked, "of that photo in the *Times* of the strip-club guy and the former governor?"

"I'd guess, and it's purely a guess, that they share an interest in watching naked women dance."

The photographer laughed.

Helen shrugged. "How well do you know them?"

He hesitated, watching her jot down *naked women dance*. "The governor and I did the fair together. I go to his birthday parties. Never met Vitullo."

"Really?" She reached into her bag and handed him a paper copy of a photo. "What do you make of this?"

He turned on a light, grabbed his reading glasses and horse-laughed, his face brightening. "That's Vitullo? This is very—"

"You can see how it raises—"

"Any idea," he asks, cutting her off, "how many hands I shook at that fair?"

"Well, that's why—"

"No, let me show you what this feels like. Here's my profile-in-progress of you. Ready?"

"Mr. Mor—"

"Helen Gulanos is a tenacious young woman born in the shadows of Ohio's dormant steel mills," he said in his best Cronkite. "She surprised her family by not only going to college but also discovering a gift for writing and subsequently lunged into journalism like a bat out of hell with a desire to scalp all the high rollers and big shots her parents and relatives had been griping about since she began understanding human speech."

"Mr. Morgan, this is so inappropriate."

He raised a palm. "After sharpening her reporting knives covering politics in the nation's capital," he continued, "she landed a job out West in an *export* city she knew nothing about. And when she's suddenly asked to write about a maverick mayoral candidate about whom she also knows nothing, well, it sure gets exciting. She gets a visceral thrill from unleashing somewhat true stories about him without once imagining what it would feel like to be stalked by herself."

"Please!" she snapped. "You said—"

"Hold on. I haven't even gotten personal yet." He cleared his throat. "She's a single mom, which helps make the sizable chip on her shoulder almost as big as her defiant mane of hair. She's raising her boy herself because a woman who can bend reality with her bare hands can do anything she sets her mind to. The boy's father simply didn't meet her high standards. Few people do. Yet just like her hometown, she's capable of great things and should never be underestimated."

"Stop this!"

He held up a finger. "It needs an ending, doesn't it? She has a soothing voice that sounds friendlier than she really is. And she has an artistic side too, as evidenced by the calluses on the fingertips of her left hand, which means she plays a string instrument, likely a violin." He smiles. "How'm I doing?"

Her face was red, her jaw tight. "For the most part," she said, after a breath, "you're inaccurate and way out of line."

"Excellent! I hoped you'd understand."

She took another breath, debating whether to leave before she said anything she'd regret. "You show a complete misunderstanding of the diligence I pour into my stories, which is surprising considering how long you've been around this game. But there's probably more truth to some of what you said than I'd care to admit. The bit about the violin is remarkable. So clearly you can be observant if you want to be, but you can also be wrong and cruel." Her eyes glassy now, she tilted her head back slightly. "My son's father dumped me, not the other way around. I was the one who *didn't cut it*."

"Sorry," he said. "I apologize for that. But see, *that is my point.* It's hard to be accurate when you're firing from the hip. Most people barely know themselves, Helen, much less their wives and friends. And with strangers, we're all guessing. You could line up a whole bunch of truths about anyone and still miss the ones that really matter."

She had no idea how to respond, so she waited for whatever he'd say next.

"Would you please tell me," he asked, as gently as a pediatrician, "how you got that scar?"

Her chest heaved as the photographer snapped several pictures from above and behind Morgan's head, the blinds casting rectangular shadows across the side of his face.

"I was following a lumber truck on the Pennsylvania Turnpike when a four-by-four sprang loose and flew right through my windshield." Her eyes swung around the room before landing on his. "Struck me right *here*." She put her pinky finger on the center point of the scar. "Unlucky, right? Until you hear that two cars behind me was an empty ambulance, which of course makes me remarkably lucky, right? Though it definitely messed up my Halloween routine. I used to dress up as Medusa just by clipping some rubber snakes into my hair. As you can imagine, it was very convincing. But see, most people don't realize that Medusa ultimately got decapitated by Perseus. So I haven't felt comfortable putting rubber snakes in my hair ever since."

He grinned. "Can I flatter you without ticking you off?"

"Not a good idea."

"You're going to be gorgeous for a very long time."

The shooter pivoted to snap photos of Helen blushing. She glared at him, then turned her bulging eyes on Roger. "That is *so* unprofessional."

"Really? You get to break me down to the cellular level, but when I state something flattering and obvious about you, I'm unprofessional?"

"Would you have said I'd be handsome for a very long time if I were a man? It's not flattering. It's just typical of the sexist crap your generation still carries around."

After a long pause, he nodded. "I apologize for acknowledging your beauty."

Another silence passes before he offered brief sketches of his three fiancées, his three children and his two grandchildren out of wedlock. Then he stretched, yawned and explained that he had to get dressed for Sy Postman's funeral.

"Check out the fridge and the cupboards," he said over his shoulder. "The people deserve to know what I eat."

"This guy," the photographer whispered, "is a piece of work."

With an unsteady hand, Helen wrote down a line she'd been holding on to for twenty minutes: *The candidate people see as representing Seattle's old money is nearly broke.*

Teddy arrived almost immediately after Roger shooed the *P-I* duo out, and he could tell by his friend's grimace that he'd seen them.

"Tell me you refused to talk to her," Teddy pleaded.

"Good to see you, my friend. Get yourself some water."

Roger slipped into his black suit jacket and followed Teddy to the elevator, both of them hobbling. "Aren't we a pair?" he said. "Looks like I'm mimicking you now."

Teddy wouldn't look at him. He pressed *G*, and they began to fall. "What'd you tell her?"

"Teddy, you—"

"Don't *Teddy* me! Think I wouldn't find out? Can't resist *any* audience, can you? Consequences be damned."

Roger smiled. "You expect me to wake up and change at seventy?"

Teddy hissed, then limped to the car, where he started the engine and handed Roger a thick folder. "Read up on your girlfriend. She hangs politicians, okay? That's her specialty."

Roger leafed through copies of news clippings about an Ohio congressman who'd been jailed on bribery charges, and whose photos made him look evil. Every article beneath her byline began with punchy, inflammatory sentences.

"Check out the lawsuits I've got in the back." Teddy gestured wildly with his right hand while steering with his left.

"Calm *down*," Roger said, suddenly upset himself.

"Annie found a web site called 'The Twenty-three Lies of Helen Gulanos!' "

"You're too close to the curb on this side."

"She ran some youth-camp leader right out of business. Tried to turn some accidental death into murder!"

"If the guy was innocent, why didn't he sue?"

"He did! You're not listening. She's been sued twice. At *least* twice."

"Well, I take it she won."

"Ever tried to prove malice? There was a front-page correction! Twenty-three lies. *Twenty-three.*"

"Watch what you're doin'!" He started to reach for the wheel before Teddy steadied it.

"What'd you tell her?"

"Stop shouting!"

"You're the one shouting!"

"Just drive!"

Chapter Fifteen

OCTOBER 1962

TOO MUCH is going on at once.

Lines back up a quarter mile to shoot up the Needle or enter the Science Pavilion as the fair bubbles over—111,500 visitors yesterday!—with the exhilaration peaking nightly now in standing-room-only raves for the Chinese opera and the Romanian dance company. And what about the cartoon sitcom that debuted in color on ABC Sunday night? Set in 2062, the Jetsons live atop a Space-Needle-like tower in a city of efficiency and leisure, with breadwinner George working ten minutes a day, three days a week. The expo's influence has apparently grown so pervasive that it's now driving pop culture.

Meanwhile, just a mile from the frenzied fairgrounds, reporters, gossips and the simply curious stake out the federal courthouse to watch tavern and card-room owners, street cops and other mystery men skitter inside, heels clacking on checkered tiles, necks bowed as they drop down into chilly basement passages and the subterranean bunker where the inquisition's being held. Policemen arrive in street clothes, some with jackets pulled over their heads, others crawling out of rusty vans, shielded from cameras and gawkers by gruff entourages as word spreads that a federal grand jury has been convened to investigate gambling and bribery and maybe even organized crime in a wholesome city now beaming with pride after Teddy broke the news this morning that the fair is *guaranteed* to turn a profit—a rarity in the expo biz, where host cities usually lose millions.

"Despite all the doomsayers' predictions of certain financial disaster," Teddy gloated, "and despite putting on a show that costs fifty thousand dollars a day and employs two thousand people, Century 21 will wind up in the black."

This leads the Seattle newscasts, though now there's competition. Nationally, New York Senator Kenneth Keating has claimed there's evidence that Cuba is building launch pads capable of hurling missiles into the American heartland. And locally, this grand-jury stunner is turning the long-rumored graft investigation into a front-page scandal that reads like a misprint. *Police on the take? Maybe in New York or Chicago, sure, but here?* Yet the evidence and consequences are piling up. Two shipping lines and four out-of-state manufacturers are reconsidering relocation plans, and the commissioner of Major League Baseball just canceled his visit.

The card-room busts were nothing but diversions, Meredith Stein had informed Roger the day after the raids shortened his outing with Elvis Presley. All they were really after were the books from Dominic's Bingo Hall, she explained. Arthur Dominic kept meticulous records on pink index cards of profits and payoffs, including recipients' names. She'd teared up after explaining that to him, and Roger knew the subject was about to change. "Please don't tell me yet," she said, rolling a stocking over her knee, "that this has all been a huge mistake."

And that was the strangest part. Sleeping with his fiancée felt like a bigger mistake than having an after-hours affair in an art gallery with a married woman. And the fling continues, as if running on its own momentum, much like the fair itself. Roger tries not to miss any of it, attending every party and show, hosting, emceeing, winding everything up toward its zenith when Kennedy will walk into the stadium and conclude this extravaganza. Yet it's getting harder to focus. Ned Gance wants to meet again, and not in a dive bar this time. He's coming to the fairgrounds, which feels intrusive. Will he finally tell him something worthwhile? Roger doubted it. He finds him, though, where he's supposed to be, standing along the western rim of the fountain, undisguised in his suit now, his pale face hovering irritably over the sunlit crowd.

"Heard from Charlie McDaniel lately?" Gance asks, lighting a cigarette for what looks like the first time.

"No."

"Seems to be missing, doesn't he?"

Roger waits for a dozen noisy women to pass, then opts to say nothing.

"It's all coming to a head," Gance says ominously. "New batch of subpoenas going out tomorrow. This might wrap up sooner than we thought."

"How soon?"

"Who knows? Maybe in the next couple weeks. They really want McDaniel. They need him *now*, see, and they want *you* to talk him into testifying."

Roger looks away, anger pulsing through him. "How could they know I know him, seeing as how everything I've told you has been confidential."

"Look," Gance snaps, "people've seen you together. And you do talk to him, right?"

"Not in a while. Don't even have his number. He calls me."

Gance studies him. "You really want us to pull your phone records? Let him know it's in his best interests, okay? We're prepared to offer him immunity. I strongly encourage you to cooperate." His face softens. "And don't forget to let the senator know I've done right by you."

Less than an hour after Roger is back shuffling through requests, Jenny Sunshine tells him that Malcolm Turner's on the line.

"Can I say something here without you getting all worked up?" the developer begins.

Roger waits.

"You're walking a curious line here, my friend, and it's not going unnoticed, okay?"

Roger runs the words back through his head and stalls. "Beg your pardon?"

"Jesus," Malcolm whines, "you think people don't know who you are?"

"Believe it or not," Roger says quietly, "I don't have the dimmest idea what we're talking about."

"No? You walk into the fanciest cathouse in the city and just smile and ask questions at five in the morning? You have a heart-to-heart at the Frontier with a lunatic who couldn't run a tavern to save his life? And now you're an *informant* for the U.S. Attorney's Office?"

The line goes quiet, Roger every bit as curious as he is alarmed.

"Listen, I'm not trying to bust your chops," Malcolm continues. "When I hear these things, seems like you'd want a friend to say something. I mean, really. You think people don't recognize you?"

"I'd think *you* might know not to believe whatever . . ." Roger's voice trails off. "Somebody just popped in. I gotta ring you back." He hangs up and waits for his blood to cool, studying his big hands as if they belonged to someone else.

That evening he's sweating in the opera house, introducing Theodore Roethke, and feeling unprepared, distracted and fumbling beneath stage lights that feel like heat lamps. From up here, all he sees is blackness, but he can hear the city's finest and the artsy out-of-towners packed in here to listen to, of all things, a poet. No crazy dancers. No mentalist. Neither Elvis nor Hope. A poet.

"You all are about to hear the best poet I know—not that I know him personally. In fact, I don't. What I mean is," he labors, "he just happens to live here. And he's a gifted man who walks on window-sills." Roger rises over the laughter, feeling a sudden desire for authenticity, at least from himself. "I've been fortunate to introduce many extraordinary people over the last five months, yet none of them have been as humbling as this man who simply seems far better connected to what matters than the rest of us. I give you the incomparable, Pulitzer- and National Book Award–winning Theodore Roethke."

Who looks as discombobulated as Roger feels, shambling onstage in a tuxedo, his Churchillian head gleaming in the lights. Oddly chatty at first, as if he were his own warm-up act, he flatters his friends, summons a weak Groucho Marx impression, guzzles water straight from the yellow pitcher and skewers T. S. Eliot and other *overrated* poets. "You see," he suddenly explains, "what I want is power!"

Roger sits in the second row in the only patch of vacant seats, chin up, craning to see, feeling the crowd's dismay, sweating profusely now, thinking Roethke might simply be too much of an iconoclastic oddball for these people, but then the man started reciting hypnotic, mournful poems, as if channeling the dead.

> *The whiskey on your breath*
> *Could make a small boy dizzy;*
> *But I hung on like death:*
> *Such waltzing was not easy.*
>
> *. . .*
>
> *You beat time on my head*
> *With a palm caked hard by dirt,*
> *Then waltzed me off to bed*
> *Still clinging to your shirt.*

The words roll through Roger, as if they were his, describing his own father. Roethke's godlike voice, hovering in the hall, feels capable of absolving him and the city and—for that matter—the increasingly dismaying world.

> *I knew a woman, lovely in her bones*

Roger flinches at the sudden grip on his collar from behind, but recognizes the touch. Her voice is in his ear now, her cheek pressed against the back of his sweaty neck. The auditorium is dark, but people can probably see—Linda, his mother, Teddy, Malcolm, anyone who wants to. Her breathy words mix with her smell. "I knew a woman lovely in her flesh" is what she whispers now. "The good cops are looking at the city council and some businessmen too. There's a banker and a developer in the bingo ledgers. This thing could go all the way," she says even more softly, "up to the governor."

Roethke stares directly down at them now with heavy eyes, swaying in the lights.

> *Thought does not crush to stone.*
> *The great sledge drops in vain.*
> *Truth never is undone;*
> *Its shafts remain.*

Chapter Sixteen

AUGUST 2001

THE SECOND ROUND of candidate profiles ran two weeks before the primary, one after the other. First the Rooney story—Lundy's thumbsucker on whether it was true the mayor was allergic to any idea that wasn't his own. Then the yawner about Christine Norheim's transformation from loaded Microsoft exec to demanding councilwoman who expected round-the-clock Microsofty zeal from her lackeys. Even the teaser for Helen's story—*Tomorrow: Why Roger Morgan Isn't Financing His Own Campaign*—generated more street buzz, with its backlit photograph of him hovering over what looked like—*could it be?*—a LEGO version of the skyline.

Shrontz, Marguerite and Birnbaum took turns fiddling with the fifty-nine-inch story. When it finally came out—with a larger LEGO photo—the case was made that Mr. Seattle's finances mirrored the city's own economic roller coaster over the past forty years. He rode the modest postfair boom through the '60s, crashed with Boeing in the early '70s, rose up again with the high-rise binge of the mid-'80s and participated in the dot-com ups and downs of the late '90s. As recently as five years ago, he'd owned a Queen Anne bungalow as well as getaways at Crystal Mountain and Hood Canal. Yet after a spate of dubious investments and his mother's move into a nursing home, he now lived in a nearly viewless $1,250-a-month apartment and got around—when not walking or busing—in a 1994 Nissan worth about $5,000. And while Morgan remained a regular at the Rainier and Broadmoor clubs, it was as an honorary, not a dues-paying, member. All of which would help explain why, according to his most recent filings, he hadn't spent a dollar of his own money on his campaign. The article concluded with his claim that he didn't feel any meaningful difference in his life whether he was wealthy or broke.

Birnbaum told Helen the story showed great instincts and precision, while Marguerite called it groundbreaking journalism. "This is the most humanic financial story I've ever read," she gushed. Bill Steele waddled up afterward. "*Humanic* is not a word. Look it up. You won't find it."

The street response was more nuanced. Some claimed it proved just how inappropriate Morgan was for the job. His fans saw it as further evidence of his authenticity and honesty, though many of them called it yet another cheap shot. A subsequent *Times* poll showed Morgan still slightly ahead of Rooney and Norheim, which provoked Omar's gadfly to finally agree to this rendezvous.

He was already deep into his curry and halfway down a twenty-ounce Singha by the time Helen and Omar showed up at the Ying Thai Kitchen. Donald Yates—whose name Omar finally relinquished—didn't rise or offer his hand, just kept chewing while instructing them not to consider ordering anything but yellow chicken curry, "and go at least four stars." His comments were directed at Omar, as if she wasn't there.

He was tall, fit and long-faced with pocked cheeks, baggy eyes and ears sprouting wiry bushels of gray hair. His charcoal suit and thin black tie made him look like an elderly extra in a black-and-white movie. When the airy-voiced waitress floated by, Helen asked for a pot of tea. "Eat!" Yates insisted, ordering another Singha. "Gimme a couple more egg rolls," he said, without looking up, then resumed gorging. "So you're the one," he added, almost as an aside, sliding in and out of a grin, "who's written all those puff pieces on Roger Morgan."

"Puff?" Her temperature spiked. "I just wrote that he's been so foolish with his money that he's practically broke."

"Yes, but with such a sympathetic tone," he said with a full mouth, "as if it just makes him all the more of a *giver*." He winked at her and grinned at Omar, then returned to his dish.

"Morgan's people," she told him as calmly as she could, "are complaining day and night."

"C'mon, now." He winked again. "People I talk to assume you're sleeping with him."

"Well," she said, "you've got some sick friends." She stood up. "Enjoy your lunch."

"Oh, sit down."

Omar made helpless soothing noises while Yates snickered. "What a theatrical reaction," he said. "Is that how Birnbaum teaches you to treat sources?" He smothered a belch. "You're not leaving yet anyway, little lady. Haven't paid for my lunch yet. Sit down." He winked yet again. "Relax."

"Mr. Yates," she said, shaking Omar's hand off her forearm, "let's see if we can have a conversation without you insulting me every other sentence or giving me any more condescending winks."

"Touchy, touchy." He looked at Omar for confirmation. "It's obvious to anyone with opposable thumbs that your paper wants Morgan to win." He licked his lips. "That's not your fault. One reporter can only do so much to puncture the fairy tale perpetuated about him for decades now. That's why I'm offering my help, to save you further embarrassment. Please, sit down."

She glared at Omar and then Yates, whose eyes leisurely panned the walls of what looked more like a residence than a restaurant. "If you have something to tell me," she said, reluctantly lowering herself back into the booth, "you should get to it pretty soon."

"Patience," he said, then spooned sauce straight into his mouth. "Let's start at the beginning, shall we?"

Helen reluctantly took notes to spare herself from watching him eat.

"He helped kill mass transit initiatives in the sixties and helped Republicans get elected. Fought the clean-air initiative in the seventies and helped Republicans get elected. Advised companies on how to get around new wetlands regs in the eighties and helped more Republicans get elected. He's always had this gift, you see, for knowing exactly how to buffalo the public. And he'll share that gift with anybody who pays him for it, which I guess defines him as a whore, doesn't it?" He mopped his face with a napkin and set it on the table between them. "Then, of course, he fattened himself up building skyscrapers, leaving us with these totems to our excess. How you figure Malcolm Turner got that height exemption on his towers, huh?"

The recounting of Morgan's alleged abominations continued right up to his public comment last year that Nader supporters had thrown their votes away. "How dare he?" Yates demanded. What Morgan had done right over the years, he told her—sneering at his efforts to save the Market and clean up the lakes—was only for his own glorification. "He's a false prince, okay? That's all he's ever been."

She'd dealt with so many unforgiving activists in D.C. that it surprised her how much she'd let Yates agitate her. "So, that's it?" She cracked her tiny purse and pulled out her credit card. "He's an enemy of the environment and a two-faced whore. Any last insights before I go?" She caught the waitress's eye and mimed her signature.

"Oh, yeah." His grin dilated in and out again before he took a bite of the remaining egg roll. "Did I fail to mention that he was taking bribes during the fair?"

Helen set her card down under her palm, watching him chew.

"Oh, so you like that?" He winked at Omar this time. "Listening to me now, isn't she?"

He then told her how Morgan had forced Seattle's Freemasons out of their building, and how one of them, a furious attorney named Sid Chambliss, vowed revenge. Before dying, he'd passed along to Yates the name of a retired Seattle cop who'd speak up if the opportunity arose. After Yates rattled off his name and that of his Spokane nursing home, and even his room number, Helen dialed 4-1-1 and got connected to the Sunset Rehabilitation Center.

"Is Denny Carmichael still in 106? . . . Yes, that's all. . . . No, no thank you."

She signed the bill, stewing on the vagueness, difficulty and vindictive nature of this lead.

"Oh, and you might ask the prince himself where he went once the fair finally ended." Yates straightened his tie. "This guy makes Clinton look like a prude. His whole past's like that, doing whatever he wants. Omar here speaks highly of you. That's why I'm giving you a head start. But if you can't get it in the paper, I'm sure Trevor Stiles can."

Helen's eyes flashed. "What're you saying?"

Even Omar was on red alert. "You promised," he said, then more forcefully, "an exclusive."

"If she can't get it in, I'm sure the *Times* will," Yates told him without looking up. "Wouldn't be fair if I played favorites, would it?"

She glanced at Omar, then gave Yates a murderous stare. "I don't think you have any idea what the word *fair* means," she said before storming outside, under the first overcast sky in weeks.

"The guy's an ass," Omar said once he caught up. "I'm sorry," he added, "but you got the tip, at least. Helen, *please*."

She sped up, trying to distance herself from him, her boot heels beating the sidewalk along Queen Anne Avenue.

"Go on, let me have it," he pleaded, catching up again. "Just *say* something. I didn't know he'd be this manipulative. I really didn't. Please, Helen." They walked side by side toward her car. "Just say something, please."

Without looking at him, she stuck her arm through his, pinning it tight to her elbow, and they strode in silence to the flashing *Don't Walk* sign on the corner where three men rolled past on bicycles, drafting behind one another like migrating birds, followed by two minivans, a woman jogger and a bus with Roger Morgan's billboard-sized face stretched over its side. His self-effacing smile seemed to say, *I can't believe I'm on this bus either.* The only words on the poster: *Vote for Roger.*

She released Omar's arm and started laughing so softly that it sounded like she was crying.

WITH SPOKANE'S AIRPORT fogged in for the last two days, the editors agreed they couldn't wait for the weather to lift. So Helen pulled Elias out of preschool and raced east out of the city before rush hour, up and over Snoqualmie Pass into what looked like cowboy country. Grateful to be out of cell range, she stepped on it, hurtling through tumbleweeds toward the Columbia. Elias woke from a nap and wanted to eat and hear stories and play games. Helen ran more questions and interviewing ploys through her head while playing guessing games with him until he said, "The speedometer says one hundred, Mommy."

"It's broken," she told him. "We're not going that fast."

"Tell me a story?"

"I'm really distracted right now."

"No story?"

"Sorry, Eli. Not now."

"Why don't I have a father?"

The dry moonscape suddenly blurred on her. "What," she said slowly, "makes you ask that?"

"Everybody else has one. Michael Ruskofsky's dad doesn't live with him, but he sees him on Saturday."

She could feel his eyes on the side of her head. "Some boys have 'em, some don't."

"Where's mine?"

"I don't exactly know."

"Should we try to find him?"

"I don't think so, Elias."

The boy pondered that. "Would he like me?"

"Oh, Eli."

"What's wrong? Why are you—"

"Of course. Of course."

"YOU KNOW all this how?" Roger asked the older man across the table.

"Huh?"

"Ah Jesus, Clint, work with me here."

"How's that?"

"At least *lip-read* a little, will ya?"

Clint squinted, tilting his unsteady head.

"Where did you hear this?" Roger shouted, drawing stares, propping his chin on a palm and leaning closer.

After another palsied shimmy, Clint said, "Yates is friends with Halsey, who plays bridge with Rosemary."

So this was how bad news got delivered these days, by a Parkinsonian, liver-spotted, half-deaf Clint Rohrbacher over a bowl of chili at Lowell's. He used to relish their grueling hikes together, but now it was hard to even catch up on their lives. What he did know was that Clint and his wife preferred birds to humans, a bias that made them allies of the Halseys and grudge-holding doomsayers like Donald Yates.

A waiter hovered over them, glancing at the two canes leaning against a chair on the far side of the table. "Can I get you young men anything else?"

"I'll be damned," Roger muttered, Clint's words still coursing through him.

"S'cuse me?" The waiter leaned closer.

"Two whiskeys."

Clint cocked an eyebrow. "It's not even three o'clock."

"Right. I forgot." Roger glanced at the waiter. "Doubles."

"What kind, sir?"

"Maker's Mark should do the trick."

Even in his physical free fall, Clint's grin was mischievous and the neurological wobble of his head made him look like he was moving to jazz nobody else could hear. They'd hiked in the Olympics a dozen times during the '70s, though Clint always relied on Roger's camera and his memory for the particulars. Their last peak was a steep scramble near the southern end of the range. They weren't fit enough to enjoy the ascent, but the tiny summit was unforgettable considering they wound up sharing it and their lunch with two beautiful young Australians.

Roger pulled out a photo and laid it flat on the table. It took Clint a few beats to recognize himself twenty-five years younger, laughing between the two festive women, then a few more to recall the moment and the setting.

"Come on." Roger looked away. "If I'd known you were gonna go sappy on me . . ."

He realized Clint didn't hear him and gave him another moment with the photo, then loudly said, "Yates still live in that shit box on Warren?"

Clint looked up, wincing. "Not planning anything rash, are you?"

Roger smiled. "Don't worry. I'm only violent when I drink."

Lip-reading, Clint snorted a laugh.

They watched massive port cranes off-loading three freighters while stout tugs shuttled in and out of the Duwamish and two enormous Asian ships, bobbing well above their waterlines, awaited fresh loads. The more he mulled over what Clint told him, the more sense it made. The Freemasons had dropped their suit after the fair, but Sid Chambliss warned him never to run for anything. And Yates and Chambliss, of course, were a natural humorless duo. Roger felt foolish for being caught off-guard like this. The routine bustling of the waterfront usually relaxed him, but not today, not with Clint's message and the lingering anxiety created by the oddly intrusive *P-I* article with the LEGO photo that had put Teddy back on the warpath.

Once the drinks arrived, Roger clinked his glass against Clint's and smiled, but his teeth were grinding. "To old friends," he said, "and new enemies."

Clint tilted his head, as if to hear some distant message. "Nothing rash, Roger. Nothing rash."

HELEN'S PULSE was fluttering as they rolled into the gravel lot in front of a large wooden building in sun-scorched fields near a languid curl of the Spokane River. They hadn't stopped for food—other than Fritos—and Elias was starting to whine. She crouched next to him beside her bug-splattered Civic, the baked land still giving off heat at nearly seven o'clock. "I'm very, very sorry it hasn't been much fun today, but Mommy has to do her job here, okay?" Her lips were so dry they stung. "And you know what? I need your help, Elias. If you're a good boy in here, I'll get you the best burger in the world after we're done, okay?"

He pretended not to hear any of this—his most effective punishment, and he knew it.

"See, I need this old man to tell us a story," she added.

He looked up, finally curious, sporting more nose freckles than ever.

"It might be hard to follow, but it'll be a good one. And I need to make sure the story he tells us is true, okay? And that's why I want you to be with me, because nobody would lie around such a smart, good boy. So just look him in the eye when he looks at you, okay? Can you do that for me? And it might be a little smelly or gross in there, but that'll be our secret, all right?"

The sliding doors didn't respond to Elias Gulanos's forty-three pounds, but once his mother caught up they opened into a small lobby and a long reception counter, in front of which an old woman was slouched in a wheelchair, her balding head listing precariously while a shirtless man holding a sack of fluids connected to a tube inserted into his bruised forearm paced back and forth, the both of them trying to get the attention of the nurse on the phone behind the counter.

"I don't give half a rat's ass about that, you hear me? . . . Uh-huh. That so? Well, you tell him he can . . ." She looked up—"Hold on"— and set the phone down. "What do *you* need?"

"We're here to see Denny Carmichael," Helen said.

"*We?*" The woman squinted, then leaned over the counter to glance at Elias. "Family?"

Helen saw the visitors' log and grabbed the pen. "Might as well be." She scribbled her name and the time. "Denny's still in 106, right?"

The woman dismissed her with wiggling fingers and resumed her conversation, the shirtless man still stammering for attention.

Helen knocked, then stepped inside the narrow, tile-floored room when nobody answered. Two loud televisions were blathering simultaneously on different channels, but a tiny bony man was asleep in the bed near the door. She watched Elias's nose wrinkle at the barrage of odors—boiled vegetables, urine, bleach. The slumbering man looked too frail to have ever been a cop. She walked over to the curtain divider and called, "Mr. Carmichael?"

She waited, then peeked behind it and found an empty bed with rumpled sheets. A toilet flushed and the bathroom door swung open to a new stench as a gangly, white-haired man toddled out, panting, shirtless and deflated, his skin sagging like a wrinkled sheet wherever there wasn't enough bone to stretch it thin.

"Mr. Carmichael?" she said, her heart galloping.

He looked at her outstretched hand and slowly took it with his wet fingers. When she introduced Elias, he stared at him as if he hadn't seen a child in years. "Shake Mr. Carmichael's hand." He stepped forward and stuck out his hand the way a trained dog lifts a paw.

"Airport's fogged out, had to drive across," she said, just to say something, and started to regret this goose chase with every cell in her body.

He clearly had no idea who she was or why she was there and looked too dazed to remember much of anything. Struggling to catch his breath, he gingerly tried to climb into bed, his right leg dangling off the side no matter how hard he strained. Finally, she gave him a hand, his calf muscle soft and loose as she hoisted it onto the mattress. He stared at her for a long moment, breathing heavily.

"Donald Yates says he's been in touch with you about me visiting. I'm a reporter with the *Seattle Post-Intelligencer.* This is my son, Elias." When he did nothing but breathe, she explained that she was writing about the mayoral race and Roger Morgan. Still nothing. His eyes swiveled so he could study Elias without moving his head.

She described her lunch with Yates, "who assured me that you had some information and were willing to help." Was this even Denny Carmichael, she wondered, then spotted a prescription vial on the bedside table. She leaned toward it, but the print was still too fine to read. "I'm sorry, sir, but I just drove four hours to see you. And I need to make sure I'm not wasting your time here. So with all due respect, my bossy editor wants to be sure you're a reliable source of information. No offense, sir, but who's the current president of the United States?"

His mouth sagged and his lips moved, but nothing came out until he said, in a grumbling monotone, "LBJ?" After holding the same bug-eyed expression for a few seconds, he broke into a bronchial laugh that sounded like he was strangling.

A whistling nurse waddled in, glancing at him and his visitors. "How we doin', love?" She stepped into the bathroom, flushed the toilet again and waddled back out. "Let's hook you back up, eh?" She fit some clear narrow tubing across his nostrils and over his ears and flipped a switch, and a small engine started humming. "Better? Daughter visitin' you, Mr. Carmichael?"

"Hardly."

She smiled. "Well, buzz when you need me, hon." A slow-motion Victoria's Secret commercial distracted her until some quiz show came back on and she left.

"So you think I'm senile," he said, breathing almost normally now, his voice raspy but fluent. He snorted through his nose. "Wish like hell I *didn't* know what was going on. So you wanna talk about Roger Morgan? That's gotta be worth something to a big newspaper."

Helen was speechless. He'd gone from zombie to extortionist far too quickly.

"At last, everybody finally wants to know about Roger Morgan," he added. "Funny how that works."

"Run for mayor," Helen said patiently, "and people want to know everything about you."

"Well, help me understand why I should talk to you instead of some other newspaper lady."

"I'm sorry, Mr. Carmichael," she said as gently as possible, the two TVs behind her merging into one annoying blare. "We don't pay for information."

"That's what y'all are supposed to say. You got a smoke?"

Her son walked up next to the bed and pointed at an old black-and-white of a boy about his age. "That's you," he said, his voice a small bell. "Isn't it?"

He studied Elias. "Aren't you observant?" he said, then turned to her. "When you got something that's worth good money, you don't just give it away. Least that's how I was raised. You came a stretch to see me. If it's that important to you, it's gotta be worth something."

Her patience was a punctured balloon. "I drove across the state because Mr. Yates assured me you'd be willing and ready to talk, and that you'd have documents to back up whatever you said. If you can't or won't, or if you're expecting to get paid, we won't waste any more—"

"Your generation doesn't bother with small talk, does it?" he interrupted. "Think I've got visitors rolling in here telling me about their vacations and bowling teams? Think there's a whole lot of friends and family checking up on Uncle Denny?"

Helen glanced at the clock next to the bed and inhaled. "You're lucky you've got air-conditioning," she said slowly. "Still pushing ninety out there."

He stared over her head at his television and what sounded like *Wheel of Fortune.*

"What's your roommate like when he's awake?" she asked. When he didn't respond, she followed his eyes and saw Vanna cheerfully turning letters on the screen. "I've been researching the 'sixty-two fair," she said. "Hard to imagine what that must've felt like. You were there, right? What do you remember about it?"

The sun dropped low enough to blast through the window and blind him. She stepped over and closed the filthy curtains, launching thousands of twirling dust motes into thin bars of light.

"Benny Goodman, eating crab at the Needle, all sorts of stuff," he said. "And the girls." Most of the teeth were missing in his jack-o'-lantern smile. "Gracie Hansen's girls. 'Paradise' something or other. Went several times. They were seven feet tall and kicking their legs. And that Gracie had a real personality on her. She toured the science exhibits and told the newspapers, 'It's great, but science will never replace sex and cotton candy.' " He strangled on his laughter again, and his voice took a moment to clear. "Elias," he finally said, "open this drawer here."

The boy looked at his mother and then back at the old man, who was tapping the bedside table with a yellowed fingernail. "See if you can find a small gold key in there."

After his mother nodded, he opened the drawer and felt blindly beneath papers, finding a paper clip, a penny, some toothpicks, an orange earplug.

"Closer to the front corner, son."

Seconds later, Elias smiled triumphantly at the little key in his fingers.

"There you go. Now stick it in the little lock on the top left of that file cabinet there and turn it this way till the button pops out."

The old man stared at Helen, puckered, then mimed smoking. She shook her head. He shut his eyes and waited until he heard the lock pop. "Now pull open the bottom drawer and bring me the envelopes with the blue rubber bands around them."

Helen resisted helping as Eli widened his base, bent his knees, slid the drawer out and pawed delicately through the files before slowly removing a bound brick of weathered envelopes and carrying it like an altar boy to the bed. Carmichael thanked him, then started tugging feebly on bands. Helen again wanted to help, but didn't dare risk distracting him. He finally removed one. Elias set the key on the bedside table and clasped his hands in front of him, awaiting his next assignment. The second band took longer, but finally a dozen brittle envelopes tumbled free into the old man's lap.

"PARK HERE," Roger told Annie once he spotted the sanctimonious Prius with its *Eco-Warrior, Pollution Isn't Pro-life* and *Nader for Prez* bumper stickers. He reached for his cane and stepped gingerly onto his bum ankle and out into the downpour. His aching hip accompanied his throbbing ankle as he groaned up the narrow flight of stone steps. With no bell in sight he rapped on the door. A light was on inside and he heard movement, though it was hard to be sure with the rain pounding maple leaves and asphalt shingles and gurgling in the gutters.

Agitated now, he whacked the door solidly with the cane handle three times, harder than he intended to, his breath ragged, his indignation snowballing. What had Yates ever done that wasn't spiteful? Roger struck the door even harder. "Donald!" he shouted. "It's me—Lucifer!" He glanced at the numbers above the entrance again, then noticed the touring bicycle suspended from the porch ceiling. Another facet of Donald Yates's sanctimony—staying in impeccable shape in his mid-seventies while reducing his carbon footprint.

He grabbed the head of the cane with his left hand, slid his right palm down to its rubber stopper, then pivoted until his shoulders were perpendicular to the window. "Think you can ruin me, Donald?" he yelled. The backswing was brief, but his pronating wrist gave him all the snap and speed he needed and the old single pane broke almost gratefully, as did the next two, though it wasn't clear which one triggered the piercing alarm. *Too doo! Too doo! Too doo!* He waited there, listening, amazed, suddenly unsure whether this was even the right house, feeling strangely exhilarated yet distanced, his body awash in adrenaline and whiskey, the cane warm in his palm.

Descending the steps was more painful, and his peripheral vision seemed to be shrinking, as if the scenery was about to go black, which made him worry about aneurysms and caused him to hurry. At street level, he saw Annie, her head bobbing behind the wheel, lost in some raucous music she played whenever she was alone in the car. He considered turning the cane on the Prius too, but his anger was already skidding toward embarrassment. He opened the passenger door and ducked inside with a mounting headache. Annie switched off the music and smiled sheepishly before noticing his expression and lowering the window to better hear the home alarm over the rain.

"All I wanted," he mumbled, "was to yell at him."

DENNY CARMICHAEL examined the envelope closest to him, then looked up. "Now find my reading glasses, son."

Elias scanned the room as if he'd get extra points for speed, then hustled around the bed to the windowsill, grabbed the glasses and handed them over. Carmichael put them on, carefully opened the first envelope, pulled out a creased sheet of trifolded stationery and peeled back the top, then grunted and leaned back, his glasses clearly no longer powerful enough. He slowly fit the paper back into the envelope and gently set it at the back of the stack before brooding over God knows what.

Helen told herself to wait quietly, that old people can't be rushed. She feigned repose, excused herself to go to the bathroom, filled three plastic cups with water and waited some more, dialing herself calm. "Can you tell us about that time period in Seattle?" she said, passing him a cup. "What was going on with the police and the gambling and all that?"

Carmichael pulled another envelope loose and went through the same routine.

"Tell us a story," Elias said, so sincerely that Carmichael's smile ruined the vertical creases in his cheeks.

He opened the next envelope, then began, "I was a policeman in Seattle, and a good one," he told the boy. "Takes courage to be a good one, you know?"

"Shoot anybody?" Elias asked.

"*Elias,*" Helen scolded.

"Yes," Carmichael said, "but I missed."

"He shoot first?"

"Elias, let Mr. Carmichael talk."

Carmichael shook his head, the breathing tubes loosening around one ear, tightening around the other. "I didn't really know Roger Morgan," he said abruptly. "Met him during the fair like everybody else. Never had anything against him. Still don't. I held on to all this just to keep my backside covered, for all the good that did me." His snort turned into a red-faced wheeze. "But I owe a guy who helped me out, see, and he made me promise to pull this crap out if Morgan ever ran for something that mattered. To tell you the truth, though, I think I'm changing my mind."

He opened another envelope, the ventilator humming away.

"See, most of us could barely afford houses. So we were always looking for ways to make a little extra. And it was already in place, see. You worked certain beats, you collected these bonuses. It helped, you know. Could be the difference between renting and buying, or maybe sending a kid to college or not. But then I got promoted to sergeant, and the bonuses kept coming." He paused, sipped his water, spilling some on his hairless chest and scooting the envelopes farther from the damp spot. He looked at Elias. "Hard to turn down free money, isn't it?" Elias nodded knowingly, and Carmichael winced at Helen. "Was coming in from everywhere, you know—card rooms, pinballs, punchboards, pull tabs, cathouses. And I was good with numbers, so they had me make sure everybody got the right amount. The beat cop took the first cut, then the sarge in charge, then the assistant chiefs, the prosecutor's office, then over to city council, see? Patrol paid directly to the mayor's office, I believe. There were separate payoffs for burglary and narcotics too, as I remember. Vice screwed the pooch, if you ask me, because suddenly liquor and food inspectors and all these other jokers were getting a piece too. Then even people on the outside. A banker, a stockbroker, you name it. And by then it was like a secret Rotary Club or something—we called it the network—and it made sense to invest as a group, you know? So we started getting into all kinds of stuff—gold and silver, racehorses, real estate. We bought land out by Redmond, then someone hooked us up with Malcolm Turner—you've heard of him, right?—who at the time was this young world-beater juggling projects and needing capital."

Helen tried to go blank-faced and pretend he was telling her stuff she already knew, but her glittering eyes gave her away to Elias, who looked concerned. "Mom?"

"Shhh," she said.

"First deal we did with Mal was a downtown parking garage, then an apartment building. This was way back near the beginning of his run, see?"

Helen kept nodding but felt like some organ was about to rupture inside her, so she was committing key points to memory, not risking taking notes. "Did Morgan and Turner receive *bonuses* too?" she asked casually. "Mr. Yates said Morgan was 'taking bribes' during the fair."

Carmichael paused, his eyes clenched in recall. "The way I understood it, he was Mal's inside guy. So, like with that apartment project near the Roanoke on-ramp, Mal told all those homeowners, 'Look, I'm gambling here. Nobody knows where the freeway's going, and if your place gets condemned you won't get half what I'm offering.' But it wasn't a gamble. He knew exactly where it was going because Roger was on that state panel. See what I'm saying? And by the time the freeway opened, Mal Turner had the most convenient new apartments around."

"How'd you come to know all this?" Helen asked, still too anxious to pull out a notebook, not wanting him to focus on the fact that this wasn't just a conversation until she found out what was in these envelopes.

"He bragged about Roger. It was all part of his pitch to get us to put up the cash. Wanted us to know he was in with the guy running the fair."

Helen leaned back and exhaled. "That's all very interesting, but you realize it's also just talk, sir, and forty-year-old talk."

He patted the envelopes.

Helen hid her skepticism. Documents so rarely tell a story. What most people considered proof was usually thirdhand hearsay and piles of meaningless paper. "So why're you telling me this? Did Morgan ever do anything to you?"

"Not a damn thing. Fact is, I hope he becomes mayor. I just owe lots of people lots of things, and as you can tell I don't have a whole lot left to give."

He looked at Helen like he was about to cry, then at Elias. He skipped over three envelopes and held one up. "Give this to your mother."

She pulled out the paper and gingerly unfolded it. On faded stationery beneath a masthead reading *New Metropolitan Properties, Malcolm Turner, Director,* and dated February 7, 1962, she sees the following typed on a manual typewriter:

```
Re: Borgata Principals
Clive Buchanan $20,000
Dave Beck $25,000
Denny Carmichael $5,000
Winston Edgell $10,000
Stephen T. Long $15,000
Ross O'Banion $15,000
Eddie Mills $10,000
Roger Morgan $15,000
Jon Reitan $15,000
```

"What's Borgata?" she asked, so she wouldn't have to keep staring at Morgan's name and the number next to it.

"The original name of the Roanoke Apartments."

"So Morgan invested in a building," she said casually. "No law against that. And if the money was dirty, why would anybody put anything on paper?"

"I think to Mal it was always just money." He watched her. "Don't recognize those names, do you?"

"I grew up in Ohio. Roger knew about all this?"

He shrugged. "Had to, didn't he?"

"Why?"

"Smart guy. Everyone said so."

"Maybe he thought he was just investing in real estate. Who's to say he—"

"Maybe." He stared at her.

Several minutes of halting conversation later, Helen mustered the courage to ask, "Can I make a quick copy of this?"

"Sooo," the old man drawled, "it *is* worth something."

"I think we've already discussed that, sir. Can I get a copy?"

His face drooped into a weary frown.

"Get Mr. Carmichael some more water, Elias. I'll be right back."

The desk nurse set the phone down reluctantly and looked up at Helen, who was acting as pleasantly as she could with all her adrenals firing. "Could I ask you to make a copy of this for me?"

"Staff only."

"I'm happy to pay."

The lady glared at her. "Good for you."

"*Please*. A dollar?"

"Didn't I just tell you?"

"Five dollars?"

The nurse glanced at the list of names, then back at Helen as if she was nuts. "For one copy?"

"And fax it too, please, to this number."

The woman looked at the number. "Fax and copy?"

"Yes. Will ten dollars cover that, ma'am?"

Afterward, Helen slipped outside and called Bill Steele to alert him to the fax and to let him know that Malcolm Turner was suddenly cropping up in her research as well.

As the excitement built in his voice, she felt herself losing control of her story, which shortened her breath and made it hard to listen when he read back the names like a strung-out cop discussing suspects.

"Fuggin' A," he said several times.

"I'll call you," she finally said, "once we're outta here."

"We?"

"Elias."

"Who?"

"My son."

"Right. *Lordy.*"

That he was out of her sight and unattended gave her a panicky quiver, and she started running down the hall before hanging up.

HE HEARD THE BELL, then the door swinging open and Teddy shouting, "Roger?"

"In the bathroom!"

"Please tell me Annie misunderstood what happened this afternoon," Teddy yelled after clomping across the living room.

"You get me a beer?"

"What did you do?"

"You getting me a beer or not?"

"What the hell? You in the tub?"

"Yup."

Teddy shuffled into the bathroom across the moist tiles, set a can of Rainier on the tub, averted his eyes, snapped one open for himself, then lowered the toilet lid and sat down with a groan. "You trying to sabotage your own campaign?" he asked calmly. "Is that our new strategy?"

Roger raised his beer toward Teddy, who still wouldn't look at him. "Actually, just trying to soak my ankle and hip a bit here, old man."

"Jesus," Teddy said. "I'm raising Cain at the *P-I* while you're out committing misdemeanors."

"The son of a bitch has been bragging so much about how he's gonna knock me out that even Clint Rohrbacher heard about it. You remember Yates, don't you?"

"No."

"Well, he's a miserable old attorney who's telling any reporter who'll listen that I'm the worst thing that's ever happened to this city."

"Think a misdemeanor's gonna look pretty good right now?" Teddy asked after a long swallow. "Think that'll give you a boost?"

"If it goes public, we'll laugh and call it the silliest accusation we've heard to date. Right?"

"Sully put the fear of God in them today. You should've seen their faces when he started listing her libel suits."

"What exactly are we so worried about anyway? What are we hiding?"

"You'd know better than me."

"What does that mean?"

"What you see as just *life* might not play that well outside your peer group."

"That I drink too much? That I've chased women, had kids out of wedlock or gambled too much? That I'm a dumb investor? That I have lunch with Republicans on occasion?"

"Yeah."

"Yeah to what?"

"All of it."

"Have you noticed how well we're doing, my friend?"

"Yeah and it's not because of your irreverence, your comic timing or the *full life* you've supposedly lived."

"Then why?"

"Because you're the goddamn father of the fair, because you're *Mr. Seattle*."

"I see, the nostalgia candidate."

"Exactly."

"You're killing me. Tell me, how is it that you've turned into the world's most timid campaign adviser?"

Teddy wiped his face. "Hanging around you is hard on the nerves."

Roger set the beer in the soap rack and sank lower in the tub. "Maybe so."

"Just win, and then you can do whatever the hell you want. But *win* first." He tilted the can and guzzled, his Adam's apple jumping. Then he sheepishly raised his chin and glanced into the mirror. "I used to be over six-two, Rog. A less honest man would have called himself six-three. Now I'm barely five-eleven. I weigh what I did when I was in high school. I avoid mirrors these days and shave in the shower," he mumbled, rubbing sections of whiskers he'd missed, "which has its downsides, in case you hadn't noticed."

"Actually," Roger said, "you're still the best-looking man I know."

"That's not what I want to hear from a naked man in a bathtub." Teddy pulled out a cigarette, then said, "You mind?" and lit it before Roger could respond, cupping his hand over the flame as if to protect it from wind. He exhaled. "So, was it fun?"

"The windows?"

"Yeah."

"To be honest, it felt terrific while I was doing it and ridiculous afterwards."

Teddy grunted. "I need something stiffer," he said, before rattling one last sip out of the can, rising with a groan and starting for the kitchen. "You want anything?"

"Nah, I'm perfect."

It wasn't immediately clear whether Teddy stubbed his left foot on the tub, or if the tiles were too slick for him to get traction. Twisting as he fell, he groped futilely for the towel rack before landing on his left hip with a yelp. Then Roger slipped when standing up, banging his funny bone so hard on the porcelain he couldn't feel his left arm.

. . .

DENNY CARMICHAEL'S eyelids were at half-mast, his voice turning groggy, the envelopes still in his lap.

She scrambled to recall what Bill Steele and the *Times* had said about the graft heydays. "Were you ever subpoenaed?"

His laugh ground toward a throat-clearing. "By the time they called me in, there'd been so much snitching I didn't stand a chance. And it was gonna get a whole lot worse if Costello talked, see. You don't know him either? Lord, you people. Rudy Costello, the pinball man."

"So he talked?"

"No, he drowned."

"Accident?"

It was hard to watch him shake his head. "Well, he drowned the day before he was supposed to testify, so what do you think?"

"A coincidence?"

"I was there." He waited for her response, then repeated himself. "I was there when this young lieutenant slugged him, dropped him in the shallows and put a foot on his back to keep him down." He looked past her now. "And I was there when they threw that tavern owner off the Bremerton ferry too."

Helen was pretty sure she'd just heard a confession of sorts to two very old murders. "And who was that?" she asked.

"I'm no good with names. Here, son, give your mother this one," he says, handing Elias an unsealed envelope.

Inside, she found a penciled list of barely legible names she didn't recognize.

She shrugged. "I'm sorry, but—"

"Roger Morgan's name came up during the hearings," he said.

She looked down at the names again. "And what does that have to do with this?"

"Someone testified that he was part of the network, that he worked with Mal Turner to hide the money."

"Okay, but—"

"You won't find it in the transcripts, but that's the list of the nineteen jurors who heard the evidence."

She swallowed, her eyes bouncing over the quaint old names—Harold, Louise, Edna. "Then why wasn't he subpoenaed or indicted?"

"Think about it."

"What do you mean?"

"The U.S. attorney was getting ready to run for Congress."

"So it was politics? You're saying Morgan was protected?"

Leaning back into his pillow, he closed his eyes.

"And what about Malcolm Turner?" she asked. "Same thing?"

He cleared his throat. "They were both golden boys."

She exhaled. "Can I make a—"

"*Take* it," he said. "I don't know why I've held on to this stuff. I don't . . . I really don't." He started sniffling. "It all seems so damn long ago now." He waved a hand helplessly. "Please, go."

To her amazement, Elias moved closer to the bed and set his little hand on Carmichael's hairy arm. He's an *old soul,* she told herself when he did things like that, a thought often accompanied by the guilty notion that he was missing out on a normal childhood. He looked so much like his father that she rarely saw herself in him. Yet the way he read people, and how gently he tried to comfort this old man, she realized, was all her.

After a prolonged silence, during which she reconsidered every significant thing Carmichael had told her, she said, "I appreciate what you've shared with us, and I will handle it very carefully, but I don't want to bother you again. So let's do this just once, okay? Are you holding on to anything else here that I should know about? What's in the other envelopes, sir?"

"Just stuff that doesn't matter anymore," he said irritably, then added, "Nothing to do with Morgan."

"Anything else about the network?"

He fumbled around until he found and pressed a button hanging near his head.

"One more time, sir, if you don't mind. Mr. Yates said that Morgan was taking bribes during the fair. And you said you were in charge of distributing payoff money back then, so was he getting a cut or not?"

He stared at her vacantly as if he didn't recognize her anymore.

"How about the names of the cops," she pressed gently, "who told the grand jury about Morgan's involvement?"

Unresponsive again, his eyes landed on her son. She reached over and placed her business card on his bedside table. "Okay, Mr. Carmichael. Elias and I are very grateful for your time. Someone from the *Seattle Times* might be coming here or calling. His name's Trevor Stiles, and you don't have to talk to him or anybody else. Understand? I don't want you to have to go through this again. You've made your peace."

There was no hint that he'd heard a word she'd said as a tall nurse sauntered in with a tray of hot food. Helen signaled to Elias to hold on.

The old man took his time examining the sliced beef and boiled peas. "It wasn't a cop who snitched on Morgan," he said before raising his fork. "From what I heard it was some guy on the liquor board, but who knows." He turned to Elias. "So long, son."

Minutes later she was back on her phone, waiting for Steele to answer, pacing outside her car, light-headed from the sweltering evening and the sense that the career-changing story she'd been training and hoping for might have just fallen into her hands. Maybe she'd even take Elias with her to Columbia to accept the award. He was old enough to appreciate it now. But this mother-son daydream crashed right before Steele picked up, when it occurred to her that this story was far too convenient and full of holes to possibly be true.

She was giving Steele the jurors' names and telling him about Rudy Costello and the other alleged murder when she noticed Elias coughing inside the car.

Steele wanted spellings, dates and other specifics she didn't have, pushing hard in his heightened state, but her mind was suddenly distracted by the image she had of Elias chewing something in Carmichael's room. What was it? She hung up and opened the passenger door, where Elias had the seat reclined and his mouth wide open, sliding his tongue around.

"What'd you eat, sweetheart?"

"I'm sorry," he said, though his tongue was already swollen enough to slur his words. "Cashews."

Which were no doubt processed in a factory, Helen knew, that also handled peanuts. In a flash, she saw that Elias already had taken the EpiPen out of her purse and had set it next to his leg, patiently waiting for her to get off the phone.

She told him he'd be just fine, removed the cap, rolled his shorts higher and pressed the needle into his slender thigh.

Chapter Seventeen

OCTOBER 1962

HE DREAMED about him again, almost the same dream, yet more detailed this time. The two of them were strolling the fairgrounds, soaking up everything like lifelong pals. Strangely, their gestures were synchronized and they were exactly the same size, smiling eye-to-eye in identical bright narrow ties and pin-striped single-breasted Savile Row suits. Moseying toward the fountain, they discussed books and cities and the threats facing the nation.

Though, of course, it won't be like that at all, which is made excruciatingly clear by the detailed itinerary in the *P-I* this morning:

President Kennedy's airplane will touch down at Boeing Field at 7:35 Saturday night. A brief ceremony of welcome is being arranged. A band will play. State, county and city officials will form a reception line.

Mr. Kennedy's motorcade will head directly for the Olympic Hotel, where he will spend the night in the presidential suite on the eleventh floor. He will attend mass the following morning at St. James Cathedral.

A motorcade will take him to the fairgrounds at 11 o'clock Sunday.

Mr. Kennedy will step out and walk to the plaza. The combined 21st Army and Fort Lewis bands will play while the President inspects the various state flags and shakes hands with World's Fair commissioners.

Roger reads that part twice. Yes. After all this, that is what he gets—an anonymous spot in the handshake line!

The President will re-enter his limousine for the short drive to

*the front steps of the Science Pavilion, where he will make an address
from a platform erected there. The World's Fair band will play.*

*Afterward, the President's tight schedule calls for him to leave
the fairgrounds in time to board his airplane at 2 o'clock. He will
not attend the closing ceremonies, which will commence at 5 o'clock
sharp.*

This entire shebang will culminate, then, in a brief motorcade, a
quick handshake and a rushed speech before he gets the hell out of
Dodge. Still, John Fitzgerald Kennedy will be here. He'll stick out
his smooth presidential palm and offer that winsome smile, while
Roger watches him work crowds, adjust microphones and go from
cordial to eloquent: *" 'Let there be light.' What more can be said
today regarding all the dark and tangled problems we face than 'Let
there be light.' "* And who knows, maybe the fair will turn his head
and he'll sense the magic and, in a glance, see the man whom Roger
hopes he'll become.

Though probably not.

There'll be no time for JFK to indulge the possibility of a new
friend. But he'll get to say something to him, though, won't he? The
moment will be so brief he'll have to pick the precise words. He won't
ask for anything, and he won't flatter. He'll *give* him something. Yes!
Not some cheap souvenir, though, a notion or an idea. But what?

Roger snapped out of it and started rooting for smaller victories:
that the weather holds, that the newspapers aren't milking the graft
scandal, that the city leaves a favorable impression. And if it becomes
a new favorite of the president's, he'll come back, won't he?

He's pacing the grounds, worrying with his feet, when he misses
the call from the White House explaining that Kennedy won't be
making the trip at all due to an upper respiratory infection. Essentially a curt note from his mother: *Jack has a bad cold and won't be
at school today.*

Roger phones East, desperately hoping the message was somehow garbled, that they'd simply wanted to warn him that he might
not be able to attend. Yet all he gets are more jolts of dismissive brevity. People are killing themselves to get to this fair, he wants to shout,
like Hindus to bathe in the Ganges or Muslims to crawl to Mecca!

But the president can't make it because of a head cold? When he calls the senator's office to express his bafflement, he's told that LBJ has the same goddamn sniffles and won't be traveling either.

He hangs up, wondering why Kennedy's really ducking the fair.

HE'S AS SLEEP-DEPRIVED on the final day as he had been on the first. It all feels like so much more than the end of a fair. People keep asking, What's next? Will the dreamers extend the monorail, build a stadium or another floating bridge? Regardless, this party ends today, and the city will return to its isolation and its escalating scandal with the Needle hovering awkwardly above it all, marking and dating this fair until some generation won't connect the two. That is, of course, if there is a future.

Today butts up against all that and more as everything spirals toward sunset. He lets the requests and complaints and goodwill overflow. *What's next?* The question keeps coming, as if he's got dozens of worldly spectacles up his sleeves. He cancels appointments, continues ducking calls and spends hours patiently making the rounds, shaking the hands of fair workers, forgetting to eat. He takes his time bidding farewell to the Belgians, French, Germans, Italians and Dutch as the grounds jam with a last-call euphoria and the biggest crowd yet. He's saying good-bye in the Spanish Village to a familiar worker named Hector when something in the man's gratitude starts Roger sobbing. Hector's tiny wife leans forward and embraces him. More people line up to shake his hand and leave him with questions that come down to *What's next?* But it's got a different tenor now, as if they also sense that the real world is strung together by delicate threads.

He notices exhibits he's forgotten about, such as a box the size of a small car, *brought to you by Behlen Mfg. Co.,* holding a million silver dollars, and another with Ford's six-wheel rear-entry vehicle. He returns to the office to change into a fresh shirt and then joins the stadium's capacity crowd of thirteen thousand people paying to witness the finale while tens of thousands more listen from outside in the gauzy light.

Jackie Souder's band marches out, playing all the same songs one last time, followed by a police drill team and high-school marching bands. He's suddenly furious all over again about Kennedy not showing. The stage is a yuckfest, but there's an emotional undercurrent now with people hugging, the senator and the governor already looking choked up. Roger had reserved seats for Linda and his mother, but can't spot them from here. He watches Teddy, tall and handsome, grinning behind his cigarette and absorbing praise in the fading daylight. And he sees Meredith Stein, formidable as ever, gliding up to engage the governor, who jackknifes with laughter at something she says. When her eyes find Roger's, he looks away before she blows him a kiss.

The senator sneaks up beside him now. "You gotta bring this thing home," he says, his eyes scanning the crowd as if counting heads. "Take it where it needs to go. Play on all this emotion here." He finally looks at Roger. "Has anybody in the U.S. attorney's office," he asks, barely loud enough to be heard, "been of any help?"

Roger hesitates. "You bet, sir."

The senator studies him.

"Thanks a lot," Roger adds.

"Well, good. Sure is a mess, though."

He nods.

"Greed," the senator says, leaning closer. "It's our curse, isn't it?"

Our curse?

Roger notices Malcolm Turner sitting on the stage next to the mayor. Who invited him? Right then the fireworks begin, accompanied by bagpipes and applause. The subsequent speeches weave platitudes, yet for once sound genuine—the politicians and Teddy all offering something different. It isn't JFK standing up there but it's oddly intimate, and the crowd roars. And it's more than just local pride, right? This fair forced itself into the American psyche and introduced this city to the world.

Roger doesn't say any of this, though, when it's his turn. Shutting his eyes, he lets the applause roll through him, the governor on one side, the mayor on the other, both men waving aimlessly, people cheering, nostalgic already, as if they know they'll never again enjoy such lavish fanfare, snapping pictures to prove they were here.

"As this fair recedes into our memories," Roger begins, "let it unleash a new crop of bold dreams and grand realities for this city and beyond." He pauses, telling himself to slow down, yet hears himself shouting, "And please join me in hoping that by creating this world community, which we have felt and relished here for six inspiring months, we have hastened our journey toward a day of peace and universal understanding!"

That sounds desperate and farfetched but he believes it when the stadium thrums with affirmation. "And in the hope of arriving at that glorious day intact and enlightened, we entrust our future to the youth of today!"

He knew what was coming, but seeing it is something else, as hundreds of children run hand in hand beneath the spotlights and the gunfire salutes as various bands unleash Tchaikovsky's *1812 Overture*. Finally, the opera star Patrice Munsel steps up beside Roger, dressed in white, her smile visible from every seat, and starts into "Auld Lang Syne," the crowd clumsily joining her until the air thunders with song. *Should auld acquaintance be forgot . . .*

His face trembling, Roger looks around and realizes almost everyone is crying too. A spotlight swings across him before mercifully going dark. After a collective gasp and prolonged silence, the crowd files out into the night.

Roger floats offstage, dazed and sleepless, shuffling anonymously out of the stadium amid the horde of strangers returning to the grim humdrum of daily life. All he wants to do now is enjoy a highball with Teddy, then go home for a very long sleep before finally confronting the unfathomable imminence of his own wedding.

"Mr. Morgan?"

He doesn't immediately register the words.

"Couple questions, Mr. Morgan?"

He finally focuses on a short young man with bushy sideburns.

"I'm with *The Daily*," he says. "Any last thoughts on the fair?"

"We just pulled off the biggest gamble this city ever took," Roger says, instantly regretting the phrase. "Every goal we ever dreamed of was more than realized." He sees the kid isn't jotting anything down. "What paper did you say you were with?"

"*The Daily.* Doing a story on the freeway too, by the way. You an investor in that apartment project on Roanoke, sir?"

"*The Daily?*" He feels the earth tilting. "The student newspaper?"

"That's right, sir. Are you in on those apartments?" This kid looks so nervous he could pop.

Roger worries he might faint. "Nobody's ever called me an investor before." He tries to laugh, but nothing comes out. "I'm . . . I don't . . . ," Roger says, not sure what to say now. "No bankers or investors in my family." He smiles, yet already feels like everything's crashing down. "Where'd you hear that, anyway?"

"Malcolm Turner."

"Really? Well, you'd think he'd know, but why's this of interest?"

"Have you been subpoenaed by the grand jury yet, Mr. Morgan?" A strap slides over the kid's shoulder and suddenly there's a camera in his hands. "Mind if I take a quick picture, sir?"

Roger smiles just in time for the *snap*.

Chapter Eighteen

AUGUST 2001

BILL STEELE was waiting in his restored steel-blue 1963 Chevelle, reading documents beneath the dashboard light, when she parked her rental car in front of her apartment, got out and carried Elias inside, asleep on her chest, his head slung over her shoulder as if his neck were broken. Steele trailed several paces behind, with his briefcases gripped in one arm, her overflowing satchel cradled in the other.

She strained her back lowering Elias into his rarely used big-boy bed and tugged his pants off, hoping he wouldn't wake up crabby, hungry or both. Mercifully, he rolled onto his side beneath the Buzz Lightyear comforter. Hearing the reassuring give-and-take of his breath, she flipped off the light and tiptoed out in time to catch Steele surveying her college-girl squalor—a black bra atop a mound of unfolded laundry and piles of worn journalism texts, as if she'd been cramming for finals. Moseying toward the kitchen, he smirked at the Orwell quote taped to the refrigerator door: *In a time of universal deceit, telling the truth is a revolutionary act.*

She hadn't envisioned this inspection when she agreed to meet here, before stranding her car in Spokane a couple hours ago—as the editors had insisted—and ducking into a queasily small twin-prop commuter jet. She'd almost dozed off driving home from the airport and felt bone-weary now. Stalling, she pondered how best to persuade him to postpone this debriefing until the morning. But it was obvious he couldn't wait, already beet-faced and whispering questions about Roger Morgan and Malcolm Turner as if her apartment were bugged.

She'd crossed into the realm of Secret Agent Bill Steele and all the idiosyncrasies and precautions that came with it. The files and brief-cases he'd always keep locked, the distrust of cell phones and editors, the mumbled bluffs, demands and showdowns—real or imaginary—outwardly appearing to be working on something no more momen-tous than a bland weather story, the only thing blowing his cover being the color of his face. The bigger the story, the more sunburned he looked.

"They all want a piece of Morgan," Steele muttered, talking faster, racing to get to whatever he really needed to tell her. "The *Times*'s I-team was told to drop everything until after the election. Everybody's working on him."

She doubted even Steele knew for certain what the competition was up to. More likely, this was part of his gambit to use competitive hysteria to get his bankruptcy opus into the paper. "Birnbaum says we should work through the night if we can," he said abruptly, which sounded doubly suspect: that Birnbaum would say it and that Steele would give a shit. "I took the liberty of showing him your faxes." Before she could digest that, he told her state Democrats were send-ing out another anti-Morgan mass mailing, with the LEGO photo captioned: *Do you really want this man playing with your city?*

After unlocking his briefcases, he laid out the clippings and personal information that the research staff had dug up on the nine alleged investors in Turner's 1962 apartment-building project. "Reads like a who's who of Seattle corruption," he whispered, then saw her expression and switched to a normal voice. "Six of these guys were indicted in 'sixty-two or 'sixty-three for conspiracy involv-ing illegal gambling and police payoffs. Just listen to who they were: Clive Buchanan, county prosecutor, Winston Edgell, deputy county prosecutor. Stephen Long, city council president. Ross O'Banion, county licensing director. Jonathan Reitan, county undersheriff."

"What about Dave Beck?" she asked, looking at the list.

Steele raised his eyebrows. "He was the Teamsters boss who ran the Northwest for decades until he was nailed for tax evasion before this all shook out."

"And Eddie Mills?" she asked.

"State liquor control board, no charges." Steele shrugged. "The prosecutor probably gave him immunity for ratting out the others. And your Spokane pal, Sergeant Dennis P. Carmichael? He was indicted, yes, but for *perjury*. So, unfortunately, your golden source here, Helen, *is* a convicted liar."

She covered her face with her hands.

"Hold on," Steele said. "All that matters, of course, is whether what he told you is true. And this looks real, doesn't it? I mean, we won't find it in public records anywhere, but nobody's required to file these things."

She explained Carmichael's theory that Turner didn't necessarily know or care where the money came from.

"Bullshit. Mal Turner's never done anything by accident. He might've just thought there was nothing to be afraid of. That's the upside to doing crime with cops, right?"

"When's the last time," Helen asked, "you or anyone else wrote about any of this?"

"Ha! Never. Every time I pitched it, they demanded some magical peg. I'd say, How about this: 'Not that long ago, this *good-government* city was run on bribes!' "

"So how'd it finally get busted up?"

"A few honest cops and an ambitious U.S. attorney. The whole thing dragged on for years. Ultimately," he added, riffling through the clippings, "only a handful did real time."

"So where does Morgan fit in?"

"Be pretty strange if he wasn't in on it at some point. Looks to me like you've found his role," he whispered. "He and his buddy Mal did the laundry."

"Mom, who's he?"

Helen turned to see Elias in the doorway. "You okay, buddy?" She walked over and squatted beside him. "This is Bill. He's a friend from work."

"My belly hurts," he whined.

"That's just the medicine. Remember the last time?" She put her hand on his forehead, then steered him into her bedroom, signaling to Steele that she'd be back in a minute.

She coaxed Elias into bed and rubbed his tiny back, but he continued fidgeting. "Want me to tell you a story?"

"No."

"Would you like me to play for you?"

"Uh-huh."

She turned out the light and strummed Brahms's lullaby in the dark. It worried her that apparently Steele had already convinced the editors that the list of investors was credible. She needed to think this through, but to do that she needed sleep. She played the lullaby a fourth time, heard her son's heavy breathing, then tilted her head back until she caught herself snoring.

"I didn't know you played the violin," Steele said when she returned. "You're good."

"Not anymore."

Before she could make the case for sleep, the phone rang on the coffee table in front of him, and he answered it as if he lived here. "Yes. Uh-huh," he said, nodding. "Uh-huh . . ."

Helen reached over and pressed the speaker-phone button.

"Unfortunately," a woman's voice said, "they're dead."

"How recently?" Steele asked, turning down the speaker volume.

"One of 'em died three months ago. The other two in the eighties."

"All natural?"

"They were old, Bill. Grand juries back then were retired folks and housewives. So they'll either be ancient or dead. I'll give it another scan, and keep looking for those missing bar owners."

"There's just one," he said, turning to Helen. "Do we have a name?"

She shook her head.

"No name yet, Elaine."

Helen gave him a tired smile after he hung up. "Look, I need sleep."

He nodded slowly. "Go ahead. I'll wait up to see if Elaine gets anywhere."

"No. Tell her to call you at *your* home, Bill."

Dropping his eyes, he clucked his tongue and slowly started gathering his files. By the time she brushed her teeth, he was finally heaving himself up off the couch.

When the phone rang again, he stared at her.

"Put her on the speaker," Helen reluctantly said.

Elaine told them she'd found two possible matches on surviving jurors in Wenatchee and Ballard. "The ages are plausible, though the Ballard address doesn't make any sense. Puts her on Forty-sixth, which isn't residential." She rattled off names and numbers and addresses, then waited for Steele's permission to go home.

He was dialing the Wenatchee man before Helen could suggest he wait till morning.

"No!" a man said and hung up.

Steele raised his eyebrows, redialed. "Take me off your damn list!" the man snapped, then slammed his phone down.

Steele grinned. "Everybody hates solicitors."

They stared at the Ballard woman's name—Lilliana Strovich. Helen glanced at the microwave clock. "It's almost eleven."

"Yeah, but she's only ten minutes from here, right? I'd go, but an old lady sees a guy my size at her door at this hour and she'll call the cops."

Helen closed her eyes and exhaled. "You want me to drive over there now."

"Or just wait for the *Times* to interview her. I raised a couple boys without screwing them up too badly, Helen. I can stay here with your son till you're back."

She gathered up her things, weariness hanging on her like a lead dress.

"I know you already know this," Steele began with the same fatherly tone she'd heard him use on kid reporters, "but you want her to think you're just trying to understand things, okay? 'Just trying to make sure that if we do put something in the paper, ma'am, we get it as accurate as possible.' And whatever you do, don't let her think it's a big deal. She's just a tiny piece of a huge puzzle we're working on, right? 'Lots of people are talking to us. Oh boy, lots. But thanks so much for your help.' Might want to pull your hair back or something. Lookin' a bit . . . revolutionary."

"*Bill.*"

"Sorry."

"This isn't my first barbecue."

"I know. Hell, you think I don't know that? And it's a damn good look if you weren't interviewing someone born in 1917."

"I need fashion tips from a guy who can't keep his fly zipped?"

He pointed at her neck while raising his zipper. "Can I ask about that?"

"No."

"Sorry."

"The blade on the guillotine," she said flatly, heading for the door, "was dull."

THE ADDRESS had to be a mistake, since this stretch of Forty-sixth was highly industrial. But after passing a marine salvage yard, a transmission shop and a pesticide plant, she spotted a cottage with fake brick siding wedged between two massive concrete buildings, roses and rhododendrons flanking the front door. The motion-detecting porch light came on as she approached, and there was little delay between her knock and the rejoinder from inside.

"Still not for sale!"

"I'm not a realtor, Mrs. Strovich," she replied loudly. "I'm a reporter with the *P-I,* and I'm sorry to call on you so late, ma'am." The curtains shook. "But I really do need to talk with you tonight."

"Well, good for you, but I *don't* need to talk to you or anybody else. Said all I'm gonna say."

Helen counted to five and knocked again.

The door cracked open. "What is it?" demanded the large silhouette.

"I apologize again, but did you serve on a grand jury here in 'sixty-two or 'sixty-three?"

"Lower your voice."

"I'm talking to surviving jurors and would very much like a chance to ask you some of the same questions I'm asking the others." She was afraid the door would close if she stopped talking. "Of course you can decline to comment, but I'm running out of time, which is why I'm here so late. Again, I'm sorry about that, but I'd greatly appreciate it if you could at least hear me out for a couple minutes."

The door opened wider and the robed woman stepped forward. *"Surviving jurors,"* she mimicked. "Even if I could remember anything, I'm not allowed to discuss it. You know that. Good night."

"Actually," Helen bluffed, "the court lifted all those restrictions seventeen years ago. And besides, if you always did what people told you, I'm guessing you wouldn't still be living here."

The woman snickered, left the door ajar and retreated. "Awake now anyway," she bellowed over her shoulder. "You can help me with this pie. My sister won't stop bringing 'em over. I keep telling her, 'Hey, it's just me here now,' but she never listens, 'specially when it comes to food or men."

Helen stepped inside a room that smelled of chamomile, mildewed books and cats. Uncertain whether removing her shoes would seem polite or presumptuous, she kept them on and took in the room. A half-full coffee mug sat on a homemade doily, a half-finished crossword puzzle on a clipboard next to the rocker, two fir bookcases crammed with embossed spines. Wall pictures of her daughter or, probably, herself, standing next to an equally robust man, their heads swiveling toward the camera in synchronized delight. She glanced at the furniture for signs of cat claws, her nose already starting to itch.

The woman carried on in the kitchen as if chatting with someone else. "What're you gonna do?" she concluded vaguely. Helen smiled agreeably, and got her first good look at the woman. Big-boned and pushing six feet, Lilliana Strovich was a sturdy eighty-four-year-old with a mole high on her left cheek and an underbite that accentuated her defiant demeanor.

"How about a cup of tea?" she asked, cutting the piecrust with a triangular spatula.

Helen hated tea. "Don't want you to go to any—"

"What trouble?" She opened the microwave. "That's the point of these things."

"You have chamomile?" Helen asked.

"You're in luck."

As if expecting more visitors, Mrs. Strovich stared out the window while the water heated, then caught Helen eyeing the pile of realtor cards in the tureen. "That's just last month. Could paper this house with 'em." She cut a wide slice of pie and slid it onto a ceramic plate. "Dig in."

Helen sat down and felt herself plunging with fatigue as she bit into the best pie she'd had since childhood. Mrs. Strovich put a steaming mug next to her plate and took the chair across the table, her eyes lingering on Helen's face before dropping to her neck scar.

"Can't get it through their heads that I don't have a price," she said. "They think it's proof I'm crazy." She grinned. "They figured there's no way an old hag would stick it out through all this construction."

"Isn't the noise unbearable?"

"Not if I play Benny Goodman loud enough."

"I don't blame you. There's nothing more annoying than moving."

"Why should I? I don't *have* to. They look at me like I'm talking Greek."

"Good for you. I *am* Greek."

The lady smiled her way back into her seventies.

Helen stopped midbite. "Must've been quite an experience being on that jury back then," she said, then finished chewing. "Hard to believe all that happened in Seattle, isn't it?"

"Oh, believe it, young lady. Offer people money, they're gonna take it. 'Specially men."

The pie soothed the itchy roof of her mouth. "Do you have a cat, Mrs. Strovich?"

"Why do you ask?"

"Just thought," Helen hesitated, "that I sensed one in here, but I don't see . . ."

The woman's eyes reddened around the rims. "Put Zoe down three weeks ago."

Helen stopped chewing. "I know how it feels to lose a cat," she lied, and didn't blink, letting her itchy eyes water.

"I forget she's not here at least twenty times a day. Keep seeing her in all the places she used to be, you know, just out of the corner of my eye. You could take out all the furniture and books and photos, and this house wouldn't feel any emptier."

Helen nodded solemnly and laid down her fork. "My sister married a bereavement counselor," she said, another lie, "and I remember him saying that losing a longtime pet can be as hard to get over as losing a two-legged family member."

Mrs. Strovich snorted. "Harder in my case, but you'd have to know my family to appreciate that. I spoiled her so much she got up to nineteen pounds."

"Someone had to help with the pie." Helen pulled out her card and slid it across the table. "See, I'm really not a realtor."

The woman adjusted her reading glasses. "That's Greek? Looks Hispanic."

"As Greek as can be."

"Nobody's asked me about any of this in nearly forty years."

"Well, we're working on a story about—"

"The former governor?"

"Actually, no. We've been told Roger Morgan's name came up repeatedly during those hearings."

The lady studied the plaster-swirled ceiling. "Of course."

"What?"

"A better question is whose name didn't come up?"

"What do you—"

"So many names were kicked around. You have no idea. Even the U.S. attorney's brother-in-law came up, as I remember. The governor at the time, Lopresti? His name came up too, I think."

"Do you recall Roger Morgan being discussed?"

"Oh, maybe in passing. You sure we can talk about this now? *Criminal contempt* is what they called it at the time."

"Nothing to worry about," Helen said. "What about Malcolm Turner, the developer? His name pop up?"

"Yes." She brightened. "And I remembered that when I read

about his bankruptcy. People like him going bankrupt? The whole country's going to hell in a handbasket if you ask me."

"So do you remember what was said about Turner?"

She hesitated. "Not really, other than maybe some of his real estate deals looking fishy."

"Did anyone try to connect Roger Morgan to Turner?"

She shrugged. "Roger was the most popular guy in town." She lowered her eyes. "Quite the looker, truth be told. Wouldn't have complained if he'd left his slippers under my bed, if you know what I mean. But you can't crave what you don't taste, right? That other fella runnin' the fair, he was s'posed to testify, as I recall."

"Who's that?"

"Tall fella."

"Ted Severson?"

"Maybe. He had a stake in some tavern on Thirteenth or Fourteenth. Something like . . ." She hesitated, then blurted, "The Nite Cap Tavern." She smiled proudly. "How do you like that?"

Helen stopped chewing. "You remember that after all this time?"

"Listen, I couldn't tell you what somebody said yesterday, but I can tell you what my husband ordered for dinner on our first date. You have no idea how many pork chops I made for my Paul." She shook her big head.

Helen felt her itch spreading to her tightening throat. "Mrs. Strovich, someone with the liquor board—it might've been a guy named Eddie Mills—told your jury that Roger Morgan was involved in a network that invested police payoffs in real estate with Malcolm Turner."

"If you say so, but that doesn't ring any bells for me."

"I'm kind of surprised," Helen said gently, "that you don't remember anything more specific about what was said about Mr. Morgan."

Mrs. Strovich bristled. "Well, aren't you something? Surprised the hell out of myself I've pulled up as much as I have."

"I'm sorry." Helen sipped tea that tasted like dirty socks, her mind scrambling. "You've been very kind to talk to me, especially this late." She pushed her chair back. "Who are you voting for, any-way, ma'am?"

"What?"

"For mayor."

"Guess." She grinned sheepishly. "He's so hopeful."

"You know him personally?" Helen asked, her voice completely nasal now.

"Never met the man. More pie?"

STEELE HELD UP a finger as she entered and pointed at the televi-sion, where unflattering images of Roger Morgan were flashing on the screen, then a slow-motion video of him talking that made him look old and intoxicated. "What do we really know about Roger Morgan?" asked the voice-over. "We know he's reckless with facts when it comes to criticizing our city's courageous police officers. We know we don't need a divisive and unstable mayor. Re-elect Mayor Rooney. Leadership you can count on. Paid for by the Seattle Police Officers' Guild."

"Wow," Helen said. "Anything else?"

"On what?"

"The news."

"Nah. What happened? Was she a juror? You talked to her?"

After blowing her nose and sneezing and blowing it again, she told him, "She was evasive about Morgan, but she definitely remem-bered Governor Lopresti and Malcolm Turner being discussed."

"My God, what'd she say about Turner?" He sat upright.

She briskly summarized the interview, its value shrinking the more thought she gave it. Finally, she sneezed. "Look, Bill. I'm gonna be useless tomorrow if I don't call it a—"

"Head cold?"

"Allergies."

"Well," he said diplomatically, "it's your story."

She knew by his tone that he was playing her.

"Just think it'd be smart," he added, while packing up, "to at least write up what we *have* and what we *need* before the drones start weighing in first thing by telling us why the sky is blue and what the story should say."

She left him sitting there with his forehead creased as she checked on Elias again and then pulled a sixteen-ounce Miller from the fridge. "Want one?"

He grimaced. "You a beer drinker?"

She cracked the can, took a deep swallow and plugged in her laptop. "Only when I write."

Then she typed while Steele paced behind her with his shirt untucked, yakking nonstop in his half-whisper, the words flowing out of her fingers with rhythm and precision, each sentence lugging its share, writing fast and fearlessly as if they've already finished their reporting and all their speculations had been confirmed.

Steele stopped and breathed over her shoulder, nodding and muttering. "Well, all we can actually say at this point is . . . No, just keep . . . Well, yes. Yes. Exactly. You *think* . . . Excellent! Keep going. *Jesus,* Helen. *Yes.*" They switched places. She read her best quotes from Carmichael and Strovich aloud as he clumsily plunked them into their narrative, leaving blanks where they'd need responses from Morgan and Turner, forging on. Then she took over again, fixing his typos and thinking hard about how the story should feel, instructing him to list the facts that needed to be double-checked and the ingredients that were still missing.

ACROSS TOWN, Roger Morgan was reading aloud to his mother. She loved these bedtime readings and the luxury of nodding off while her son was in mid-sentence. But tonight she'd had coffee after dinner in hopes of staying awake until the book was finished. He was a bit late, though, so he wasn't even to the final chapter when her eyelids began sagging.

" ' "Your potion, Harry," said Mrs. Weasley quickly, wiping her eyes on the back of her hand. Harry drank it in one gulp. The effect was instantaneous. Heavy, irresistible waves of dreamless sleep broke over him; he fell back onto the pillows and thought no more.' "

Roger tucked her in—and even that hurt his swollen elbow. He flinched when he saw the stack of *P-I*s next to her bed. She's reading the papers again? Then he turned off the bedside light, switched on the green night-light he'd bought her and slipped silently out the door.

WHEN SHE FINALLY stopped typing, her fingers numb, she realized Steele has been silent for at least an hour, sprawled across the couch, his legs dangling over the arm. That a reporter his age still was so excited about stories suddenly seemed so endearing that she felt selfish for being reluctant to share this one with him.

She wrote her way out of that guilt and others as well: out of her recurring insecurities and shameful mistakes, her single-mom martyrdom, her embarrassment over her simple parents, her current exhaustion and every other thought or impulse that wasn't helping make this draft as compelling and powerful as it needed to be.

Reading through it a second time, she typed parenthetical commentary in the text. She needed more proof of nearly everything, but she could feel the story's potential rising inside her as the freeway quieted to just an occasional car and then nothing, a span of rare silence followed by rain that began like a murmured prayer and built until it sounded, in Helen's ears, like applause.

THE NEXT AFTERNOON they were waiting for her and Steele in Birnbaum's office. Even the publisher was slouched on one end of the couch with his thin white beard and his tiny eyes fixed on her.

She speed-read the other faces. Marguerite looked oddly evasive. Webster and Shrontz and a few high-ranking mutes were gloomily sipping coffee. They clearly wanted to avoid the fishbowl so their reporters wouldn't gossip about what the publisher was doing in the newsroom.

What *was* he doing here? The only time she'd met him he'd waxed in clichés about the pillars of a decent paper—fairness, vigilance and a duty to inform, the generic publisher's speech that reporters want to hear.

Helen felt that fragile high she often experienced right before a crash and struggled to look relaxed as Birnbaum opened with: "Well, Helen, I hope you can understand just how awkward and embarrassing it was for me and Mr. Alexander to be blindsided this morning with allegations about your past."

Her mouth dried up. "What do you mean?"

"Morgan's attorney and campaign manager came in here and tried to make the case that you're not an objective reporter and to request that you be removed from working on any future stories regarding his candidacy."

"Oh, please," Steele muttered.

"*Bill,*" Birnbaum snapped.

"Neither Shrontz here nor anybody else was aware you had *two* libel suits back in Ohio, the most recent of which was just settled, correct? A settlement that included front-page corrections, didn't it?"

Helen tried to find her voice. "That was—"

"Can you see how that makes us look a little uninformed? Perhaps we would've been able to do a better job of defending you if—"

"It didn't occur to me," she whispered, "to bring up some of the most stressful moments of my life during a job interview." Shrontz had sunk into such a deep pout he wouldn't look at her. "We were sued by a jailed congressman," she said, gaining volume. "The guy sexually harassed his staff and rigged contracts for companies that a judge later determined were linked to the mob."

The stress and thrill of that story, she realized, still flickered inside her. "I said he was arrested for a DUI, which is what the arrest stated, though the courts later reduced it to what they call a *wet neg,* basically the same thing, though of course I wish I'd clarified that." She tried to clear her throat and ended up coughing. "Still, they never should've run those corrections the way they did, but I was gone by then."

Steele handed her his coffee. She sipped it, rotating the mug so they couldn't see her fingers twitching.

"Okay, Helen, but as you know, there's more." Birnbaum glanced down at a Post-it note. "There's a web site called 'The Twenty-three Lies of Helen Gulanos!' in which another target of yours accuses you of getting things wrong and ruining his reputation."

"Gregory P. Conover," she said, her skin tightening, "is a psycho-path who ran a boot camp for troubled teens in central Ohio. After one of the kids died of dehydration, I looked into Conover's past and found that two other teens had died of easily avoidable causes at a camp he'd run in Utah. It seemed relevant." Her vision pulsing, she lifted her hair off her neck and flapped her blouse. The man had screamed into the phone that he would *destroy* her.

"Take it easy, Helen," Marguerite whispered.

Looking at Birnbaum, Helen saw that more was coming and sud-denly feared that she wouldn't be spared anything today.

"They also claim," he said hesitantly, "that you got your biggest story in D.C., the one about that South Carolina senator's penchant for porn, and these are Ted Severson's words, by sleeping with an aide on his staff."

She shut her eyes and let the words bang around in her chest.

"This is bullshit," Steele said. "Why do we care what—"

"*Bill,*" Birnbaum barked.

"I did have a relationship with a guy in Senator Honeycutt's office," she said softly, "but that was after I reported and wrote those stories."

"Did he father your son?" Birnbaum asked. "I'm sorry, Helen, but that's the allegation."

The room quieted. Finally, she said, "That's not your business."

Birnbaum stretched his neck, tugged at his tie. "I'm sorry to agi-tate you. I really am. But these are things we had to discuss. You understand, right?"

She gave no response, but what she realized was that the time-lines of the story and the romance—from flirtation to conception—would never matter to anyone but her.

"They haven't said they'll sue yet, but if you write anything else they don't like, they clearly intend to drag all this into the light. Wouldn't you say that was the drift, Stan?"

The publisher nodded, but since he'd been doing this pretty much nonstop, its meaning was hard to gauge.

"Can I say anything yet?" Steele asked, rolling his left shirtsleeve up past his elbows.

"Bill," Birnbaum said, "this isn't—"

"Let him talk," the publisher told him.

"If I haven't pissed anyone off in a while," Steele began, rolling up the other sleeve now, "I figure I'm not working hard enough. But maybe that's just me. What I do know is that we've all written sentences and stories we'd love to have back for one last rewrite. That said, after sitting behind Helen for almost a year it's obvious— regardless of what anyone *claims*—that she's one of the most diligent and gutsy hires this paper has made in the past decade or so."

"Nobody's saying—" Marguerite began.

"Think about it," Steele interrupted. "What message would you send if you give Morgan to someone else? And why would we possibly"—he was looking directly at the publisher now—"want to surrender a war we're currently winning? You think the *Times* wouldn't have run her Morgan stories, much less the one we've got in the works? While I was passed out on her couch last night, or early this morning, whenever it was, Helen was pounding out a draft—a very rough one—of what we think we know so far. And, trust me, we understand this needs a whole lot of confirmation before it's ready, but just listen."

The publisher sat up and Birnbaum jingled some keys as Steele slowly read the opening five paragraphs, which to Helen sounded premature and reckless.

"He changed his name?" Birnbaum blurted. "Has that ever been written before? How long have we known that? But what about the sourcing? You've got a convicted liar, an old woman and—"

"I said it needs work, but after hearing its *potential,* can't we agree that this might explain why these hacks are trying to smear Helen and scare you off a story we haven't even finished reporting yet? And as far as these people trying to run *our* newsroom, I say, and this comes from the heart, fuck 'em."

After a prolonged shuffling of legs and rubbing of faces, the publisher quietly said, "Yes." His face tilted upward, his eyes brightening. "Yes!" he repeated, louder this time. "Fuck 'em!"

Everybody was nodding and blushing now. Marguerite raised her arms as if they'd just kicked a field goal. "*Fuck* them!"

Chapter Nineteen

OCTOBER 22, 1962

THE PECULIAR DEATH of Rudy Costello gets little attention the day after the closing ceremonies, when the vandals and vultures descend on the fairgrounds wielding sledges, prying nails and loading trucks as if this was merely a circus being packed up—Space Needle and all—that would be reassembled next month in Barcelona, Geneva or Tokyo. Most of it is trash anyway, yet there are plenty of exotic artifacts—Filipino lamps, Chinese dolls and so much more—amid the instantly nostalgic shrapnel of placards, trinkets and brochures. Coverage of yesterday's finale rules the newsday, of course, so it isn't more than an aside that Mr. Costello, who owned the contracts for the county's 1,217 pinball machines, drowned in five feet of water beside his fifty-three-foot yacht in front of his Lake Washington mansion.

Roger can't place the name or picture the face, in part because he's distracted by reports that the northern span of the freeway from Roanoke to Ravenna will open earlier than expected next month and that the mayor pledged to tighten gaming policies and eliminate what he calls "the poor image of law enforcement." Roger's digestion of all this is further disrupted by Jenny Sunshine, who informs him that a tall, officious-looking man came looking for him but declined to leave his name.

"How tall?"

She reaches as high as she can.

"Did he say when he'd be back?"

"He wanted to know when you'd be in, and I told him I had no idea," she says playfully, "seeing as how this is the first day of your new life."

He hastily sorts his office into piles before realizing how badly he doesn't want to be here when Ned Gance returns, then grabs his coat and heads out to do what he's been putting off for months now. Riding the monorail downtown, he broods over what he'll say, every combination of words sounding so inadequate. He steps off and trudges along Fifth Avenue toward Frederick & Nelson with the gait of a man who doesn't truly want to get where he's going.

From a distance, coat in arm, he watches her unlock glass cabinets, cheerfully showing necklaces to one woman, rings to another. He is tempted to postpone this drama, at least for several hours, or maybe even another day, until he admits to himself that he's leaning toward leaving town tomorrow. Finally, both shoppers waddle out.

As he closes in on her, she looks as pretty as ever, with the sort of radiance only found in someone who is genuinely happy, and he feels a reflexive desire to add to her joy, to surprise her by taking her to lunch wherever she wants to go. When she spots him, however, it's not with the look of a fiancée but the cordial mask of a saleswoman. "Can I help you?"

"I'm sorry," he begins, plummeting immediately to where he needs to go. "I shouldn't have waited this long."

"You don't have to do this now," she says levelly. "You've already said it a million different ways."

His words catch in his throat and he clears it, astounded she's this composed, as if all this fine jewelry gave her strength. He stalls, looking at necklaces beneath the glass until he sees the fourteen-karat Space Needle charm for $39.50 and his own pinched expression in a small oval mirror.

"If you'd been paying attention," she says softly, "you'd have noticed I haven't sent the invitations out yet."

She tries to slide the ring off, but it catches on her knuckle. She spins it around once and studies it, as if making sure it's the right one. "I don't want to marry you either, Roger. I want someone who adores everything about me."

He wants to help her with the ring or say something soothing but can't seem to do anything but watch as she tugs futilely. "Please," he whispers, "just keep it."

She doesn't seem to hear, then looks up not with anger but something closer to sympathy. "Don't worry. I'll find someone to love me."

Right now he wished it was him.

She pulls on the diamond again and then looks past him, her taut lips sliding into a magazine smile. "Hello there, ma'am. Can I help you?"

Afterward, he drifts back to the fairgrounds and bounces around the clean-up projects, unable to let go of this spectacle, he realizes, until it's entirely gone. Apparently the mayor is caught in this same vortex, because he's here too, gushing about how swell everything was.

"Where's this gonna end?" Roger asks softly.

"What?" the mayor asks, his smile lagging behind his startled eyes. "Where what ends?"

"I hear council members took money. Head of licensing too." His voice is quiet, but he's moving closer. "Where's it end?"

The mayor's lip trembles. "Look." He pulls both pants pockets inside out. "Nothing but lint, Roger. Okay? Never got a dime, I swear. Christ almighty . . ."

Two hours later, he's reliving his ineptitude with Linda and taking off his coat to help demolish a ticket booth when the planet stops spinning. "Within the past week," President Kennedy says on every television and radio station in America, "unmistakable evidence has established the fact that a series of offensive missile sites is now in preparation on that imprisoned island."

Roger and a swarm of workers are huddled around a small transistor outside the food pavilion as the president states the obvious: "The purpose of these bases can be none other than to provide a nuclear strike capability against the Western Hemisphere."

Of course, Roger tells himself. It wasn't a stupid head cold that kept the man from the closing ceremonies.

Kennedy explains his plan to quarantine Cuba by inspecting all seaboard shipments, then drops this gauntlet: "And finally, I call upon Chairman Khrushchev to halt and eliminate this clandestine, reckless and provocative threat to world peace." Roger's mind hurtles ahead so fast he misses the next line. All those gushing accolades he'd thrown out last night about *peace and universal understanding* were already being exposed as so much happy horse shit. A more apt speech might have concluded: *We threw a ridiculous six-month party on the eve of the apocalypse, but thanks for coming.* Finally Kennedy closes with this comment about his Soviet counterpart: "He has an opportunity now to move the world back from the abyss of destruction."

PSAs follow the speech, encouraging everybody to load up on food, water, flashlights and radios. "The head of the family should have a plan of action, so panic can be avoided. If war comes, every man should be prepared so that we may survive to win and rebuild the nation."

Afterward, there is a quiet moment of awe similar to people's reaction when they stare into the Grand Canyon for the first time. Roger pictures Murrow in mid-inhale, squinting at him as if he were a toddler. *Boeing makes you a bull's-eye, of course. But you already know that, right?*

When a 707 thunders overhead, vertebrae crack in thousands of necks. Roger drifts into the numb crowd around the International Fountain and stands silently among them, absently noticing the yellowed maple and alder leaves dangling loose, the slightest puff testing their resolve.

"Mr. Morgan."

He recognizes the voice but keeps his eyes on the leaves, wishing like hell he'd already left town.

"Mr. Morgan," the tall man says again.

"Does the federal building," Roger asks, still staring upward, "have a bomb shelter?"

"I have no idea."

"You should look into that."

"Will do. But have you heard from McDaniel? We need him to testify *right* now."

Roger turns and sees that Ned Gance is paler than ever.

"You understand this is serious, right?" Gance glares down his nose at him. "We were supposed to interview Rudy Costello yesterday, but perhaps you heard he didn't make it to his appointment. You want to know something else that article didn't mention? Rudy was a competitive swimmer in high school."

Roger hears this last bit but it doesn't stick because he's busy recalling a night in Club 21 when Mal Turner introduced him to a tanned and bloated man named Rudy, who shook his hand with moist, meaty fingers, one sporting a massive onyx ring that looked like it wouldn't come off without a hacksaw.

"So you can understand," Gance says, "why we're a bit worried about your pal Charlie."

Roger watches people hugging and crying and walking in circles.

Gance steps closer. "They want to subpoena you too, see. They've waited until the fair was over, at my personal request, but I can't hold them off any longer. I only have so much pull, you understand?"

All of Roger's suspicions click into place. Gance has been a double agent since the beginning, earning points with the U.S. attorney for everything he's squeezing out of Roger while making the senator think he's doing him all the favors.

"Why?" Roger stalls. "What could they possibly want to hear from me?"

"They want you to explain what McDaniel told you, and what you saw at the Dog House, and what you know about how the city works, that sort of thing. This is a broad investigation, understand?"

"Have you guys even figured out who's running this goddamn thing yet?"

When Gance reaches inside his coat, Roger braces for a subpoena, but it's just his tiny black notebook in which he jots something, then says irritably, "What *thing* would that be?"

"The network, or whatever you want to call it. Who runs it?"

Gance leans forward, his neck bowed. "There's no godfather, if that's what you're asking. There's just people who live and work here. People like your police chief and your county prosecutor and some of your other friends."

"*My* friends?"

"Have you invested in an apartment building, Mr. Morgan?"

Roger's voice gets small as the air pressure drops. "What?"

"Having trouble with English? Do you or do you not have a stake in the construction of an apartment building on Seventh Ave.?"

Roger stalls, amazed, wondering if Gance had botched the address. "No," he says finally, "do you?"

Gance reshuffles his feet like a man getting ready to swing a bat. "Tell you what, I'll do what I can to get you blanket immunity."

Roger forces a laugh. "From what?"

"For your own peace of mind. Blanket immunity: think about it. It's not easy to get. I can't guarantee it, but I'd do my best, especially if you bring McDaniel in *today*."

Roger jingles the change in his pants pocket, realizing that Gance, like everybody else, is just guessing. "I don't think so," he says.

Gance cocks a thin eyebrow. "How's that?"

"I don't need any more of your so-called favors. Your boss has no legitimate interest in me, and he's well aware of the risks of over-reaching. If I'm wrong, come find me."

Roger waves aside Gance's rebuttals and legal advice and strolls off, eyes on the ground, heart thumping, his thoughts hopping from Gance's warning to wondering what percentage of the city can squeeze into bomb shelters to reliving Linda's emotionless response as another plane roars overhead, and all eyes, including his, swing upward.

Chapter Twenty

SHE COULD TELL when the depleted night shift gravitated toward the newsroom TV that the mayoral debate had begun. Joining in, she listened to their mockery of the candidates. Rooney and Morgan looked exhausted. As the questions mounted, their answers warped into snide attacks on each other, an unsightly fracas in such a mannerly city. Norheim was the only one who seemed reasonable. A slight shift in countenance or tone suddenly made her look and sound more appealing, competent and *original* than the surly men smiling painfully on either side of her. The newsroom banter faded until Helen was finally staring at the television alone, realizing with a low groan that this was the fifth straight night she'd stranded Elias with another teenage babysitter.

The story had gotten away from her. She liked to work fast, but with just nine days left before the primary, everybody was rushing her. Management's fear of getting sued had been trumped by the more unthinkable dread of getting scooped, especially with the *Times* dropping more bombs about Vitullo and his strippers backing Rooney. The latest installment featured read-aloud funny quotes from anonymous dancers who said all fifty-six performers at Vitullo's three clubs were offered $700 in cash for every $650 check they wrote to the mayor's campaign. Told she was among Rooney's most generous contributors, one of the girls was quoted as saying, "I never even knew Mr. Chubby's real name until I wrote that check." A local weekly stole the next news cycle by offering Norheim a front-page endorsement if she came out of the closet and admitted she was a lesbian. The race was so close now—a virtual three-way tie—that every newspaper, radio and TV station was firing off whatever they had. Given that only two candidates would survive the primary, nobody wanted to be left holding a scoop on someone who soon might no longer matter. As Marguerite kept telling Helen, "Carpe diem!"

She'd spent most of the past four days skimming grand-jury transcripts and tracking down cops who'd testified. One former sergeant politely declined to talk and then, the second time she called, suggested she leave him alone. When she then knocked on his peeling front door, he looked at her through a swirl of whiskers and slurred, "Get off my porch, you communist slut." Another retired cop who'd testified in '62 told her he didn't recall hearing anything disparaging about Morgan other than that he preferred married women. She tried to find the U.S. attorney who'd led the crusade only to discover that James Stockton had been dead since 1971 after a forgettable six years in Congress; his deputies and assistants also had vanished.

Frustrated, Helen had driven to Olympia one afternoon to scan lobbyist and campaign records for anything the capital reporters might have missed. There was nothing, though, as if Morgan's decades of hands-on politicking had left no fingerprints. She looked up every state record involving Malcolm Turner's corporations, hoping for something Steele might have overlooked—such as additional lists of investors. Again, no luck. The more reporting she did, the more incomplete the story felt. Yet Steele and the editors were in giddy lockstep, convinced they were on the brink of connecting two of the city's biggest stories in decades. When Helen gently asserted that they needed more to link Turner's and Morgan's sagas than the allegations and foggy memories of a bedridden perjurer and an eccentric Ballard woman, Steele countered that neither accuser was vengeful and that his bankruptcy sources were independently confirming—off the record—bits and pieces of all this!

He'd also warned her that the grand-jury transcripts were a dead end, claiming he'd scoured them five years ago when they were finally made public, but she doubted he'd had the patience to scan them adequately. So, rather than skim them in a reading room at the federal building, she'd paid for all 6,221 pages to be copied, and Shrontz hadn't even flinched at the $311 bill. *Full speed ahead!* Yet the boxes surrounding her desk were a mess, with many pages out of order or missing. After reading Eddie Mills's unenlightening transcript, she became preoccupied with the informative yet incomplete testimony of his liquor board colleague, Daniel Bottenfield. The first five pages of Bottenfield's October 25, 1962, statements provided the most detailed accounting she'd seen of the payoffs. Yet his final two pages appeared to be missing. Researching him, she found a brief article and a photograph when he was appointed in 1959 but no mention of any potential wrongdoing. By the time she unearthed his most recent address, he'd been dead for eighteen months. Returning to the courthouse, she requested the box containing Bottenfield's original testimony. Page 6 was missing there too, but not page 7. To her disappointment, it looked to be nothing more than a page-numbering gaffe, with page 5 flowing seamlessly into page 7, which referenced a "crime network" several times without ever mentioning any names. Yet thumbing through police testimony near the back of this same box, she came across a seemingly stray page 6—which included a pyramidal flow chart titled "The Network." At the bottom were the Racketeers—gamblers, prostitutes and bookies. The next level up were the Organizers—card-room and bingo-parlor owners as well as cops and politicians. The top tier, the Financiers, included bankers, realtors, jewelers and developers.

After copying this diagram, she'd sped to Ballard, where Mrs. Strovich once again mistook her for a realtor. There was no offering of pie this time, and she was further rankled when Helen pulled out the flow chart and asked her to try to recall what Daniel Bottenfield had told the jury about the network. Her recollections turned fuzzier and surlier the longer they talked.

Finally, Helen cut her off. "Please don't play forgetful again, Mrs. Strovich. It's just not convincing." She laid the black-and-white image of the double-chinned Bottenfield on the table. "This man used this diagram in his presentation," Helen said, trying to imagine the scene. "And he probably explained, in a very meticulous manner, exactly how and where the money got invested through realtors and developers and others who helped turn dirty money into seemingly clean investments."

"If you say so," Mrs. Strovich finally replied, her eyes lingering on Bottenfield's photo, "but I don't remember him at all."

Helen studied her. "I find that really hard to believe. You've already told me how appealing you found Mr. Morgan. I'd think you'd remember what was said about him."

The woman's eyes widened. "*I* think it's time for you to leave."

"Please just answer one question, and then I promise to leave you alone: To the best of your recollection, did Daniel Bottenfield or any other witness ever suggest that Morgan and Malcolm Turner were messed up in the city's so-called crime network?"

Mrs. Strovich got up and carried her empty mug to the sink. "Yes," she said quietly, after running the water, "but there wasn't any proof."

"Was there talk of subpoenaing them?"

"See how you are? You said *one* question. And like I already told you, there was all kinds of talk."

Helen gathered the photo and the diagram and stood up. "Was there any about Roger Morgan, in particular, that he was protected, that it was a matter of politics not—"

"Of course there was." She nodded toward the door. "Now away you go."

Helen was back into the transcript boxes now, reading more testimonies while Steele whispered like a clandestine lover with his sources and tinkered with their draft, clunking it up with old-school jargon—*a four-month investigation by the* Post-Intelligencer *has revealed that* . . . Running short on time and options, Helen called Morgan's assistant once again to insist on a sit-down interview either after tonight's debate or sometime tomorrow. Impossible, she was told, his schedule was already overbooked with a reception at the Space Needle and a full day of events. Exasperated, Helen hung up and watched Steele stomp red-faced toward her desk with something he couldn't wait to share.

THE FAREWELLS were even slower than he expected, with a growing line forming to bid him good luck and good night, the older men flaunting their remaining vigor by not letting go of his hand, their eye contact equally intense, astigmatism to astigmatism, some choking up, others resorting to clumsy backslappy hugs. And the women, damp beneath old lace, wrapped their flabby arms around him and smeared lipstick on his cheek, a few openly crying, many of them exasperated, gingerly shifting from arthritic knee to swollen foot, exhaling, plopping back down and fanning themselves, coming off as irritable or impatient though he knew they were just in pain and wanted to be home and alone already, most of them well past straining to look younger than they felt.

This had been Teddy's brainstorm. One last chance to honor and loot their wealthiest supporters to help buy some last-chance TV ads, all of which made him feel like an unimaginative shyster milking the same old marks once again. When a thin widow festooned with pearls and diamonds shuffled to the front of the line, Roger knew this good-bye would come with advice, her husband having served six terms in the legislature. "You've gotta arrange buses for the retirement homes, Rog." She was repeating this instruction for a third time—"otherwise they won't get to the polls"—when he noticed Teddy impatiently skidding his walker toward him.

Without excusing himself, Teddy bored in close and hissed, "She's *still* on the goddamn story and wants to talk to you *now* even though Annie already told her you didn't have time." His chest heaved with exasperation. "Bill Steele's here with her too."

Roger glanced across the SkyLine Banquet Room and spotted them.

"I'm gonna tell the beauty and the beast to beat it," Teddy said between breaths.

"No, say we'll be delighted to talk to 'em up in the restaurant once we finish up here. I'm not about to rush this line, though. Tell 'em that too. And let Nancy know we'll need a quiet table." He pivoted back to the widow, dropping his head to hers. "I apologize, Opal. You're absolutely right, my dear. Buses and more buses." He kissed both her cheeks as she slid an envelope into his suit pocket.

Forty minutes later, he and Teddy found the two reporters yakking on their phones—coiled and amped, sipping ice water in the spinning dining room at a window-side table. He smiled and shook hands.

"We appreciate you taking the time, Mr. Morgan," Steele said.

Roger nodded graciously, the reporters' urgency relaxing him, and turned to Helen. "Please tell me you've been up here before."

"First time."

Her smile was more of a wince, her skin pale, her voice nasal. Either she was sick or, he realized, a whole lot was on the line here. He chuckled. "I forgot, you just work here. But would you like my mini-tutorial anyway?"

"We've actually got quite a few questions and not—"

"Sure," Steele interrupted her. "That'd be terrific."

"Okay, well, this used to take exactly fifty-eight minutes for one full revolution. They sped it up to forty-seven minutes in 1993 so they could get more diners in and out because, you see, people tend to leave after just one rotation. Upside? More business. Downside? More people get motion sickness, especially if they're facing the wrong way like you two." He self-consciously noticed the background music had abruptly switched to Miles Davis. "All forty-eight of these windowpanes are washed automatically." He heard himself stalling. "Fortunately, nobody has to dangle out there anymore. Maybe a dozen people have jumped off the observation deck in forty years; the three who did it without a parachute didn't survive. This whole thing was built in four hundred and seven days for four-point-five million. Almost half its weight is underground, which hopefully makes it earthquake- and hurricane-proof." He tapped his knuckles on the table twice. "The elevator gets here in forty-three seconds and descends at the speed of a raindrop, though you're welcome to take the eight hundred and thirty-two steps if you prefer."

HELEN FELT at an awkward disadvantage. Morgan seemed so comfortable in this preposterous building that he'd imagined and built above *his* fairgrounds and *his* city, which from up here looked more like the blinking motherboard of some massive computer than a breathing metropolis of more than one million residents. As he pointed out various skyline relics—such as the red Roosevelt Hotel sign—Steele was obviously fascinated and starstruck. Why wouldn't he be? He'd waged his entire career in a place where Morgan was a living legend, regardless of his merits or deceits. She checked her watch just as the first deadline passed and wondered with a panicky flicker exactly what the *Times* would have tomorrow. They hadn't run anything in days, and the longer their stories held, the bigger they loomed in her mind. Her skin and throat were both itchy. She hadn't slept more than a few hours a night for nearly a week and felt oddly volatile, as if she might weep before the questions began. It occurred to her again that tonight's babysitter was far too young. Did she even warn her about peanuts? What was her name again? Teresa? No, *Tara*! She exhaled. "Mr. Morgan," she interrupted gently, "We need to—"

"Of course you do."

"Do you recall," she said, going straight at him, "investing in an apartment building with Malcolm Turner in 'sixty-two on Roanoke near Broadway?"

His grin startled her, as if he welcomed the topic.

"I do! In fact," he said, leaning back toward the window, "in just a minute or so it should swing into view. Right, Teddy? One of Mal's earlier buildings, I believe." They all scanned the northeastern skyline, craning to see which illuminated box he was pointing at. *"There,"* he said, "isn't that it?"

Teddy swiveled his neck and grumbled, "Beats me."

Somehow it had never occurred to her that the tower might still be standing. Its plainness made her feel disoriented and slightly queasy.

"Even the Mal Turners of the world start small," Roger explained, as if she'd been thinking aloud.

"New Metropolitan Properties," Steele interjected, as if he were simply there to jog memories. "That was his company at the time."

Roger hesitated and then glanced at Teddy, who was fixing Steele with a drowsy scowl. "Oh, yeah?"

Helen shuffled papers and turned one sheet around so Roger and Teddy could see it in the candlelight. "Here's the list of original investors in that building."

"God almighty," Teddy groused.

The maître d' set a bourbon on ice next to his elbow. "Anybody want anything else?" she asked pleasantly. "Music all right, Mr. Morgan?"

"Perfect."

HE WATCHED HELEN jot *music, hostess, perfect* and *Miles Davis?* as he pulled reading glasses from an inside pocket, fixed them low on his nose and slid the sheet closer to the candle. The table quieted to tinkling ice as Teddy swirled his drink and Roger slowly read the nine names and the dollar figures next to them. It was hard not to audibly groan. He needed to stick a knife in this day. He'd been irritable in the debate and rushed his gratitude with the donors. He never should have agreed to this interview.

"Do you know," she asked in a quavering voice, "what all those people on that list besides you, Eddie Mills and Dave Beck have in common?"

Roger took a swig of water and refocused on the names.

"Recognize anyone?" Steele said.

"Certainly, Mr. Steele. Anyone my age in this city—"

"They were all implicated," Helen said, "in the gambling and graft investigation that began during the fair."

"So *what*?" Teddy growled.

Roger was simultaneously fascinated and alarmed. What was he being accused of? He knew Dave Beck had invested in the apartments, but he threw money all over town. Then, for the first time in decades, he recalled that kid reporter asking him a similar question at the end of the fair. But nothing came of that, right? And that insufferable stiff from the U.S. attorney's office—Gant?—had also asked him about Mal's projects, but again that was the last of it.

"Ms. Gulanos," he finally said, "it's been a very long day. So what *is* your point, beyond insinuating that I should be embarrassed to show up on a forty-year-old list of names I've never seen before that might well be fraudulent?"

"We're really just trying to understand things here," Steele blurted.

"We've been told," Helen said slowly, "that New Metropolitan Properties served as an investment arm for a *network* of city cops, officials and businessmen who profited from graft."

"Yeah?" Roger said, his cheeks burning. "And who told you that?"

"Several sources, sir," Steele answered.

Helen glanced at her colleague. "Denny Carmichael's on the record," she said, turning back to Morgan. "He was a police sergeant back then."

"Jesus H. Christ," Teddy snarled.

Roger smiled tightly. "Let me see if I've got this straight: some senile liar told you I was involved in something forty years ago that I wasn't involved in, and now you want me to comment?"

"Forget who said what," Helen instructed him. "You served on the state's right-of-way committee for the freeway project, didn't you?"

He didn't respond.

"Did you or did you not," she continued, "tell Mr. Turner where the freeway was going so that he could buy land at a discount and put up an apartment building?"

"Let Sully handle this," Teddy barked. "Don't say another god-damn word."

"Mr. Severson," Steele said gently, "we're just reporters doing our jobs."

"You're goddamn jackals is what you are!" Teddy snapped. "Put that in your paper! Write that down! You don't have the . . . Don't you have any decency?" He gripped the arms of his chair and strug-gled upright.

Roger grabbed his shoulder and settled him back down, reeling from the realization that he'd rationalized his little insider tip so long ago that he'd forgotten the twinge of guilt that had accompanied it at the time. Worse yet, he'd deluded himself into thinking it would never rise up again, much less so shamefully in the blazing light of the present. "Easy, my friend," he said, stalling. "Easy."

"Easy, hell!" Teddy's bloodshot eyes flashed insanely in the candlelight.

"Please," Steele offered, "we're making a genuine effort here to give you an opportunity to respond. We're doing everything we can to be fair."

Teddy dropped lower into his chair, snorted and set a twitchy hand on the table, then retracted it.

"Yes," Roger finally said, as calmly as he could. "I was on the right-of-way committee, and I did tell Mal where I thought the free-way was going."

"Roger!"

"Teddy, relax." Then to Helen, his eyes brightening: "There wasn't any mystery where the damn thing was going to anyone who was paying the slightest attention. The meetings were very public."

"But what did you think you were doing?" Helen asked, holding up a hand to stop Steele, "when you gave him the tip and then invested in the building?"

Roger's eyes bulged. "I was doing everything I could to help this city grow!"

Helen waited a beat, then said softly, "And you did well on that and the subsequent projects you were involved in with Mr. Turner, didn't you?"

"So success is now a crime," Teddy muttered.

"I'm not ashamed of working with Mal," Roger said, "if that's what you want to know. I parted ways when I thought he went too far and was building too much, but without people like him this downtown never would've happened. Everybody wants to kick him now that he's down, but when Mal owned these buildings, he answered the door when you had a problem. Who owns them now? New York investment trusts and stockholders who couldn't care less about this place."

Teddy tried to tap a cigarette out of a pack, but his hand was too jittery. "Why tell 'em anything?" He pointed the pack upside-down and finally shook a Pall Mall out. Two more fell on the floor.

"Did you ever receive any money directly from that so-called graft network?" Helen asked Roger slowly.

"Of course not." He picked up the cigarettes and resurfaced. "Never. The question itself is highly insulting."

Teddy pulled the candle toward him and lit up with some whistling inhales.

"C'mon," Roger said. "You can't smoke in this section."

Teddy inhaled defiantly, then exhaled over Helen's head.

She leaned toward him beneath the smoke. "You don't have a concealed-weapon permit for that gun of yours, do you, Mr. Severson?"

He blinked at her and said in a low rumble, "If there were permits for fairness and decency, yours would've been pulled long ago. So arrest me," he added, "or fuck off."

Roger grinned. "See why I love this guy?"

"Yet you knowingly pooled your money," Helen said, as if there'd been no interruption, "with money you knew was dirty."

"No, I certainly did not, Ms. Gulanos. And you've presented absolutely no proof that it was."

"I spoke to a woman," Helen said, "who served on that grand jury in 'sixty-two and says that at least one witness claimed you and Malcolm Turner provided investment opportunities for members of that graft network. And she's no enemy of yours, sir. In fact she intends to vote for you."

He forced a laugh. "People will say anything."

"So you've never heard that before?"

"No, I sure haven't. Who'd she say said that?"

"A Dan Bottenfield, who was on the liquor board at the time."

Roger shook his head and chuckled. "Another Mason."

"What're you saying?" Helen asked.

"I was the one who had to break it to the Freemasons that we needed to occupy their building for the fair, okay? Their attorney vowed to screw me some day, and maybe that day's finally come. He was pals with Donald Yates—you might be familiar with him— who also was a Mason, as was Bottenfield. Hell, your lying cop in Spokane was probably one too. Do you understand what's going on here? You're a tool in a misguided vendetta that's older than you are." He laughed. "So, keep all that in mind while I tell you a little story."

"Sir," Helen began.

"It wasn't a request."

He relaxed himself by slowly explaining how he became aware of the bribery investigation during the fair. "I was afraid it might make the city look bad at just the wrong time." He plucked the cigarette from Teddy's fingers and dropped it into his water glass. "But the more I saw and heard, the more it seemed like a kind of rot. At first, you think it's just the outer rim of your porch, right? Then you realize it's in the siding too, and—Christ almighty—actually it's in the posts and beams. I don't know that we had a bigger gambling problem than other cities our size, but graft is a sickness. And we had it bad. I was appalled—but certainly not involved, no matter what anyone told you."

"Did you know Rudy Costello?" Helen asked. "Or a bar owner named Charlie McDaniel?"

His mouth opened, but he didn't speak.

"Denny Carmichael says he was there when both men were murdered, before they could talk to the grand jury."

Roger stiffened and began to say something but then stopped.

"So you got to know Malcolm Turner," Helen abruptly said, "when you were trying to build the Space Needle."

He settled his gaze on her, still picturing Charlie McDaniel so vividly in his mind, then said, "About then, I believe."

"So he helped finance it," she speculated excitedly. "He helped pay the mortgage on this thing, right?"

"Well, no." Roger felt completely off-balance now, his eyes drifting to the pleasingly familiar jumble of buildings below. "We had a hell of a time getting financing," he said, resorting to storytelling again. "People forget that. There was no public money for it, and the banks wouldn't consider it without a big private stake. The four principals lined up pretty quick."

"But Turner, or perhaps his New Metropolitan Properties, were secondary investors through Jack Vierling's company, correct?"

"Well," Roger began cautiously, "I don't remember that level of detail . . . or see how it matters."

"*None* of this matters!" Teddy snarled.

"Mr. Severson," Helen said, swiveling toward him, "your name came up during the hearings too."

He demolished an ice cube with his molars.

"The grand jury was informed," she continued, "that you owned part of a tavern and card room called the Nite Cap that was bribing cops."

Roger's eyes widened in amazement, and he waited with the others for Teddy to quit chewing ice and respond.

"You people are unbelievable," he finally said, glancing at Roger. "This interview's over."

He saw the truth of this charge in Teddy's eyes before he scooted his chair back toward his walker. Is that why he'd dropped out of the governor's race after such a promising start in '64? Roger felt queasy. How deep had it all run? Was everybody—even his best friend—using him back then?

"Where did you go immediately after the fair, Mr. Morgan?" Helen asked.

He hesitated, then said, "Nevada."

"To see your father?"

"The goddamn interview is over!" Teddy snapped.

"Where'd you find him?" Helen pressed.

Roger stood up to give Teddy more room. "You obviously know."

"So you visited him. What was that like?"

Roger put both hands on the table and leaned over her. "*Stop this.*"

"We just tonight received the criminal records and newspaper articles," she said softly.

"Do you really think you can tell me anything about him that I don't already know? Why would you—"

"Because they're jackals!" Teddy barked, halting conversations on the other side of the restaurant. "Have you people no judgment? This is a great . . . Roger's a *great* man!"

"Teddy"—Roger held up a hand—"please."

"No! They're just exploiting your honesty." He bared his teeth and pointed at Roger. "I don't even like his politics, but he's the best man this city could hope for!" His voice warbled. "Can't you see that?"

"Excuse us a minute," Roger said, and guided him toward the elevator.

They were both writing frantically in their notebooks when he returned. "Sorry about all that," he said. "We're through here anyway, right?"

"Mr. Morgan," Helen said, "we both greatly appreciate you answering all these questions at the end of a long day, but we have a couple more."

He didn't object, but remained standing and stared past them at a retreating ferry that looked like a bright skyscraper knocked on its side and sliding west. "I'll agree with Teddy on one point," he said. "You people don't reward the truth. So let's leave it there and hope that in the morning light you'll realize your reporting's full of misconceptions and speculations and that none of this is of interest or value to readers or voters." He pushed through a hip twinge and stepped away from the table.

"Mr. Morgan," Steele asked sheepishly, "did you vote for Barry Goldwater in 'sixty-four?"

He shook his head. "I voted against Johnson."

"And Reagan?"

"My voting record is my own business, but I did vote for him once and regretted the hell out of it."

Steele nodded. "Any other regrets?"

"Thousands. They're just not the ones you want me to have. Now, good night. I'm gonna help my friend here."

"I'm sorry," Helen persisted, his back to them now, "but when you headed to Nevada after the fair, were you alone?"

He walked ahead several strides, his back stiffening, then spun on his heel like a much younger man. "Don't ask questions to which you obviously know the answers. It's just asinine."

Chapter Twenty-one

OCTOBER 1962

HE'S SEEING HOW FAST his new Impala will go, driving through Nevada toward the California line, pushing the pedal until the needle crosses 120 and the horizon gets hard to pinpoint, everything at once blurring and seemingly standing still as he reaches for the bottle of warm champagne between her bare thighs. The news broke this morning. Khrushchev had blinked and the standoff is over! He howls now with a complicated joy that includes more than the thrill that the earth will continue spinning. He takes a swallow and then passes the bottle back, smiling at her now, her face half-obscured by wind-whipped hair.

They'd bought a cheap room at the Stardust and spent a week indulging long nights and late mornings. They gambled, won plenty, lost more. And during some woozy moments, it almost felt like the fair was continuing down here in the desert, though a drearier version, with some of the same acts playing to listless crowds and with none of the solidarity or panache. Just the opposite, actually. Yet it filled the void—didn't it?—and offered an escape.

Her husband thought she was flying to Palm Springs to comfort her high-strung sister. He'd figure it out but ultimately forgive her, she'd told Roger just before he approached the fifth of seven Las Vegas addresses for *Robert or Bob or R or B Dawkins* and was relieved yet again not to find anyone resembling his father. Once he checked with the police, though, it got easier. They directed him to the local jail, which gave him the phone number for the state prison, which was exactly where his bogeyman awaited him in a pungently sanitized visiting room.

Neither of them could muster much conversation until Roger shared a bit about the fair, telling him how big of a deal it'd been for the city and downplaying his role to essentially a VIP chauffeur. Bob Dawkins did his best to look fascinated, but his eyes were foggy and Roger soon realized his father was going to ask for money. Yet what a relief to see him so diminished! Skinny and shrunken, shabby and balding, round-faced and groveling. His voice was the only thing left.

"They've got a casino in here called the Bullpen," he'd said, lighting up. "Amazing, isn't it? A casino in prison? And I'm good at craps. Extremely good, actually. You spot me a thousand, I'll send you twice that in a week. Should be outta here in a month anyway, two at the most." He sounded as certain as a stockbroker assessing the market. "And when I do, I'll hook you up with a guy who can double your savings just like that." He snapped his fingers and cracked the same grin Roger had seen in the mirror too many times.

"Let me show you something." His father brightened as he pulled out a deck of cards so worn you couldn't make out the casino's name on the back. "Shuffle, cut and pick," he said, flashing his gummy smile. Roger did the drill and slid a card to his side of the table without glancing at it. Then his father performed the same flamboyant high shuffles Roger recalled from his childhood before turning five cards faceup like a veteran dealer and rubbing his palms in mock concentration. "What do you think you're doing, mister, with my jack of clubs?" Roger wouldn't flip the card, so his father did it for him and followed that with a wink and a slick account of all the lucrative options he'd be weighing once he got out. "In the meanwhile, though, I could sure use a couple bills." The number kept falling until it hit twenty dollars. Roger never said no, but he didn't give his father any money either.

Speeding north out of Carson City through this sun-broiled moonscape, they toasted Seattle as if they were newlyweds moving there. And they saluted Kennedy, too. It had been weighing on Roger more than he realized, this fear of nuclear annihilation. Otherwise, why would he feel so liberated? Of course, seeing his father had something to do with it. That he wasn't curious about what Roger was making of himself lifted the burden of so many imagined expectations.

There also was the comforting call he'd had with Teddy, who told him the grand jury had closed down and that its indictments would be announced soon. But as much as anything there was the exalting possibility that he finally had figured out what he'd do next.

He would meet with honorable men in dark rooms like his grandfather used to and have long thoughtful conversations about what was best for the city. He'd be a midwife for good ideas. He'd make it his business to advise people, a notion that makes him giggle now, given that he's driving drunk with a married woman in her underwear. But he's high enough on this plan to be bouncing it off Grandpa Morgan in his mind when he feels the front right tire grab the outer lip of asphalt and hears her scream, the vehicle swerving then rocking on its shocks through mercifully flat dirt. When it fishtails to a lurching halt, her head swings dangerously close to the dashboard and she stops screaming and starts laughing and can't quit as he steps out and strolls around the car, thrilled that they're somehow still intact. Settling back into his seat, he apologizes gently and repeatedly before shifting the Impala into gear and rumbling back toward U.S. Route 395. Meredith Stein is still laughing.

Chapter Twenty-two

HELEN LISTENED, steeling the courage to insist they either hold the story or pull her name off it, but they were thawing her with praise, raving about all the phenomenal reporting she and Steele had done. It's just postpartum blues, Marguerite assured her. The prevailing sentiment was they'd be fools not to run this now. Hell, the *Times* would have run it days ago and already be whoring for a book deal. Or, as Birnbaum summarized, "The voters deserve to know everything we know *before* the primary."

Everybody but Helen was buying in.

Steele had reorganized the top of their draft the night before, after she'd reluctantly gone home sick. He claimed the editors had done most of it, but his prose was as singular as everything else about him and he obviously was the one who'd turned her thoughtful look at Morgan's secrets and contradictions into an old-school hit piece. Regardless, it was full speed ahead now, especially once Steele announced the *Times* was piecing together a similar story for Sunday.

"I just feel like we're opening a watermelon with an ax," Helen said, hoping to avoid another coughing attack. "Why not hold it until after the primary, just to give us enough time to tighten everything up? Even if he loses, it'll still be relevant."

"With any big story," Birnbaum sympathized, "there'll always be screws you'd like to tighten one more turn. Isn't that right, Bill?"

Steele grunted on cue. "Tell me about it."

"You're a perfectionist," Marguerite added, "but you're spent and you're sick, okay? Let us do our job here. You've got to trust us."

Helen felt like she was the only one who hadn't read this script in advance. "What if Morgan's right about this being a vendetta?" she asked softly, everyone leaning toward her now. "I mean, I checked it out, and Yates, Bottenfield and Carmichael *were all* local Free-masons. And shouldn't we worry that we might be killing off our best candidate? Doesn't that factor in anywhere?"

The editors glanced at Steele, as if he'd already briefed them on her conspiracy theory and growing affection for Morgan.

"Instincts," Birnbaum said vaguely.

"Look," Marguerite said, "it's easy to get too close to your sub-ject, especially one this charming. That's why we've got Steele on this thing to give us a more detached perspective. All this stuff about his father alone needs to be printed *right now*, Helen. If you'd feel more comfortable with Bill's byline on top, we could—"

"*Absolutely* not," Steele protested. "This is her baby. I'm just happy to be the stork here."

Everyone laughed except Helen, who started coughing and couldn't stop.

SHORTLY AFTER MIDNIGHT, Roger is clicking Refresh again and again on the *P-I* web page. Having heard rumors that it was coming out each of the past three days, he'd checked every night at midnight after learning that some stories were available that early. He knew even a hostile newspaper wouldn't try to hang him on the eve of an election. So, without a Sunday edition, the *P-I* had just Friday or Saturday to squeeze it in before the primary. And Saturday was the least-read paper of the week, so either it would get posted in the next hour or they'd hold it until after Tuesday. If he could just survive the primary, he thought hopefully, an attack afterward might even work in his favor. *Roger against the media! Roger against the cops, the unions, the state party! Roger against the world!*

He hit Refresh again, and at 1:18 a.m. the story popped up. The headline made him dizzy—"The Secrets of Roger Morgan"—and the old photo staggered him. It took him a few breaths to recognize himself in a chummy-looking foursome with soon-to-drown pinball mogul Rudy Costello, soon-to-be-indicted county prosecutor Clive

Buchanan and soon-to-be-skyscraper-tycoon Mal Turner. He'd never seen this picture before, but the backdrop and the fact that Mal had hair told him it was shot during the fair inside Club 21. The only one not smiling like a lotto winner was himself, as if he'd sensed bad things might come of this moment.

He attempted to read the article on the screen, but his vision blurred. When he printed it out, the type was too small and the ads disorienting. Finally, he grabbed a magnifying glass and started on the printed version. He read the first paragraph, backtracked, read it again, then did the same with the next two, a hummingbird fluttering in his chest as he tried to picture any of this on the front page of a newspaper in a few hours.

He read the same three paragraphs again through his mother's eyes. Unable to get past them, he called Teddy. "It's online," he said when his groggy friend answered at last. "Please tell Judith I'm sorry."

"How bad?" Teddy grunted.

"Feels like it's about somebody else."

"What's it say?"

"I can't get through it. You try."

"I'm not . . . What's it say, Rog?"

"That I'm a big-time shyster just like my old man."

"You don't sound right," Teddy grumbled. "Get a glass of water or something, then read me the top. Probably isn't as bad as you think."

Minutes later, Roger started reading aloud:

Colorful mayoral candidate Roger Morgan legally changed his name when he was 18, in part to distance himself from his father, whom Nevada police would later dub "the king of Las Vegas con men."

"What?" Teddy blurted. "You never changed your name, did you?"

"Let's keep going."

"Well, shit!"

Twelve years later, Morgan was running Seattle's 1962 World's Fair and simultaneously helping launch the controversial career of mega-developer Malcolm Turner by giving him insider information

about the future path of Interstate-5 through Seattle, which led to the
construction of an apartment building at 911 E. Roanoke St.

"What a load of—"

"Just listen."

A document obtained by the Post-Intelligencer, *during its four-*
month investigation of Morgan's often mysterious past, suggests
most of the original investors in the Roanoke Apartments were city
and county officials later indicted on assorted graft charges stem-
ming from illegal gambling activities involving a payoff system that
amounted to monthly bribes to city police during perhaps the worst
spate of municipal corruption in Seattle's history.

"This is so outrageous!" Teddy hisses.

Morgan says the freeway information he shared with Turner
was already public knowledge. Yet records show that Turner bought
the Roanoke property at less than 10 percent of its appraised value
before the release of the report boosted property values near future
off-ramps. Morgan says he never knew who Turner's other investors
were or where their money came from.

Teddy growled inaudibly.

Turner, who went on to build four of the city's ten tallest sky-
scrapers before facing bankruptcy proceedings and related lawsuits
earlier this year, refused to comment other than to say, through his
attorney, that he never knowingly accepted investor capital raised by
criminal means.

More than 80 people, mostly city police officers, were indicted
by federal and county grand juries in 1962 and 1963, six of whom
showed up as investors in Turner's apartment building, which still
stands on Roanoke Street. According to this internal document,
investments ranged from $5,000 to $25,000 per person. Morgan's
contribution to the project at the time was $15,000—or about
$105,000 in today's money.

Commercial real estate analysts interviewed by the P-I *speculated*
that Morgan and his fellow investors at least tripled their money
when Turner sold the building in 1965 for $847,500. While Morgan
and Turner were never subpoenaed or implicated during the city's
graft probe, their names surfaced at the federal hearings during dis-

cussions of graft money being "laundered" in real estate investments, according to one of the jurors, Lilliana Strovich, a Ballard woman who says she intends to vote for Morgan on Tuesday.

Roger then raced through a series of quotes from former policeman Denny Carmichael about the widespread investment of graft profits with Turner, a young developer at the time who'd boasted of his connections to the man running the fair.

"Unbelievable," Teddy mumbled. "This is un—"

"Hold on, there's a lot more."

Born Roger Morgan Dawkins on April 28, 1931, Morgan dropped Dawkins from his legal name after graduating from Sedro-Woolley High School, where he was voted "best smile." Morgan said he changed surnames to honor his grandfather Thomas Morgan, a history professor at the University of Washington, rather than to distance himself from his father.

Robert Ignatius Dawkins spent eight years in prison before dying of a brain aneurysm in 1966 at the age of 69. Dawkins's signature con, according to press and police reports, was to claim he'd owned a restaurant chain in the South and was now just trying to help others get rich. He had a friend, he'd say, who'd stockpiled gold and diamonds that he would sell to him at bargain prices. As The Las Vegas Review-Journal *wrote in 1958: "Dawkins was known for his ability—some called it a gift—to talk people into doing just about anything." One city detective dubbed him "the king of Las Vegas con men."*

"You want more?" Roger asked.

"No," Teddy managed after a long pause. "I don't think . . . I don't know what to . . . Look, make a list of all the crap they got wrong, okay? And we'll go after Helen and the *P-I* with everything we've got. It's just a disgrace."

Roger listened to silence on the other end, then heard a cigarette igniting and a windy inhale. "It's over, Teddy, isn't it?"

"You don't deserve this."

"Neither do you, my friend." Roger wanted to get off before Teddy broke down. "Apologize to Judith for me for waking her up. I hate to bother that woman."

He hung up wondering how soon he needed to get to his mother's to intercept her morning paper. He read the article all the way through for the first time. It went on forever. There were plenty of inflammatory photos as well, including one of him and Malcolm Turner holding cocktails and laughing, and also a mug shot of his father that made their likeness unmistakable.

What amazed him as much as anything was that Helen Gulanos could be brutal. And in that thought, he found hope. The story strained so hard to be damning it was bound to generate sympathy from people who never would have voted for him otherwise. His mind casting about, he recalled how many years it took him not to worry about someone calling him Roger Dawkins. And while he knew that his father had tricked people out of money, he'd never heard he was the *king* of anything. And it amused him in the abstract to think of those shabby Roanoke apartments and Mal's other projects as money-laundering operations. But was it true? Or had Helen just got it all wrong?

After reading the article again, his outrage grew. Pacing barefoot, talking into a recorder, he listed all the errors, exaggerations and speculations. He called Mal Turner's cell phone for the first time in years, but his mailbox was full. He started typing an e-mail to Charles Birnbaum, the editor of the *P-I*: *Do you really want to go to court with this innuendo?* Yet as he reread his bluster, his anger receded. Suddenly blackout weary, he squinted at the clock before collapsing on the couch. A three-hour nap, he told himself, then he'd go see his mother.

He woke four and a half hours later, yanked on yesterday's clothes and without breakfast trudged the nine blocks to her retirement home. Passing a 24-Hour Fitness, he saw dozens of healthy youngsters exercising, their skin glistening like fresh fruit, as if to remind him that he was nearly dead. Moments later, he was standing in front of his mother.

Freshly bathed and smelling of baby powder, she was sitting upright in bed with the front section of the *P-I* folded neatly at her side. He experienced a momentary hope. She'd always refolded the sections so carefully that he never could tell if she'd read them or not.

"Come here, Son," she told him. "Look at you." She pressed a button and the top half of the bed rose up with a whir. "Just look at you." Her skinny arms reached out for him. It wasn't her acknowledgment of what had happened that broke him down, but rather that this was how she'd always calmed him.

THE MOOD TURNED raucous in the Olympic Hotel ballroom when the first vote tally showed Roger five points ahead of Rooney and eight up on Norheim. Only Teddy and a few insiders realized how meaningless these 8:05 p.m. numbers were, since the polls just closed and these were all mail-in ballots cast long before the *P-I* stink bomb. But it was hard not to feel the bounce or hear the chant—"Ro-ger! Ro-ger!"—or indulge the possibility that the unpredictable electorate, as scholars and pollsters liked to call the voting mobs, might just tell the *P-I* to screw itself.

Thousands already had in word or deed. Protesters old and young alike had boycotted the newspaper building in shifts since the morning the story broke, shambling back and forth with signs proclaiming *Lies!* and *Shame!* and *Gotcha Journalism!* City historian Walt Merrill went on two local TV stations to blast the article as "assassination by association." Such a story, he argued, "violates any semblance of fairness, particularly considering it ran just four days before an election." Rumors also suggested the paper had received a record number of cancellations. The flip side, however, was a surge in newsstand sales and new subscribers. And Roger knew the overriding problem was that so many people had read it. The worst part, though, was word of mouth, thirdhand accounts from people who hadn't read it but stated as fact that Roger was a crook who'd done time in Vegas and changed his name to hide his crimes.

Tonight, though, people kept telling him, was another story. All he needed to do was finish second and he'd be on the November ballot! And by then the *P-I* story would be forgotten. People didn't look to newspapers for guidance anymore, he was told, and after his second beer he started to believe it.

He knew that most of his supporters here, particularly the young ones, couldn't imagine him losing. And as the ballroom filled with this refreshing mix of college kids and retired folks, he recognized the importance of body language and willed himself to talk, look and move like a winner.

Since the polls opened this morning, Teddy had directed his rag-tag crew of volunteers to make reminder calls to registered voters in key precincts. Meanwhile, Roger talked to everyone in the ballroom, increasingly invigorated, even flabbergasted, by the turnout. He'd considered canceling this gathering altogether and joked about changing his name again and moving to Argentina. But given that the hotel had donated this space, he saw this evening as a chance to at least thank everyone.

Right now, it felt like a victory party. He overheard reporters commenting on how festive his gathering was compared to Rooney's and Norheim's more subdued soirees. And the ballroom just kept filling, with a TV crew now interviewing ninety-six-year old Hazel Molchan and then eighteen-year-old Ryan Tyler about why they were still so gung ho about Morgan. And it wasn't lost on the press when former governor Ed Lopresti shuffled inside to shake his hand, along with other assorted city icons and activists who'd taken the trouble to be seen with him tonight. Clearly, attacking Roger was an assault on their version of history too.

By 8:50 p.m., the party tightened and so did the new vote tally, putting him a point ahead of Rooney and three over Norheim. Roger knew these votes were probably cast before lunch in precincts closest to the courthouse, and since that should have been his territory, this slippage was even more discouraging. Teddy sent a runner to the courthouse for the precinct turnout stats, so he could compare them with 1997 numbers. Then, based on the disparities, he passed out cell phones and divvied up calling assignments in Wallingford and Queen Anne, where turnouts were low and Roger should have fared well. The kids looked excited but confused. *The polls have already closed, right?*

"As long as ballots are postmarked today, they'll count," Teddy told them, explaining that there was a post office near the airport that stayed open till midnight. "Tell 'em if they haven't voted yet, we'll come right to their house and pick their ballots up and mail them ourselves. Annie will organize the pickups. Do whatever she says."

Teddy hobbled back into the center of the room on his cane, turned on the microphone and started in on his Ed Sullivan impression, which if not particularly good was perfectly timed. People were desperate for diversions. Standing hunch-shouldered, with the backs of his wrists on his hips, talking in the distinct pitch and hesitating cadence of the long-dead showman, Teddy started listing off his guests tonight. "And what do you know? There's Elvis . . . Presley . . . himself."

With this cue, and to awkward applause, Roger swaggered to the stage and grabbed a stool.

"Mr. Presley? How do you feel about Roger . . . Morgan's chances tonight?"

Roger played with an imaginary bouffant of hair, then mumbled, "Well, uh, Ed, can I call you Ed?"

"Feel free to call me Mr. . . . . Sullivan," Teddy replied.

"Well, uh, Mr. Sullivan, are we talking about Roger Morgan's chances at the polls or in the sack?"

The applause was more strained during his Bob Hope impression, and by the time he'd finished his LBJ routine he was looking for an exit, when he spotted Meredith Stein in a purple dress and black scarf. Stranding Teddy, he walked directly over to her, not caring about the gossip and surprised by how touched he was that she'd come.

"You need to call me," she told him.

He agreed and wanted to say more, but suddenly was overrun by others wanting a piece of him, people he assumed already would have abandoned him. Even Jonas Lange was here.

"First political event I've ever been to," he said, shaking Roger's hand. "You got a raw deal," he added through clenched teeth. "Patricia would have found a dozen ways to make the *P-I* pay, not that I know how to do you any good. Just thought I'd at least be here."

"How you managing without her?" Roger asked.

Jonas shrugged. "Like any other amputee, I guess."

Then it was Linda Bancroft heading toward him. He hadn't seen her in at least fifteen years, but easily recognized his first fiancée by the exaggerated swing of her arms. The older she got, the more her simplicity appealed to him. She hugged harder these days too. And, amazingly, Malcolm Turner himself had broken out of his embattled reclusion, showing up in a sharkskin suit to navigate a crowd full of his critics and bankruptcy victims. Yet he came, and now was striding toward Roger with his hand extended. Democrats, Republicans, apoliticals, Christians, Jews, agnostics, everybody paying their respects. They were *all* here, though he noticed the savvier ones exiting before the next pile of votes got tallied.

His elderly supporters switched from wine to coffee as the crowd thinned, though the youngsters were still guzzling the free liquor. The 9:50 numbers were as devastating as Roger expected, showing him trailing Rooney by five points and the councilwoman by three. A chant erupted anyway. At first he was shocked they still didn't get it, but then realized that in fact they did and were sticking it out regardless. By 10:45, the crowd was down by half and the kids were astonished when the latest count put him eight points behind Rooney and six back of Norheim.

He conceded in time for the eleven-o'clock news, earlier than Teddy thought he should, but he knew the numbers would only get worse.

"Do you regret running?" the KING-5 woman asked.

"You kidding me? I got to converse with so many people I would've never met otherwise, people who share my affection for this city. The whole thing was a wonderful and humbling adventure. And in the grand scheme of things, despite disappointing these generous people behind me, this isn't all that big of a deal. This city will continue to be among the greatest, and I'll continue working for it every way I can. We tend to overestimate the importance of who's in office. And I guarantee you that in a couple weeks people will come up to me and ask, 'How's your campaign goin'? Go get 'em, Roger! Give 'em hell!' And to those people I'll say, 'You bet I will.'"

"Anything you'd like to say about the impact of the controversial *Post-Intelligencer* article?"

Roger winced and bit his lower lip. "It didn't feel fair or accurate to me. I didn't recognize the man they wrote about. Life is a challenging and often inexplicable odyssey that doesn't translate easily into newspaper stories. If that article was all I knew about me, I would have voted for someone else too."

THREE WEEKS LATER he was emerging from yet another funeral. Just sixty-two, Jenny Sunshine left behind a weepy husband, four kids and eleven rambunctious grandchildren, all of them crammed into the front rows at the University Unitarian Church. Having been asked to speak, Roger recounted her first day at the fair, when she dropped a pot of coffee in his office and couldn't stop laughing. He dipped in and out of several other mini-debacles that were no match for his secretary's high spirits. "She was supremely gifted in the happiness department."

Afterward, he felt oddly exhilarated, as if his fever had finally broken and he was himself again. He had Teddy in the backseat and his mother in the front. They were both ready for naps, but he wanted to take a drive.

It had taken him more than two weeks to get over the sting of the primary, yet somehow getting skewered in the press *and* losing so dramatically had boosted his stature. And it was inspiring that people still wanted more of him after seeing his life cast in such a dismal light. More strangers than ever were hailing him on the streets, and he was getting more speaking requests than he had since the '70s. The Rotary and Kiwanis were no-brainers, sure, but the Historical Society, the League of Women Voters, the Mountaineers, People for Puget Sound and Washington Conservation Voters? Some invitations, no doubt, were driven by sympathy or morbid curiosity, though people suddenly wanted him—needed him—to explain their city to them, to help put its historical seediness into perspective, especially in light of the *P-I*'s series on Mal Turner and the graft heydays. *Find me a great city that wasn't built by visionaries and scoundrels* was one of his favorite new lines. Two authors and a literary agent called to see if he was interested in doing a memoir. The sky was a flawless, cheerful blue. He felt stunningly good.

Teddy and his mother were both snoozing by the time he drove past the Needle and popped up on the Viaduct, with glassy skyscrapers to the left, serrated mountains to the right and sparkling water in between. He nudged his mother, the curl of her spine exaggerated by the seat. "Mum," he whispered. "Look, Mummy." He slowed down, flipped on the hazards, jostled her again.

She finally woke up, blinking slowly. "Oh, this is so lovely."

He thought about trying to stir Teddy then decided to let him sleep. Seeing the Bremerton ferry approaching the Coleman Dock now, he patted his pockets and pulled out his phone.

SHE WAS PICKING blackberries with Elias and Omar a few blocks from her apartment, where the aggressive vines had taken over a vacant lot next to the Burke-Gilman Trail, the drooping berries so ripe and heavy they were falling on their own and leaving purple explosions on the paved path. Loud chatty women sped past behind shaggy retrievers on long leashes, followed by bicyclists as colorful as tropical fish, two pierced teens on skateboards and a solo exhibitionist on a unicycle wearing nothing but Converse high-tops and purple body paint. Helen's cell rang, and she was startled by the incoming number.

He hadn't returned any of her three calls since the story ran. She'd typed him a quick letter the night it went to press, admitting how disappointed she was with its tone. The letter momentarily salved her guilt, though she didn't intend to send it, particularly not after the congratulatory raves from the publisher and so many others poured in. Marguerite called the story a "wing walker," whatever that meant, and several *Times* reporters and friends in Ohio and D.C. had gushed over it. Yet in hindsight, to her it felt more like a stepping-stone to the next bell-ringer.

The morning it ran, Helen and Steele started receiving anonymously faxed lists of private investors for almost every Malcolm Turner construction project over the past four decades. These lists suggested that all his buildings were financed, at least in part, by local investors, mostly cops, who'd been implicated in graft investigations.

On the Monday following the primary, Steele's story detailed how Turner's bold strategy had finally backfired when the dot-com bust left him with a million square feet of empty office space. Among his many creditors were more than two hundred "investor friends"— many of whom were now suing him in hopes of liquidating his assets and seeing some return on the $160 million he owed them. Yet it was this continuing thread of dirty money, not the bankruptcy saga, that made the story explosive. A graphic re-creation of the downtown skyline showed Turner's buildings in red beneath the headline: "A City Built on Bribes?" That provocative question, coupled with Helen's sidebar on the construction and financing of the Space Needle, had people looking at their city differently.

It was hard for her to dig up more than thirdhand accounts, but she still told the story, as best she could, of how the Needle was built on an extremely tight timeline. After the city and county refused to help, Morgan and Severson found private backing from four well-known local tycoons, including Jack Vierling. Yet, as Helen pointed out, there were also "silent partners" who helped repay the $4.5 million construction loan, including young Malcolm Turner, who was overseeing Vierling's real estate ventures at the time. Vierling's son told her that Turner had come up with a fourth of his father's share. To her astonishment, Turner discussed it with her as well. In a terse six-minute phone chat, he confirmed his involvement but wouldn't say how much he invested or where he got the cash. "I was doing my damndest to help, you understand? And I was honored to be part of it. I wasn't asking questions. Find me anybody who does background checks on their investors. When people have given me money, my typical reaction has been, 'Thank you very much.'"

These articles swelled in Helen's estimation until she began considering them the sort of public service journalism she'd marveled at in Pulitzer anthologies, a notion bolstered by the *Columbia Journalism Review*'s latest issue, which lauded Helen and Steele for *knocking out* a city legend running for mayor, and for exposing the possibility that much of Seattle's spectacular skyline—maybe including the Space Needle itself—had been built with tainted money.

Finding her *Dear Roger* letter days later on her office computer had given her shivers. She'd deleted it, clicked into her trash and killed it again, appalled she'd written it even in her weakened state. But now she was healthy, rested and invigorated, beneath a sky so blue it hurt to look up.

Amazingly, the city was starting to feel like home. She'd jogged around Green Lake with Omar and the cheerful masses last weekend, then let him take her to the symphony, which was so good it made her cry. He'd also found her a deal on a Ballard apartment with a sunset view that she couldn't wait to show her parents. It really was happening. She was falling for this place. She took lunch breaks at the Pike Place Market and heard herself asking strangers, "Have you seen the mountain today?" It was creeping into her, this cheery notion that something exceptional was going on here.

She watched Omar playing with her boy as if they were recess pals. It was definitely Morgan's cell number. Perhaps ringing her by accident? People's hips called her all the time. And if he was trying to reach her, it would no doubt be hostile. She told herself to let the call pass into her voice mail, but then cleared her throat and picked up.

"If you haven't done it yet," he said without introduction, "you and Elias should take the ferry to Bremerton while the weather holds. If you take the seven-o'clock boat, you'll see the sun drop over the Olympics. Fabulous trip, if you haven't made it already. Captain's name is Matt Schultz. Tell him you're a friend of mine, and he might let Elias steer a little bit."

He gave her a moment to compose herself and respond, but she just kept clearing her throat. She wanted to tell him that on deadline she'd successfully insisted they cut any mention of his three illegitimate children even though he'd confirmed their existence. Finally she simply whispered, "Thank you" right before he hung up. She felt emotion rising toward her head.

"Mom? What's wrong?"

Elias had taken this nurturing tone with her ever since she explained that his father was a short, clever man who'd never loved her. She crouched low enough now for him to drop a large, perfect blackberry into her mouth.

IN LESS THAN sixteen hours, two Boeing jets will slam into the twin towers in New York and thousands of people of all races, ages and incomes will spontaneously gather beneath the grand old Space Needle to cry, stack flowers and hold hands. Roger would have loved to see his fairgrounds pulling the city together yet again, even to mourn, but that won't happen.

RIGHT NOW he's walking down Union Street trying to pinpoint why he feels so good. Part of it had to be the phone call. As his grandfather used to say, it's hard to beat the glory of forgiveness. Plus he'd given his mother a ride, and at the last minute had summoned the right words to send off Jenny Sunshine. And it's early September, his favorite time of the year, with a crispy hint of fall and the smell of dying leaves amid all this photogenic stillness. It's his favorite time of day, too, with the city getting off the clock and bicyclists weaving through traffic and people strolling freely onto buses and ferries and into bars and restaurants. His boom-bust city is rebounding, and that has always lifted his mood. Jobs and wages were up in August. The port's also expanding, as are Amazon, the bio-techs and the Gates Foundation, which now is merely attempting to rid the world of preventable diseases. Seattle's thinking big again.

Most of his mirth, though, he realizes, can be attributed to Meredith Stein, who's waiting at the bottom of this hill to show him Annie Leibovitz's latest exhibition—seventy-five black-and-white photos of women.

He checks his watch, thrilled that he remembered in time to hear the first pitch. He sticks his earpiece in and listens to Niehaus describing Ichiro's pre-batting ritual—the deep knee bends, the pinch and lift of his jersey at the right shoulder, his right arm extending with the bat vertical, like an archer aiming his bow at the pitcher, then dropping the bat across his body and assuming his stance, ready to swing at whatever gets thrown. Inside, outside, head high, in the dirt? Doesn't matter. He'll swing. And he does so now at the first pitch.

This skinny Japanese rookie has done the impossible by making routine groundballs exciting. This one bounces twice, fast and low to the right of the Angels' shortstop, who rushes his backhand scoop because the ball came off Ichiro's bat, and every player and umpire and savvy fan knows it's going to be really close. Niehaus's voice rises excitedly as the ball thumps the first-baseman's glove at the same instant that Ichiro's left foot hits the sack. It's only the first at bat, and just an infield hit, yet Niehaus makes it sound like a game winner.

The day is bursting with promise, and Roger struts painlessly down the hill, noticing all the orange markings where high-speed Internet cables will be buried beneath the pavement. Why plant miles of wire in a city that is home to the cellular revolution? Why not be the first wireless city? This thought triggers a flurry of others. Why not turn this into the greenest city on earth? Buildings with triple-paned windows and automated blinds, rainwater reservoirs and sod roofs. Yes, yes, and why not lead the way on electric cars too? Hell, why not collapsible electric cars? And instead of all these light-rail boondoggles, just expand the damn monorail. And do it now! He'll counter stupid initiatives with smart ones if he has to. Better yet, he'll pass his ideas on to young dreamers who can reinvent this city with their bliss. Yes, yes, yes! And what about putting on another fair that dares to look decades ahead? Why hasn't he thought about that before? He'll get all the brainstormers involved—Gates, Bezos, Glaser, McCaw, come one, come all. He sees his young city out front once again, sailing faster than the others into the radiant future.

In his mind, it's already happening, and he's running these ideas past his grandpa now, and soon he'll hear what Meredith has to say about them. Is he finally ready to commit to a woman? He laughs aloud. He's seen her twice in the past week, and knows he's falling for her yet again. From here, he can actually see her waiting at the bottom of the hill next to the museum. It's got to be her. As wide as she is tall. He can't wait.

Then it's just a pop and a rapidly expanding headache, but he knows. And in this instant of knowing, he imagines his funeral, and Teddy breaking down, and so many people who expected to go before him saying, *Good God, he was so young,* but nobody knowing, not even Teddy, what to say into the microphone because he's not there to say it for them. His vision dims as the sidewalk rises up to catch him. *Not now!* He can't help but want more. He hasn't been to Buenos Aires yet. And who's gonna read stories to his mother? He wants *more*! Just a little bit . . . *more.*

By the time she gets up the hill to him, a dozen others are already there and several have dialed 9-1-1. A bearded young man has attempted CPR, and he's trembling because it didn't work. And a thin older woman has recognized the famous Roger Morgan and is shouting his name over and over again.

Meredith is panting as she takes off her sweater and folds it beneath his head, which looks unharmed. Kneeling beside him, she places a finger on his neck to be sure, though she knows. She strokes his forehead and finger-combs his bangs the way he likes them and starts humming to stop herself from crying. For a moment there is nothing but the sound of her humming, then seagulls shriek nearby, a train whistles across town, a jet rumbles overhead and the city carries on.

AUTHOR'S NOTE

While much of Seattle's 1962 World's Fair is accurately portrayed here, this novel is the result of research mixed with imagination. Some celebrities have cameos in this story, but most of their conversations are invented. Also, Roger Morgan and Teddy Severson are my creations and were not based on men who actually ran the fair. Last, Seattle endured an elaborate bribery scandal in the 1960s and early '70s, which was condensed to suit this novel. Similar liberties were taken with more recent newsflashes.

Books that helped conjure this story include *Century 21: The Story of the Seattle World's Fair, 1962* by Murray Morgan; *On the Take: From Petty Crooks to Presidents* by William J. Chambliss; *Pugetopolis* by Knute Berger, *Seattle Vice: Strippers, Prostitution, Dirty Money, and Crooked Cops in the Emerald City* by Rick Anderson; *Meet Me at the Center: The Story of Seattle Center from the Beginnings to the 1962 Seattle World's Fair to the 21st Century* by Don Duncan; and *Seattle and the Demons of Ambition: From Boom to Bust in the Number One City of the Future* by Fred Moody. *Seattle* magazine, circa 1964 to 1970, inspired as well, as did interviews and journals of fair executives Eddie Carlson, Joseph Gandy and Ewen Dingwall.

ACKNOWLEDGMENTS

Thanks to Gary Fisketjon for his editing prowess and to Jess Walter for his writing camaraderie through the years.

Others who generously helped include Kim Witherspoon, Valerie Ryan, Matt Willkens, Diane Valach, Paul Berendt, Jay Rockey, Gabrielle Brooks, Knute Berger, Roger Sale, Janet Peterson, Mark Matassa, David Tye, Karen McKenzie, Nick Budnick, Lorraine McConaghy and, as always, Denise and Grace Lynch.

ALSO BY JIM LYNCH

"*Border Songs* has the kind of ambling, provincial whimsy found in Richard Russo's small town tales and the hard-bitten optimism that colors Larry McMurtry's. . . . A gifted original novelist." —*The New York Times*

BORDER SONGS

Set in the previously sleepy hinterlands straddling Washington state and British Columbia, *Border Songs* is the story of Brandon Vanderkool, six foot eight, frequently tongue-tied, severely dyslexic, and romantically inept. Passionate about bird watching, Brandon has a hard time mustering enthusiasm for his new job as a border patrol agent guarding thirty miles of largely invisible boundary. But to everyone's surprise, he excels at catching illegals, and as drug runners, politicians, surveillance cameras, and a potential sweetheart flock to this scrap of land, Brandon is suddenly at the center of something much bigger than himself. A magnificent novel of birding, smuggling, farming and extraordinary love, *Border Songs* welcomes us to a changing community populated with some of the most memorable characters in recent fiction.

Fiction

VINTAGE BOOKS
Available at your local bookstore, or visit
www.randomhouse.com